JANET TODD was born in Wales and grew up in Britain, Bermuda and Sri Lanka. She has worked in Ghana, Puerto Rico, India, Scotland and England. In the US, at the University of Florida and Douglass College, Rutgers, she became active in the feminist movement and began the first journal devoted to women's writing. She has published on memoir and biography, as well as on authors including Jane Austen, Mary Wollstonecraft, Aphra Behn, Byron and members of the Shelley circle. Her lifelong passion has been for female novelists, both the little known and the famous.

A Professor Emerita at the University of Aberdeen and Honorary Fellow of Newnham College, Janet Todd is a former President of Lucy Cavendish College, Cambridge, where she inaugurated a festival of women writers and established the Lucy Cavendish Fiction Prize. She lives in Cambridge and Venice.

A Man of Genius

A Man of Genius

JANET TODD

BITTER LEMON PRESS

BITTER LEMON PRESS
A co-publication with Fentum Press

First published in 2016 by
Bitter Lemon Press
47 Wilmington Square
London WC1X 0ET

www.bitterlemonpress.com

A CIP record for this book is available from the
British Library

ISBN 978-1-908524-59-1 (hb)
ISBN 978-1-908524-71-3 (trade ppb)
ISBN 978-1-908524-60-7 (eB)
ISBN 978-1-908524-82-9 (ppb)

Designed and typeset by Jane Havell Associates
Printed and bound in Great Britain by TJ International Ltd, Padstow

For Anita Desai

'Great men are meteors designed to burn
so that the earth may be lighted'
Napoleon

-»-<-

'even as we idolise the object of our affections,
do we idolise ourselves . . . we walk as if a mist or
some more potent charm divided us from all but him'
Mary Shelley, *Valperga*

Contents

London

'Annabella looked at the corpse. Hands and head separate. Blood had leaked from wrists and neck. Fluid covered part of the distorted features. The open eyes were stained so that they glared through their own darkness. A smell of rotting meat.

'By itself the face was unrecognisable, yet she knew it was her father's. What was a father? A man begot a body but not a mind. She prodded the head with her foot. The blood must have congealed for her boot remained clean.

'Had she killed him? It wasn't clear. She rather thought she had. She was sure she'd not cut him up. She hadn't the strength. She would order the bits thrown in the Arno to mix with filth from the city. She turned away.

'How many people do you have to murder before it becomes habitual? Before you cannot remember which corpse is which and who is its dispatcher?

'She wiped old blood off her hands with her handkerchief. Her maid would wash it clean.'

He'd come silently into the room and read from behind her. He smiled.

Ann felt the smile. 'I will cross out the fluid and rotting meat,' she said without looking up.

The Pursuit

1

She met Robert James in St Paul's Churchyard. The bookseller J. F. Hughes held a dinner once a week for his distinguished writers and a few hacks. She was invited to leaven the party with what a prized pornographer called 'femality'. Mary Davies, who wrote children's primers for numbers and letters, was absent. Hers was a more respectable trade than Ann's gothic horrors but Mr Hughes judged Ann less prissily genteel in men's company.

An Italian was there. He said little except when talk veered towards argument. Then he remarked there was a sundial near Venice that claimed to count serene hours alone. How good, he added, to take notice of time only as it gives pleasure.

'That sundial had not the English art of self-tormenting,' said Richard Perry, an intense, gentle man introduced by Mr Hughes as a reviewer and former bookseller.

'It's surely not so easy to efface cares by refusing to name them,' said Ann.

Nobody pursued the point. Signor Luigi Orlando felt no need to facilitate further.

Later, much later, she wondered why Robert James had been invited. He'd published nothing of consequence beyond that amazing fragment of *Attila*. Did Mr Hughes believe in his promise as fervently as his friends did? As he did?

At first he'd been silent and she hadn't much remarked him. During the introduction she'd failed to note his name, being too engrossed in her own. Then, as afternoon turned to evening, and wine and conversation flowed, he'd started to dominate the talk, to catch and keep attention. He spoke animatedly. She knew who he was then.

'Why don't we make our language anew? It would transform life as Napoleon transformed Europe.'

He drank to the bottom of his glass, then waited while Mr Hughes's man refilled it and wiped the bottle's neck with a white napkin. It was already streaked with red but the formality compensated for carelessness. Nobody spoke during the little ceremony. They waited, as an audience waits during the interval for the actor to begin again.

'There's one matchless original of language. True?' Robert James looked about the company. Richard Perry sought his friend's eye and nodded. 'So scholars argue that purity lies in the past, at its inception. Then it proceeds to corruption. I say, No. Language moves towards purity. Use it, try it out in all its forms, even its interjections and conjunctions – slowly it will emerge in splendour. It is all to come.'

What was he saying? That wasn't the point: it was the glint, the glamour.

'Politicians speak only in debased words. They talk of the past, they're retrospective. They know nothing of futurity. They impose on language, kill its iridescence.'

His voice rose, then he paused as his body continued expressing itself in little movements, wriggles, of hands and torso.

Was Mr Hughes happy just to listen? Probably, for he must have known he'd invited an entertainer to dinner.

'The cause of reason and truth is menaced not by the democratical spirit – there's no collective, it cannot exist – but by the stupidity of those who think to inflict on others their stale ideas.'

He was darting his eyes on and off his listeners, while sweat bubbled from just above his eyebrows. 'The legal robbery of government is not its taxation but its opinions. Every man must resist.

'And every woman too,' he added looking at Ann, 'for she brings to man's courage her fortitude, her tact to his intellect.'

She hardly registered what he'd said of woman – tact wasn't her strong point – for his eyes had been on her. But she heard the rest well enough and was surprised.

Politics excited nobody, not now in 1816. So old-fashioned, so very much the last century. Revolutions and wars were over. People were weary.

Even the French had given up thinking.

Yet here, on this night, the company listened and some of them, she was convinced, had been truly engaged. That was genius – to go against all expectations. It was doing what this man had already done in *Attila* when, with strength of his own will, he'd flouted common knowledge and made an ogre of the popular mind into a force of miraculous nature; Attila the Hun had become the destroyer not of numberless victims but of a diseased old order.

She'd read that work and admired its almost repellent force.

Unusual for her to seek out this sort of writing. But she'd been invited in by a stray remark overheard in Mr Dean's office, that there was something gothic in the brutal conception; it sparked her interest.

As he spoke and day waned, Robert assumed other voices, making points through mockery and caricature, more and more exaggerated as his audience grew increasingly responsive. He did the orators, the parliamentarians, the German royals; then, for entertainment, just types: ham actors, lawyers, money lenders, women of fashion, Irish seducers. People put on silly voices when nervous. It wasn't so with him. He became the voice he spoke. He exposed and skewered his victims. Did he also make them lovable in their comedy? Or himself?

A sudden desire swept Ann that he would do her dead father Gilbert in the accent only this man could assume. For something here, now, caused that unknown, unheard parent, all recounted words to her – but what words! – to surge up into her mind. As never before in all his absent years. It was a mad wish. She remained silent.

Perhaps she was so enthralled because she'd drunk more than usual. Mr Hughes declared the wine a present from Cadell, a publishing name to impress his guests. It might well have been stronger, though to her taste it was as coarse as any from a Cheapside inn. But it couldn't be the wine for, when not caught up in the listening and the laughter, she was just a little repulsed. Possibly Mr Hughes was too – his response was difficult to gauge. In company Robert James might be, at base, a show-off.

Suspicion faltered. Her eyes stayed on him, his balding head with its rim of fair, slightly reddish hair cut in Caesar style, his pale grey eyes, much paler than hers. It was not a colouring to admire. Never anyone's favourite in abstract. Her heroes never had it. Yet his face, the fleshy lips and thinner pronounced nose, arrested her as no other had done. It was becoming The Face. Even then.

She'd been introduced by Mr Hughes, who'd made the usual jest about her name, St Clair, so apt for a writer of gothic novels. The name was an embarrassment, she said and smiled. Mademoiselle St Clair or spinster Ann from Putney.

He listened attentively and laughed. That afternoon she looked well. As time passed, he seemed to notice her especially, noticed something about her. Gilbert had been all eyes for Caroline from the start, so her mother's story went – and who, even if only half-aware of a drama beginning, could escape such deep-laid wordy memories?

She'd once yearned to be loved by these lover-parents whose look turned only on themselves, but that was long long ago. Now, at this moment, she was pleased just to be noticed: those pale grey eyes brightened everything like the coming of a shiny morning. Its light sank through her brain to her depths.

Next day she was back at her writing. She'd furnished her small lodgings comfortably and was not dissatisfied with her mode of life. Her novels were short, repetitive, requiring no deep thought, just a lot of plotting and knotting of loose ends. She had to remember what she'd said in pages already delivered, that was all. For, unlike the great *Attila*, her works could never be fragments. And nobody read them twice.

She made no claims, nor wanted to.

She earned enough money to pay her rent and keep happy the

butcher and the baker and the laundress and the paper seller. Clothes were no special love, but for the winter she would have saved sufficient for a decent new pelisse.

Better than being a governess or companion. How could she ever have been one? Oily emollience, infinite agreeableness a prerequisite.

'You haven't pleased me,' said her mother when she'd once mentioned that plan. 'How would you please anyone else?'

Caroline had a point there.

Now Robert James. He changed everything.

She spied him next at the Temple of the Muses. He was ahead of her over on the other side of the broad room in a crowd of men including Richard Perry from Mr Hughes's dinner. Even from there she could sense he was the centre of the group, the Author, the cynosure.

She was hurrying to reach where they stood when she was stayed by Mary Davies, who was seeking a picture of a robin for her children's reading book. She asked Ann's business. Mary and she didn't greatly care for each other, yet they met often; they had their work in common, and companions in labour have sometimes merit over chosen friends. In fact Ann too had come to the Temple to find inspiration; caricature gave her ideas for what might be done with the human body in her monkish torture chambers. She was disinclined to tell Mary this. By the time she'd answered vaguely, she could no longer see Robert James.

But now she knew where he visited. So she happened to pass that way the next day, and the next. But she didn't see him at the Temple of the Muses again, outside or inside. The boy at the counter was driven to ask if she was looking for anything in particular for she'd been there so often. How many days was it that she'd gone out of her way like this? Memory delivered the number but she needn't dwell on it.

Two weeks later, *The Horrors of the Mountain Abbey* was finished and she was walking past St Paul's with the completed manuscript in her bag towards Dean & Munday in Paternoster-Row when she did really see him. It was he. She knew she was often too forward, but now she hung back. This was strange. And after so many detours to encounter him. Perhaps it was because the cathedral bell clanged in her ears.

Then by coincidence she was at tea with Mary Davies and in he walked, along with Richard Perry.

'We have met,' he said smiling as Mary Davies came forward to make an introduction.

'We have,' she said. 'I think you had recently returned to London, Mr James.'

He must often have been absent or she'd have seen him. How could he not be noticed?

'Yes,' he replied. With only a trace of the lilt she'd discerned at Mr Hughes's dinner. 'I travel a little, on the Continent and Dublin.'

He'd said Dublin, she remembered, but he'd not mentioned other cities.

'You are Irish?'

He nodded gravely as if she'd offered a deserved rebuke and looked her straight in the eye. 'But do not hold it against me, Miss St Clair.'

When the first cups of tea had been drunk and Mary Davies's small hard cakes crunched and the general talk on new plays, books and music had subsided, Robert was back on the dullness of the present post-war moment, adding this time the failure of England to have a proper revolution. It had, he said, peaked too early. If it had waited, it might have gone beyond France, shown the world a real ending of thrones and domination, of regurgitated thought. Napoleon was a great man, yet he could not avoid his French heritage.

Mary Davies pulled her scarlet Indian shawl tight round her shoulders to express discomfort. Her young brother had died fighting this bad man in the wars he caused, but she was too polite openly to protest. 'Would you care for more tea?' she asked, raising the pink china pot.

Robert was undeterred. For whom was he speaking? For his friend Richard Perry – or for her? It must be for her: she had quickly surmised that Richard Perry was a frequent, captive and captivated auditor.

The French had ruined it all, sullied the noble ideas of liberty and equality in government and art. England had colluded. No one had now the stomach to change anything. He'd once thought to go to America. But it was all money there, it was money they'd fought their masters for. Money! What was money? So now, so long after all this chaos and error, this was the place for real change, for complete revolution. He thumped his broad chest, then struck his forehead. 'Here.'

Richard Perry smiled and nodded, his intense eyes sweeping his friend's features. He knew enough not to interrupt Robert James in full utopian flow.

What did he really think of the ideas rather than the man? What did she?

Surely she thought nothing at all. Just watched and listened, enthralled by the sound of his speaking.

So many years of hearing Gilbert's impenetrable words repeated by her mother like psalms and litanies to a Sunday congregation. They swept over and through her infant, childish, then adolescent head as Caroline fell into an almost religious reverie.

It irritated her daughter as physically as any eczema with its pustules on her neck and ears.

This talk was quite different, of course.

Mary Davies was thoroughly annoyed. It was not conversation for the tea-table and mixed company. Thoughts pinged and twanged over the pink, gold-rimmed cups in only one direction and in a most ungenteel manner.

The guests left all in a rush. Mary Davies was further offended that her friend didn't stay behind to chat woman to woman and exclaim on this odd vain man. But, though Ann professed independence, Mary always thought her too concerned with men and their talk.

Richard Perry, a widower, was in a hurry to visit an only sister who'd just borne a son in Clerkenwell. So Ann and Robert were left walking off together in whatever direction he pleased.

Ann and Robert, she thought, not bad in a romance.

So it began.

2

He cared about clothes. He wanted them to seem negligent but he took trouble. She didn't much mind for herself. She'd disliked Caroline's finery, her turbans and garish coloured shawls. But she loved to see *him* well dressed.

Now he wanted to dress her. She demurred. She was not beautiful. He didn't disagree. Instead he said that beauty could go rotten and become 'loathsome', more than ugliness. More than adders and toads.

He had a family allowance, not large – she rather surmised than knew this – or maybe Richard Perry said something. But he went off and bought expensive material for her, pea-green, striped and shiny. He let the material slither through his fingers while he closed his eyes.

He came with her to a dressmaker to have it made up so that for once – so he said – for once she would have clothes that fitted well and were stylish. She could be smart, she had the figure for it. Why did she not take more trouble? He sounded like a mother, she thought, and giggled.

Then he became the dressmaker and was amusing, just for her. Later he bought her an intricately sewn blue silk scarf. It suited her colouring, he said.

She would try to take trouble and did so for a while. His admiration mattered.

She had told him – why, for she'd not before spoken much of her past? – that father Gilbert had loved material things, the cabinets of curiosities. He knew the names of shells: the magician's cone, the glory-of-the-seas, the precious wentletrap, the nutmeg snail – the list had gone on but she remembered no more now, the words had come with no images attached. He had carried her mother – with difficulty she said Mother instead of Caroline, sensing a social conservatism below the radical talk – to Montagu House for the purpose. Caroline could still remember those shells. It was part of her tribute to the dead. 'Name them to me, child, those curiosities,' she'd demanded after her relating.

'I will show you the curiosities of the mind,' said Robert James.

When she had a toothache and found the cloves no help, she was about to consult a dentist. He threw up his hands in protest. 'Medical men know nothing. Keep away. They are all quacks.'

Perhaps. Often her mother had consulted Buchan's *Domestic Medicine* while Martha, her old Putney nurse, had provided more homely remedies that almost always worked – in time.

Robert was scornful. 'Poor little hen,' he said. 'Martha indeed. There is only one sure treatment for any body part: electric shock. It shakes the frame and jostles the teeth. What could be more healthy than a jostling? Or would you rather place roasted turnips behind the ear as my great aunt did in County Cork? Maybe a toasted fig between the gum and cheek?'

He was off, for he had become the dentist and was unstoppable. 'Perhaps some vomiting, a purging of what is unwholesome, some leeching might help, Madam. Or perhaps a hot iron on the tooth which I personally, Madam, would apply. Or maybe something a little less common, more unusual and special for a special patient: might I insert three drops of juice into the ear on the side the tooth aches? They could remain there an hour or two, while I, Madam, would stroke your hand for comfort. If all this fails, we will gently pull it out without disturbing a single nerve. Personally I always think a little excellent wine shared with your physician is much to be recommended, though taken without advice one might, I admit it' – he clapped his hands and then stroked his hair, 'one might become plethoric. Madam, I abhor home doctoring. Leave it to the professionals. There are so many injurious effects by people using their common sense and calling things by simple names. It will not do, Madam, it will not do. Not a one of them has a real understanding of physic. The eel of science, Madam, will not be caught by the tail. It will not, it will protest.'

His gestures were so comical, so typical of the type he mocked that she had to laugh. She was flattered he did it for her. And it *was* for her, she the only audience of a man who could enthral a crowd of men.

Sure enough the pain died away.

He brought her a lily, some lilac, a rose, and all together. How could they have all been in season? But she remembered the scents mingling, so heady that they went beyond flowers. That was the point, he said. All making one.

But why would separate smells mingle to make a better? Common sense would argue . . .

'Reason, my little Puritan, is the critic and interpreter of nature. Then intuition finds dark corners in the mind where reason stumbles. It is not common-sense to rely on common sense,' and he pranced around holding a flower in each hand. He twined them in her hair and looked intensely at the result. Then very gently he stroked her cheek with the lily's softness until she sneezed.

They went to the theatre, but had to avoid Edmund Kean, all the rage among the vulgar. He'd once given his fragment of *Attila* to Kean to read aloud to auditors. The great man had turned his inward tragedy into fustian, the kind of melodrama Robert particularly despised. Horrified, he'd torn the pages from the little actor's surprised grasp.

She knew the story. She'd heard it from several sources.

So she took Robert to *The Castle Spectre* with its bleeding nun and devilish seductress. No pretension there to high art, no bathos where no heights. He was bored.

Better bored than furious, she reflected.

What he liked, it seemed, were new tricks, the famous gas lighting at the Lyceum and Drury Lane. She couldn't share his joy: an evening in gaslight made her chest heave and her eyes water – the effect lasted for fully three days. He loved too the mirrored curtain which showed the audience itself; they saw it later when they went down to Lambeth Marsh to watch the jugglers and harlequinade of the new Royal Coburg. Such simple entertainment was, Robert declared, more real than the sensational stuff strutted by Edmund Kean.

Her cousin Sarah was quietly amused when she saw the new pea-green gown and heard of the visit to Lambeth Marsh. She knew Mary Davies a little through some acquaintance of Charles's sister and, from the trail of gossip, learned that Ann and a male companion had been seen walking in Hyde Park together, close together, and talking all the while. Mary Davies had been restrained: no hint of the dislike she'd felt at the behaviour of her boorish guest.

'Are you in love?' Sarah asked playfully – on important matters like family and children her broad face became prettily serious, not now. 'I know there's a man in the case.'

'He's not exactly in the case, an acquaintance,' Ann replied. 'You know me. I've done with that sort of thing. I'm growing an old spinster. I shall soon adopt the Mrs style. Gregory Lloyd was enough.'

Yet on the tip of her tongue to say that this was so very different. 'I just want to make my own living,' she said.

'You know that I cannot believe you,' smiled Sarah.

'I've always known I might have such a relative,' Sarah Hardisty had said when years before Ann had fallen into her life from another world. She laughed as she often did to punctuate her thoughts, 'but our mothers quarrelled. I was told yours was rather, shall we say, unusual?' She glanced anxiously at this new cousin.

'We shall indeed,' replied Ann, smiling back. 'But I haven't seen her for years.'

'I'm so sorry.' Sarah was about to reach for Ann's hand when the other's expression stayed her.

'Don't waste pity. Caroline and I are better distant. She never approved of me. She was full of Gilbert as if I had had nothing to do with either of them.'

Sarah was bewildered. With a shock she understood: it was her aunt who was Caroline. She'd never heard any woman call her parent by a Christian name. It was very strange. 'Oh, I'm sure she did, somewhere, underneath. You are so clever. And besides, mothers always do.'

'Do what?'

'Love, so in the end they approve.'

'Is that your experience with your little brood?'

Sarah's fair face puckered. 'Well, yes, I suppose it is.'

'No favourites among them, one you care for more, one less?'

'That's a different thing.' She stopped, then grinned. 'I expect your mother was impressed by your writing, cousin Ann – it is Ann not Annie? You a woman making books. That is something.'

'Now there you are quite wrong, Sarah. We parted long before I did it for a living.'

A shadow crossed Ann's face. 'She thought I was stupid. She said it often.' Her eyes focused behind her cousin. 'I had a weakness in my chest, an asthma, and when it came on me I breathed through my mouth. Caroline – I was not to call her Mama except when told to in public – left me standing as she spoke about my father's mania for astrolabes. I was just ten years old. My mouth fell open. Caroline saw it, stopped in mid-sentence, stood up and screamed, "Close your mouth, you stupid girl. You look like an idiot, an idiot I say. Get out of my sight."'

The telling of this distant, so demanding memory was too savage. Ann was ashamed. But there'd been something in Sarah's placid face that urged her on when she'd better have been reserved.

She swallowed, ground her teeth a little, smiled and tried to rescue the moment. 'I believe, if she thought of my future at all, Caroline wanted to see me married to a powerful – yes powerful – gentleman, the mistress of a mansion where she could preside as a lady. But how . . .' Ann trailed off.

Sarah chuckled with relief – though her eyes remained serious, her pale face showing a fading blush. 'What mother does not want that for her daughter!' She paused. 'Do not you think, dear Ann, that perhaps we daughters want something of the sort for ourselves when we are out of pinafores?'

'Not me.'

'Possibly so, cousin Ann. Or perhaps you thought you might not have it.' Afraid she'd offended, she added, 'Not that you could not, but that you had not the way of wanting it enough. You have said as much.'

'I doubt many men could have made me happy or would have wished to, and I don't know how I would have made them so.'

Sarah had no response. She tried to keep pity from her eyes. She'd seen the bitterness in her new cousin; it made her angular where she'd be better round and smooth. She herself was used to adapting. It was what women did, what her mother had taught her to do, and what in time her daughters would do. But she already knew enough of Ann's eccentric life to see she lacked a useful model.

'Tell me about what you write,' she said much later. 'You have hinted but not described it to me. I think it so bold a step to take. I could never do it.'

'Do you really want to know?'

'I really do.'

They were in the small snug back parlour beside a cheery log fire. Sarah sent the maidservant for more hot water and settled herself further into a comfortable armchair. 'Sit back, Ann, you are at home here.'

She did speak — haltingly at first, then more loosely.

Suddenly Sarah clapped her plump hands. They made hardly a noise beyond a soft fleshy thud. Then, with her usual little chuckle, she asked, 'Do you base the books on your own life?'

'No,' smiled Ann, 'no, no, of course not. They're full of horrid adventure, lots of blood and corpses; my life is not. I'm too plain, too complicated.' She laughed. The habit was catching. 'Yet, if truth be told, I suppose, though they rarely know their fathers and I too . . .' She stopped. How odd to feel this rush of emotion, 'you know, Gilbert . . .'

Sarah looked anxious. Her cheeks flushed bright red.

Ann was puzzled. Her cousin must still find these Christian names too strange. She'd not expected her to be so sensitive. 'Perhaps too, sometimes, Caroline, my mother – perhaps she has crept into the books as the Stepmother.'

Sarah patted her hot face with the back of her cooler hand. She remained flushed.

This introspection, this thinking aloud and about oneself and one's childhood, was perhaps too much, thought Ann. Could she be irritating Sarah by running on – though her cousin was too polite or kind to show it? But no, she'd caught pity in her face, not irritation. Or – and the thought struck her suddenly – perhaps Sarah hadn't wanted to be so long separated from her babies and was embarrassed to admit this to her childless cousin.

Was this the alternative to Caroline? Was this kindly milky flushed being what a mother should be?

Sure enough, Sarah soon excused herself and went to check on the nursery. A small child played with pieces of material in the corner, making hats and gloves for a rag doll. Charlotte? When she returned Sarah kissed her. Then the nursemaid came to take her upstairs. The child objected and cried out but was picked up and carried off still protesting.

No, it struck Ann suddenly, Sarah hadn't meant to ask about mothers and fathers at all. Her cousin was referring to imaginary *lovers*. Of course. How slow she was! After all, she created these tales for yearning women. What else were stories for?

When Sarah was seated, she rushed on again. 'Some people might have expected me to feel shame displaying myself, but my name is not on the page. In any case I don't feel any – any shame I mean.' She paused and looked at Sarah. 'I know what you're thinking. A man would see this as too independent, too encroaching on the masculine sphere. But I never claim there's anything in my work that has merit beyond a moment's read.' She hesitated. 'Besides, what does it matter what a man thinks?'

She looked at her cousin enquiringly. Sarah caught her eye but remained silent. Her face had resumed its usual pallor. She picked up her basket of sewing and chose some little pantaloons to mend, her chubby fingers expert at feeling what tears could be repaired, what consigned a garment to the box of rags so useful in a house of infants.

Ann waited. 'All right then, so it might? In any case it gives me a regular income,' she went on quickly as she saw Sarah searching for a way to respond. 'It's not so different from millinery or teaching in a school. No one thinks that not feminine.'

Sarah still sat tranquilly sewing, saying not a word. So Ann rattled on. 'I'm very fluent. All I have to do is vary elements. I never run out of plots.'

Sarah bit the thread to break it and looked up encouragingly. She had absolutely nothing to say. Neither she nor Charles had ever read any of this sensational stuff.

'You make some surmountable trouble between delicate heroine and handsome hero, but only after the girl has been nearly frightened out of her wits by the villain in his gloomy castle.'

Sarah looked up and gazed at her cousin. Strange indeed to have a head full of such things – on a body sitting familiarly in her back parlour. She would ask her novel-reading friend Jane Lymington to procure a volume from her circulating library; then she could glance into it and compliment her cousin when the right moment occurred. She smiled.

'Sometimes,' Ann went on, warming to her talk, 'I've wondered what would happen if the heroine chose the villain and pushed the hero down an abyss or shut him away like an idiot in a madhouse.'

Evidently the idea, the words, were simply too strange for Sarah. She pricked her thumb with her needle, frowned, bent her head and licked the blood, then pressed the thumb against a rag from her basket.

Could there really be disapproval?

'No one reviews my little productions, you know, Sarah. No one has to say to me, "Pray Miss, put down your pen and take up your needle." I write to earn my bread, that's all.'

Sarah looked up then and laughed heartily. 'My poor cousin, my poor Ann, why these apologies? I have never thought to be an independent woman. It's not possible for me and I do think women are made for marriage and the home, and to be cared for. But I can admire those few who don't take this common path. Charles is less admiring I think, though he much respects and will love you, cousin Ann. Only I wonder whether it is possible to find content without following what our nature wants for us.'

Before Ann could reply, Sarah hurried on, 'But come, I hear the twins stirring. Please to see them after their rest. One of them is lisping words and both coo so prettily. You cannot but be charmed.'

She was never quite charmed. All those wriggling limbs, all that mess, the incontinence. But she visited the house often.

Why did this early conversation ooze into memory so many years later? Surely not because of that awkward defence of her way of living. Had Sarah anything to do with Robert? Doubtful. Ann expected compassion not shrewdness from such a lactating, sewing, buttressing being. At the time, that is.

No, it was what she'd said to her cousin about the might-have-been plot. It raised a question. Did anyone in life *choose* the villain?

3

Was Gregory Lloyd the preface to the meeting at Mr Hughes's dinner?

Because of him she was no virgin.

She set little store by the change. There'd been no unwelcome price to pay. But there were those out in the world who put great weight on such activity, productive or not. She knew that.

Whether he was seen as fall or freedom, Gregory Lloyd was the fault of the Putney house. As isolated as if on a rocky isle off Essex. In fact it stood a mere stone's throw from the crowded public bridge.

Caroline had a pair of widows for occasional gossip and cards, Mrs Graves and Mrs Pugh. They usually visited one at a time. Then they could talk simultaneously, Caroline of her irritating child, the guest of her relief at childlessness and her better-preserved furniture. Mostly they spoke in agitated undertones of shocking scandals from the newspapers. They loved the extravagance of royalty. Such pleasure tutting about the blubbery Prince of Wales and his malodorous princess, Caroline of Brunswick.

Young Ann sat in the corner of the room with a book on her lap letting out sneering breaths.

Apart from these women there was no community round them; not even a distant uncle or great aunt visited.

Once a year her mother put a peacock-feathered ornament on a large turban leaving a fringe of false red curls, arrayed herself in a rainbow-coloured shawl, reddened her cheeks with crimson, looked in a small silver-edged mirror, and then entered a hired one-horse chaise. She was going to town 'on business'.

To the Strand, she'd say grandly for Martha to hear, to the main office of Moore & Stratton.

The turban was because Gilbert had admired the headdress. He'd been to court and seen royal ladies in turbans of black and coloured velvet with high feather plumes; Gilbert cared nothing for pomp but he knew the ways of men and women in all degrees.

On other rare occasions, similarly turbaned and shawled, she'd take herself and Ann to church for form's sake. They were never detained by the vicar or the vicar's wife, who pursed her lips as her eyes rested on Caroline's extraordinary garb, then slid away when they caught Ann's sullen gaze. Caroline was the daughter of a rector in Hereford but she made nothing of this to the vicar's supercilious lady.

Mostly she was content even on Sundays to loll in her chair, sketch flowers and objects brought to her by Martha, and leaf through the *Lady's Magazine*. This was intended for her alone. So at dead of night, Ann padded downstairs to read it by a very flickering candle. She looked only at the stories, ignoring the romances but ingesting the monthly monitory tales.

Through these she learned that to suffer with patience, to rise superior to misfortune and to repay unmerited ill-treatment with benevolence were virtues which provided happiness and recalled the licentious to paths of duty.

She tried 'benevolence' on Caroline for several days. Caroline thought it 'insolent'.

Ann believed she failed because 'licentiousness' was not her mother's prevailing fault.

The impotence of such edifying stories confirmed her preference for Mrs Radcliffe's monks and brigands. These she found in books from the circulating library which Susan Bonnet, another unpopular but less saucy girl at school, borrowed from her mother and lent to Ann. *There* was a world to live in, since Putney was so disappointing.

Once Caroline and Mrs Graves took her to visit Mrs Wright's waxworks in London. A woman with unlined face stood in antique dress. Ann thought her alive and they laughed. She never went to

Vauxhall but it was more real in memory than Mrs Wright's waxworks.

Of course it was, for Caroline had told her of it: over and over.

We had supper at nine in a superb box, such an elegant collation, and so expensive. All so fine, even the thin ham, the lights, a thousand glass lamps, and we bathed in a glow so that it became fairyland. I was in my Indian cotton with ruched lace, my crimson-and-yellow shawl and . . .

Ann had tasted the thin ham. It lingered on her tongue.

Despite all these memories, Gilbert was, except for his words, largely absent for his daughter. She'd glimpsed him in a faded picture set in a locket. Sometimes this hung round Caroline's neck, but usually it lay in a silver box patterned with two stags, their noses touching and their antlers fanning out to form silver trees. The box was kept on the spindle-legged table beside a bottle of eau de cologne and a single flower in a china vase.

The child had been told never to put her fingers on the box for they would tarnish the silver.

Ann asked to look at the picture in the locket to see if she resembled Gilbert. At this Caroline, usually so sedentary, rose up and stepped towards her, almost as angry as when she'd stood before her open-mouthed. 'How dare you?'

But Ann was now fourteen, not ten, old enough and sufficiently well read in cautionary and gothic tales to know that Caroline was not like other Mamas. She stood her ground.

'I would look like him,' she said with tears in her voice but not quite in her eyes. 'Why should not a child look like her father? I must have his hair or teeth or complexion . . .'

Caroline sat down again and put her head in her hands. 'You, you are not worthy to speak of him in this way. He was like no one else. How could you resemble him?'

Martha had once hugged her and said in a voice that came from deep within her bolster of a bosom, 'Don't judge your Mama too harshly, Miss Ann. It is a terrible thing to lose a husband and so beloved. The poor mistress cannot even bear to have a portrait of him about the house. She has a broken heart.'

'But didn't I lose a father?'

'You didn't know the loss, Miss Ann. It's different.'

'She hates me.'

Martha sighed so that her breath rippled from her great bosom and rolled down the folds of her belly. 'Don't say that, Miss Ann. She cares in her way. She gives you masters to make you a lady too.'

'Too?' gasped young Ann into Martha's linsey-woolsey breast. 'I won't be a lady. I won't be like her.'

Children say that kind of thing. They make absolute statements and think they can conform to them. They don't know they're already formed.

Then Martha, warm, ample, beloved Martha, who'd sewn her clothes and dampened her sobs in her early years, Martha who'd crept up the stairs with a bowl of buttered bread in hot milk for the older dry-eyed child shut in the attic, remembering to avoid the stair that would creak and give her away to her mistress, this dear Martha went to look after a sick sister, whose husband had just been killed at sea near Barbados by the French.

Caroline let her go without a murmur.

So, when Ann met some sectarians on the wooden Putney bridge, she joined them. Just like that. Despite the shadowy clerical past, there'd never been much religion in Caroline's house; one god seemed as good as another to her daughter. She was eighteen now.

William Bates, the founder, was a man of the inner spirit, a Quaker originally but wanting something even less constrained than Quakerism. He'd inherited money and a house with a little land and a well-stocked library in the village of Fen Ditton near Cambridge by flat marshy fields. There, with his friend Jeremiah Ellison, he would form a community of equal beings, to join in prayer in each one's own way, study, work together and share everything. Each would do what he or she could and expect the same of others. They would be vegetarians. Betty, ten years older than Ann, had also joined, along with three other men.

Caroline snorted as Ann packed her bags with her few clothes and books. She would be rid of the burden of supporting the girl. What had been the use of the Italian lessons from Signor Moretti and the music from a dismal harpist who hated teaching, when Ann had a character so contrary?

Wanting no made-up tales of elopement or disgrace to entertain the Mrs Graves and Pugh, Ann told Caroline her purpose.

Her mother raised her drooping lids: her greenish eyes sparkled as they did whenever she was in a passion. Ann would learn soon enough that men and women might be equal in theory, oh yes, but there were ways in which they weren't and *never* would be. She shuddered to mention their power. She closed her eyes against the thought.

Sexual congress, Ann supposed, having learned a good deal from the letters section of the *Lady's Magazine*. Much her mother would know of that!

Ann was too big to be slapped and too unschooled to argue. She left Putney, treading the bridge's wooden planks, not looking back even once.

Yet she took a precaution. The office in the Strand where Caroline went on her annual visit was the anchor of the Putney house. As she moved through her separated years she told them of her whereabouts. In case.

The community lasted longer than anyone outside, and perhaps inside, expected.

'We will work four hours a day,' William Bates said. 'That should take care of our needs. We will sell the excess farm produce and sew rough clothes to make an income. The rest of the time we will pray, read, discuss, explore our inner selves and commune with nature.'

Ann's enthusiasm waned as she found the housework, the cooking of so many root vegetables, the organising of communal linen, becoming women's work despite the talk. They had outside help for washdays and harvesting, but there were divisions of labour, and not to her advantage. William Bates was attuned to the flat land for he'd been raised nearby. He loved the earthy fare of turnips, swedes, beetroot and parsnips grown on his own fields. But on dark days Ann looked bleakly at the sodden low-lying ground; she even yearned for the suet puddings and lamb stews of Caroline's impermanent cooks.

Among the men was young Gregory Lloyd.

Lanky, tall, very pale, with nearly white hair. Almost grotesque, she thought him at first. A widowed mother, now dead, had raised him. Their situations felt similar. So they became friends, amorous. Both were at an age when anyone will do. Sometimes they lay in the long grass.

As time passed he grew fonder and fonder, taking every chance to touch her as they went about their work. He said they should be married one day. But by now they'd anticipated most aspects of marriage in the fields near Grantchester and it seemed a limp affair to Ann. Besides, there'd been no consequences – and why else did one marry?

He appreciated everything she did. The unfamiliar approval became oppressive. He was earnest about the praying, wanting to make them both spiritually deeper. She asked why they couldn't live like other people and was as embarrassed as surprised by her words. He was hurt. He wrung his thin hands.

She then made an even crueller remark: 'We are still living with our mothers.'

None of this suited the spirit of the community. William Bates wanted them all to be chaste and amiable, to avoid lascivious looking and doing, but he must have noticed something going on with Gregory and Ann, though they kept their 'congress' to the fields.

It was worse when she lost the little faith she'd mustered in the first heady months before housework chafed her.

She'd been walking back from town one winter's evening along the Cam when the night came on too fast. The towpath was little more than a muddy track in places and, careless of the danger, she lost her footing and slid on her back into the river. She was caught by growth just under the surface. It tangled round her legs and snaked into her shoes.

For a moment she thought she'd drown, thought dramatically that a short life was unkindly over. And all because a heavy cloak pulled her down into the cold water.

Then she found a foothold on a stone and pulled herself up out of the vegetation and into the slime of mud and wet nettles on the bank. Shivering and shocked, she stumbled along in the darkness, teeth chattering and head whirring.

By the time she flopped into the hall, her clothes wet and dripping on the flagstones, her face streaked with dirt, she knew she no longer believed even in the vague god of that house and would stop making any effort to do so. She'd been saved on the riverbank but not by anything divine. Rather by some effort on her part and mainly by luck that her foot had caught a stone. Bad luck, a little less effort, would have seen her drowned.

Gregory rushed to help her as she staggered into the house. He held her tight. 'Thank God,' he said.

'No, not that.'

She pulled away. He thought her hysterical.

Gregory was loyal to the community; yet, as the years went by, he, like Ann, grew restive, no longer immune to a world outside the house and grounds, no longer so keen to engage in discussing his faults – with so few to present. He would walk down the muddy bank of the Cam into the city and watch the university men strutting around, hear their taunts of the poorly dressed like himself, their arrogance. He would gaze at the bookshop, the learning denied to him, though quite as clever as any. At the house they studied without authority; they had good teachers, people William Bates and Jeremiah Ellison had known in their past lives, learned men who arrived to demonstrate the globes and microscopes. They knew more of science and natural history in that draughty mansion than the college scholars in their courts and towers, but it didn't give them what the Latin and quaint theology delivered: self-confidence in the World.

The time for tearing down the unholy trinity of church and king and college had gone. They lived in the wrong era. William Bates admitted it.

Then Betty left – after some incident with Jeremiah Ellison, Ann never knew exactly what. William Bates came out of his pious reverie to take notice. She and Betty had not been close, simply tolerating each other and sometimes making common cause over the unshared housekeeping. But it was hard to be the only woman.

The others planned to invite in an older widow met in Ely market who'd seemed drawn to their way of life. But, before they did so, Ann decided to leave. Then one evening just before she packed her bags, William Bates was too honest about the inadequacies of those who depended on his spirit and diminishing inheritance, and the group disintegrated.

He'd not taken particular note of Ann through their years together but he was more astute than his idealism suggested. As she prepared to make her own way outside, he addressed her. 'You have a heavy burden, Sister Ann, you have not had enough loving kindness in your life and you are in much need. But you do not, pardon me dear Miss St Clair, know where to look for it, on earth or beyond. You will be in my prayers.'

She didn't say, don't bother – after all he'd kept her these past years. But it was intrusive when other people summed one up.

What was the use of this memory? Not a lot for the later time, but it did, she thought for a while, put it into glowing perspective.

For Ann and Robert had made love.

In truth they had not quite made love at once. He wanted to do so, she even more, and they'd been through the motions. But he'd arrived too fast. He'd been upset. He'd not withdrawn to save her honour. He knew she was no virgin; he admired her for it.

It didn't matter, she said.

He seemed so sad. This trivial thing, not necessarily to be repeated, resonated in a symbolic world she couldn't reach – a world in which all parts served a whole, were the whole, and where each if not perfect diminished the whole.

That made things way more dramatic.

She wanted to put her arm round him but knew then – once she must have had more tact with him – it wouldn't do. She made herself small and demure. She waited till he put his arm on her and only then did she comfort him with silence. That was right.

She liked such moments – after a crisis – when tears, had they flowed, would have stopped but could continue falling gently inside.

He took the voice of a lover a few times. She understood the message.

His warmth was huge, his median temperature way above a human average. He enveloped her like a massive fur coat. He was taller than she was but not tall for a man, stockily, powerfully built, the hair on the top of his head partially gone in a distinguished way. His legs were a little too short for his torso but she didn't notice that in the beginning. And afterwards, even that made her fond, like everything else about him. He stirred her as a spoon stirs in thick cream.

At Margate on a day's outing to the seaside, after she'd taken a donkey ride at his bidding, they stood in the cold water together, embracing. Then they lay against a sand dune with reeds sheltering them a little from an unkind west wind. She watched the wind play on the strands of hair at the nape of his neck and burst with resentful love. The dear head.

They walked holding hands along the sand below chalk cliffs as the waning moon rose and the light faded, the darkness engulfing everything except the back of his hand from the light of his pipe. When it went out he struck his tinder and it glowed on his face as well. Then they held hands again.

There was dust or sand sticking to some hairs on his neck. She brushed it off and he looked away.

They tried once more. He spent too soon again and against his breeches. He was angry. She repeated that it didn't matter, but that was wrong. 'It does matter,' he snapped and got up. He left her dazed. He'd given her such amazing pleasure and she was grateful, for no one had bothered before or known how. Poor Gregory.

In Grantchester meadows she'd felt the grass prickling her back through her muslin dress. Gregory had been entirely rapt. He'd once been stung by a wasp, which made a welt on his fair skin with long trails of red like tiny threads travelling from it up his arm. It didn't concern him. He hardly noticed.

But Robert was attuned to prickles and weather and everything around. Somewhere a dog barked or an insect hummed unmelodiously in a nearby tree: it was enough to disturb him.

He cared not one whit about privacy. What space he occupied was his entirely. He took his clothes off and threw them aside, not with the haste of desire but indicating their casual unimportance. Yet they *were* important, very much so. A dark-blue jacket, the whitest shirts and fine thin breeches.

He was never naked with his hairy chest, those densely covered shoulders. But there was movement under the skin as if his flesh formed the surface of an ocean of boiling underwater currents.

On her own body she noticed where the veins would soon show

below the skin, when Caroline's hands would become hers, a parchment telling an unavoidable true story. And legs? She'd never seen, or didn't remember ever seeing, Caroline's no doubt portly legs. Hers were thin, unshapely. But whatever Robert touched – and he touched her parts so gently, so amorously – that part of her became valuable and beautiful.

Her hand was too cold, he said. And in any case he didn't like being caressed – there.

'It doesn't matter,' she said once more.

He looked coldly at her. Surely he could make this a comedy. Was there not a voice of the Member? Why did he not turn his humour on himself?

She'd heard that some men wanted a woman on top or to come from behind (she blushed to think it), not in the wrong place of course, not that. But rather like animals, cats and dogs and so on, not facing each other. She thought she'd mention the idea delicately to Robert. But was she ever delicate enough? He was uninterested. He saw no problem, he liked holding her breasts, sucking them, kneading them.

It was generous. Her breasts were her best feature. He once said he would like to have had them himself, but he didn't do the Voice of the Breasts either. What would they have said?

They both smiled. So that was that.

Then they had a quarrel. She forgot the reason, it was unimportant. It was a terrible unexpected thing. It must be their last, she told herself. She could prevent it in future. She would see that she was always swept up in the listening and the laughter, never provoking. She, the insolent daughter, would be the submissive lover.

Yet it was after this quarrel, so devastating she thought it would end her life, that they made successful, rapturous love, achieving their pleasure together in a rush of tears and clasping. He nuzzled into her breasts and was happy.

She was always entranced. There was no one like him. She felt him all through her body from her neck to the pit of her stomach and down her legs. He was so far beyond thin Gregory Lloyd, and even wordy Gilbert, that he was altogether another kind of being. To be noticed for what she said or did, even what she was, to be wanted – yes loved perhaps – was really too much. It was to crave beyond her deserts, and yet she did crave and hope. She was what Gregory called her in their final days together, when she was leaving him and would not say why: bewitched.

'Ann,' he said, 'Ann.' And it thrilled her that he said her common name. He made it sound like Annabella.

Without having arrived there with words, with none of the amazing devotion Caroline had reported from Gilbert, she knew well enough she was burning up with desire, bodily perhaps but even more – what? – spiritual was wrong, mental was wrong. She only knew she'd caught something febrile. She welcomed it like a baby tiger into the cosy lodgings of her mind.

Was it Love? Was this the thing she'd been reading about in the circulating library books since she was a sulky schoolgirl in the Putney attic, the thing Caroline boasted about when she bored her daughter to death with her stories of Gilbert – there they were, these equally spectral parents, intruding again – the thing she, Ann, had used in her tales to wrap up the true plot of torture and horror, a passion taken for granted as if it were the easiest thing in the world to feel, quite distinct from those fearful states of terror, grief, disgust, obsession? Was it?

She wouldn't answer. What she knew above all on her pulse was that she had increasingly to see Robert James or be nothing. This new velocity of life took her breath away as thoroughly as any childhood asthma.

Emotions were bodily like material words: he showed it in himself. Desire was substantial, it was no flimsy thing that could be filled by thought, or destroyed by some small physical failure. The body is just a vehicle for the soul. So he said. This was not the thin religious concept she'd heard enough of in Fen Ditton, so she told herself. What then was it?

Energy coursed through everything, and especially through his body. 'Listen,' he said one day in Islington fields, holding her arm and twisting her round, 'listen to the rustling, the whispering.'

She thought he meant little creatures, maybe mice or voles, but it wasn't that at all. It was something quite other that she was supposed to hear. It was the world resonating in him and round him. You could if you listened hear an echo of all the past.

Everything was more intense in his shadow, the water more glittering, the sun more violent, the waves on the sea more purely blue-green, the river, the ripples on a puddle more sparkling. A glass of water caught the sun, a weed in the crack between bricks in the courtyard: both sprang to life when he looked at them and she looked at him.

He was a single sharpened shard cutting through a spongy surface. Then the surface shimmered.

He kept drinking tea so strong it exploded in the mouth like gunpowder, enough to keep a weaker man awake for days. She couldn't drink a tenth of it. She admired him even for that. Though when he slept soundly but jerkily, filled with tea, wine, a little brandy and laudanum, he snored to bring the rafters down. Even if she'd been a good sleeper she couldn't have slept against such uproar.

When he stayed the night in her rooms – having just occasionally achieved that ecstasy which was as nervous as sexual and rarely mutual – he remained noisily in the bed. While she, sometimes weak with desire, silently got up to spend most of the dark hours on her narrow couch by her desk.

It was convenient for early-morning work. She could reach her paper and pens from where she lay and make dungeons and lascivious brigands in the raw early-morning light.

Outside, the night-soil man trundled by with his cart of filth.

He loved an audience, a discipleship. Men were drawn to him. Grave, gentle Richard Perry, who almost worshipped him; huge Frederick Curran, who'd known him at Trinity in Dublin, both being pleased and furious to be among the first Catholic students there; Suffolk-born John Taylor, who'd interrupted law practice to paint water-colours of the English coast, most delicate when the artist was in liquor – his face mellow then but with harsh undertows increasing as he sobered; John Humphries, who, like Richard Perry, digested books for journals, a man's man who avoided women's eyes; boyish, raw-faced Henry Davies, quiet, earnest, with a little of Gregory's yearning look but more intensity. All of them and others who came and went, hanging on his words.

They took her in as a disciple – no, like an appendage. She was grateful. It was warm in this manly fog of alcohol, sweat, tobacco and talk in the Castle and Falcon or the Swan Tavern or The Queen's Arms in Bird-in-hand Court in Cheapside. Other women occasion-ally hung on sleeves but they were never part of the inner circle and Ann didn't see them as separate beings. Of the men she should have liked Richard Perry most, for he was more gentle to women than the others and he adored Robert, but there was something disturbing there, some core best not deranged – she heard he'd lost a young wife, perhaps that had marked him. No, if she had to do with anyone beyond Robert James, it would be with big Irish Fred Curran. Once she fancied Gilbert might have looked like him. He gave his flesh to Gilbert and Gilbert responded with his eclectic words.

Robert had so much promise – far beyond what he'd already done as a young man. Everyone said so. He had fire in his brain, he would make a difference in the world. They were lesser beside him. He draped his personality over the company like a bright bespangled cloak.

He didn't care for politics, he'd said so often. That was not it; he cared so deeply the quotidian was neither here nor there. His 'politics' were capacious. Anarchists and radicals were old-fashioned. They wanted simple things: money, fairness, equality. They had had no vision, no Vision. They were Protestants, secular Protestants,

Separated people. They lacked the grandeur of the universal, of transcendent thought. It took a lapsed Catholic to see that. *Urbi et orbi,* after all.

Back in that quotidian world Richard Perry and Frederick Curran both suspected Robert was being watched. Fred Curran said he knew he'd been followed – and Robert was a bigger fish. Activities on the Continent? Were they not both Irishmen, obnoxious to English authority, any authority?

Robert James denied it, but he was suspicious in strange ways none the less. Sometimes he sensed men lurking in corners of taverns or in dark hallways.

Ann registered Fred Curran's words. She asked Robert how he'd got into trouble with 'authorities' and where it happened. He looked at her for some moments, then away, and let out a deep breath.

'Who said that?'

'Richard Perry.'

'Richard Perry knows nothing.'

Politics didn't matter. Only poetry of philosophy, philosophy of poetry – purity of language which is its beauty. He'd tried to say something of this in *Attila,* showing brute power grappling with words, but he'd failed. He knew that. The form was wrong.

'See, see,' he said, holding her hand and letting his thoughts ripple through his body and into hers. 'Do you see? The metaphysics of beauty develops the concept of the beautiful in its pure form. It's abstracted from particulars, through the unity of the elements which appear – always appear – where the Beautiful truly exists. Of course, of course, they're so intrinsically contained in the ideal unity of the idea that each demands the others. Only words contain them. See?'

She had no impulse to say Not quite – certainly not while his burning hand held hers.

'This is an abstraction insofar as it can only be realised by unaccommodating Truth. A pure concept as such can have no objective existence. But – and this is important – it's not to be seen as a mere form created by thought; it's the foundation and content of its truth.

This principle is always right. It must be.' His eyes shone. 'In a new kind of poetry that isn't just poetry, not just writing, much more than that, I can capture this very thing, this principle, this purity.'

Then, with Richard Perry and Fred Curran in a room in Gray's Inn which Curran treated like his own, though Ann never knew whether he actually lived there, Robert simply continued his talk, as if different time and place and audience had no need to interrupt the monologue. 'Of course there's an essential difference between the concept and its realisation, and the former is, if you use the language of logical thought, assigned to the category of abstraction. I discredit this point of view, I erase it.' He lit a cigar — one of several given to him by generous John Taylor — waved it around in his hand, then thumped the table with the other. 'It's obvious that the concept itself is truly present as it's realised, as a creative and moving soul and the soul lives in its potent words.'

They would go on listening, sometimes talking, sometimes just agreeing, long into the night.

And she, Ann St Clair, server of gothic pap, would be among them.

So they trundled on for another year. Genius, Robert said, was a dream of the old century made into fulfilled desire in the nineteenth. Ann was now less thrilled by this idea than she'd been initially.

Robert never said he was a genius — he didn't have to. Wasn't a genius the master of antithesis, and wasn't everything he said antithetical? So there you were then.

In which one of his voices would he have said this if he'd said it? she wondered later. Would it have been the Fantasist or perhaps the Poet? The Fantasist who wove together self and the external or the Poet who pulled twine from himself? Was it the Poet who had that throbbing need to go back and back into his past thoughts and lay them on chairs and tables and beds?

He was beyond fantasy and poetry, though he had to use their terms. His words, words as counters of the self, they were the Thing. 'Not that the words are the things, you understand, Ann, don't you?' he said. 'Imagine that words could be physical, not words as we know them, concrete words. These words are truth, a violent truth, because they shatter the obvious, the superficial, that is how they are concrete, heavy and dangerous.' He would make poetry that was equivalent to philosophy and beyond. Not philosophical poetry — not doggerel for superficially enquiring minds. No, poetry — always qualified by 'if it could be called poetry' — that was the same as philosophy, that expressed the comedy and sublimity of the world.

He would march through ventriloquism, not just the individual voice of an intricate conqueror but the language of everyday man, to reach a something beyond, an absolute.

Of course he could do voices, for, to go further than every man, he had to be a sort of Everyman, he said. Richard Perry said, Yes, yes, Robert had a marvellous plastic ability. Henry Davies added quickly, for he'd rehearsed the lines, 'We all have bits of others in us. You show us and make us more ourselves.'

There was plenty of such talk. But Ann saw no equivalent work, nothing since the early wonderful fragment composed so many years before. Only writing would be a permanent record of his present imaginings and make Robert's mark on the world. Was she affecting the great work, just a little, by her presence?

Or was Robert beginning to fear and she'd caught his fear? The task he'd set himself, or had been chosen for, was so great. Should he compromise, try for less?

He'd said something of the sort not specifically to her but rather to all of them and only once, in the early hours of a Sunday morning. They scorned the idea. He could do whatever he wanted. He'd shown that already.

Of course he could. So he abandoned his act as tortured sacrifice to emerge triumphant once more. Richard Perry patted his shoulder.

Always he went to the universal. Yet at home alone, even so early in their time together, even as she almost worshipped, to her the ideas seemed brilliant fragments. After all, his marvellous tragedy had been unfinished, unacted. He made a virtue of it, for great work could not be closed. But still, it remained true, it was partial, and he knew it. She'd always lived with scraps and splinters of truth and she suspected that these were all there were. That was no problem for her; under all her froward ways she'd always been humble.

They were sitting drinking and eating in the Queen's Arms in Cheapside one winter's day, not caring who would pay. Curran had brought along a young woman called Lydia, his cousin's friend. She was making sheep's eyes at John Taylor, who'd been introduced as a lapsed lawyer as well as an artist, a man in whom she sensed possibilities from his smart address near St Sepulchre, mentioned in passing. Otherwise she was bored. The men had drunk a lot, the women less.

'The inner and the outer come together in a visionary world,' said Robert. 'The art describing it is never overblown, always austere by definition.'

John Taylor laughed, flecks of froth were sticking to his beard. Lydia ignored it and smiled at him. 'We do not deal in mere ephemera,' he said, 'not we.' He waved his hand. 'We are free, uncircumscribed.'

'We none of us want to be regulated,' said Richard Perry.

'Well we are. We are mastered twice over,' said Frederick Curran, who was the drunkest of them and felt the melancholy of his state. He seemed unsure of the purpose of his bulky person.

'We are,' said Robert.

'Oh no, not this Irish bragging again, always the grandest victim,' said John Taylor. He hiccuped.

They all laughed but Ann saw that Robert and Fred Curran were a little hurt. To her mind there was something uncomfortable, discomfiting about John Taylor. He admired Robert – they all did of course – but not as unconditionally as Richard Perry and Fred Curran.

Robert tapped his forehead and addressed it, his eyes swivelling to the ceiling. 'The head is austere.' He loved the word tonight and elongated its syllables.

'Exuberance can be austere,' said Curran airily, having difficulty with the 'x'.

She might have thought it rubbish, but not here.

'Anything but the whimsical, the sentimental,' said Robert. 'When thought is correct there's no difference between fact and fiction, dreams and experiments, science and poetry. Look there' – and he pointed to his brow – 'it contains a universal grammar, words are its servants. A single form is near infinite, a single word, all in there.'

'A single drink,' laughed John Taylor, who'd mastered his hiccups and now raised his tankard for someone to pour in more liquid. Dark blue paint stained his knuckles.

'Of course, a sip, ship,' said Curran lifting the jug unsteadily towards him. 'Drink is ritual.'

Lydia gave up trying to attract John Taylor – maybe he was nothing but an artist after all – and was pulling at Curran's arm. He jerked it away. 'Do you know that my mother has been sewing a fantastic garment to be worn on judgement day?'

'That is a serious business,' said Robert. 'I am the tailor of the garment.'

'Oh you,' shouted John Taylor, 'me rather. You are just an old alchemist.'

'I am,' said Robert, 'and one day you will see gold.'

'I have no doubt of it,' said Richard Perry. There was no mockery in words that might, in another mouth, have seemed scoffing.

Ann coughed. Richard Perry glanced at her, then turned away.

'To the unknowing everything is hieroglyphics,' said Robert and raised a hand in blessing.

Lydia took no pains to stifle a snort. Having failed to move Curran or charm John Taylor, she'd gone past boredom. She was irritated and wanted to leave this gang of childish men

Robert looked at her pretty pinched face. 'We have distorted bodies because we have distorted words,' he said. 'We can free the one with the other. No need to be enigmatic, secretive; it's all open, clear as light and day, bright as the sun.'

He addressed Lydia directly. 'You are just there, suspended between life and death, past and future, here now. And this "now" is no more important than the other "nows".'

'What's he saying?' said Lydia in a hoarse whisper to Frederick Curran. He ignored her.

'It is always the present,' said John Humphries, who was content in his companionable silence but liked to ease where he could, especially when women spoke when they should be silent. He relished the chiming bass voices of men even in their cups, but winced at the higher register of females – it was like cats mewing. Henry Davies, so eager now to please it almost took his speech away, looked round trying to focus his eyes; he started to say something to his blurred companions, then thought better of it. Nobody heeded him.

It was John Taylor's turn to have the drinker's gloom as he waved his blue-stained hand, raised his head and closed his eyes.

'You are only a painter, you are naturally dark,' said Robert.

'I am lugubrious melancholy,' shouted John Taylor, his eyes still firmly shut. 'I am not dark. I shine in the night.'

'Then you are drunk,' said Robert.

John Taylor collapsed into a bearded sack.

'Don't brood on it,' said Robert James, 'Everyone is drunk some time and a good number here – except of course Miss St Clair and Miss Um . . .'

Lydia hissed 'Minogue, Miss Minogue,' but no one heard or paid attention.

John Taylor inflated again. 'True, true I am that. I am magnificent. My skies and seas are a marvel. My skies are divine.'

Frederick Curran reached across Richard Perry to pat John Taylor on the knee. 'They are pure,' he said, and the 'p' sent spit on to Richard Perry's waistcoat.

'Divine, spiritual,' said young Henry Davies, content at last that he could expel his remark.

Richard Perry ignored them both. 'Purity matters,' he said, looking at Robert.

'It does indeed. Purity is boundless, it is love and truth.'

John Taylor deflated again and was suddenly on the edge of sleep. This time his eyes closed involuntarily. Henry Davies, his raw face shining with excitement, nudged him without effect.

'Sleep the inscrutable,' said Robert gently.

'We are the saints,' said Frederick Curran as if pricked to speak.

'They are the Puritans,' said Ann.

'Oh the pedantry of Protestantism,' said Robert, waving his tankard at the others but looking at her. As he looked he smiled with a soberness only for her.

She felt warm, included in all this rich nonsense. Robert James was becoming her own Gilbert, not exclusive to be sure, but more publicly admired. That *she* could be admired by a man admired by others was so very sweet.

'Images are power,' said Robert and sent his boy, an Irish lad with white eyelashes, for more drink and more of the beef suet pudding they'd been consuming earlier. It was not his dinner to command, but no matter. Who was the host, who the guests, who the entertainer?

'Bless you,' said Robert, again raising his hand and waving it at the group. 'Bless you all. We all have grace.' He paused a moment, then looked round again. 'That moment of my conception. Imagine how the clouds moved, the earth convulsed. My poor father and mother. They were hardly material to it.'

'I paint,' said John Taylor, suddenly waking up, '*I* revive the dead.' His eyes closed again.

'Life is a mnemonic,' said Robert, 'a grand gesture pointing at something else. I extend myself into it but I am not enclosed by it.' He leaned over the side of his chair, then swung back. 'I become like you.'

Curran was growing less drunk, more aware of Lydia scratching on his arm. 'Should we go to the theatre?' he said abruptly.

'To that pitiful place? It's for fools,' said Robert. 'They might as well wear Grecian masks for all the feeling they show. There's been nobody since Garrick.'

'Did you ever see him?' asked John Humphries.

'Of course not. That's why he was so great. You didn't need to.'

Lydia felt her moment of escape disappearing. She looked from one to the other and tried not to catch Ann's eye, assuming a woman who kept such company would be no help.

'We usher in our own theatre,' said Robert.

'Such innocence. To think of theatre speaking in the head as you do,' said Frederick Curran. There were tears in his eyes as he looked at Robert. At least she thought so.

'Innocence doesn't speak, it is *infans*,' said Robert. 'It is impervious, pointless, almost unborn.'

Suddenly Robert sang out in a resonant baritone a line from the Latin hymn to the martyred innocents. He stopped abruptly.

'I think,' said Richard Perry, 'that we who are alive are a bestiary. We live in a zoo.'

'We want ecstasy but can't reach it or hold it if we could,' said

Fred Curran mournfully, his slurring tensely controlled.

'Ecstasy is blind,' said Robert, 'we want clarity rather. That's the point of art, it blazes and clarifies, not intoxicates.'

Fred Curran looked abashed. 'We are all emissaries of something else,' he muttered.

The candles were spluttering. They had not been replaced. When more drink and food arrived it was nearly dark. They set to consuming it, continuing to speak to the group, to each other, or to themselves, it did not seem to matter. Polyphony or just cohesive noise?

She said things she didn't remember because she mainly remembered the words of others. How deep the melancholy had been!

Sometimes he seemed short of money, perhaps when his allowance had run out. She was never quite sure where this came from. His family – the maligned Catholic progenitors in County Cork, or a Dublin relative? He borrowed freely from his friends. They were never grudging. She remembered saying so.

He gave generously, indiscriminately, to beggars. Then his face went moist as if he identified thoroughly with them or with his own act. He gave too much to the wrong ones. Wasn't this more generous, more profound than her calculating way, thinking of deserts?

Imagine, he said, that our words, the truths of philosophy, could form sentences that had physical substance. Marble words. He'd said 'concrete' before. Was it the same meaning if not the same substance? How about it, Ann?

He held her waist and swung her round her tiny room, dislodging her papers on her writing desk and scattering them on the floor. They'd been placed ready for the printer's devil. She hoped he wouldn't pick them up and read. When he didn't, she was in a tremble he would tread on them. She really couldn't write that stuff again. Besides, all her quills were blunted and would spit ink.

'It's not the words that are the things, don't you see?'

No, of course she didn't. Did anyone else know what it meant, really meant?

She'd told him now that she lived in splinters. A shame of course, but she could live with shame. He'd no such need and certainly no practice.

She mentioned Caroline and Gilbert – delicately, she hoped – and he didn't probe. She wanted to repeat more of Gilbert's words because, though not at all to the point, they'd lodged in her child's brain. Perhaps he might explain or modify them and the emotion they'd begun to raise.

He said he'd severed himself from his past. Yet it repeatedly rumbled into view, the boyhood, the potatoes, the priest, the garish altar, the raucous faith, the easy politics of resentment. Ireland was an English idea, he said to Fred Curran, who agreed.

With the genteel he was sullen, hating social chitchat. But he grew so effusive over wine, good or bad, and strong ale taken in company with men he liked. They spoke excitedly or listened with simple exclamations. Such joy then.

'Gilbert,' Caroline smiled dreamily, 'used to say that I thought him so strong because he was big and expansive. But really he was – he often said as much – weaker than I, far weaker. I was the strong one and he needed my strength. My intuition was better than his reason, more right, even my judgement. Sometimes he was confused and didn't know something till he was with me. Then he knew.'

Ann would be picking her nose by now and staring at the ceiling or hanging her head elaborately. But she was unseen.

'Only then did everything grow clear. I had strength from my own mind, you see. Then he would say so very lovingly and over and over again, "What I do know is what I desire and need and love. I want you more than anyone in this wide world. No one else will do." That's love, girl.'

It was boring for a child of eight to be told this once, let alone twice or thrice. Yet these over-used words must have been sinking in even as she was angry that Caroline hadn't ordered a new frock to be made for her to go to school and look like Other Girls.

Gilbert was no help at all. She decided not to try his words on Robert James.

Yet something not to do with Gilbert, something fantastical that Caroline knew, perhaps remembering some leftover tract from the radical '90s, might connect with Robert. It was a woman's right to initiate just as well as men's.

Had Ann imbibed the idea with mother's milk? But no, it was a ridiculous image. Caroline had employed a wet nurse.

Not mother's milk, then. But she felt sure that Caroline had at one point said that women need not wait for men and that her forwardness did no harm with Gilbert.

It wasn't easy. Like discovering a new continent, not knowing on what plants to place your feet as you pushed into the undergrowth without a light.

There were no conduct books to tell you the words. Their advice all of a piece: hide your feelings, fool the man who'd likely enough fooled you. But Ann was no young inexperienced girl. She should have the right words to handle this. For, with all the love she felt sure he felt and knew *she* felt, he made no further move to bring them together, not exactly marriage, though perhaps . . . but just together.

'I don't want to leave you,' she said, her heart pounding with such daring.

Then simply, with his grey eyes fixed so kindly on her, expressing infinite intimacy, he'd replied, 'Then you should not.'

What other man would have been so very right?

Her desire, the craving, continued. Out in the world, in the street or in a shop or market, Ann had that thrill in the pit of her belly when a figure with Robert's outline came closer, turned to a surge of joy if it was indeed he.

Was desire too consuming? Were human beings meant to go at this speed? Was she? Was this aching elation a kind of sickness? She refused to answer. She shut off part of her mind. The rest of it hurtled onwards, together with all her body.

More of that stimulation, that titillation that he'd once so generously given to meet her physical desire, might have helped. Though now, in the solitariness it occasionally caused, it could turn to something akin to pain, made almost shameful when she saw through her pleasure his tender but unmoved face.

More sleep would have made a difference. But she'd always been a poor sleeper. Even as a small child when Martha did her best to combat wakefulness with her single lullaby of 'Baby Bunting'.

Caroline had a clock – an heirloom, she said, though it didn't look so old – that chimed and whirred through the night. Caroline wound it herself, not leaving it to a servant. Ann asked Martha to try to stop it but Martha would not go against the mistress – she respected Caroline because she sat on cushions and was idle, like a lady should be.

'You won't sleep,' said Caroline to her, 'you fear dreaming. It's a sign of a bad conscience in a child.' She never believed this: the day was simply too short for thoughts. You had to use the night.

He decided one day they should eat strange foods, strange to her – the kind her mother's cooks, the Hannahs and Marys who never stayed for long, would tell her to throw to Jonah's pigs. Caroline had liked only English food. Wistfully Signor Moretti had described the Roman confluence of garlic and oregano and olive oil when Ann had sat in his stuffy rooms trying to master irregular Italian verbs, but he'd not cooked for her. She'd mentioned the mélange to the second Mary, who laughed and laughed, then went on wrapping her suet pudding. When she'd had to feed herself after the years of root vegetables in Fen Ditton, she'd bought a lot of chicken and cured meat.

Robert saw food as expression, a language with which to engage the body.

So he threw out her white bread and sent his pale boy to bring back dark rye instead. She'd thought it peasant fare but no, not this tasty rich bread, eaten with onions cut in rings and salted herring.

She didn't enjoy it. She disliked the lingering smell in her lodgings, too. Was Robert's taste superior to hers? Of course.

That night after dinner he was the Fashionable Lady from out of town, from Tunbridge Wells, who wasn't sure this was quite the smartest place to be. And she laughed and laughed, for he was so good at being other people.

'You are so marvellous at this, your characters are so believable, why don't you write a novel?'

He looked at her in bewilderment.

Did any of it come from memory? she wondered. Did he mock acquaintaces or were his imaginary people born of fragments in his capacious head? He recollected his family differently at different times. His father had been a bully, he said, and he the son had walked out on him shouting, 'I want nothing from you.' His simple quiet mother had been saintly; she adored him. That was what he said. But he also said that his dull mother had pulled down his clever father, who would have been — what he would have been was unclear. Instead, he'd remained a country doctor and who would not drink to excess with such a fate and such a dismal wife? And she? She in her dullness and despair turned more and more to the priest and her love for her only son.

She had some delicate pots, Chinese, French and Meissen, inherited from her own mother. He'd learned to hold and value them and know about their making: about candling and dipping, crystal glaze, gum arabic and vitrification. He found Ann's cups too thick-rimmed and coarse for his use, so he bought her new fragile bone-china ones from Spode. He pointed out where the hazy colour shadowed from green into grey. It was at that point, the numinous, that things happened, he said. 'It's like the sky and sea, John Taylor's painting, what he tries to capture, you don't know where one begins and the other ends.'

As she looked at these fragile vessels, she felt his eyes and fingers on them as if she'd been what he caressed, as open and as empty to be filled.

It was fondling. He fondled her. She responded. It was her fault that she, only occasionally now but with such pain, grasped after more.

With Robert the commonplace was insight. Always the senses must be intense as if candle lights were stars. If he drank apple juice from a coloured glass, it became the gods' nectar.

He prized a gold Swiss watch. It had been an old priest's — he didn't explain why he prized it since he'd abandoned the beliefs of the giver.

He loved to look at its unequal hands moving round the dial. He could sit on a sofa and stare for minutes on end at these hands on the watch's face. She marvelled at the absorption.

Was it laudanum he took, alcohol, mercury? Or was it just a grace?

He knew he had a temper. In school in Cork he knocked down a boy who'd insulted him. He didn't consider it unusual, either the arm that hit or the temper that propelled it. He was not a violent man, he said. He was simply tense with intellectual excitement. And volatile, he knew that. He either sang or was petulant.

Always he was one hop and a skip from outrage, but early on Ann thought she knew his dangers. The quicksand would appear before her and she should and could jump aside. So she believed.

They went on a walk in the country out beyond their usual paths in Islington fields but still close to town, not far enough away to lose all sight and smell of London. She was enjoying the fresher air, but he was morose; the muddy earth was dirtying his new blood-brown boots. He didn't want them stained with paler soil.

The scene ahead was picturesque. He forbade use of this modish word – or rather he laughed at her when she used it. But it was true. It was like a detailed watercolour: a hawthorn in a foreground with a gentle blue-and-green slope behind, the grass blurring to set off the sharply delineated twigs for the focused eye.

'For heaven's sake, shall we go home?' she said at last.

'Yes, why not,' he said. 'It's filthy here.' He prodded a weed with his cane.

'But lovely.'

'If you are properly shod it might be but I'm not.'

'I did tell you to wear something stouter.'

'Can't you ever leave me alone?'

'We wanted to be together.'

She felt ridiculous tears rising to her eyes.

This was not the first time. When it happened, to counter it she found her voice becoming deeper, slower – and consequently more irritating. When he could hide his vexation no longer, he would mutter; then, if they were in her rooms, go out, slamming the door. The women behind curtains in the other apartments would listen for more. She was sure of it.

Once in general talk – they were in the lodgings he shared with Richard Perry – at a moment when Robert was not listening, she'd said something on the edge of critical about his temperament; Richard Perry watched her in silence as the talk flowed on. Then, when the night was deep and conversation no longer general, he took her aside. 'He is beyond wonderful,' he said, earnestly engaging her eyes. 'You may not understand it enough. Not because of his tragedy, one that could never be finished. But because of what he is. I owe him my life. He saved me. Let me tell you some time. You are close to him? I would like you to know.'

So, when he was eating again in her apartment, he seized his moment. Robert left to see Frederick Curran about some matter in Cork, and Richard Perry waited behind. By now she'd learned some listening skills though she dreaded a long tale. She settled herself in her chair. She liked Richard Perry more now than at first, mainly because he so much liked Robert: he buttressed her feelings – and simplified them.

'It was some years ago. I was a bookseller then, not a reviewer. It was before my business went bankrupt. No matter, I have a different existence now. I had to journey to Hamburg in the dead of winter. I took passage with a trader going up the Channel into the sea. It lost its way among shelves of ice on a sandbank off Cuxhaven. It sank. Three of us including the master managed to pull ourselves on to this sandbank while the others were drowned in the icy water. I think some tried to make for the shore instead. It was just after Christmas, before the twelfth night, a night I always remember for it was when my wife died.'

She was about to comment when he prevented her by adding, 'It was sad but we had not been married long, not become used to each other.' He wanted no interruptions.

'The three of us, the master, a sailor and I, had managed to pull towards us some stores that floated past amidst the pieces of ice, a small cask of wine and some biscuits and cockles. I had a few nuts which I'd put about me when I knew the boat was in trouble. On this fare during nearly a fortnight we all managed to live. But the sailor had been longer in the sea than I. He was always weak – I think he sustained some splinters from the ship's side when the ice hit it. At the end of two weeks he died. To tell truth I resented the nibbles of biscuit he took, for I knew it was only postponing the inevitable. He died without my noticing. No rattle or convulsion, just one moment breathing, the next gone. The master seemed to give up after that though he'd been the bigger and the stronger man. The cold was so bad you couldn't tell whether either of them died for lack of food or froze to death. Anyway the master followed his man in a matter of hours. We'd huddled together for warmth. Now my mates were dead.

'In the day I crawled round on the icy sandbank eating a few cockles but never managing to lean into the water to catch a fish. I am not a country or coastal man. My bookselling business had been in Holborn, the skills you need there are quite different. I was a boy in Lichfield and have lived always among houses. At night I thought my blood would freeze if I slept long, and it would have done. So I stretched out the body of the sailor still bearing warmth, then lay on top of him and pulled the master over me. You might think they were decomposing – you turn up your nose – but they were not, the cold was preserving them, they were quite intact. I smelled nothing. But of course my own nose was no longer sensitive. I had to rub it often against the cold.

'The body on the top grew colder than the one beneath, so the next night I changed them round, do you see? Putting the sailor on the top and the master underneath. And so I went on, while eating up the rest of the biscuits and the cockles – I hate them still, it's an unnatural food for men. And then. Such a fright I had. I'd known the sandbank was icy but thought the ice was only on top, and that the whole was fast tied on to roots in the earth and close enough to the shore to be seen one day. But then to my horror it began to move. I had for some days detected a little warmth in the daytime air, a little less absolute cold. Now I saw that my sandbank was no such thing; it was just a piece of ice and I and the bodies of the sailor and the master were drifting out to sea. I had prayed, I suppose – yes, often, but perhaps not enough – and counted my sins. I was never a pious man though I've always gone along with something. I don't think my feeble prayers were answered, but I don't know. I have not Robert James's assurance on this. I was spied by a boat. It was from Schleswig-Holstein.

'They hauled me in, made me warm, fed me small bits of mush, for I could take little – I had not eaten at all for some days. They listened to my story – or rather understood the gestures I made, coupled with some little German I'd learned for my business. I could see horror in their faces. Indeed I mirrored it then, but I cannot say I felt much while on the sandbank. Fear I felt in plenty but not horror. Those dead men gave me their warmth. I would have done the same for them. I was sorry I didn't say farewell to either as we sailed away. The bodies of the men who'd saved my life were pushed off the ice and made to sink. The pilot was superstitious I think for, though without clerical authority, he mumbled some words as they sank which sounded like a bit of the burial service. It's strange they have no worry about sending bodies to the fish but need to mumble something while they do.'

At the end of his story he gave a chuckle from the relief of telling, then continued.

'On land in Esbjerg, for my sailors were going there, half-starved still, my mind almost dead, senses quite bewildered, I met Robert James and stumbled out my story. Where the boatmen had fed me little pieces of food, he fed me special delicacies and, more important, he fed me just enough of hope and life to make my mind start to live, to work again, not grow fat but at least begin to stir. He treated my mind as if it were his own, do you see? cared for it, nurtured it.'

Ann was silent, thinking of Robert and his kindness to strangers, to men. Why not always to her? Was her story not good enough?

Watching her unusual silence, Richard Perry feared she might be squeamish. He wished he'd not said so much, but either he told all his story or none of it.

She roused herself. 'Oh, Richard,' she said.

The sympathy unleashed more. 'Do you know he, Robert James, had tears in his eyes when he saw me. He took new lodgings to accommodate me and cared for me like a child, a beloved brother.'

She still felt some resistance.

'But he didn't actually save you,' she said, 'that was the boat and the German sailors.'

'No,' Richard Perry said, 'no, you are wrong there. It was Robert James. I would have been mad without him. And what good is life without a mind? He made me human again. He is a wonderful man. There can be no one like him.'

In the end resistance dissolved and she swallowed the words gratefully.

'He stayed with me in those cramped rooms in a bleak coastal town day after day, week after week. Just for me.'

'That was kindly done.'

'Yes. And to make me comfortable he said it was right for him, said it suited him too, for he was in hiding from authorities, in Denmark, maybe Copenhagen, no, rather a nearby island, he didn't say clearly where he came from, probably many places. None liked England, too swaggering in her power. Maybe he helped her enemies. It would have been the English authorities after him. Imperial arms stretch far, he always said. He wasn't even using his right name. He told me it but I was not to speak it then; I was to call him Peter O'Neil instead.' Richard Perry smiled to encourage response. 'But in fact I had little occasion to use this subterfuge. I could hardly speak to anyone for many weeks and I never went out. Neither did Robert. He sent a man to buy what we needed. I think he may have said these things for my sake.'

He was back in that time of secret intimacy, two men snugly shut up together. 'He sent out for good things for me – to tempt me to eat,' he repeated.

She was struck by the strange naming. Peter O'Neil.

'He uses his own name now?'

'Oh yes, the danger is passed. And he has moved from politics. They are of this ordinary world, and he is beyond it. He always was, but he thought once that some preparatory change might be political. That was why he began his great work to show what energy might do in the world. He knows now he was wrong.'

Yet he retained strong views of that despised world. He loathed the mad King George and his flabby son. Ann remarked that Napoleon was no longer the taut young hero but had cradled his paunch long before being toppled from his throne.

Robert scoffed. 'So many false images the English make of someone they couldn't conquer without the help of half the world.'

'But they, we, have conquered him all the same. He was just a show in Southampton. He walked up and down on his prison ship for everyone to see before they sailed to St Helena. How will he cope on an island without courtiers and audience?'

'I could do it. I could have been a hermit,' said Robert.

'You could have been a monk,' Ann countered. 'I think you fancy it.'

His face creased into a tender smile, 'Well, a cardinal,' he said and held out his hand with his fingers splayed for kissing. She knelt down and put her lips to his flesh. 'You look like a cardinal.'

'Indeed, yes,' he said, 'my other self. To be called *sua eminenza* and have jewels on my plump white hand. Delicious.'

She was standing again. 'And decadent.' She thought of her cardinal villains gazing at her sobbing girls.

'You mean Catholic, my little Puritan.'

'Well yes. Papist.'

He listened to her – sometimes. It was not perhaps in the way Caroline had described Gilbert doing: listening in rapture, touching hair and skin reverently, looking into eyes whose colour could not be told. She banished this memory with her old childhood scorn, for she'd known that Caroline's eyes were dirty green. How despicable to repeat these words to a child! How irritating that she remembered them now in so different a world.

When with a glass of wine in hand Robert James gave her his attention, she told him what she'd not had time to tell even her cousin Sarah Hardisty, or which perhaps it had been best to repress, for Sarah was conventional regarding the church. But Robert was encouraging.

'I lost the little faith I'd found in the community through a fall when no power outside saved me from drowning.'

He studied her intently, his wonderful grey eyes on her alone, then he exclaimed, 'Bravo. It's a good step taken when you see no one's at your elbow. My mother told me that everyone had a special guardian angel by their bed. I called mine Percy. He was mine alone, though perhaps he'd had other little boys before me, I didn't think of that.'

Had he ever suggested marriage? She wondered this when she remembered the early time, when she went back and back to it as to a heaven glimpsed but on whose threshold she'd somehow missed her footing. She thought he had, but as a throwaway remark to please. But it would have been sincere – for after all he didn't try to please.

Much later, very much later, she asked him if he'd said something of the sort and could say it again.

He could not, he could not repeat himself, he was no lapdog to sit in the same position day after day. He was a passionate man.

Through all the turbulent months she felt Sarah's presence, warm, stable and comforting.

'I have really met someone special,' she said once towards the beginning after they'd taken tea with Sarah's friend Mrs Lymington, and Ann had waited till this bubbly laughing companion left them together alone in the drawing room.

What a thing to say, how bald a statement! Any moment now, she would answer herself, How delightful! as Robert said when he became the Holborn Lawyer, How exquisite, Madam!

'You – you, but I thought you were so happy alone,' laughed Sarah pressing together her chubby hands. 'I always knew it. It is the giver of the pea-green gown?'

'No, Sarah, I didn't say I was. I happened to be alone. I was and still am content.'

'Oh, more than that. You are so independent. What you said about going to live with those people in Fen Ditton. Wasn't that a remarkable thing for a young woman to do? We thought you a marvel, Charles and I, when we heard of it – I didn't tell him quite all, cousin Ann! To leave home alone. I would never dare. But now, how delightful!'

'I'm still independent, Sarah.'

A fine thing, independence. Sarah saw housekeeping money. The rest trivial. She wouldn't trade it for an umbrella held over her head in the last weeks of pregnancy when she had to prop up her sagging belly with her two hands.

To Ann it was money for warm clothes and snug lodgings. It was the going out and in without asking leave, the familiarity with

London streets, the travelling alone in stages or hackney carriages, and the knowledge that the right money must be proffered to avoid being cheated.

There were things she could *not* do. She couldn't carry her heavy box when filled with books – but many a fine gentleman couldn't do that either. She couldn't sit alone with a tankard of beer in a tavern and become invisible. She couldn't watch the world go by as a man could; couldn't overhear, move, travel inconspicuously. Her skirts were always vulnerable. A man might protect her, but he couldn't give her freedom when she left his arm. There were always limits to independence for a woman.

'He is different,' she added.

'Well, tell me about him.'

This was so kind, for she knew Sarah wanted to be elsewhere hearing little Charlotte tell her lessons. Yet she couldn't respond.

Was he handsome?

She had no idea. Bald as a coot, someone might have remarked, and he did sometimes dart like a coot, but no coot had his brooding stillness when he chose.

No, he couldn't be called handsome by anyone, certainly not a maker of heroes with dark eyes, slim hips and tousled curls. Yet there was something about even that fair head, certainly about that face, that you stared at again once you caught sight of it. By now she had it firm inside her skull, burnt on to the back of her eyes: she saw it quite clearly in dark or light.

Then there was the genius thing, the talent, call it what you will. How explain that?

She thought to repeat a line or two of *Attila*: '*A curse may weigh heavier than lead but is light as feathered quill on the sun's . . .*' – no, it would not do. Perhaps some of the words spoken to her? But nothing emerged in a credible or creditable way. He said he couldn't bear the tyranny of other people's thoughts, of ready-made creeds. She luxuriated in *his* thoughts but couldn't, it seemed, repeat his words and make them significant.

Difficult even to mention his sense of the numinous. 'Do you believe in God?' she said at last, noticing that Sarah couldn't bear much longer the conflicting pulls of needy cousin and importunate child.

The tension dissolved. 'What a thing to ask,' laughed Sarah. 'Of course, everyone does.'

Then up she went to Charlotte, who was calling from the stairs while the nursemaid tried to restrain her.

Ann waited. She really wanted to explain. It was so important that Robert see Sarah, that these two people on whom she set such store should be acquainted and impressed with each other.

'He is lots of people,' she said lamely to Sarah when after too long she returned, surprised to see Ann still sitting where she'd left her in the drawing room. 'He can imitate – no, he can become other people. It's truly very funny.'

Sarah looked doubtful. She let out a deep sigh; her lips puckered. 'Oh, cousin Ann, do be careful. You are cleverer than me in so many ways, but you know I think of you in this sort of matter a bit – forgive me, dearest – well, a bit like a child.' She blushed, then went on before Ann could speak. 'Bring him here, let us meet him. Charles will like to have another man at table. They can talk of manly things. I make a good venison pie. You know that.'

Yes, as any reader of a life could tell, it was a foolish idea. She'd known how sullen he became in commonplace company. He couldn't possibly have appreciated how much this ordinary couple in ordinary Phoenix Street meant to her. Why in the world had she risked putting the author of *Attila* on show?

All were dispirited. She threw out subjects, urged Charles and Robert to speak by imploring looks. But it was no good. Robert, so lively with her and in the tavern, was morose and uncommunicative. His mood spread over the table and dulled the blue-and-white china and dainty glasses. She wished he'd do his funny voices, but he sat silent and unresponsive.

It was as well. Would Charles and Sarah have found the Billingsgate butcher amusing or the fashionable Mayfair dame or the Irish priest in Brighton or the unctuous Holborn lawyer?

And indeed, if she were honest, she knew he'd begun to tire himself with his invented people. He spoke more and more only of his ideas, in his own voice. And these ideas were not for such company.

As soon as minimal politeness allowed, Charles excused himself, he had to see someone urgently. It was probably true – he was no expert liar – and he could have done nothing if he'd stayed. But Ann was hurt.

The evening dragged on until Sarah declared she could no longer bear the needs of the twins pressing on her. Ann heard no cries, but she supposed only a mother was attuned to faint sounds.

After that dinner, etched on her mind, she remembered Sarah saying nothing for a while. Then, much later, while they were drinking tea near the Haymarket or in her lodgings (the cups were not Robert's bone-china ones, and there were almost imperceptible cracks so they couldn't have been at Sarah's place – her cousin was proud of her perfect china and never let the children handle it), she had said somewhere – it didn't matter where – she'd said, 'I cannot say anything of your Mr James. He didn't like me, I'm sorry – for your sake.'

'No, that's not true. He just doesn't know what to do in families, he has very little social talk.'

A pause followed, then to her surprise Sarah said, 'Do not stay there, dear cousin Ann, if it is difficult for you.'

'That's not fair. He was not on good form that evening. He can be such fun, you know, such laughing times we have.'

'Of course,' Sarah had interrupted, then or later? 'He *can be* charming. Dearest cousin, he is not for a woman like you, not for all of life.'

Ann agreed. Yes, of course. Yes, who needs such a man? Who needs another person at all? Who needs?

But had Sarah, the docile, maternal Sarah, actually said these words? Or did she, Ann, think that Sarah should have said them? What sort of woman did Sarah think she was?

When they met again – and she was sure it was after, long after, because she'd begun another book (time could be measured in plots) – they didn't speak of it. Was it for comfort that Sarah grumbled a little – and this for the first time – about her domestic, her solely domestic, life? Was this a gift, an offering, to the cousin who was about to have such a fall?

The children were certainly more present than on her earlier visits. The little house in Phoenix Street was full of wet and dry clothes, wool dolls and toy wooden carts, noise, the damp flannel smell of small people insufficiently contained at either end. It was perhaps because they sat in the back parlour rather than the drawing room. Had Ann called without invitation or warning, to try to see this scene?

Sarah seemed to have less time for chatting than usual. Charles was good, but he was not there all day, not there as much as she would have liked.

'All these children. I don't know,' she said suddenly. 'I love them of course, but has my life been better for having them? I am with child again, five in eight years. I don't know.' She shrugged. 'There's no choice.'

'Well, there's always a choice,' said Ann without thinking.

Sarah gave her a serious look. 'You didn't marry,' she said. 'Or rather you haven't married. You can't share a bed with a man and have a choice. Do you understand?'

'Yes, of course I do. But he could, couldn't he? You know. Interrupt, well, something of the sort. Or so I understand,' she finished lamely.

'He could but he didn't and doesn't choose. And I don't know much about it. It is not perhaps for a lady. Or for a gentleman like Charles.'

'As I see.'

'Anyway,' Sarah got up and began folding some little garments that had lain over the fender to air, 'there they are now, they are with us and we love them. They quarrel and tumble and make up, and even with Jennie to help I run after them all the time. But then, they are my life. They are what I am for.'

'They are not your life, Sarah. Come on. You gave them life, they owe you something in the end, a bit of freedom from time to time.'

Sarah laughed and threw off her serious mood. 'It's the other way round, dear Ann, as you will one day know.' She added 'perhaps', for her cousin was getting older, it was not quite so inevitable now. 'I owe them or at least that's how it has to be. They will be launched one day. William will be going to sea when he's eleven, so he says. And, you know, I will miss him most dreadfully.'

Everyone loved was a hostage to fortune, thought Ann. A tie, a rope, a chain. Best to have a scissors, a knife or axe to cut loose when needs be. Well, she would always have that. She'd loosened herself from Caroline, wrapped Gilbert up inside her, snipped off Gregory Lloyd and, if she could do that, why fear anything else? Or had her mother cut her loose? It really didn't matter.

Outside her lodgings and the tavern where she and Robert so often met his friends, the ordinary world went on as before. People sauntered by, smoked a pipe or two, read a newspaper, tugged at a child with its nose at a sweetshop window, stepped over horse dung or tripped into it, clung to a wall as a pompous carriage rattled by.

But she, wherever she was, lived on a different plane from those who did these commonplace things, people who bought vegetables in the market or looked over prints in Clerkenwell.

'Don't you dare try to muzzle me.' There must have been a first time when he said these words. She should have known then that he was a fierce animal. What made her think she would be its tamer?

Had she ever tried to be? To contain perhaps, yes, at moments to prod him into a common sociability, to urge him into ordinary behaviour, into what she thought of as normality.

'Can't you just be like other people?' she used to ask. On the first occasion remembering with a surge of unwanted heat poor Gregory Lloyd. She hoped he'd found a family.

And he replied, 'I am not other people. I do not live by their rules. You know that. Why did you want someone like me? You try to reduce me to the commonness you admire.'

He was right. Truly she didn't know what normality was, and wouldn't have recognised or wanted it. So did she try to 'muzzle' this extraordinary being? Her hands twitched as she pursued this self-analysis.

She knew where she was faulty. After some time, much time, she'd heard his sentiments so very often that, when he would give no tenderness, no pleasurable comfort of the sort she craved, and when she was tired from work and anxiety, and he went on talking and talking as if his listener were of no account at all, then and only then she would show her boredom – as she had to Caroline. It irritated him for he'd not changed. Was this muzzling? Probably in part.

Her mental longing for him survived intact, even her sense of his uniqueness, his spiritual power – but yet the boredom showed, just at times. When she tried to make him say the false ordinary thing that eased a path through life, those necessary lies, he could not: this was not muzzling, this was pricking him to bark. No wonder then he growled with his eyes.

He could be greater than he had been, more wonderful. So he must not be hampered by anything or anyone. Not by her boredom or her nagging. She knew it.

And yet.

And yet, even Richard Perry might have known there was something wearing out in him, something that might not, finally, let him go to the ends only he could see so clearly, where difference between all knowledges was annihilated. Did Richard Perry or any of his friends suspect that his heat was the remains of youth being consumed, that *Attila* had perhaps been his jagged peak? How long can promise last?

She sometimes wondered whether there was a deep problem for Robert James. Something huge like Sin or Sacrifice. These were words to conjure with. He'd rejected them but they lingered. Of course, for it was not simple wholly to rid oneself of the ingrained. There was always residue, something left in the mind's sponge. Left after he'd made his *Attila* to ravage his church. He'd turned his back on his Catholic God – but had his God turned his back on him? When she phrased it like that, she rather prided herself on her antithesis.

Was he his own Pope now? Was he keeping, deep in himself, the purpose that his Catholic God once gave him when he stood near the altar or lay in bed with his special angel? She hadn't the courage to ask. But yes, she had – and she did – but shouldn't have done. Should, should.

'You know you should have been an actor,' she said once.

'And you should have been a schoolmistress.'

She didn't like that.

There were times when he pulled away from her embrace. He was so much stronger than she was, there was no contest. At these moments he wanted no one's touch – even if she, embarrassed but not enough to repress her feelings, was swooning with desire for some gesture of affection.

Then the repulsing was rough. He would say when she protested, 'I cannot handle you like glass. I must be free.'

'But surely not free from me and what we have.'

'Just free.'

Whatever did that mean? She knew such words were wedged between them and should be allowed to do their work. But it was no good: if it was delusion to hold on – mentally, for he could certainly shake her off his firm body – she still could not let go. Desire intensified with each rejection. There was a conundrum.

It wasn't wonderful that she knew so little of men. Her ignorance sent her into the pit with no tools to dig herself out, as surely as any of her reusable gothic Lucias and Elenas. But would she have tried to scramble up if she'd known more? She doubted it. There was something sweet about being down there. Cousin Sarah could know nothing of it.

When they quarrelled over something, an interruption to his life, to his Work, he towered in rage. 'You don't like it but this is me, my true self, the bare, the naked man.'

Later she would ponder that emphasis – not on nakedness but on 'man'. Such a ringing word. 'Woman' was no match for it.

She began keeping a diary to assess happiness and misery. Knowing that not one single day would have a mark alone for happiness, trying by this paper record to persuade herself this was not as it should be. But instead congratulating herself she was living this purely miserable life. Not everyone could do this.

Out of the blue, out of the black, rather, he snapped, 'Shut your mouth, shut everything. Just get out of my way.'

Each time it happened she was stunned.

The violence was never named. It was the shedding of tension, of too much sparking inner life.

Once in a tavern he kicked a dog and knocked over a glass bottle that shattered. And the dog, which was old, fell into the sharp pieces and was hurt. Robert crouched down beside the beast he'd kicked and carefully removed the glass from the wound in its matted fur. He didn't notice at once that the dog dirtied his smart double-breasted coat with its blood and saliva.

Then – only she'd not seen it follow – then at some point, some point carved into memory but not quite clear as to date and time, he hit her hard with his clenched fist. He wished he had not, he said later, but he knew it was her fault. Hadn't he taken up with someone who professed independence, a life apart, and here she was, become so clinging, so moistly entwining, so much a Woman after all.

She could not fault the logic.

None of his friends knew and she wouldn't tell. John Humphries would have crowed, women were always trouble; John Taylor would have waved his stained blue fingers and scoffed at her feebleness, knowing that a man created his great work only when no woman hung on his belt; Richard Perry would have grieved and disbelieved anything cruel of his hero, despite her bruises. All of them would have hung together and stared at her.

It was better that he leave, he said. And he almost did. But then he relented at her urgent pleas, for where would she be without the habit of him? How could she live without the dear scrolls of hair at the nape of his neck?

When he gave in, agreed to stay, she was deliriously, painfully happy that he would be with her again. Although it ached from where his fist had landed, her body jumped up and down in glee.

In spite of reason, all pain, she actually – and she knew this – found his rages heroic, like his consuming, his talking. They were larger than life. Nothing like them had been experienced. Not in the cold intense rooms of William Bates's mansion, not in Holborn lodgings or along the streets of Somers Town, not in that little Putney household with the negligent mother rising only to some cutting rebuke or a box on the ears, nothing grand, just emotion and irritation. This rage was masculine, wonderful and appalling.

What would Caroline have made of it? What would she have thought of Robert?

He was no Gilbert, for Gilbert had never been angry with his beloved. Yet, despite this distinction, she knew that Caroline would have loved Robert. He would need only to have kissed her hand and smiled directly into her eyes. He had such charm, such glamour. He would have won her, as Gilbert had done.

'He is special,' said Frederick Curran in his Irish way. 'He can be angry,' he added, when she'd asked obliquely. 'But with such gifts, you know.' Even Curran hesitated. In these cases, of such gifts, such riches in the mind, there must be frustration, the sharp spear must make a wound. Who could withstand it? He *should* be angry, didn't she know that?

As for Ann, she said he was not himself when it happened. He didn't mean it. His thoughts were so powerful, such possibilities he had, how could he choose and not follow all? So passionate. He couldn't help himself.

And, after all, wasn't she provoking?

Following the quarrels when he'd vowed never to see her again and had actually left, so that she feared she really had lost him, she – she hung round the doors of places he might be, just as she used to do in the beginning, following paths and lingering where she thought he'd come. She even dressed differently, as disguise, so that she could scurry away if about to be discovered.

What on earth was she doing?

Perhaps such following, such spying, such prowling, had seemed exciting when she'd first done it. Now it was downright silly.

He was drinking more wine and brandy than ever, taking more laudanum for some ache in his head which he said moved round his skull, choosing stronger tea, his body tauter and more tense, then almost shaking. Sometimes she thought he might explode.

'I must get out of England,' he said. 'I must get out of this damned country, with its buying and selling, its hoarding and bartering, its government of fools.'

She remembered how once he'd so enjoyed mocking the absurd Regent and his vulgar Princess Caroline, doing her funny German voice with spitted consonants. Not now.

His anger came more often. She was his victim, though she kept the word for her stories. She had, he said, made herself into this pitiable thing. It was not a role she had to take or that he wanted her to take. It was a woman's way.

He put venom into the word 'Woman' as he inflated the word 'Man'. The rights and wrongs of woman, indeed? The wrongs women had no right to inflict on men, he said. He was all for women's independence. Oh yes. Absolutely. Then why did she not have it? It would free men, free him.

He must get away from her, her clinging love. It was too agitating, he couldn't work under it.

But then there were her tears, her endless tears. When they'd first met she'd boasted she didn't cry and faint like other women, real women, women in her books. Now there she was lying on the bed sobbing. She did it, he was sure, to reproach him, to destroy his peace.

She should have thought how to handle him; he would say this often enough. She could see where trouble lay. But she was so inexperienced, what had she to go on? She chastised her past as if it had been a wrong choice.

'Why do you talk so much?' he'd demanded of her as her clichés streamed towards him — so he called her words. She had, he agreed, required no special notice for her chatter, only a little tolerance, which he wouldn't give. She really didn't deserve it, or rather her words did not.

Did he find her dull? He despised anything tranquil and yet no more than she could he live always in rough seas. Or could he? Did he enjoy the exhilaration of constantly bobbing about on this stormy water?

She sometimes tried to keep up with him, stimulate herself to his level, to the place where the hairs on a hand grew large and waved like fronds of fern. But she couldn't drink deeply or dissolve the white powder and down it in one go. If she tried, then next day she had a pain that coloured her room; she could hardly breathe the purple and orange air.

His headaches went on. Then he held his brow in his two hands and said nothing. He simply resumed himself when they passed. He did not, he said, lose his self, his Self.

And over and over again he said he was going to organise words in a new way. He would clarify paradox, so that ideas and metaphors, particulars and thought, would be one, no separation, no distinction, all merged in a glorious act of pure expression.

Yes, yes, she thought. The same thing. I've heard it. Why does he not do it?

The fire was burning low in her grate, no curtain drawn across her window through which the waxing moon could be spied with clouds racing across it. Neither of them got up to feed the fire. Instead they stared at the dying embers. She was tired, tired out, tired to death.

Once as a child he'd had himself electrocuted to see how it would feel. He'd let the current course through him. He'd felt vibrant.

Perhaps he'd never been the same since, just full of sparks. Perhaps touching him she'd taken on some of his electricity, only instead of making her more alive, it had singed and dulled her.

Sarah didn't raise the matter again and Ann didn't visit as often as she used to.

On one occasion, Sarah remarked, 'I worry about you, cousin Ann. Charles and I think you are bilious. Maybe there's superfluous bile. I am no doctor, but there is something not right. There's a yellowish tinge to your skin. You're thinner. We think you are not well.'

It was cover for a deeper commentary but she didn't wait to hear more – or encourage further diagnosing. Sarah was near her term and was sensitive to bodies.

Despite such turmoil, she finished *The Cavern of Horror; or, the Miseries of Camilla*. It was set in the echoing caves of Illyria, wherever that was, full of blood, spectral encounters and the triple swoon. It was probably her worst production, patched with bits and bobs from her more adroit work. She couldn't be ashamed for she'd put no life into it. Much life was not necessary, but some wasn't amiss, and she'd have preferred at least to add some polish to the surface.

Her mind had been elsewhere, and her obedient pen continued scratching the paper, with very minimal skill.

Mr Dean might have found the work wanting, but he took it in silence and counted the sheets, as he always did. He'd been in the navy and ran his publishing business as a tight ship. He and Mr Munday were not laggard in paying, she appreciated them, but sometimes she wondered if they ever did more than skim her work and number the pages. In this instance it was as well but at others it would have pleased her to think she entertained an idle hour for these men. She rather suspected Mr Munday admired her; he'd once asked her to take tea with him and they'd had companionable talk about what men and women wrote and what they chose to read.

Robert threw away so many sheets of paper, used up so many fine feathers of goose and swan and raven, so many words he'd written and rejected, because he would not leave anything behind that wasn't perfect. Even the fragments of *Attila* were deficient now, a mere shadow of what he wanted and would produce. He would catch the universal style when he'd tried out all styles, all selves, as he'd once tried out the voices. He would get the tone.

But she knew he feared.

He was serious about leaving. Even he could admit he was on edge these days. Out of England he might be calmer, his strings of life less taut. And if Robert James went, so would she.

But why? In heaven's name why? She'd looked at her diary of marks, added up the contrary ones, and saw no record of 'happiness'. The fact did not alter her travel plans.

She knew her love was flecked with revulsion, both from him and from herself – for what she was becoming under the influence, not of his personality exactly, but of her dependence on it. She wouldn't look too closely: for she couldn't combat the deadly longing, the sweet need for him.

She was like a babe that clings to a cruel mother who bites and burns and tortures it while kindly onlookers try to pull it away to unwanted safety.

The image swam into her mind and she did her best to banish it. Quite wrong: it didn't and couldn't answer. After all, there was something so utterly ridiculous in her attitude. You really ought to laugh.

Cuddly Martha said, as the child burrowed into her soft flesh gasping out how much she hated Caroline, 'We all need a mama, Miss Ann.' Martha held her so close and for so long she smelled the sweet sweat from the deep dark armpits. This was what a mama should be. A warm body with few words.

Well, she wasn't getting that anywhere else.

Robert brought her no kin. But he would have said, if he'd ever thought like this, that he'd delivered something better: a chosen circle of devoted friends. Yes, she relished the warmth of being part of it.

But she never knew how to move inwards. She was there only for and through Robert.

Besides, she was jealous of them. He should be only hers. There was a paradox. But down there, by the confines of consciousness, she knew full well his glamour would diminish without them. If he were taken away from London, if she had him alone, wouldn't he be lessened?

And another danger. If she abandoned her comfortable life in London, she must never imagine she did it all for him – it would be too big a burden for anyone to bear or be given.

She'd wanted to travel ever since Signor Moretti's book of Italian scenes had roused an appetite for dry, sunny places – why else did her heroines tramp through pine forests and canter over hot dusty plains if the idea of foreign lands hadn't stirred her deeply?

So why not take this chance to go to a distant country with a man so beloved?

She dropped the baize over the *camera obscura* of her mind before it could investigate and sharpen the image of questions best left indistinct. Travelling with the uncaged tiger.

He seemed to have some money left from his allowance. Perhaps enough to take him where he wanted. She never knew. She'd be paid what was owed to her by Dean & Munday before they left, and she could send work back and receive drafts through offices – there must be such in foreign parts. For now it was possible to manage on what they had – if they travelled carefully, thinking of the pennies. Well, she should have abandoned that thrifty idea as soon as formed.

There was always excitement in the idea of going, changing places, leaving everything behind.

Even if you took most of your heavy baggage with you.

She suggested Germany or Denmark, since she'd heard he'd been there and might have friends in place.

'How did you know?' he asked. He must have disliked being discussed when absent, for he gave her a cold, almost angry, look.

It was a poor suggestion. He wouldn't have chosen such dull Protestant countries. Hamburg – a snivelling, constricting town. She knew his prejudices by now. Not there, then. Despite the rye bread.

'What about Ireland?'

'You are wilfully tormenting me,' he said with half a smile. 'If we go, we will go to the sun. For what other reason does one travel?'

'I'm not sure I have enough money for a long journey.'

'Money, money! I have money. We will spend it. We will go to the end of the world.'

As he said it, the light from the setting sun through her window caught his face. It looked older, more distinctly lined, simultaneously tight and flabby. She loved that face the more for the tale it told, but also she felt – for the first time – it might evoke some pity. He would never forgive even the shadow of pity.

To the end of the world they would go, though where to get passports?

Italy, it had to be. France was no country without its Emperor. There'd been an Italian at Mr Hughes's dinner, Luigi something. She suggested asking him about expenses and lodgings in Venice. It would be cheap now, in a conquered city that had lost its power and purpose.

Robert waved his hand and grimaced. Byron is there, is he not? A man so proud to be a lord. Terrible. He would go nowhere near that mountebank.

Telling herself not to mention money, she mentioned money. He erupted. So Protestant, he said. 'Protestantism is all about money, making money out of other people, grubbing, grabbing, cheating, littleness. I want nothing to do with it.' And out he went.

It hadn't been a sectarian matter, just whether to pay the butcher before they left, the real butcher not the one whom he'd once so comically imitated; the one who sold the meat they'd eaten in her lodgings these last months.

And what about Robert's unpaid boy?

Luigi Orlando was easily found and brought to the Swan. Since he'd discovered exiled Italians, he was no longer so often around the English but, through Richard Perry, he'd met John Taylor and admired his misty watercolours – to such an extent that he'd been offered a bed in the artist's spacious north-facing rooms near St

Sepulchre where the light was just right for painting. His time with edgy John Taylor and his Italian friends had made him less peaceable, more outspoken than when they'd first encountered him.

'Venice is, of course, not what she was,' he said. 'A colony, pah!'

'You don't like Venice?' asked Ann.

'I am not from Venice originally though I lived there many years. I am Veronese, a foreigner, always that. But now, since the French invasion, we are all strangers.'

'A city of great painters,' said John Taylor, who'd been drinking in the Swan much of the day, 'great men. I forget their names.'

'Leonardo da Vinci is the only one,' said Robert.

'Our Venetians did not admire him,' said Signor Orlando. 'He stayed only a year and you know what they wanted of this great artist?' He paused for effect. 'To build defence to keep their money safe. They caricatured his *Last Supper*.'

Luigi Orlando was about to go on, for he enjoyed mocking a city which made him feel provincial, but Robert interrupted.

'Do you know, Leonardo made a mechanical lion? To show Florence's friendship to the King of France it moved its legs towards him, opened its chest and presented French lilies. Something eh? Art, science, politics and ostentation all together. The great artificer.'

Frederick Curran cared nothing for paintings or automata. He refused to let a promising political argument evaporate. 'It was not the French that killed Venice,' he said to Luigi Orlando. 'The old monarchies always win. Nobody must dent their privileges and power. How could the French be anything beyond what they were allowed to be? See, Robert was showing us in *Attila* how the System conquers in the end.'

'The French do not rule Venice now,' snapped Luigi Orlando, misunderstanding Curran's tone. 'It is the Austrians.'

'Just so,' said Curran, 'you are given to the old regimes, just so.'

Luigi Orlando was about to reply angrily, when Richard Perry interjected, 'The Venetian republic was something admirable.'

Fred Curran was undeterred. 'Not at all, not a proper republic, not a revolutionary republic, just an old elite, an oligarchy trading in secrecy and deceit, no liberty in its stone bones. Greed. Do you know, Venetians betrayed each other by stuffing malice into a gaping lion's mouth? Better to marvel at Leonardo's mechanical beasts.'

Before Luigi Orlando could respond, Robert waved his hand round his friends. 'Perhaps after all we will go and see. Can it be worse than this stew-pond of London?'

'Liberty,' pursued Curran, 'was as repugnant to old Venice as it is to the imperial court of Vienna. Venice is Ireland.'

Luigi Orlando was puzzled but calmed by the last notion. 'We set up for neutrality,' he said. 'It was a stance without power, it was weakness. Our rulers were absurd.' He spat on the floor. 'The serene republic was swept away – whoosh – ' (and he pushed the glasses on the table towards Fred Curran) 'because it was led by donkeys. The French and Austrians rode their backs. Now our taxes go to foreigners. Once the Venetian sequin was honoured through the world, it was of pure gold. Now it is nothing. The invaders have killed our city.'

'It died because it wanted to,' said Robert. 'It wished for death. States die when they want to die, like people.'

'That is too heroic, my friend,' said Luigi Orlando, 'they were outwitted – they, the great republic, were of no account to France or Austria. They played every hand badly.'

'Ah, but they had an heroic conqueror,' said Robert. '"I shall be an Attila to Venice," announced Napoleon. There's nothing like the former Emperor for magnificence.' Robert drank long and heavily to indicate the talk was over. They all thought of his heroic fragment.

Had Napoleon simply coincided with him, Ann wondered, or upstaged him so completely there was no more to say? Or could he be quoting the fallen Emperor without irony because he saw them now as two of a kind?

She turned away. 'I shall be an Attila,' she thought. Imagine saying that! What woman could even quote it, say it aloud?

It was evident they were going to Venice, despite Lord Byron and his doggerel.

'Why not,' he said, when she asked later, 'the place of Leonardo da Vinci, why ever not?'

'He'll benefit from a change of scene,' said John Humphries when she met him walking along the Strand. 'Bright skies, Italian beauties.' He turned briefly to Ann and gave her, she thought, a mocking smile.

She realised how heavy her heart was becoming, how daunting was the prospect – unless Robert had some hidden reserves, how little money they had to undertake so long a voyage and stay in foreign places.

But she couldn't break away. Whether consumed by love or hatred, she simply knew he must not leave without her and her heavy heart.

She would tell cousin Sarah in a message sent to her address in Somers Town. But only when all arrangements had been made and the post to Dover booked. Sarah was busy with the new baby and the twins still so young: that must be her excuse.

She knew her cousin would be appalled when she heard; she'd have many anxious talks with Charles. They were unmarried; he was not right for her; she was taking a most dreadful risk; she must be restrained; Charles would come to talk to her; it was madness.

10

She busied herself round London getting passports and passage for at least the first lap of the journey; other documents must be obtained or countersigned on their way. Did Robert understand? She asked him several times.

How did any man with a strong arm put up with this?

First, passports for Mr and Mrs Robert James, Ann James. Fred Curran knew about such things. He knew the value of having different identities. So she'd requested papers in these names as well as others for Miss Ann St Clair. He had a friend, an Irishman from Ulster, who could help in such matters. He'd already helped Robert once and would do so again. Curran didn't elaborate. Peter O'Neil? Everything cost money, of course.

She bought a plain ring from the Soho Bazaar, put it on awaiting comment that never came. A ridiculous thing, marriage, and yet: Mrs Robert James. It was the best honorific. Well, she smirked to her mirror, she'd earned it.

Then, ring on finger, to the French embassy to get passes to travel through France to Italy. Everything took time and effort and money. Robert abhorred the new France but it wasn't easy to avoid it without more expense. Spain was as bad.

They should take the military route over the Alps, said Fred Curran. His usual steady eyes flickered as he made the suggestion. Created by Napoleon, he added to please Robert. Rocks blown up with gunpowder to wrest a road out of the mountains.

From Robert's response to this temptation, he knew what he'd lately feared: his friend was ill equipped for the journey. He was nervous and too excited one minute, at another apathetic. To Frederick Curran he declared the adventure simply a voyage through rocks and water to nothing.

Did not a road formed of scattered rocks appeal?

'Better than scattering limbs,' said Ann.

Frederick Curran gave her a swift uncommon glance and turned away before she could respond again.

They made abortive attempts to leave through Calais. But the boats, the tide, the fares, always something was wrong.

The waiting agitated them. They had to leave soon for both their sakes.

Finally they went. Not from Calais but on a sailing smack from Brighthelmstone heading for Dieppe, trunks and boxes stowed away, clothes for the journey and for Italy, his slim pile of papers containing what remained of his manuscript of *Attila* and good blank sheets for what should come. Her own few papers she kept apart, putting them in a floppy hemp bag which could be shoved under beds and behind chairs, then pushed into a trunk for moving. She did it as instinctively as she coughed on opening a stuffy wardrobe. Yet the bag held nothing of consequence: a few plans for future tales, addresses of Sarah, of Moore & Stratton, of an office in Paris where Mr Munday had said a bill might be changed if payment had to be made and she was nearby – a kind thought that had, to his surprise, made her giggle.

The boat was called *The Swift*. It belied its name as it strolled across the water in the limp breeze.

As England faded Robert leaned over the ship's wooden rail beneath the slack canvas, biting on his tobacco pipe. He could be alone with the sun or stars.

Ann looked at him and sighed. She was with him, that's what mattered. She could neither follow his intensity nor accept his apathy. Both intrigued, worried, excited and overwhelmed her without allowing her a share.

For the first time she had him entirely to herself. What would she make of the gift? The weight, rather. But had she ever really had his body? She sighed for how much she'd made of so few satisfactory encounters, how much desire had to stand in for performance.

He of course had her entirely. Not since childhood when she manoeuvred through and round Caroline's moods had she been so beholden to a single person, so responsible for sustaining their temperament. Would she be tempted to misuse the power?

She was rightly frightened. But the colourful paint of adventure varnished her fear. She, Ann from near Putney Bridge, who'd lived a life in London and flat lands, was going to see the Alps where sedentary Mrs Radcliffe, for all her sublime describing, had never been.

It was early September, not the best time to be setting out on a long journey.

She had Thomas Nugent's grand tour guide for the Continent. It listed sights to be seen by the cultured traveller, usually one more affluent and attended than they were, but at least it told them where to stop and stare.

Robert pushed it away irritably when she placed it before him – on more than one occasion. What had 'sights' to do with him? There was the natural outside world, a poor jumbled thing, and there was the language that formed it. To harness that was to harness the world.

Yes indeed. But the world was on its own now. He could not and would not deal with it. He could not hear it.

Why did she not mind her own business?

Now they were alone together, it *had* become her 'business'. She said as much but he didn't hear, or pretended he didn't.

How could anyone not be excited that even children spoke French? But Robert had travelled on the Continent before as she had not, though the enthusiasm for rye bread and Richard Perry's admiring tale suggested rather out-of-the-way voyaging.

To her relief, their papers functioned well on the way to Paris. There they must be countersigned by the Austrian ambassador. Robert held the documents and the money, it was a man's right. She knew better now than to ask him too often if he'd obtained all the signatures.

They passed through Paris in a blur of rain and mud and hostile glances. Some years since Wellington had finally defeated Napoleon. But glamour remained with the defeated hero. Not every Frenchman had loved the self-made Emperor for turning the Revolution into imperial conquest. But no one appreciated England's part in the ending of such a gorgeous adventure.

In Fontainebleau Ann wanted to visit the royal château. Robert was in no mood. Not even when told of a table where Napoleon had signed his abdication. A fellow passenger described how the Emperor – for he was and always would be that – struck the table with a penknife to aid his thoughts. Robert liked the detail but had no wish to see the marks.

Going south they passed ruined châteaux and convents: made into manufactories. The result of a mundane peace. Some surviving aristocrats were back with the return of the old monarchy but not to their castles and landed power; rather, to a shared world of money and bourgeois trade. The 'nation of shopkeepers', as Napoleon had termed England, had infected France.

Industry was less picturesque than castles and lords.

Often they stayed at the best inns. Ann wanted to conserve money by seeking the cheapest and suffering bedbugs and fleas. She looked disapproval but said nothing. It was the kind of loud 'nothing' he especially hated and in which she often indulged.

His lowness enveloped everything. What had caused it? Doubt, she supposed. Doubt of himself. Could he ever do what he wanted, fulfil his purpose, embody his vision, do much more than write an inspired fragment?

This Vision, this thing apart, was hungry; it needed to be fed. It was taking from his substance, like an unborn child within a starving woman.

She was not even trying to feed it from outside, even had she the right sustenance.

Once devastated by imperial wars, the villages were now recovering, seeking a living in the old way: by fleecing travellers.

'It would not have been so under Napoleon,' said Robert James.

They were eating stale oily food in an inn close to where the land began to rise steeply. In the distance were outlines of mountains, at intervals indistinguishable from clouds.

It was old talk. In the past she wouldn't have contradicted, but the context had changed. She was weary of agreeing or being silent, tired of the tension of another's mood, tired of her own contingency. 'I thought Napoleon betrayed the Revolution,' she said.

'Glib, glib. You are wrong. Energy is always to be welcomed.'

'The Revolution was energetic. It ended in massacre, in Terror. Look now, nothing is altered.'

He was impatient, his hands grabbing and pulling strands of his residual hair. 'The ideas are separate from the people who mauled them. The upheaval occurred on shaky foundations. Napoleon took the moment and made it great. Even *you* might see that. He was wrong-headed, he was a man of action but a genius, the rest were little men.'

He wanted to lapse into silence, as she well knew. She wouldn't let him. She niggled at him, a lurcher worrying a bone.

'But they believed in equality. He didn't.'

'That sort of equality, pulling down the exceptional, the great, produced the guillotine. If the people had risen up on behalf of truth and greatness, it would have been different. They didn't. It was for envy and bread. But, still, they acted; that's more than you have done. The English are puny. It's the legacy of Protestantism, it brings down everything majestic and beautiful. You, they, abuse language.'

'You are still a Catholic,' she mocked.

'It has nothing to do with being Catholic. Didn't I create Attila, the scourge of Catholics, routed by their nauseous cant? I speak of the moral relationship to language, the universal. I have told you often enough.'

Often indeed.

She was too weary to go on. However he protested, it was all Roman, all magic, all preposterous, all achingly grand.

After eating, Robert went outside. She saw him sitting on a stone bench, a breeze blowing over a face gone slack. She went over to him and clasped his limp hand.

Could they not be quiet bodies? He was too tired to respond or pull his hand away.

Was he ill? Or disturbed, a little mad? What did that make her?

At the Hôtel de Genève in Poligny he turned on her, using force conserved in long silences. 'Go away, go away,' he said. 'I don't want to be with you.'

Could it be clearer than that? If there'd ever been love, surely it was dead now. And yet . . .

She could not be without Robert James.

It would be to lose her essence: Caroline without her Gilbert. If she would avoid this horror, she must adapt to another's richer existence. That was what love was, wasn't it? She was Mrs Robert James, even without his or society's permission.

All that nearly repulsed her still tugged at her heart whenever there was a chance she might lose him: the balding head on the muscular body seemed disarming weakness grafted on strength; the short legs a manly refusal of the sportsman's effeminacy; the pale eyes telling of a creative spirit that looked through not with. The inside was all-important, the body a shell covering wonders.

What sort of object of desire was this and what was it to do with her?

Comforting comfortable ordinary Sarah could have helped perhaps in this dilemma, had she allowed her. But she'd not let her cousin try, or try hard enough.

She'd overheard her friend Mrs Lymington say something when they all met once at Sarah's house for a child's birthday celebration. Mrs Lymington had said, 'He would not last long with *me*,' and tittered. She'd strained her ears to hear Sarah's reply but failed. Jane Lymington couldn't know Robert, so she was responding to what Sarah said of him.

Could simple cousin Sarah be wiser than she was? She'd said as much. Ann assumed she spoke in jest.

Once when Sarah had sat with a plump twin on her knee, pulling at her hair and pushing against her swollen belly, Ann tried to tell her cousin something of what was happening. She approached the topic warily. She eschewed the word 'horror' and came nowhere near explaining the abject state she was often rebelliously in during those last weeks in London.

Sarah had laughed, then smiled, 'Surely as the writer of tales with mouldering castles and clanking chains you'll know what to do with a little real-life difficulty.'

Now, so far away, over so much water and so many dirt miles, she understood Sarah's delicacy. How kind to stop her confessing what must in memory give pain.

They ascended the mountains, following the road through deep valleys, by rocks and craggy summits. When she pointed out the sublimity of the lofty heights and slopes with firs and torrents, a sublimity worthy of Mrs Radcliffe at her soaring best, Robert was dismissive.

The mountains were a tomb, he said.

Even she knew sublimity was better in *The Mysteries of Udolpho* than through the window of a jolting carriage. But still there was this tremendous thing, just outside.

It was not Robert's tremendous thing.

'Do you want to visit Voltaire's house at Ferney?' she'd ventured near Geneva.

'No, I will not pay that compression of vanity such a compliment.'

What had caught Robert's attention was the hydraulic machine powering the city fountains.

She remembered how he'd admired the gas lights and mirror curtain in London while scorning the plays; he'd been enthralled by Leonardo's mechanical lion. Could more of such marvels have taken him out of his lethargy, even out of his treacherous poetic self? Could he have been amused quite simply, with toys? Like a child.

Then a hitch. The passports had not been signed by the Austrian Minister at Paris or indeed the French Minister of the Interior; Robert had left them in the offices and picked them up later, but hadn't checked they'd been signed. He was impatient; it was not his fault. No one had queried them as they passed along through city gates. Why now?

More expense, for a messenger must ride to the sub-prefect of the district to get permission. It arrived after long delay with a warning that the pass was only partial: there would be constant harassing on the rest of the way out of France and into Italy.

Snow, white and green ice, porphyry rocks, grottoes and archways of granite failed to move him beyond the remark that it was all earth unmade. Only the signs of Napoleon roused him: the greatness of the vision that had caused these rocks to be blown sky high with gunpowder. Engineers had done the deed but they answered the will of one man who had the intellect to understand and conquer the virgin snow and ice. *He* ordered the explosions.

For the last stage in the mountains they took the early-morning charabanc shared with several passengers, mainly Germans. It was still expensive even then for there had to be guides, mules, riders, all needing to be paid, six livres here, nine there, divided out, but still.

Down and down they went, paying to have their trunks ransacked by guards at every stop, down through gorges into where vines were curiously trained from tree to tree. Robert continued gloomy. She felt little better, her female problems troubling her. It wasn't just strength that men had over women.

Italy at last – and the most rapacious customs men.

They had to stop longer than they wished in Milan to get their papers in order. Even she lacked much energy for sightseeing but out of habit she suggested the cathedral, open from sunrise to sunset according to the guidebook. He was uninterested. She proposed other churches, other palaces. He didn't care for tasteless extravagance, not for art as duty.

'I am sick of travelling, let's just go to Venice, and finish the comedy.'

So they traipsed on through rice and grain fields and vineyards, through towns, some bustling, some deserted. She tried out the Italian learned from Signor Moretti and found that his Roman tongue was not currency here. Or perhaps he'd left so long ago he'd fallen behind the times. She couldn't easily catch the lilt that might have made her words intelligible. Robert picked up language to speak, but made little effort to understand.

Might he warm to these more vital people? Not even their courtly manners, the gentle bows and kisses of the hand, animated him, although he was not displeased to be treated with more ceremony.

They stopped in a small town by the Brenta, delayed yet again by something not quite right in their papers. He'd found an Englishman, no, an Irishman – dear God, an Irishman – and he was drinking wine with him. The Irishman said there was an English colony in Venice. It was a dismal place of shifting foreigners. He'd left it for good.

She doubted it was dismal. It glittered spectacularly in Mrs Radcliffe's novels. She tried to look forward to gliding down the Grand Canal to the shining sea even if she did it alone. Better if she did it alone.

The Irishman went on his way to Bologna. She'd caught sight of a picture of bare buttocks garishly tinted in pink and red, so assumed he dealt in unsavoury prints. He left Robert drunk and inflated with talk. When he got up he stumbled and fell on to her. She caught him, then fell herself.

'See what you've made me do,' he said.

What was the matter with her that she put up with this, resented it and got back on her hind legs to beg again? Was female independence so ludicrous, so unnatural as cousin Sarah thought, that she was clinging to its opposite as to life itself?

Could she fear being alone in a foreign land? Doubtful, for she'd negotiated most of the journey and could do it again.

Best not think too much.

Venice

11

They were on the sea in the dark for the final lap of the journey. A flickering lantern dangled and swayed from the prow of the boat. They were rowed past buildings: more like rocks untidy with undergrowth. They smelled of people, of human waste.

So this was it. Venice.

No one spoke. They entered a wide stretch of water. The Grand Canal?

The boatman glided to a dripping wooden post, then stopped. He leapt into the mist. The boat bobbed dangerously. He said something they didn't hear. Robert trembled with irritation.

'What damned thing is he about now?' His face was turned to the bank.

The boatman came back with a girl muffled in a dark cloak. He dumped her on to the boat like a bundle of rags. '*Sorella*,' he muttered and took up the oar. The bundle twined round his leg.

They were out on open water again. Where could they be going? Across the Adriatic in a flimsy open boat? To meet Barbary pirates, Turkish corsairs?

They were too poor for kidnapping. Perhaps they were being returned to the mainland, the trip a paid-for manoeuvre to collect a droopy sweetheart.

After a few minutes, more dark houses loomed, with light flickering from them. Oil lamps yellowing the edges of shuttered windows? The boat glided down another, narrower stretch of water.

By now her eyes were used to the dark but she could still see little, and the mist, though thinning, remained dense. The stench was strong, fishy, acrid, but less human. She tried but failed to close her nose. Some people could do that.

The boat – was this a gondola? She'd described their sleek glamour more than once but could this cramped shabby craft be one? – came softly to rest by stone steps. The water splashed over them trailing dark green fronds. She looked down. Only two large steps rose above the waterline, blackened by the green slime.

The boatman disentwined himself from the pile of girl's clothes, and gestured for them to get out. He wasted no words.

'*Inglese*,' he'd said when they first boarded his craft, then spat. It surprised her. This easy hatred had been a French habit – explicable in France after Waterloo and its Emperor's humiliation. What had the English done to Venice?

She recalled Fred Curran's words: given Venice to the Austrians. Not England alone of course, but all the gangsters who carved up Europe after Napoleon's fall.

Probably it had nothing at all to do with politics; it was rather that they were strangers and not rich enough to be fleeced.

The boatman was rapping on the narrow door of a tall house. He left Robert and Ann to get out of the unstable boat as best they could. The girl appeared to be asleep in the scrambled cloth.

Robert clambered over the rim before she could warn him, slipped on the slimy step and fell, dirtying the green greatcoat that had stayed unharmed through half of Europe.

Hitching up her skirts she bent down, intending to kneel on the cold step. Even then the moving fronds nearly edged her off. Her stockings were thin and wet against her pressure. She struggled to pull herself up. The water sloshed against the stone slabs and went over her shoes. A rat plopped into the canal.

By the time they both stood on the pavement they could hear foot-steps in the house.

A heavy woman in late middle age came to the door, pulling back a rusty bolt that screeched, then thudded into place. By her flickering oil lamp she seemed even darker than the man in the boat. She said something in a harsh voice. This was not the language of Signor Moretti. A dialect, perhaps?

Signora Scorzeri looked at what the boatman had delivered. He picked up people, often foreigners, from Mestre on the mainland, and ferried them to her door – the last had been two giggling Frenchmen scarcely beyond twenty but with enough money to take her middle floor for the winter months, perhaps longer. She preferred foreigners: she could charge them more and they were less fussy about her cooking.

This couple was not prepossessing. Had they been dragged behind the boat? Yet there was something about the man. He bowed over her hand. She softened.

Then hardened. They'd arrived with no servant, not even a woman. Unusual for the English. What money could come from bedraggled people who kept no man or maid? A couple of trunks were being unloaded from the boat but there were no bandboxes, no parcels declaring the acquisitive traveller. What had such people to do here? Probably they were fleeing something.

She stared at them, narrowing her black pebbly eyes. She doubted they were married. They had a look about them.

Still, she would take them in – her top rooms had been empty these many months – and she signalled as much.

'Names,' she said in heavily accented English. 'Give names.'

'Signor and Signora James, Anna and Roberto James,' said Ann.

'Jamis,' said the woman.

'James,' said Ann.

Anna and Roberto: they sounded operatic as Ann and Robert had once seemed romantic. Even as the falsehood was wearily repeated she liked to hear it.

The man bade no farewell to his passengers as he stepped back into the boat. Normally he informed the authorities of foreigners he ferried over from the mainland, but he doubted he'd bother in this case. The *sorella* woke at his footfall and twisted herself upright like a growing vine round his torso, her head swathed in dark scarves.

They followed the *padrona* up sloping steps of damp uneven stone, leaving a ragged boy scarcely in his teens to carry up the trunks. At length they entered a large, piercingly cold room with a high ceiling crossed by dark, crudely cut wooden beams.

She'd thought Italy would be warm. Another lie of poetry and novels, the warm south that wasn't warm.

It was only November. It must get worse.

The woman had given up speaking Italian or, Ann supposed now, Venetian at them and simply gestured with a weary hand at the three rooms.

The bed was immense. It smelled musty. She felt her chest constrict. Robert disliked her weakness and would be especially morose if she complained. By hawking and coughing in the morning she could rid herself of the effects.

A big bed had one use. She could hug the far edge, not to avoid Robert's embraces — it was long since he'd offered those — but to get away from the loud snoring that shook his frame, increased, then ended in a start of wakefulness before the whole cycle began once more.

The soft blue silk scarf he'd bought her so long ago in London had during their long journey been folded into a cover for her ears. It slipped during the night and was no proof against the final crescendo when Robert lay sprawled on his back.

Tonight she was so tired she managed to fall into a dream-filled sleep even before she could put the blue scarf in place.

A few hours later both were awake and in the sitting room. Robert had opened the shutters on a silvery-grey, less misty morning. He was standing at the window letting in the colder air with its smell of seaweed and salt. The sound of water banging on stone and wood entered the room. It made it seem part of the wet workaday world. Robert responded. 'Perhaps here I might do something.'

'Of course,' she said, trying to catch her breath. Her chest was still full of bad musty air.

He went into the small adjoining room which they both assumed he'd take for his writing. He came back: 'But coffee, coffee.'

Coffee cost money. Each chocolate drunk, each tea and glass of wine delivered, each coffee taken stole from the bread and meat that were surely more essential. But she was not a demanding coffee drinker. He'd noted the fact back in London, touching her nose lightly with his forefinger before leaping off to find the drink without which he could not act, compose, even live. It should be taken in men's company.

He went out while she unpacked the few necessary items from the trunks, then as usual stored her hemp bundle under the bed. She hoped that Robert would find his coffee on this strip of island, wherever it was, and some men to drink it with. Else it would be a sorry homecoming.

When he returned she knew he'd drunk something, perhaps coffee, perhaps a stronger drink. She smelled rankness in the air from his breath.

'It's all vegetable patches,' he said. 'We're among peasants with hoes and chickens, clam fishers who crawl in the mud and scarcely bother with shoes and stockings.'

He went into the little study, sat down at a rickety table and brought out his travelling desk, his pens and ink and good paper.

She tiptoed in to remove the greatcoat from the high-backed chair on which he sat to smoke. She ought to work on the water stain from last night, then hang it freely to air. But she probably wouldn't. She often imagined domestic acts she had neither the patience nor skill to undertake. Still, it was better out of 'his' room.

'The weather is disgusting,' he said and turned to her with a weak smile.

He looked pale and still tired.

'Just make a warmer sun,' she responded.

'That's hardly the aim.' He paused, his face rippling a change of mood. 'It's not some sort of gloomy vanity, you know.'

'I know.'

She sensed the danger. He grunted, then poised his pen above the paper. She left the room and pulled the door to – gently and as far as it would go. There would always be a crack.

12

It was time to sort out how they would live here.

'Here' being where exactly? An island near the Venice she'd seen in Signor Moretti's book. Probably the pictures were as misleading as the accounts of Italian weather.

She'd find out how much the surly *padrona* was going to charge for giving them bread and coffee in the morning and a little fish for dinner or tell where these things might be cheaply procured for her to cook. She would learn how the washing was to be done, how she was to exist as a woman with all a woman's wants. She went out to explore.

Moving, she felt warmer and, as she came from the narrow path by the side canal, she saw a wide stretch of water. The day had cleared and across the water to her right were the shapes she'd expected, the campanile, the colonnades and gothic windows of the Doge's Palace, the round solidity of Salute, Signor Moretti's woodcut pictures made stone.

The silver was now more intense and her spirits rose, as, just for a moment, she hoped Robert might find some peaceful energy and she enjoy a little tranquillity.

But wouldn't he discover it all a colossal cliché? Those so illustrated buildings? It was too contrived an 'English' scene for any fragile imagination. She herself liked a cliché.

Pray God that other cliché, Lord Byron, had left his palazzo. Let him be gone with his entourage of monkeys and badgers and dogs and parrots and whores and infants – or whatever else the scandal sheets reported about his person – let him be gone far far away taking his vulgar fame, his reproachful facility, his sneering pride out of Robert's dark orbit.

Though, truth be told, she herself would have relished a sight of him in his gondola with whore or bear. She wished she'd been in the English crowd watching Napoleon strut on the prison ship in Southampton before setting sail into exile.

No matter: little difference between remembering what you'd seen and remembering what you'd imagined seeing.

To her, Robert's imagination was now a physical body to be nurtured and cared for, like a difficult disturbed child. She'd intended to be its nurse and comforter; instead, in her darkest moment, she felt she'd become its dependent, a kind of parasite or tumour growing out of it. Caroline's moods inhabited the house, changing shape but always with a mouth that might at any moment cry out and demand the attention she could never adequately give. Nor *wanted* to give in that case.

There she'd be in her little attic room in the dark except for the single candle with which her cold fingers traced the words of the filched magazine, and Caroline would summon Martha to bring her at once to the warmer drawing room. Her mother would be sipping pale tea in impetuous need of an audience. Then Gilbert would emerge with all his knowledge and experience from Caroline's prodigious memory.

'He travelled, girl, to see the habits, manners and customs of men. He spoke of France and Germany, but he knew of unseen places. He said' – and here Caroline leaned towards her bored young daughter – 'that a Japanese, to vindicate his ruined honour, will murder himself; and his adversary, scorning to be less pure, will entreat him to live long enough to behold him follow the honourable example.'

'How did my father die then?' said the child Ann.

Momentarily bewildered, her murky green eyes flashing, Caroline had barked at her to go away, to go now for she wanted rid of her there and then, shouting after her as she fled back upstairs, 'It's not for you to pry. He loved all things graceful, not wayward, girl, like you. He died as he lived, a gentleman.'

Her Italian was understood enough for Ann to discover most of what she needed – bread, fish, possibly where to get a little fruit from the few stalls along the *fondamenta*, the quayside of the main canal. They were set back in narrow, bent houses before little fields, patches rather, of artichokes and beans.

No one replied to her in Signor Moretti's tongue. Indeed they hardly replied in words at all but simply sat on benches and looked away when she accosted them. They were jovial enough with each other on this low-slung island as if they were all in families, which she supposed they were, all exchanging greetings, touchings, demands, courtesies. But the sociability didn't envelop the stranger, even a harmless smiling one as she supposed herself to be. She felt discouraged and disapproving.

She returned to the apartment with a few flat cakes, fishy biscuits and something like sardines in strands of vinegary cabbage. She couldn't imagine Robert eating this but it was all she could find on this first excursion, and it seemed a local food.

As she entered their rooms she knew something wasn't right. She braced herself.

Putting her eye to the crack along the door she saw he was pacing up and down his little study, talking to himself in splutters. From the smell oozing from the room she realised he'd lit one of the expensive cigars John Taylor had given him before they left England.

He didn't immediately come into the sitting room and when he did – to go down to the privy outside – he said nothing to her as he passed. He was holding the half-smoked cigar between the fingers of his left hand.

When he returned, she spoke. 'Is it no good?' She couldn't help herself.

'Of course it isn't. Did you think it would be?'

'I suppose I hoped.'

Her body had tensed.

'*You* hoped. But I'm not sure how much *you* care.' He stopped, put his cigar to his mouth and puffed. 'I need peace, yes, and calm, but also good company, conversation, a place of ideas and ferment. Do you think I'll find it here among these water rats?' He gestured towards the window.

'There must be other people,' she pursued. 'We're not so far from the Grand Canal and the palazzi where foreigners, writers, interesting groups must congregate. There may be Venetians you could get to know.'

'Venetians,' he spat out. 'I don't think so. What have they ever produced? Dreary pictures of saints. No vision.'

'You haven't looked at them.'

'I didn't come here to stare at antiquated stuff. From the dead past. What has even Titian's work to do with me, with now? Damp, pock-marked. Look at this place.'

'Let's take a boat over to St Mark's anyway and see the cathedral.'

'Sightseeing' – he threw rather than flicked his ash across the room – 'that's all you've wanted to do since we left England. You don't know a place by looking at what others tell you to see.'

'We haven't seen anything yet.'

'Stones, just stones, an empire of ruins. I will not live in a petrified world. It's in the mind things happen.' He jabbed at his head with his right forefinger.

The gesture reminded her of Caroline twirling hair round her little finger in jerks – like a small child, Ann had thought. She grimaced.

'Oh yes, mock it. I know what you think of my work.'

'It's not true, don't be so cruel.'

'Don't start, don't be pathetic.'

He strode back into his study. She swallowed the tears and phlegm from the night in damp bedding, and felt a most comforting self-pity.

There was something about being alone, excluded, that was so familiar, so homely. 'I never wanted you,' Caroline had said when in a pet. 'And I never wanted you,' Ann had replied before fleeing upstairs. You knew where you were with someone like this.

Over the next days she wandered round the city, following hints from Nugent's guide. She looked foreign among the painted people. Their faces were not always masked as in pictures of Venice in Signor Moretti's book but invariably rouged and tinted as if to defeat the greyness of their weather. She liked looking at them; not so different from glancing at fashion plates in Caroline's magazines. If they noticed her, they'd have thought her frumpish.

Curiously there appeared little shame at surrender of a thousand-year republic. There was more bustle in triumphant London, more purposeful busyness. Yet here people in the piazza and *campi*, along the dingy *calli* and *rive*, went about their lives quite assured. As if this little provincial conquered town were the centre of the world. It was a great skill.

'Signora,' said a voice, 'I see from your small book of travel you speak English.'

She didn't hesitate. 'Indeed, that's all I do. I thought I spoke a little Italian but time on La Giudecca has convinced me otherwise.'

She looked at the short, slightly built, clean-shaven and pleasing young man. A taller older one, fair with a faint moustache, possibly a small beard, was with him, close to his shoulder studying a news-sheet. Only the younger one spoke.

'Oh, those people do not talk Italian.' He laughed.

'That I gather. But you speak very good English.'

'I have been in London.' He held out his hand. 'Giancarlo Scrittori.'

She took it. 'Ann James, Signora Robert James.'

The young man came round so that the weak sun would not be in her eyes.

She glanced at the older man, now partially obscured by Signor Scrittori. He didn't speak and was not introduced; he made no move to push himself forward or to walk away but stood completely motionless, paper in hand.

Obviously they were not, after all, acquainted, for the younger man didn't look at him. Curious, for there was too little space between them for strangers.

She'd hoped there'd been two men – it would be more seemly to have a stray introduction within a group. A single man accosting a woman alone would not have been quite decorous in Holborn or Putney; she doubted it was so here.

'I apologise for approaching you but I wish to help – this is my city – and to take an opportunity of practising my not so good English. I am wishing to start a trade with English people in things of luxury, little boxes, miniatures, some glass trinkets from Murano we call *margaritini*. No, do not fear I am trying to sell you something,' he added as she drew back. 'For this I need a good English.'

'It sounds good to me, very good already.'

'You are kind. But now, what are you wanting to see?'

'Well, the sights, the obvious ones I'm afraid. I saw illustrations of them in a book of Italy I borrowed when a child. Indeed I have described them.'

Why say this? Was it better to be responding to a stranger as a spinster hack or a married woman?

'You are a writer, then? My name should make me one but I am not.' He smiled.

'Well, sort of a writer, nothing great or very imaginative,' she said quickly. 'Just, you know . . .' She trailed off.

'Well, no, I do not, Signora,' he laughed again, 'but maybe you will tell me as we look at all those things you have already so excellently described.'

'My husband is . . .' She stopped.

He noticed the pause. 'Perhaps I will meet your husband, he is a writer and not "sort of a writer" I think.'

'What makes you say that?'

He grinned. 'You have said about writing and not really writing, so I can conclude you are married to a great writer. The English are good at genius. We are not so – how shall I put it? – so very concerned with the attitude. We love skill, fineness. I myself deal in miniatures, small lovely things, not made by genius but much – what is the word? – craft. Though I have a relative, a sculptor, who might be what you wish.'

How unexpected he should discern so much, this stranger casually met.

While they were speaking she noticed again the taller man she'd assumed to be Signor Scrittori's friend still standing close by studying his paper at intervals, perhaps watching them as well. She couldn't be sure for he remained partially against the sun and his features were not fully revealed. Not enough to understand expressions. A stranger, she supposed, from the paler skin and something in his bearing and clothes. Dutch, German perhaps?

Did he disapprove of a foreign woman making such easy contact with an unknown man and one so clearly younger than herself? Maybe he was censorious. Or was he just glancing at her as a man might?

She smoothed her hair across her brow beneath her bonnet. Her clothes were drab but the blue silk scarf always brightened her face.

Perhaps he was English and heard her speech with Signor Scrittori.

When she looked again, he was gone. Probably he'd stood in his own thoughts, unaware of others. Men often did this.

The day was altering. Colour was seeping into the sky. In the puddles on the stones the water glinted. From a high building with gothic windows a woman was singing mechanically, cleverly, without passion. Technique only, no imagination, she caught herself thinking in Robert's words. What relief, how sensible! She raised her eyes and smiled at the young man.

'You are a godsend – you say that? I read the word in your newspaper.'

They had become familiar as they walked along towards the Rialto after their visit to the basilica. 'There is a young girl, my aunt, my distant aunt you would say, wants me to give her some lessons in the English. Her gracious mother has most particularly asked, but I have not the time and not the craft. Perhaps you might like to take my place and have from her some woman's hints of our city in return? You would be doing much service.'

A good idea to earn some money, yet she was dismayed that her need was so obvious.

They'd now crossed back over the Rialto bridge and were walking in the direction of the Jesuit church from where she planned to get a *traghetto* to Sant'Eufemia on La Giudecca. Near San Toma he stopped. 'This is the palazzo where she is living,' he said. 'What better time?'

He reached up and grabbed the bronze knocker and handle. He banged it against the door twice and the sound echoed in the distance. There must be a cavern behind the ornate wooden door.

After a lengthy pause footsteps could be heard, along with some other noise, like a cat or irascible gull. An old woman opened the door, seemingly with difficulty. She was followed at once by a pretty girl with startling and startled eyes – rich, dark and deep, set in milky cheeks. They contrasted with the blue and grey of the day. A full flash of a mouth smiled. It was a long time since Ann had looked on someone as young – and pure. So strange a word to come to her mind, though so often on Robert's lips. The girl, child really, opened her mouth to show pale even teeth. Her own, though a little yellowed, were good for her age, sensitive but not broken. These were white porcelain.

Giancarlo Scrittori inclined his head and spoke. 'May I, Signorina Beatrice, introduce an honoured friend, Donna Anna, Signora James. We have a proposal.'

The girl took a moment to construe the words, then smiled a wide lilting smile, gestured politely and stood aside.

'*Permesso*,' murmured Giancarlo Scrittori as they began to follow the girl and the more reluctant old woman into the *portego*, the wide hall of the palazzo. It appeared immense and glinting, the floor made of coloured, highly polished stones set in cement. Ann had seen nothing like it. A footman scuttled from one door to another.

Suddenly they heard voices from somewhere far into the interior. They stopped. Then what she'd supposed a seagull cry hurled through the space above their heads, followed by a female voice mounting higher and higher from a low soothing murmur; then a sound of metal scraping on tiles.

'Not now,' said the girl, still smiling. She pushed Giancarlo Scrittori back towards the front door. 'Next week.'

Her face kept the same expression as Ann too was propelled over the coloured floor through the door and on to the stones outside, the girl still courteous but insistent, the elderly maidservant close by framing her from behind. 'So sorry, Signora,' she said, 'so very sorry.'

Before even the usual farewells could be exchanged, the door had closed. Giancarlo Scrittori walked on with Ann. He said nothing at all.

She stepped off a *traghetto* on to the island, then steadied herself. The water in the canal had been choppy and there'd been too many in the boat for comfort, all precariously standing between the oarsmen. She walked slowly along the *fondamenta* watching her feet over uneven flagstones and puddles. It was easy to trip.

She was reluctant to go home – home, an inappropriate word for the cold, tense apartment. She stopped and stared into the sky.

Her eyes followed a gull swooping and circling, then settling domestically on the water. The bird was buffeted by waves and boisterous wind as well as by the swirl from passing boats. It was swished up and down but never dislodged or seemingly discommoded, the closed feathers unperturbed in its nervous environment. Were the webbed feet working strenuously underneath the calm feathers or did the bird have some skill in suffering so calmly, whether from boat swell or gusts of wind, with no ruffling?

She was admiring the bird's self-composure when a group of six or seven seagulls suddenly landed beside it. All joined together and screamed raucously, flapping at each other over some blood-soaked stringy entrails she could only partially see from the way they were tugged about. They must have been thrown out by a butcher. Or did these birds find some small living thing and kill it and tear it apart with gusto? It was enough to make one laugh.

13

That night Robert said that words could be dissolved into a pure void. What would be their sound?

This sort of thing used to seem wondrous though obscure when she'd sat in admiration before him.

She knew the sentiments by heart: they simply arrived in different combinations. In any case there was no truth to them, for language always lies, so could not be pure, solid or dissolved.

Still, from his saying the words at all and in whatever order and however dubious, she concluded he was in a good mood. This despite disappointment at the peasants with their clams and bare feet. He must have found men to drink with, to listen to him though understanding not one word. But he'd not trouble over that. He'd prided himself on no one truly understanding his *Attila*.

Boredom fought with desire to keep him amiable. Which would win? She knew already – she was bad at keeping quiet when tired to death. The tallow smell in the room was pulling at her lungs. It had no effect on Robert, although she noted that familiar clutching at the breast, a gesture he made with his left hand alone. But that was part of his rhetoric, not pain: well, not that sort of pain.

'When I was out I met a young man who . . .' She paused. The momentary eagerness in Robert's eye was absurd. He wanted her to say that this casually met young man, this Italian whom no one knew, had admired his fragment of *Attila* and been struck by his universal ideas which were now known only to a coterie in a few northern districts of London. This impossible dream: the potency of *his* language.

Why on earth did she know this? And if she did, why allow the response? It had been the sparkle she'd not even tried to keep out of her own eyes that had led to this hopeless delusion.

She resumed quickly. 'He said I might get work teaching English here – perhaps to children.'

The light faded from Robert's face. He turned away and shrugged. 'If you want. You always want money, don't you?'

'*We* need it.'

'We might. We've used up most of mine.'

'We both contributed.'

'Oh yes. You counted. You're good at keeping accounts. Life balances for you, doesn't it? What you can get out of people.'

'That's unfair and you know it.'

'Don't tell me what I know.'

'It's a manner of speaking.'

'Well of course, mistress of banality. What sort of young man?'

She didn't answer at once.

'Just an ordinary young man from Venice. He was trying to be helpful.'

'Meaning I'm not?' He picked up his dark green-coat with its now indelible water stain and moved towards the door. 'Enough,' he said. 'The stars are shining in my gloom.'

'Thank God for that,' she mumbled. Her muffled anger swirled round the room.

A week later she met Giancarlo Scrittori again as agreed. If she'd not known it unlikely, she'd have thought he'd spent his short time in London reading those pap gothic novels with which she herself was so familiar.

Perhaps, though, the bizarre arrangements had been made simply to allow him to chatter on, so covering with many words the oddity of that aborted visit in San Toma. For nothing had been said of what had happened at the palazzo doorway, nothing to deaden the howl from that cavernous house.

To make sure they found each other, that she had a respectable place to wait if for any reason he was detained on business or something interrupted the encounter – he doubted this would happen, but you never knew, a customer . . . he'd trailed off – he'd suggested the basilica. They would meet in the interior of San Marco. But it was dark and huge, and one could wander round it for many minutes without achieving even an arranged meeting. There needed to be a place.

'Put one foot on the lamb which eats a willow branch and the other upon a goose. There I will be.'

She'd enjoyed the game. She'd not told him clearly what she'd done in London, but perhaps he'd assumed correctly, or expected something gothic from all English visitors nowadays. Whatever the case, the assignation was amusing and she'd arrived just a little early to take time to position herself.

Inside the basilica she hesitated. What would a mosaic goose look like? There were many animals here which had never walked the earth. She strolled round for a quarter of an hour or so before spying a likely candidate. And close to a willow-eating lamb. She stood on the spot.

Giancarlo Scrittori was almost upon her before she noticed him, so fixed was her concentration on the feet of a stylish saint cased in scarlet hose and bright sandals.

'I have my pupil now ready for you,' he said gaily. 'All is settled. You know, you saw her, she is a young girl of impeccable family. She wishes to learn the English well so she may read Lord Byron in original.' He smiled. 'That is her idea, of course. Her mother has told my aunt that she thinks it must be improving material if it is written by an English milord, and I bowed to assent with her. She hears tales of his life here but I' – he gestured – 'disabuse her of them. Signorina Beatrice is the sister of a great sculptor.'

'I would be happy to. She is a pretty girl.'

He looked at her keenly. She blushed. Was she so starved of a little ordinary politeness?

Ah, the young man was noticing her drab clothes. Her garments were unsuited to a palazzo with great rooms.

'I might try to find a new jacket for this work, Signor Scrittori.'

He smiled encouragingly as to a child. 'Yes, yes, Signora. I know just where you must go, Campo San Paterian, a cousin of mine. We can be there and we can practise my unsatisfactory English as we go.'

'You know very well your English is good and it sounds just perfect to me. With such a nice lilt. But yes, if your cousin has ready-made clothes, I am happy to come with you.'

He worried he'd insulted her. 'So many ladies here buy such clothes when they have need of them speedily,' he said. 'Dressmakers take their time.' He still appeared anxious that the supposed need might have offended. Then he chuckled. 'Your English has more words and more chance to express what you do not mean, I think.'

'Don't worry. I both need and want a ready-made jacket, something a bit brighter to fit with the brightness of Venetian ladies.'

He beamed. 'You have a phrase, when in Rome? Which will settle for Venice too, I think.'

They had come out of the basilica and were in the Piazza San Marco.

'It is grand. This is as I pictured it.'

'You mean unlike La Giudecca? But you know this is partly new and it is not our creation.'

'No?'

'No. It has been Napoleone who has made it so grand. They say he called it the drawing room of Europe.' He pointed away from the basilica. 'See that arcade, all new, made by the French who like grand things. We are more – how do you say? – homely.'

'I don't think that's at all the right word for your palazzi, if the one I glimpsed is the standard.'

'There's a real palace behind the arcade, with a great ballroom for the Emperor's stepson. Look there. They intended a great statue of Napoleone as Jupiter but he was fallen too soon. Now his place is bare.'

Although they were by now threading their way through the crowd, Giancarlo Scrittori was not diverted from his theme. His tone and face registered no passion; yet he had to speak his protest.

'The great Canova himself was shocked. He remonstrated with the Emperor but to what good? The French have only French ideas. They make everywhere France. They sent our basilica horses to Paris, then knocked down our palaces, our convents and churches, all destroyed as if they are without history. Now there are wide French streets where there should be noble houses.'

He checked she was listening as his voice rose above the cries of hawkers, his expression continuing amiable while he spoke bitter words. 'He dredged the waters for his big ships and now we flood.'

'Didn't Venice always flood, Signor Scrittori?'

'We flood more.'

'I hear the new island cemetery of San Cristoforo is beautiful.'

'They move away our dead and leave us here, the living dead.'
He fell silent.

Best, she thought, to give no more compliments to the French.

'I accept that the lighting is better,' he said after a pause. The French think they are enlightened people; they will force others in the light too.'

He smiled, proud of his joke in English.

'And the Austrians?' she asked as they passed two German soldiers smoking on a humped bridge.

'The Austrians returned our bronze horses.'

The shop was in Campo San Paterian near San Luca, with a small front and long back. It stretched into the darkness. On both sides bales of cloth were stacked high on bricks.

A weak sun shone through the door and, as her eyes adapted to the gloom, Ann could see the pattern on the colourful fabrics, some the Indian design so fashionable back in England, others more classically geometric. Shawls in black, red and silver were draped over bales. She didn't care for gay shawls. Caroline had been so often swathed in them, while her friend Mary Davies had thought them the most feminine of items.

'I want something serviceable.' The word puzzled Giancarlo

Scrittori. 'I mean something I can wear in two seasons, not too warm when the sun shines or cold when it freezes, something that will last.'

'I see. But, Signora, that is a sad use of clothes. You have a body for that. Clothes I think should make you happy and show your spirit.'

She smiled. 'I like the idea of a jacket that will gladden my heart. Let's see if we can find the kind of garment that will delight and last at the same time.'

The cousin Tommaso was looking on, rubbing his hands, perhaps for something to do while they spoke in English, perhaps to work on his own cliché – so Robert would have said.

A vision of old merry Robert flashed before her. He could have done Tommaso and the charming Giancarlo Scrittori to a T. He'd made amusement from the predictable. Now he was as boring as any he'd imitated. How strange she couldn't use his predictability to help them both.

She snapped out of her dispiriting thought: the two men were staring at her.

'The signora has a colour in mind?' said Tommaso.

'Perhaps a brown,' she began. But, as Giancarlo Scrittori looked downcast, she added, 'a bright brown, more terracotta, more orange.'

Tommaso went farther into the gloom of his narrow shop and ranged through the garments hanging on pegs from wooden rails. He passed over some brown ones – or what seemed brown in this dim light – and came forward with a *turquois*-coloured short jacket of thick knit material, wool and a little silk perhaps.

'This would suit the signora,' he said. 'It is a colour not for the signore here but for pale people. It is beautiful, is it not?'

'Yes it is,' she said, 'it is lovely but not brown.'

'Try, please.' He gestured to a darker corner behind a torn brocade curtain.

'Well, it is not what I had in mind.'

She went obediently to try it on. It fitted well.

'It is I think too expensive,' she said doubtfully.

'It is a little expensive,' Giancarlo Scrittori acknowledged. 'But good wearing and it will be a jacket you can use wherever you go. It will be you.'

'How much?'

Instead of answering, Tommaso wrote a number on a scrap of billing paper, crossed it out and in that age-old custom of the salesman wrote a lower figure below. 'For you Signora, since you are a friend of my good cousin.'

'It's still too much,' she said.

She began taking off the jacket.

Giancarlo Scrittori gestured to stop her. 'My cousin can give you even a better price and you can pay part from what you earn from the little Signorina Beatrice. The Savelli will pay well, I promise.'

'But if I don't please them?'

'Signora, you will please, I know it.'

So it was done and the jacket was packaged up.

As they walked back, Giancarlo Scrittori sought to entertain again. Perhaps he wished to get some opinions off his chest he didn't care to share with fellow citizens.

They progressed away from the main sights. There were gaps where houses had been demolished or had fallen down leaving terraced rows like mouths of broken and missing teeth. They turned into another humped road or *rio tera* where a canal had been and was there no longer, then into a large paved square.

Giancarlo saw her disappointment. 'The French did this,' he said. 'They demolished much but the Austrians are blamed for all.'

She looked at one palazzo half-destroyed and newly so. 'But this cannot be the French, they left four or five years ago, surely.'

'This we do ourselves,' he replied. 'We Venetians. Some people do not want to pay the taxes and would rather destroy their homes.'

'I believe the French are now less hated than the Austrians,' she ventured.

He glanced at her as if to enquire about something but he thought better of it. 'I read it in *The Times* I think, before we left England. Or perhaps I heard it from an Italian man we met in London, an acquaintance of my husband's, a Signor Orlando.'

He made no comment. He had received a rather bitter letter from Luigi Orlando recently but there was no need to tell everyone everything.

They were walking now towards the Gesuati. Ann was relieved that their way was far less crowded than near the Rialto and the Piazza. She turned once, thinking there was someone too close whom her friend must know. But the man withdrew into a side *calle*. This uncertain closeness happened often in a city of too many people and too little space.

At last he broke the silence. 'There is truth in it. The Austrians are, we think, rude to us – perhaps – sometimes there are insults exchanged. We think that on their surface they are dull-minded. Is that the word?'

'Perhaps "dull-witted" would be better.'

'Well, dull-witted, earnest, not the kind of people we Venetians usually like and think we are.'

He fell silent again; then after a while he continued, 'The French were not liked but were not so unpopular. I think to agree with you. My fellow citizens are quick and clever but not wise. They did not quite hate the French despite their looting and sacking – many common people welcomed them as liberators. You know they turned out nuns and orphans on to the streets?' He chuckled. 'But you, I think, do not become so anxious over what you call Papists.'

She smiled. 'We don't approve of harming orphans. Nuns I grant you are not so popular, except in dark novels. We love them there.'

She felt tired and was glad to stop talking and listening. But yet, when the moment came, she was sad to see this pleasant young man walk away. She turned to seek a *traghetto* for the choppy ride home.

She returned to La Giudecca and entered their apartment gingerly. She placed her jacket in her hemp bag under the bed beside her few now rather crumpled papers.

Next morning when she set out to find the palazzo near San Toma, she took it with her in a basket, then changed quickly just after stepping off the boat on the wooden planks. When she'd earned some money she'd pay off what she owed, then, when she'd earned a little more, of course wear it for Robert to see. Why should he not?

It was not so wonderful a garment, nor did it shout expense. Indeed it was very ordinary, she thought as she looked closely at its secure, inelegant stitching in the brighter daylight. Yet it would not pass without comment in their dingy apartment.

Better if it had been a jacket for Robert. Perhaps parents were like this with children, especially demanding ones. Happier to see them fine clad and shod than themselves. Was it love, selflessness, excess humility or fear? Robert would have said it was not love but control of another, her control.

He was very concerned about control – it was the worst thing in the world.

14

She'd come to the Palazzo Savelli without Giancarlo Scrittori: he had some business to do, he said, but she suspected he wanted her to go alone. He wished both sides to be impressed

The palazzo didn't disappoint. It was full of glass, the chandeliers intricate, elaborate Murano, mainly white with touches of pink in the mantels. They hung, huge fossilised sea anemones from a waving sea of dark wood rafters. On the wall were ornate mirrors in panes, some flecked with rust spots, all distorting, exaggerating or decanting the scenes before them. It was hard for Ann to know where she was. Impossible not to see oneself in different postures: made now picturesque, now grotesque, always obscure.

Her ungloved hands had coarsened from too much washing in cold water, but here in these tarnished mirrors the roughest hands were smooth and indistinct. Ann was not displeased to look down at hers when she'd removed her gloves.

She'd been shown in by a diminutive manservant, followed at once by the old woman they'd seen before – well, not so old, she now noted, someone very unlike her mother with her rouge and false hair. This woman had embraced ageing in her black garb, voice and stance. She was helped by an absence of all front teeth.

Then a footman, slightly shabby despite magnificent powdered wig setting off his brown face, ushered her up a wide flight of marble stairs with walls of fading frescoes. He left her in a large gloomy room after muttering what she supposed was a version of her name in too many syllables. Heavy curtains shaded the windows; the paintings in their ornate gilt frames were hardly visible in the dim light, darkened further by poor placing and layers of dust.

A woman in shades of elaborate black was seated on a sofa of faded crimson velvet embroidered in dark silk swirls. Her face was pale and lined, framed by black lace.

Not unkind but not prepossessing, a little haughty.

'I am the Contessa Savelli,' she said in heavily accented English. 'You are Signora Jamis. Please to sit. I speak not much English.'

Ann sat on a lower facing chair upholstered in the same faded velvet. A young twinkling voice interrupted the silence. 'Signora, we are most content you are here.'

It was the girl she and Giancarlo Scrittori had met the last time they visited the house. Now she was ready for courtesies. Again, as with Signor Scrittori, no mention was made of the first strange meeting.

'Signorina,' she replied. 'I too am content.'

There followed more Italian pleasantries, which Ann was unsure how to answer, the girl speaking in her light musical way, the mother in lower tones from a smiling mouth beneath remote eyes.

Then the Contessa left the room. Ann rose as she went. She glanced at a ceiling fresco of pink and white cherubs displaying undulating stains on plump flesh.

'Let us go to another smaller place. There is good light,' said the girl. 'We will sit near a window. There you hear the sound of water.'

'I would like, Signorina, to do exactly what you have in mind. We have an hour for conversing or reading, what you will.'

'Beatrice, please.' The voice fell like a warm spray over them both.

'And I am Ann S–' She stopped, realising she'd almost used her maiden name. How absurd.

Frederick Curran said it was always best to be more than one person. She presumed he meant on paper.

'But that is not so correct,' laughed Beatrice. 'You are the Signora.'

'Yes, I suppose so. I am old.'

'Not old Signora, no, just older than I am and you are married and will teach.'

The girl was all sunshine, all smiles and shifting music. It was impossible not to respond.

So they chatted and nodded and chuckled and Beatrice wrote down phrases in a small notebook exquisitely covered in an intricate geometric pattern of muted red and cream. The hour passed in a flash.

At moments the wintry sunlight on the canal beneath was reflected through the arched window on to the carved ceiling and from there to a tarnished mirror: then all was moving, dazzling on the patched and shredded green damask walls. 'You make more of the sunlight here,' said Ann.

'Possibly,' replied Beatrice.

When at the end of the session the Contessa, with her mingling of stateliness, anxiety and polite hospitality, came in to check that everything had proceeded well, she must have seen the success of the lesson. Perhaps she was glad the new teacher had amused her daughter, who, Ann knew now, was quick and might become easily bored.

She'd passed some test. The Contessa would be honoured if she and her husband – a famous English author, she understood – would attend for a social evening. Not in the next weeks, for the Marchese would be in town and would want her company. The Contessa gave a smile both proud and deprecating. 'And my son, you will have chance to meet the Conte if he will be seen.'

An odd phrase, perhaps it came from inadequate English. It chimed with Beatrice's mention of this young man who was and was not in residence. Ann supposed he lived elsewhere for part of the time. She saw that the girl gave her mother a quick glance as she spoke of him. There might be sibling jealousy.

She hoped no invitation would ever come, that its suggestion was just polite formality. Perhaps she should have set up for widowhood, so that a husband need not be produced. But in that case she'd have dressed in sombre black (widows did not wear *turquois*-hued jackets). And Giancarlo Scrittori would need to have kept quiet. Had she really mentioned *Attila* to him? She must have done. In any case it was too late to be a widow or a spinster. She prayed the event would not happen.

She took a *traghetto* across the Grand Canal, heading to the Palazzo Grimani near San Luca. Giancarlo Scrittori had told her that the *poste restante* was located there. In her bag she had three letters for England, two with return addresses of the *poste restante* on them.

One was the customary notice to the Strand office of Moore & Stratton telling of her whereabouts. She never knew who received these notices but nothing was ever returned, so she assumed the firm was still in business.

The second was to the booksellers Dean & Munday. She doubted they would give the credit she requested since she was sending no work, but it was worth a try: beyond food and rent, she and Robert were in need of almost everything else that separated them from the Albanian beggars who snatched at their cloaks on the bridges. This was the important letter and at intervals, when she could not pass that way herself, she would send Signora Scorzeri's ragged boy to the *poste* to check for a response.

The third one, with no return address, described for Sarah the Venetian sights in the language of a guidebook. Ann had had no pleasure writing it and her cousin would have little interest reading it, but the letter would declare she was alive and thinking of Sarah and her brood in London. She would write again in a month or two and convey just as little.

She kept from Robert her trip to the post: he distrusted authorities anywhere and the office was notoriously connected with the Austrian rulers. Besides, she was increasingly eager to keep a few things to herself, even if only a bag under a bed and a furtive visit.

The next lesson suggested to Ann that young Beatrice had read rather more in English than she'd admitted. Perhaps her dignified mother did not approve of novels.

Initially the girl indicated she'd been honoured by the Contessa with an English work of Mrs Chapone, *Letters on the Improvement of the Mind*, a most interesting volume, she added. Her mother had received it from a distinguished friend who'd met the celebrated Mrs Chapone on a visit to England in happier times when Venice belonged to itself. Beatrice lowered her voice when she spoke of the city's past.

But on a second meeting it was clear that her young pupil had failed to reach the end of this improving work. She was a great deal more acquainted with the gothic stories of Mrs Radcliffe, borrowed it seemed from a girl called Mariotta rather than from the Contessa's distinguished lady friends.

'This is a book your mother accepts?' asked Ann, turning with pleasure the familiar pages of *The Mysteries of Udolpho*.

Beatrice looked worried. 'Is the English not pure, Signora?'

'Yes, the English is pure,' laughed Ann.

'Then all is as it should be,' smiled Beatrice. She was, she said, ravished – perhaps not the best choice of word – by the plot. Who could not be? It was so exciting, so marvellous. The girl gave her little tinkling laughs as she mentioned the passages that related to her native city.

'Do you remember them, Signora?'

'Yes, I do Beatrice. I think I was a little influenced by them when I thought of coming to Venice.'

'No, no,' Beatrice put her hands over her giggling mouth. 'Her pictures are no guide to Venice. It is not the city we inhabit.'

'I didn't think they were but it's hard not to keep them in the mind.'

'That is good, Signora, for you would be disappointed if you expect to see with Mrs Radcliffe's eyes. It is art, yes?'

'It is art.'

The girl opened a volume of the book which fell easily on to her writing tablet. Clearly it had been much read.

'I will tell it to you, Signora, and you can correct my accent on the words.'

Ann nodded assent.

Beatrice sat upright on her brocaded chair and held the book high.
Like a schoolchild on a stool with its spelling slate.

*Nothing could exceed Emily's admiration on her first view of
Venice, with its islets, palaces, and towers rising out of the sea,
whose clear surface reflected the tremulous picture in all its colours.
The sun, sinking in the west, tinted the waves and the lofty mountains of Friuli, which skirt the northern shores of the Adriatic,
with a saffron glow, while on the marble porticos and colonnades
of St Mark were thrown the rich lights and shades of evening.*

Ann forgot she was supposed to comment on pronunciation. She was
enjoying the syncopated rhythm that Beatrice brought to the familiar
prose. So it was the girl who interrupted her reading.

'This is difficult, Signora, when the lands of Friuli are so distant
to the east and their mountains out of sight. You know,' and she
placed the book on her lap to gesture with her hand, 'mountains are
very pleasing to the Signora Radcliffe. She finds them everywhere,
even on the plains along the Brenta River. The Piazza San Marco she
calls St Mark's Place, like a square in London.' She tinkled a laugh.
'And my accent, Signora?'

'I had not thought of it, Beatrice, you read so well.'

'For your Mrs Radcliffe all the palazzi are magnificent. It is not
quite so. Rotten wood and broken stone do not sound so well as
marble.'

Ann couldn't read her mood. 'It helps to live in your own palazzo
to judge,' she ventured.

'Our palazzo was once beautiful but not so much now. You have
seen how the mirrors dirty – I forget the word . . .'

'Tarnish.'

'Tarnish, yes. All of Venice is tarnished. We have become poor.
Mama had to sell some of her portion, a necklace of pearl and rubies.'

'Mrs Radcliffe writes from her imagination, Beatrice.'

'There is one real thing,' pursued Beatrice. 'The wicked Montoni has a magnificent *salotto* but his other rooms are bare because he cannot furnish them. His grand appearance is a mask.'

They were both silent.

'Mrs Radcliffe's Emily writes a poem whenever she is moved by a scene. You might try to write verses in English yourself, as an exercise.'

'No, no,' replied Beatrice with a start, 'one artist in the family is enough.'

15

It was after Christmas, during the long preparation for *carnevale*, that the formal invitation from the Contessa was given, and Robert had to be produced.

They formed a small party, chosen Ann assumed as suitable matches for commonplace English visitors. There was of course Giancarlo Scrittori. His familiarity with the family surprised Ann. Strange to her that the man who dealt in baubles and whose kinsman sold ready-made clothes in a cramped and overstuffed shop sat easily at the table of a proud contessa with her drawing room on the *piano nobile* of a palazzo on the Grand Canal. Sometimes Beatrice called him 'my cousin'.

Another guest was Signor Verezzi, an elderly man with full curling white eyebrows and wispy head hair; he appeared to be a distant but poor relation of the deceased Conte. A second younger man, Signor Besan, had thinner, more aggressive eyebrows. By his gestures he made it known he came from the Contessa's side of the extended family. He had a pugnacious chin which, when he arrived, had been paralleled by the beak of a black mask. From their courteous but curt greeting, it seemed the two men were much acquainted but not close, perhaps not in political agreement. There was also Signora Zen, a sort of companion perhaps or even poorer relation or earlier governess to Beatrice – Ann was never told – there to swell the numbers of ladies but not expected to talk much when men were present. She was introduced without elaboration of role or status.

In all it seemed a very un-English combination. But then, Ann reminded herself, she knew little of aristocratic English families. Seen close they might be as bizarre as this.

The wintry light was thin in the glassy rooms. The usual seeping Venetian cold was felt equally in rich and poor apartments, but here the china and silverware glinted in the glow of wax candles and open fires, and everything had a patina of warmth. Despite having grumbled at going out for dull, mediocre company and some ominous fumbling with his necktie before they left, Robert was expanding with the full-bodied Friuli wine.

When all the guests had been assembled for some time, to Ann's surprise Beatrice's brother was produced. She'd been told he would be present, but his absence from the welcoming party persuaded her that this elusive figure had dashed off again to gamble or hunt on the mainland, or whatever noble young men did in Northern Italy. He was presented by his full elaborate name.

No further civilities were demanded of the new visitors for at once the Conte, a tall bent young man, turned from them and looked into one of the mottled mirrors, perhaps at himself, perhaps only at reflected light and darkness. Ann briefly followed his gaze.

As they began the meal the Conte continued a disturbing presence. He scowled at Robert, then looked with conspicuous inattention round the room when he spoke either in English or in his rushed inaccurate Italian. The Contessa gently cajoled her son to bring his consciousness to the table. She made matters worse, as she must so often have done. Giancarlo Scrittori engaged both mother and son when he could, used perhaps to facilitating in this great house.

Robert's Italian was not fluent, but Beatrice in particular understood enough when he lapsed into English to make an animated point, and his animation in whatever language was engaging. Even Giancarlo Scrittori, whom Robert treated frostily, leaned forward to catch what he said of philosophy and art and immaterial beauty. He hazarded a few responses, but Robert refused to engage with him. Giancarlo Scrittori was either too polite or too attuned elsewhere to notice. Ann listened to the words, made unfamiliar to her through watching new auditors.

Did she feel pride at the company's response? A little perhaps, but more resentment that he entertained others – and that she herself had dared to become wearied by his act.

As time passed, the Conte Francesco Savelli began to get the drift in Robert's mélange of languages – he'd even begun to add a little French to make himself understood. Francesco seemed to thaw, then he warmed. 'Yes,' he suddenly said. 'Yes, yes, *certo*.'

And before the third plates of the meal were even removed, he rose and crossed to Robert's chair, then pulled him by the arm. His mother protested but smilingly – evidently indulgence was her most successful mode with this clever, troubled son.

Suddenly Francesco jerked Robert to standing. 'Come, come now, you must come to see my suffering Madonna. Come now.'

Only Robert was included in the invitation but to make the event less strange Beatrice also got up. Used to her brother's sudden spurts of activity, she called over to Ann. 'Let us go too, Signora, you will want to see the wonders my brother has carved. Pardon, Mama.'

So, leaving the Contessa, Giancarlo Scrittori and the other guests – except for Signora Zen, who got up and followed silently – they trooped out of the dining hall and down the marble steps to the hallway. An ornate wooden door opened on to a large room in semi-darkness.

Francesco sprinted in and lit the candles, in such a hurry he spilled wax over a table and burnt his finger, exclaiming but still rushing on excitedly. 'You will see,' he kept repeating. 'My Virgin you say.'

They entered the dimly lit room. Unshaped massy stones and gnarled pieces of wood were strewn about the floor. Heads of boar and wolverine adorned one wall and on a high table were bottles of what looked like pickled frogs, moles and a half-formed human foetus, all glinting in the candlelight and waving gently as Francesco brushed past them.

The carving he beckoned towards was covered in a white damask cloth. It made the shape beneath appear a giant upturned crab. They stood and stared as the young man fingered and twitched the cloth. Then just as the waiting became oppressive, with one violent jerk of his arm, he flung off the covering. Like a magician entertaining an audience with his live rabbit. But what was produced with this gesture was more monstrous.

It was a bronze, a dark metal pile: a ravaged rock on which straddled a human form with strangulated face.

Instead of the usual beatific and smooth-faced, cradling Mary, Francesco had created a woman without her son, no infant nor grown man; a woman left ageing, alone, bereft, horrid in her uselessness, anticipating no reunion in heaven, tied to crude unyielding rocky earth.

The sculpture delivered a message of dreadful grief, grief made inelegant and ugly. This was no moving *pietà* for watchers but angular jagged anguish, the face wrenched back and the arms in grotesque gesture clawing at the air. A woman shrieking in silent metal.

Ann glanced at Robert. She had worried about his reaction – he was no lover of the plastic arts. But he was transfixed, his nervous body momentarily still. Then, changing into his usual expressiveness, he put his hand out to feel.

'No,' said the Conte, shocked into sudden movement, 'not to touch. She is hard, not to be caressed.'

Robert jerked his hand back as if stung, but Ann could see he was not much offended. His pale eyes, a little bloodshot from too much wine, were bright and eager. 'It is, as you say, wonderful, magnificent.'

'*Si si, magnifico.*'

They stood in silence.

'My brother,' said Beatrice at last, breaking the mood, 'my brother is very talented.'

Francesco gave her a quick scornful look and grabbed the white cloth from the table. He was about to fling it over the image again when he was interrupted.

'No,' said Robert, 'no, just a moment more please.'

Without smiling Francesco stayed his hand, rubbing the cloth between his fingers.

'It is a masterpiece,' said Robert, 'the cleverness of portraying this grief without the body of Christ, so that it is grief itself, pain itself that you have depicted here, pain of the body and spirit but through an absence. Only this lifeless metal forced into such active shapes could catch it.'

He was speaking largely to himself using only English. Francesco Savelli understood little of his words, but he was now watching Robert with hooded eyes of almost doglike adoration. Beatrice and Ann grew uncomfortable. For both of them in different ways it was all too naked.

Then Beatrice spoke again to urge her brother to put the cloth over his work. Ann understood. Surely it was better covered.

They climbed back upstairs, Robert following the two women, with Signora Zen coming after like his shadow. The Conte stayed down in his studio. As they left, Ann could see his form slumped over the candles which he was putting out with a flick of his fingers, as if even this showing had been too much. Nobody urged him back to his mother's table.

'My brother the Conte is very gifted,' Beatrice whispered to Ann again as they mounted the stairs, 'but there is something in his head not so, how to say it? not so comfortable, so comforting to him or to anyone. He becomes very excited and then his work goes so well but at other times he is down the bottom of the steps. He has these melancholy moods like a – ' she paused for a word, 'like winter coming. Nothing stops them. He howls. Poor Francesco.'

'But not so poor perhaps if he can create such things.'

'Oh yes, he is well regarded in Venice. But he puts over his creations his white cloths and like tonight shows people for moments only. He is a strange one. Mama worries herself over him. She becomes quite sick with it. When Papa was alive he used to take Francesco to our estate in Friuli and try to make of him a hunter and a man, but he comes back much worse, sometimes growling like an animal, more often sunk into such black feeling he is sitting down there doing nothing. He curls up his arms and legs like a mouse in a nest.' Fearing the wrong image Beatrice curled up her own hands and nestled them in her breast to make her point. It was a poignant gesture. 'Mama was in agonies. Now, as you see, she – how do you say? – humours him.'

'Yes, perhaps that's it.'

They entered the dining room and a little later Robert followed. He'd heard Ann and Beatrice talking but hadn't wanted to listen. Signora Zen slid silently in behind and took her place.

Robert's exultant mood was over.

Back at the table there were marzipan sweets, candied fruit, almonds and oranges, and dessert wines in coloured glasses.

Ann was on edge. She made no effort to hide her glances from Robert. She hoped he would drink no more. He knew that quite well.

He was no longer speaking, except when spoken to, but he remained polite, even attentive to the Contessa. Ever the moderator, Giancarlo Scrittori tried to engage him in conversation or bring him into general talk, but he shrugged the young man off.

Signor Verezzi and Signor Besan, who'd kept their heads bowed through much of the meal and their mouths working greedily – they were evidently used to the dramas of the house – were released by the Conte's absence and enough wine to get their own back on the English guest who'd been so talkative while they'd been silent.

'The Austrians sent a coach and four horses to the patriarch of Venice. To draw him along the water!' Signor Verezzi laughed out his words. Then he glared at Giancarlo Scrittori, who bowed his head over his glass. He too knew the habits of the company.

'They have given us new judges,' said Signor Besan, his jutting jaw becoming more pronounced. 'Contemptible.'

'It is as well to respect one's masters,' said Signor Verezzi in English.

Robert looked up, letting a scornful expression settle on his face before he lowered his gaze. He seemed about to speak, then perhaps feared he couldn't muster the language. The Italians were switching between their own and English, but it was not easy for foreign guests to intervene.

Ann spoke to prevent Robert. This way of acting had already infuriated him in London. 'There is at least peace,' she said.

The Contessa cleared her throat to take up the point but, before she could speak, Signor Verezzi went on, now addressing Ann and

Robert directly, 'We live by the Austrians but they are another race of people. Peace, pah.' Then more quietly, under his breath, he added, 'Better to give hatred and contempt as Signor Besan suggests. Better not to plan and act.'

The Contessa put her arm gently on his sleeve and smiled a gracious smile to the company.

'*Affenarsch*,' muttered Signor Verezzi, who, Ann saw, was much affected by the wine. He was not to be silenced. 'We are poodles of Vienna.'

'The French never tried to get into our minds. They just took the art and trinkets and went away. Napoleone brought a giant despotism – ' Signor Besan's speech made the Ss slur and he stopped, swallowed and concluded in a loud voice, 'We are now tethered by midgets.'

'Certainly, *certo*,' said Signor Verezzi. 'We must ask leave to piss in the canal.'

Giancarlo Scrittori kept his eyes on the table, seeming to investigate the weave of the damask cloth.

For the moment Signor Besan abandoned any effort to intervene. He nodded, catching the Contessa in his eye.

'Peace is important,' said the Contessa.

'The peace of death,' Signor Verezzi continued, throwing the words directly at Giancarlo Scrittori, who raised, then lowered his eyes again, studying now the handle of an ornate fork with its Venetian lion mark. It might have been an intricate jewelled dagger laid out for sketching. Beatrice, who'd been silent, sent an encouraging look towards him.

There were matters here Ann couldn't fathom. Secrets and tangled webs she failed to discern against the candlelight. The Contessa must know how things played between these three men. Why invite them to the same table? And why with her and Robert?

'Look at the state of our houses. We cannot afford to repair them.' Signor Verezzi waved his hand round the brilliantly candled table with its silver and glass glinting in the flames. 'The palazzi will fall into the canals and the canals will fill up. It will become a town for visitors to stare at. Mudbanks and seaweeds at the last. A wreck floating out to sea.'

'Venice is one big prison,' said Signor Besan, 'like all Italy. We are a manacled people and you English sit with our oppressors.'

Robert was still silent, so again Ann felt she had to answer, 'But not all of us, surely,' she said.

'All Europe is in despotism,' said Signor Besan, more slurred than ever. 'But there will be change. I say it. The bayonet in the hands of idiots does not rule for ever.'

The Contessa roused herself, this was not good public talk. She glanced at Giancarlo Scrittori, then back at Signor Besan. 'Signori, please, we talk no politics at the dinner table. It does not go with food.'

A silence followed.

Suddenly Robert spoke, looking only at his hostess. 'You are right, Contessa. There is no purpose in this for we are all slaves.'

Ann was as surprised as Signori Verezzi and Besan. She hoped he would not go on.

'Venice was not conquered in a thousand years,' said the Contessa with finality.

'But she has made up for it in the last decades, Austrians, pah!' said Signor Verezzi.

'They do not even attend the opera,' said Signora Zen suddenly. 'It was half-full last night.'

As they left much later in the Savelli gondola through a cold clear night, after what seemed to Ann hours of men drinking and women pursuing their desperate small talk, Beatrice remarked, 'We will have our lesson tomorrow, Signora. It may be that at last we will get to Lord Byron's tales.'

There, after an evening of avoiding it, was the Name. Living with Caroline should have taught Ann never to feel secure.

'So that is what you do to earn the green jacket. Read that rubbish to a young girl.' Robert was undressing in the chilly bedchamber, flinging down his clothes as if they'd offended him.

'That's unfair. She wanted to read him. We aren't there yet. We read Mrs Radcliffe and talk.'

'That's the height of your teaching?'

'They pay well.'

'And we live off this activity through the patronage of that coxcomb Scrittori? We are eating, you would say? Well remember, Madam, that we have eaten my substance for a good long time.'

'I am not saying that. I know.'

What she wanted to say, to shout rather, was that the jacket – and when had he seen it for she'd not worn it this evening? – was *turquois*-coloured, close to blue perhaps but not green.

The spiral began. They were both almost too tired for it.

16

After the brilliance of late winter it had become grey, with flurries of snow that stung the face. Ann walked the *calli* and *rive* muffled in wet wool. It was clammy against her skin. Her skirts had grown heavy with the water she could never quite avoid in this saturated town.

Then the weather changed again. Snowflakes glittered and disappeared. Humidity evaporated over the water. Everything was on the move. Seagulls swooped down near the quays or were tossed about in energetic air waves if they tried to rise higher. Or they bobbed on the churning canal as sudden winds spurted over the lagoon. When they were stilled for a few minutes, long-billed sleeker birds arrived to skim and dive in the shimmering water.

Sometimes the sky was blue, sometimes azure, sometimes almost bleak, livid, while the lagoons held extremes of dark green, creamy indigo and a thick leaden. The waters were shallow and yet at such moments they seemed to hold great depth: their coloured layers leading to an unfathomable darkness, even to a fancied fanciful nothing.

One unstable, almost spring day Ann stood on the wasteland behind the vegetable patches and boatyards on La Giudecca looking over choppy water under the fluid sky. It must, she mused, be filled with the rubbish of centuries, drowned sailors, collapsed huts, sunk boats, the luxury that Venetians so loved to paint and flaunt.

The wind dropped and the water grew smooth. The sky lightened. Her spirits lifted just a little with the brighter weather. Near her feet she saw nervous fish to-ing and fro-ing in the clearer water.

Out in the southern lagoon a boat with a faded orange awning seemed stranded on the sands beneath the water. It twisted a little whenever any craft nearby, or even distant, made a swell that reached it, however faintly. There was no fishing from it; indeed, as far as she could discern, it held no person at all unless the dark patch at the end was an unmoving head. A boat carrying a corpse all alone? San Cristoforo was far away in the northern lagoon and it was not heading for the burial grounds on the Lido; there was no ritual of death that such a little boat could form.

As she watched it turned slightly. The morning was now growing misty, the sun coming through a veil and making the sky the sort of light blue that cloaked the Virgin in faded Renaissance paintings. With the higher tide would the boat float quietly into the mist beyond Chioggia, out to the Adriatic and on till it rotted and fell with its dead body eaten by gulls into the sea, the bones filtering down? Or would it be beached on the sands of the Lido or Pellestrina, leaving a corpse to disintegrate on the stones of the new sea wall fronting the Adriatic?

It would rot and stink on the blocks until discovered by a *cavaliere*. He would hold his elegant nose and turn round his horse, then in time nonchalantly alert the authorities to a broken boat and a rotting body near the dunes. Leaving before his name could be asked, for no one in this secretive town wished to be questioned about anything by anyone in authority.

She reined herself in. Was she moving into her own plot? Would she imagine herself the corpse in the boat? More likely the shape was a pot to hold clams taken from nearby nets.

Perhaps these morbid fancies made the ordinary more bearable. She shook her head at the notion. Instead she thought something more disheartening: that the dead boat, the smelly corpse, the murder, the fever, the plague event, whatever might have caused the death, if death there'd been, the abandoned and broken heart, the dunes or the deep sea — nothing was so bad as what waited for her.

She was being dramatic, but drama, like morbid imagining, was comforting.

She walked quickly from the side of the south lagoon over the waste ground to the *fondamenta* by the large canal. It was not far. La Giudecca was a mere strip of islands.

She was rowed across the canal with washerwomen towards the Gesuati planks. On the water, even for this short and now habitual crossing, it was hard for a person once as landlocked as she had been not to feel a little exhilarated.

She was at the Palazzo Savelli at the appointed hour. The be-wigged footman let her in. He smiled in greeting. She knew now that his handsome face was ruined by the absence of front teeth. Did the Contessa not care for the dentist's skill when it came to her servants? Or were the toothless ones kept as foil to Beatrice and her pearly teeth?

The girl and she had become friends, as far as one could across years, place, background, culture and language. They'd started to read those *Oriental Tales* of Byron that Beatrice had yearned for; she was gripped by the story of a man part dashing pirate, part incon-solable lover. Ann had no more respect for the sensational stuff than Robert but enjoyed a good plot. It reminded her of her own work. More about men – but change the sex and style of the author and where was the difference, she a hack writer of cheap gothic, he a cele-brated poet – and a lord?

'No,' said Beatrice to her enquiry. 'There is no more interest in Milord Byron here now, as a man I mean, not much since he became *cicisbeo* to La Guiccioli and followed her to Ravenna like a pet spaniel. The talk of the English – and I think you do not mingle with them?' She moved her pretty head in enquiry. 'No? Well I tell you, the talk is again of the *principessa*, the Princess Caroline. You know your people are here making discoveries these past years. The Prince – he is King now, yes? – he tries for divorce.'

Beatrice took in a sudden breath and glanced quizzically. 'You look so uninterested, Signora, but I will try to amuse you by telling you all about it. It will be such a good practice for my English.'

Caroline had gossiped with Mrs Graves and Mrs Pugh in Putney, agitating their monotonous days with scandals kindly provided by their silly but entertaining rulers. Ann hated these half-forgotten memories. She was still a child in that.

'The talk is of the servant again,' Beatrice continued undeterred by Ann's withdrawn expression, 'a servant who has long time been more than that, Bartolomeo Pergami. Italians like to be included and he is an Italian from nowhere and from no very good family, so it is more not proper.' She stopped and looked directly at Ann. 'Perhaps, Signora, you do not care for gossip at all?'

'"Involved",' she said, 'not "included". Everyone likes some gossip, Beatrice, when not malicious.'

'Is there such a thing, Signora? No matter, I will tell you what is much said.' She moved her chair a little closer.

'The Princess was at the Grand Britannia, the hotel, you have seen it? She was staying there since a long time. She made the impression.'

'Yes, I did hear that,' said Ann, feigning now more interest than she felt. When they first arrived Robert called the scandal a foolish story concocted by Italian informers about a German whore and her English whore-master.

'But then,' Beatrice was saying, 'then, Signora, she left the Grand Britannia and went to live in a private palazzo. So near here it is impossible not to know, and news travels up and down the Canal Grande like I cannot say what, a waterfall that goes both ways.'

She smiled at her invention. Beatrice was growing up, thought Ann. She would soon overtake the gentle Giancarlo, who, she rather suspected, had some interest in his pretty cousin. If cousin she was, for it seemed a rather inclusive concept in Italy.

'Her bedroom – and this we have from Signora Valauri, who lives very close – it comes off the big *salotto*. One side there is a door to other rooms. Here Signora Valauri closed one eye – blink, I think, no? – and moved her shoulders thus. She would say no more, but asked who was in the rooms. Then Mama, who was present and usually not so interested to hear gossip, at least not when I am beside her, mentioned the Princess's other gentlemen, so she must know more. Signora Castelli joined her and asked too – she is a little vulgar, I think, though she comes from a most noble family – "Where did all those gentlemen who were said to service Her Royal Highness sleep? Where was Hieronimus, where was the boy William Austin, Captain Hownam?"'

'My, my, Beatrice, you have an amazing memory for names, even strange English ones. You have everything pat.'

'Pat? Is he another lover?'

Ann was surprised that this – and there was much more – amused the Contessa, who, from the little she'd seen of her, appeared an austere, intentionally stately lady.

Beatrice surmised her thoughts. 'Mama does not leave the house often because of the Conte. She and her friends do not always have gossip but some talk like this makes the *tarocco* table less dull. In the old days when Papa was alive and before everything changed, we had a chaplain in our house and Mama talked much to him of Francesco when he was a boy and already a little strange, but he is long gone from us.'

After pausing, she added sadly, 'Mama prays much but it has made so little difference. Signor Verezzi tells her so.'

Ten days later Ann was by the booths on the Rialto trying to buy some cheap material to be made up as a nightshirt for Robert. She had no skill to mend the superior, now worn-out, garments he'd brought from London. There she was accosted by Giancarlo Scrittori.

'Oh, Signora Jamis, why do you not come to my cousin Tommaso's shop? You disappoint me.'

'His stuff is too good for what I am after today,' she smiled.

'No, no, he will give you a nice price. And, see, you are now wearing the *turchese*-coloured jacket that is so becoming to you.'

'No, really, I am content for now to look in these cheap stalls.'

'Let me buy you a coffee and a cake. I hear such good things from my young cousin Signorina Beatrice that I would like to do something for you. We – you and I – had meant to meet I think some time to see more sights and I to practise my English. But you are busy?'

'Well, I often am, but not now. I will come with pleasure.'

They stood at the edge of the *trattoria*'s marble counter and drank the strong grainy coffee that seemed air and sustenance to Venetians.

She noticed Giancarlo Scrittori was holding an English newspaper, *Street's Courier*, limp and much handled. How had he come by it? Was Giancarlo connected with that English society Robert was so keen never to know?

He saw her looking at it and moved his hand to wave the first sheet. 'You are watching my paper, I think, and wondering how I am with it.' He grinned. 'There is no mystery. It was passed to me by Giacomo, my friend, who had it from the Santangelis, one of whom is an agent for Sir Edward Colefield, who had it perhaps from his client or Sir Alexander Trotter. He is here often and brings newspapers, mainly *Gazettes*, when he travels. It is not old and is full of what you English so like, the royal investigations. You may have it.'

She thanked him but made no move to take it.

'You do not smile as much as you did when we first encountered each other. Signora Jamis, I think perhaps the work does not suit you.'

'Oh, it does,' she cried at once. 'I love my lessons with Beatrice.'

'As I told you before, I could get you more pupils. The Savelli are a very good recommendation to anyone.'

'Maybe soon but please not just yet.'

'Perhaps our Venetian climate is not good for you. It is colder than you English want it to be. But soon it will be hot, very hot, perhaps then too hot.'

She was hardly listening now. Wondering instead about links and families and kinship and webs, about gossip and news and subtle networks of secrets.

Giancarlo Scrittori fell silent too, mistaking her abstractedness for unease at the sight of his English paper. He was used to being looked at askance: he was thought to befriend the Austrians and in truth the paper had come through them. He was relaxed in his stance. It had its uses, especially with his noble cousins and their loose-talking relations. But a price had been his fierce quarrel with a good friend, Luigi Orlando. Orlando had flounced off into exile.

To Giancarlo it seemed the Austrians had introduced much order into a town that needed it. Filled in the most stinking canals, put railings round some treacherous steps. He approved. He didn't care to get his boots wet or risk stumbling into fetid water when a little in liquor. If they paid him something for his support, that helped too, for buying and selling was hard work across nations.

He would make the Englishwoman easy again. She was so often alone, never with that vain husband who'd ignored him at the Savelli dinner while showing off to other guests, even to the ridiculous Signor Besan. He'd no wish to meet him again and he took some trouble not to do so; the town was small and everyone met almost everyone somewhere when it was left to chance.

If he ever did and was provoked beyond proper endurance, he'd be forced to tell him in smooth unruffled Italian how absurd his *Attila* was: to make a man of unbridled fury into one of intellect and genius. It was to obfuscate reality, perplex only the simple-minded. Despite their conquering habits, the English *were* simple-minded.

'Let me show you a new place, behind the Frari.'

'Thank you but no, not now.'

He was not put off. 'I remember you liked the gold staircase of San Rocco so much. If not today, then another, we will go there again. Perhaps you may bring your husband.'

'Perhaps,' she said. 'But Robert is not so pleased with Venice now as I am.'

Giancarlo Scrittori knew to be silent. He inclined his head and took his leave. Before he did so he thrust the English newspaper into her hand.

She was not sure why such a relic of England discomfited her like this, even beyond the mention of a Caroline. None the less she read it on the *traghetto* on her way back to La Giudecca, the rising and dipping of the boatmen's oars making her eyes flicker over the paragraphs.

The stern Duke of Wellington, who'd vanquished Napoleon for decent English values so short a time ago, must have shuddered at this inelegant and lewd display by his unappetising royal masters. It was amusing all of Europe.

In the ups and downs of the water passage she learned of Significant Things. The Princess, it seemed, had travelled by night, bumping her short fat body for eight hours at a time. Then she'd rested in the heat of the day – on a Turkish *sofa* in a tent. All England and half the Continent lolled on this sofa.

A serious query: did it have bedclothes on it? Did she remove her skirts and shift to lie there? If she did undress, was she under a blanket? On or under?

Ann's eyes flickered over the rest of the news-sheet. A few current events, some naval skirmishes off Cyprus but almost all just naughty secrets revealed, the insalubrious spectacle of a great country delving into the intimate life of a woman no worse than her persecutor.

By the time she arrived on La Giudecca she was less disgusted. With such disarming details of sofas and blankets and undergarments, the account made her countrymen rather lovable, comic even. Most of the testimony came from Italians, and the gullible English lapped it up like innocent puppy dogs.

Caroline. The name had lodged in her brain. The Princess was an entertaining fantasy as much as Byron's Giaour or Corsair. Her Caroline was not so different now, her coloured shawls and turbans registering in her daughter's mind like the royal sofa. Had she been married like the unfortunate Princess? For sure there'd been a coupling and a child born. Legitimate or a child of passion? A child of passion from Caroline? A likely tale!

Anyway, a child of old age. Too old, too old for the cooing and dangling young girls do with babies. She'd been bored by an infant. She said so. Had she wanted a son or perhaps a beautiful daughter to admire her? Or no child at all? The whole thing a horrid accident.

All this oppressing memory from the consonance of names. What had Caroline to do with the Princess? And what had Robert to do with Caroline and father Gilbert that they so often now reared up where his presence was everything?

Entering ungreeted into the apartment, she saw herself as a bat in the morning air with no sense of the night's resting place. She sat on the bed and let all her mental monsters cruise about her head.

In a town so attuned to the coming of the plague, the pest in all its forms, the cholera, the putrid typhus, the great and small pox and all manner of water-borne diseases, there was always awareness of bodies. No wonder Venice was known for its gorgeous fabrics. Mostly only the face – though this, too, was so often masked – discovered the otherwise hidden distemper.

Robert had become familiar with Italians on the island and across the canal, even with some foreigners. He was not particular. People greeted him in the *calli* and the *campi* more than they did Ann. Did his face tell them there was something wrong? He didn't look conventionally fevered, yet he had a feverish quality. Perhaps liking his affability, they failed to notice his increasing nerviness. Probably – if they thought at all about a stranger – they judged it typical of the English.

She too had changed. She'd become almost gaunt, with some strands of grey in her chestnut-coloured hair, though she was still far from forty. It didn't matter. She had no audience.

One day beyond the Rialto by the newly opened Jewish ghetto, where she'd gone to buy some cheap Marseilles soap, she spied him at a distance. He was standing smoking, leaning on a parapet wall and gazing along a small canal. What could he be doing by the ghetto? Even from where she was she could see that his body was twitching nervously. Though his frame was ample, there was now little flesh on it except where the belly swelled forward unhealthily. He was not what he had been in London, that sturdy being so present in himself.

Then some weeks later she'd been sitting alone at a table in a small *campo* north of San Marco in deep shade, her back against a cracked stuccoed wall. On the opposite sunny side, Robert was with a group of men. He had a sty in his eye which irritated him in the apartment but here simply rendered him purblind. By the look of their clothes the men with him were local labourers; Robert was throwing at them words in Italian they couldn't understand while making wide gestures. One man outlined the shape of a voluptuous woman with his hands and moved his thighs. They all laughed.

What was it that made others come to Robert? She had not a tenth of such power; had she been turned into a man she would still not have had it. What gave some people influence to pull others towards them – even if they burnt them when close – while others, all well-meaning and eager, stood solitary?

Another unkempt man joined them, greeting Robert in English. An artist, for he held a large easel from which dangled the torso of a skeleton. His voice carried across the *campo*. Robert spoke in a lower tone but she could still hear something of his words; her mind filled in gaps.

'I am sick of the town and its cursed women,' said the artist.

'Women are a curse,' agreed Robert. 'They cling like limpets out of malice.'

'Bitches on heat,' said the artist. 'I married a whore, fucked her too often and got two brats. Along with a whole family of maggoty sisters and aunts.' He rattled the bones. 'Look at this skeleton. It's a woman, the bit you need. I can put this cunt wherever I want. That's how it should be.'

He produced a bottle of liquor from his deep pocket. The owner of the table couldn't have approved but perhaps he'd already made enough on his wine to allow indifference – or wanted no trouble from drunken strangers.

'I was trepanned into coming here, lugged over the Alps. For what? I've been so cursedly stupid.'

Where had this hatred come from? She'd loved him in part because he treated her as an equal, was immune to difference, finding (she'd thought) no sex in souls and minds.

Like her father in philosophical rather than romantic mode – according to Caroline – like utopian William Bates, like thin needy Gregory Lloyd, so many men. Did any of them truly deliver? Here before her this easy misogyny was trotting out as man's second nature.

Then she heard the name Bianca, *cara Bianca*, and a guttural laugh from the artist. She was sure, no, not sure exactly.

Another woman? It couldn't be.

But of course it could. Robert was often away much of the day and into the night. What did he do? Just because she'd seen his slow decay, the waning of capacity for pleasure with her, didn't mean others who'd not known him in the past couldn't be attracted. She of all people understood how he might appeal.

A vile and muddled jealousy seized her, so that she almost got up and broke cover. But she stayed still. For if she were seen now that they were half-drunk – the labourers had just left the two foreigners at the table – there would surely be a public brawl of words. More?

How could he keep such low company? She'd never heard him speak so coarsely in England, not even within his circle of drinking men. Had these ruffians replaced the scholars and writers of London, Richard Perry, John Humphries, bluff Frederick Curran, all of them clever men? Had brilliant John Taylor given way to this rattler of bones?

Cara Bianca? Maybe she'd heard something else altogether. She let the name dance round her head as she kept herself in the shade until they were gone. She was sodden with self-pity.

By the time she reached the apartment on La Giudecca she'd resolved to eradicate the name, making it an ear's error. Perhaps he'd said *carabinier* and her demented mind had translated it into what she feared.

Why fear? How could this be something to unsettle her? The relief she'd once felt at no more strained and irritable attempts in bed had dissipated long ago; but there was a difference between knowing Robert worn dry for her, and being replaced.

In the apartment he made no mention of an artist with a skeleton's torso. Indeed he hardly mentioned anything of his life outside. They rarely talked. Yet one day he'd spoken of a Signor Balbi, a distinguished man, a traveller – a cultured, patriotic Venetian, friend apparently of Signor Verezzi. She couldn't place the name at once. Then remembered. The Savelli dinner.

Cultured and patriotic? In the past he'd never have coupled these words. Was it meant as a reproach to her and her friend Giancarlo Scrittori?

This Signor Balbi had taken him to see the painting of a hornless rhinoceros brought from India by a Dutch captain to exhibit in cities through Europe. In the picture a young man held high the creature's horn, its animalhood, the aphrodisiac, while the poor mutilated beast munched glumly on dry straw. The painting had upset Robert but he'd contained himself with Signor Balbi. Look at yourselves, he'd wanted the rhinoceros to shout, this noble plated animal, so different from all others. Made into a raree show by dullards! Such is the fate of the extraordinary in the ordinary world.

To her, though she never saw the painting, it held a different message. The creature was called Clara. She was exhibited unmasked, unclothed, while the men who watched and exploited her were hidden behind a panoply of power and arrogance.

Apart from Signor Balbi, she knew well how Robert's standards for company had fallen. The Italian labourers, even a dilapidated artist, might be explained, but not the English visitors, the kind of insufferable boobies he'd caricatured in the old days, mercilessly reducing them to their banalities.

Was this haphazard socialising a sign of sickness in the head, something deeper than the affliction in London that sent them scurrying across the Continent to run up more debts? Had he in despair given up distinguishing? Was that what Bianca – if she existed – meant?

She couldn't judge: she had such slender experience of him in a commonplace world.

Unusually, they were walking together when they met the Bigg-Staithes. The man was a jowly English squire from Hampshire with a florid face: he seemed always about to deliver a joke he couldn't remember. His pretty diminutive wife assumed she and Robert an ordinary couple. She tried to talk to Ann.

Venetian fashions so strange. The masquerade costume she'd worn at carnival with a pink sequinned mask, imagine! Moving her little hands in coquettish gestures and scratching the air with puce gloved fingers, she explained rounded sleeves and gathered bodices. Then she registered Ann's dowdy clothes, felt her apathy, and abandoned the talk with a little giggle.

She was charmed by Robert. He was all movement and all for her.

To these nondescript tourists, he made remarks on England's sorry state as if they were thinking beings. Ann was embarrassed for him. One side or other must in the end be disabused.

The theatre was proposed. Robert spluttered. The London theatre dealt in vapid stuff, performed by crude actors answering money-grubbing managers. He was hasty and dogmatical, not brilliant at all. What had happened to him?

Bigg-Staithe was impressed and determined to remember the opinion. 'But here,' he said, 'here the very town is theatrical.' He'd been told this many times by his expensive guide Altonello. Surely the theatre in Venice could not so heartily offend a man of such taste as Mr James.

'We do need amusement,' said his wife, stroking Robert with her eyes. Lightly she placed her gloved, beringed little fingers on his arm, then put both hands together in front of her face in a pretty gesture of prayer.

'Yes,' agreed her husband eagerly. 'We will go to the Teatro San Luca. Our guide told us we must go there.'

Why did Ann not leave then and go home? Women could always summon a headache. Was there jealousy, some impulse of fear she might lose Robert to this frivolous doll? Surely not. Losing would be release. In any case no one else would take him on – or would they? She reddened, recollecting 'Bianca'.

It was an *opera seria* for the benefit of a prima donna they'd never heard of. Altonello, paid handsomely for his advice from both clients and theatres, declared she was the rage in Venice and Vienna and was kept in magnificence by a rich and concupiscent signore from Milan. She was singing part of Rossini's *Otello* with its happy ending. Robert snorted. Othello, another great man whom Venice destroyed.

The diva sang in a silvery voice that travelled out into the night and rolled over the waters before returning to the ear. Despite her dislike of the story, Ann was enchanted. Robert expressed ennui by smoking and squirming. All technique, artifice, nothing, no heart, no art.

'She sang very well,' said Ann as Mrs Bigg-Staithe tittered and fluttered her fan of black sequins and white feathers.

'A child with a good voice. Nothing more. You do not go to the place where she sings. You are on earth all the time.'

'Perhaps you are not a devotee of music, Mr James,' ventured Mr Bigg-Staithe, eager to know what Robert thought of everything, to learn what he himself should think. Opera was a painful penance: he would like licence to say so.

Robert shrugged. 'I love music, Mr Bigg-Staithe. It's the highest art; it comes straight from the mind. I once journeyed many miles to hear Beethoven, the Napoleon of notes.'

Mr Bigg-Staithe looked surprised – it was odd to invoke the little Frenchman in such a manner.

Ann said, 'Venice doesn't suit Beethoven's music. Here they like the *buffo* as if they know they can't scale the height. But they do that very well.'

Robert looked at her with an expression Mrs Bigg-Staithe never saw. 'Oh yes,' he said, 'they must make a joke of what they can't achieve.'

Was he speaking of himself, he looked so despairing? He made no jokes now.

Where were the images that buoyed him up, his creations? In the past he'd said that it was not images, not even words alone, that mattered in themselves, but the emotion that allowed them to surge forward in the right order. If that emotion were disturbed, then all was disturbed. If there were no transformation through words, what then? What if now for the first time he felt his life invaded by his body? If he did, he would reject the idea. He would never be vulnerable.

As they separated they turned into couples by force of habit. In the light from braziers by the water, Ann saw the Bigg-Staithes in their fine warm clothes arm-in-arm, a gorgeous vibrant double beast in the chill spring air. She and Robert stood apart, quite different animals.

'Venice is suffocating,' he said suddenly when they were both awake and exhausted in the night, he because he woke himself from deep sleep too often and she because she couldn't sleep when he did; the spurts and groaning of his breathing had become worse these last weeks.

Though it was cold she had to get up. She sat on the edge of the bed, a thick old shawl round her shoulders.

Robert grunted and rolled over on his side. 'Genius is destroyed by littleness.' He swung his legs on to the floor, throwing aside the heavy coverlet. He sat up unsteadily. 'Littleness, Madam,' he shouted.

Despite Giancarlo Scrittori's best efforts, it was not easy always to avoid unwelcome encounters, unless one kept to the vegetable patches of La Giudecca or the high-sided *campi* of the ghetto. So now, near the Accademia gallery where a barge sold dried and stored fruit from the Veneto and a *traghetto* waited to ferry people across the Grand Canal, Ann, Robert James, the Bigg-Staithes with their guide Altonello and Giancarlo Scrittori all met by unhappy chance.

There were introductions but the Bigg-Staithes showed little interest in an Italian neither rich nor patrician; Giancarlo Scrittori was polite, Robert sour.

Mr Bigg-Staithe took his lead from his new friend. He grumbled about the difficulty of being paddled everywhere and the ugliness of so much of the decrepit town.

They had been to the Gesuati church, directed there by their guide. He'd proposed they should see this fairly new, sumptuous building mainly because he intended afterwards to lead them to his friend's *taverna* on the Grand Canal.

The Bigg-Staithes were dismayed; no picturesque nuns or monks tramped the aisles. The order had been suppressed and the place turned into a parish church, the monastery a boys' home. Mr Bigg-Staithe left some coins – Altonello made sure of this – and hastened out, his wife on his arm.

'So disappointing,' he remarked.

'A copy of Redentore,' said Robert, 'and that's a barren treat. The church is nothing here. If the French had stayed, there might've been some compensation for the loss.'

'But the Tiepolo on the ceiling,' said Giancarlo Scrittori, 'is – '

Mr Bigg-Staithe interrupted, 'Venice is nothing,' he said and looked for encouragement from Robert. 'Well, nothing since the Austrians.'

Ann glanced at her friend. He was silent but gave a little bow.

When the party began to move on, she remained behind with Giancarlo Scrittori, ostensibly to discuss something about their common friends in Palazzo Savelli. Altonello pricked up his ears at the name but it was too late and the group dissolved.

For the first time she saw her friend openly disturbed. The mildness usually in his eyes was gone.

'It is so easy, so facile, to say these things. Why are they, so many people from your country and others, here? Why? How do we have so much opera, whether they enjoy or not, so much art, and yes such comfort and prosperity, for we are not so poor before or after the Austrians? Is it only something good to be making wars and killing people for cities you don't need – is that what being something in the world is? If we do not patrol land and seas and order people to pay to pass, are we less for it?'

Before she could reply soothingly, he'd regained his affability. 'After all,' he said, 'the Austrians returned the bronze horses, a little battered but that was not their fault.'

She glanced at him quizzically.

'I know I have told you this already but it is a fact that always brings me back to myself.'

They walked a little in silence back towards San Trovaso. Then Ann spoke, 'My husband,' she paused, it was never easy to use the term, 'meant I am sure no disrespect to Venice. He really knows little of its politics. He is so used to denigrating rulers and authority of any sort. It is his own country he despises. I cannot answer for the others.'

Giancarlo Scrittori smiled urbanely. 'Then he should not meddle.'

Ann supposed the word misused; perhaps he meant 'judge'.

'Yes, a man may laugh at his own. England is perhaps not now so easy to mock, though. It is rich and triumphant.'

'I don't think everyone in England feels triumphant or rich. You will have heard of soldiers killing starving people at St Peter's Field last year.' She paused. 'And, after all, he is not English.'

Giancarlo looked puzzled, but did not enquire. He'd not quite taken mental leave of the vexed subject. He remembered the dinner at Palazzo Savelli and remarks young Beatrice had later made to him of this irksome man disturbing her brother with what neither understood.

'He is wrong about Venetians being dominated by the church till liberated by the French. Always we were independent of popes, even when we made them. Mohammedans, Jews, Armenians, Orthodox, Protestants, all have worshipped here without hinder. No heretic was burnt. Can you say this for your country?'

'I say nothing. You have no need to argue with me.'

'I am so sorry, Signora, but I become defending.'

'But not angry?'

'No, never angry with a lady.'

Yet she too wanted to protest. She hoped she could rely on her friend's restored amiability. 'For women it was not so good a place. Convents where you locked away your nubile girls to save a family fortune.'

Such relief to argue without fearing an explosion! She hoped she'd not gone too far.

'Ah, Signora, you have some right there but not all.' He looked intently at her. 'An unhappy marriage can simply be annulled. Your sad Caroline and cruel George would not have their trouble here. That is why you entertain us with your divorce.'

Again she was seeing another side of Giancarlo. He'd seemed so simple, so refreshingly superficial. She sighed: did she never understand anyone?

'I will leave you here,' he said. 'I live back near San Barnaba.' She gave him an enquiring look. 'You have perhaps heard? No? Well, no matter. I have no wife or family with me. And many men like me live in San Barnaba. But I am not what they used to call one of the *barnabotti*, the poor noblemen unmarried and too poor to take much interest in affairs of state. I, as you see, earn my living. I am not of the favoured families like my cousins. I am no indiscriminate supporter of my city, indeed there is much wrong with it. But I do not like it traduced in ignorance.'

'That is the very point. That is why you need take no offence. It is done in ignorance.'

'What I say is that, yes, we were in decline in the political world but we were moving with the times, we did not accept the old ways as we used to, there was much hot argument here. We were ready in mind if not in bodies for the French.'

'And the Austrians?'

He gave her another serious look. 'As I say, they are here and they bring order. You have heard of the secret Carbonari? No, well, they try to make much trouble. Only the powerless will be hurt if they do. I think your husband knows.'

He broke into a smile, relaxing as if the anxious thoughts had simply swum away on an outgoing breath.

Ann smiled too. She knew that, whatever the Carbonari might be – something like the Masons she supposed – there was no *cara Bianca*.

When they parted, she'd no desire to return to La Giudecca. She had things to buy at the Rialto and towards the opera house of La Fenice. She was unknown there and would not be pressed to pay her bills.

As she walked beside the great mass of the Frari church, an impulse, an urge for more delay, took her in. Giancarlo Scrittori had carried her to see Titian's *Assumption* in the Accademia di Belle Arti where it was placed in a poor light: a fitting response to its smoke-damaged and dirty surface. Its move there from the Frari had been on the orders of Napoleon, who intended later to transport it to Paris with his other spoils. Unlike the bronze horses it had not left the city. But nor had it returned to its home. As she sat looking towards where the great altarpiece should have been she let her eyes unfocus while she thought of the absent picture's fiery soul: such longing expressed in the watchers of the miracle.

Robert had said – only once, for it contradicted everything else he professed – there was disproportion, a chasm between what we desire, what we must express, and the world we see and what we can express. Into that chasm we will fall and be swallowed up. No one can step over it.

18

Robert was ebullient and rather drunk. He held a bottle under one arm.

'Signor Balbi met a man who's intimate with that poseur Byron. He says no word of him except that he is fat.' Robert laughed. 'Fat, fat. Oh wonders! So vulgar a lord, so lordly a vulgarian.'

She laughed.

'Like his cobbler's verse.'

Robert let out a loud *Ave Maria* in the fine baritone voice Ann had not heard since long before they left England. 'Signor Balbi is the better man. He travels. And not to ravish every female he finds.'

He rooted in the big canvas bag he now carried everywhere. It gave him the look of a haggard painter or ill-fed artisan, the tools of his craft over his shoulder. 'Tonight I'm going to show that slovenly wench downstairs how to cook. I've been to the Rialto and bought us two quails and a chocolate bon-bon for little Rosa.'

With what? she wondered. God in heaven, with what?

Before the quails, he'd persuaded Signora Scorzeri to cook her speciality, a pasta with a sauce of onions, pine nuts, anchovies and raisins, all in wine. It was cheap and tasty. Robert had seen its potential, and demanded of course more wine, more anchovies, more of everything piquant within it. He never stinted. How had he made her do all this when they must owe so much? Had he given her something substantial at last? If so, where did the money come from? His initial funds must have been exhausted long since. Or was it his admiring of little Rosa? Or just his 'charm'?

'Light candles,' he said in excitement, though it was not dark. 'Lots of candles.' He was like a terrier, all his body, his paunch and hairy chest and bald head wriggling with excitement. Had he a tail, it would have wagged. The thinness showed, the flesh nowhere taut.

It all tasted good, all excellent, the pasta neither too dry nor too wet, the meat firm, sauce just spicy enough. As he had insisted.

He fussed over everything, making sure she had the right amount of liquid with the quail, that the vegetables were firm enough, that there was wine in better glasses than usual. He must have talked the *padrona* into lending them these special vessels for the evening.

The meal had taken so long to prepare and to adjust to his liking that it was late when they finished. Ann was tired. Robert went on drinking. She couldn't and wouldn't keep up. She wished – and not for the first time – that Richard Perry or big Frederick Curran, even John Taylor or John Humphries, were by to keep him company and take from her the weight she'd once so desired to shoulder alone. He needed men around him.

'My lesson is quite early tomorrow; Beatrice has a fitting for a new gown, so I will have to go to bed soon,' she ventured.

She saw him deflate.

'Ah, your work,' he sighed. 'Woman's work.'

'Well, it's not really my work as you know. I've not done much of that,' she began.

'No,' he interrupted, 'you cannot write here, is that it?' He flung out an arm with the glass a quarter full at a precarious angle. It was hard to keep her eyes off it. 'And I, do I have work?'

'Of course you do.'

'My writing is different from yours? You cannot do yours but I should do mine?' The hand came back and he emptied the glass.

'I didn't mean that. I don't set any store by it, you know I don't.'

'But it happens whether or not you set store, doesn't it,' he said with that ominous mildness she knew so well.

'It happens with you, Robert, sometimes, and that is what matters.'

'Does it?' he said bitterly. 'Does it?'

She was touching him, he thought, intentionally provoking him, playing him.

She felt the quick fear and, to her shame, the dreadful elation.

His anger was mounting as speedily as his good humour subsided. As always, she felt terrified yet privileged to be involved in this supreme rage as it rose.

Looking from outside even as she cowed before the coming storm, she wondered if she believed in this idea of special talent or genius, and of genius justifying everything. Were they all caught in a bogus faith which demanded other people's suffering?

'This stinking sewer,' Robert exclaimed, pushing away his chair, 'I have to get out. Out! Always with you it is not enough. I get you wonderful food and you, you . . .'

'I said only that I had to work.'

'Work, work.' He turned round to her. She backed away into the darker corner. 'You set up for insipidity, mediocrity and then whine. It's pathetic. Look at you wincing. You do that cowering so well. I am assaulted by your fear.'

She pulled herself together and came forward. She could have retreated. She knew that. 'You wanted to come to Venice. You said you couldn't write in England, it stifled you. Its hypocrisy and complacency.'

'Don't parrot my words.'

'I'm not, I agreed with you. But remember we could have gone to France or Ireland, anywhere, if this place wasn't right.'

'You know I have no wish to see Ireland again.'

'Even County Cork?'

'No, not ever.'

Yet she felt him relax just a little at the name. She remarked gently, 'I can hear that touch of Irish in your voice even now.'

He still looked cross but the face was settling. She had used this trick before. Would he resent it this time?

'I speak as I speak,' he said, 'I am from nowhere now, I speak all the places I have been and none.'

'Well, there are traces.'

She had moved back towards the table and the spindly cold bones of the meal. She forced a smile.

'Perhaps,' he said, tired. Then he brightened. She was putting together the plates in a homely, self-aware, feminine way. Did he like that?

'I do sometimes think of it, especially in this bog of a place. The soft sweeping fields, waves breaking not limping on the shore like here, and – ' he looked at the debris of the good meal, 'potatoes.'

She went on stacking and tidying the plates to take them downstairs in the morning. It was too late now. So the room would smell of food through the night.

'Let's go to bed,' she said. His anger was gone but so was his exhilaration.

Yet, before they started to undress, as he stood by the window and she by the table, before she could at all prepare herself, something happened, an impulse and surge of emotion darting through the room. She must protest.

'Don't try to muzzle me.'

There it was, the *so* favoured word. As he snapped, he revealed his yellowing teeth and a little froth emerged at the edge of his mouth. How could he so repeat himself?

She went over to him and held on to him, trying to catch his eyes.

'Let me go,' he said. 'I hate those dumb pleading spaniel eyes of yours. I've seen them before. Are you a dog?'

She held on tightly. 'Let go,' he said again.

She would not.

Then he pulled back his left arm and punched her hard in the face. She let go then.

Her eyeball sank in her head. She fell back – to the ground, only a little involuntarily. She lay still.

Then he kicked her hard in the ribs twice and went out, slamming the door. 'You damned woman,' he shouted.

It was the third – or was it the fourth? – time this had happened. No, it was the fifth. She had been over the events so often that times had merged.

After an interval she asked herself why she was lying there on the floor. A rib might be cracked, but might not, and she would have to get up at some point. Why not now? Tears welled up of course. Ugly tears.

Why had she not been prepared for violence? The community in Fen Ditton had thought every day of death so that they'd be ready when it came. Why didn't women think every day of what they would suffer just as surely? William Bates would have been better telling her to meditate on this rather than praying for her. And she — why had his training not taught her to be more scrupulous in examining herself? How had she become so mesmerised by abjection? Was it to be as far away as possible from Caroline with her easy, selfish life? Was it to refuse that one final warning: that men could do more than you ever imagined?

As for Robert, he was still raging as he stamped on the last step on his way downstairs and out. Provocation was just as brutal in effect as anything an arm or leg could do. He almost wished he'd kicked her to death, or at least kicked much harder and in that face to silence it. What right had this woman, any woman, to invade him, to think she could control him, hold, cling to him? He had given up a lot for her. It was always a mistake. It was not the first time he'd made it. He had come back over and over again when he ought to have stayed away. He knew that now.

He walked much of the night. The sunrise made his eyes water. He felt himself in its blaze, his promise fading as this beauty burgeoned. Was hope lost? I will begin writing again tomorrow, he told himself. I will cull poetry out of this accursed prosaic life.

Beatrice was waiting for Ann, who was just a little later than usual. 'I have to go to the dressmaker's,' she began. Then she saw Ann's face and her wincing walk. 'Madonna! You are injured, Signora?' she said with alarm.

'No, it's nothing. I fell down the stairs.'

Beatrice gave her a quick, pained look.

'Truly,' said Ann, 'it's very dark on the steps in our lodgings, slippery and easy to fall.'

'Didn't your husband steady you?'

Ann reddened, the colour mixing with the bruises. Beatrice turned away; it was a tact born of years round Francesco Savelli. 'But if you feel well enough we will have our lesson. My cousin Giancarlo is very keen I learn from you. He says you have much pure language.'

'That's an odd thing to say.' Ann would have accompanied her words with a smile if it hadn't hurt. 'He has been most kind in introducing me to you.'

When she returned to La Giudecca and mounted the dark stairs she avoided seeing Signora Scorzeri, often out with her beloved Rosa. That so far was the only good thing about the incident, its possible secrecy. The jolly Frenchmen had gone from the apartment below on a tour of Tuscany, and no other lodgers had taken the rooms while they were away.

How much had the *padrona* heard last night? She would have recognised raised voices in any language, and the tumble, even perhaps the heavy foot. Especially after her good dinner. If she had, would she not have come out to stare at the result this morning?

They were both subdued and said little. She hoped Robert was ashamed but doubted it. How could he be? It was against his nature. He was still angry.

'I never liked it,' he said suddenly. 'I never wanted to be here.'

'Well, we are. And you sometimes think it beautiful.'

'Beautiful like a dead woman. A dead woman who deserved to be dead.'

'You talk in clichés now.'

'I've caught the habit.'

Let it pass, she cautioned herself. 'Why are you so rude?'

'Don't start.'

For once she didn't 'start' but simply left the room, hastily pulling on a warm cloak. She must go out, however chill the weather. He said nothing of her bruised face.

She looked out at the small side canal, then walked holding her aching ribs with one arm towards the great lagoon at the end. It stretched to the sandbanks of the Lido, the islands, the low-flying birds, the fishermen's stakes, the *briccole*, the quiet boats far out. She'd come in the months to love its desolation, its mixture of nothingness and excess, its tame wildness, with sea and sky like the beginning of creation, yet nowhere more lived on and in, more touched by men, nowhere more created and uncreated.

John Taylor might have caught it as he'd caught the low East Anglian coast and sky, with his light blue- and green-washed colours. Yet she couldn't imagine him in Venice.

She retraced her steps and came out on the other side looking towards the city. She took a *traghetto* over to San Marco, then walked towards the Rialto. The walking hurt but the air through the muslin over her blackened eye was comforting. Normally she went there to find the cheapest fish for Signora Scorzeri to cook when it was the weekend and the tetchy *padrona* refused to do the shopping. But it was far too late for that now. Today she went just for the going.

She paused on a bridge and looked down at the murky water of a narrow canal. Another woman stopped momentarily, then a man brushed past her, stood for a while close by, then moved on. She didn't look up. What had she to do with any other beings?

'I'm glad I had no child,' he said that evening as he pushed away the dry baked fish.

It was as near to an apology as he could get. He didn't look at her. He'd responded to her bruised face as if to an insult.

'I could have tormented it as I'm tormenting myself.'

And me, she thought. And Me.

As she lay on the bed alone – Robert had gone somewhere, it didn't matter where – she was overwhelmed by a rush of humiliation, a deep *physical* shame. How could she be like this and not act?

But what act was enough? What was in any way equal to her massive passivity?

In all her imaginings she'd never invented anything so morbid, so hopeless for her helpless heroines. They always triumphed by sheer goodness – and beauty. Only the bad, the vicious, those provoked beyond decent endurance, had to act.

Yet what act was available for the weak, however vicious they'd become? Not for them the great fist, the iron-hard foot, the sword, even the pistol with its single shot. No rousing combat, exhilarating strife so beloved by men, or why glorify the simple-minded Napoleon?

If you cannot hit and fight in the open, you have to work furtively.

Her bruised mind dwelt on the crime of vulnerability. How ever to make amends? A furtive killing perhaps.

A soothing fantasy. But how did one actually use a stiletto? Surely it could be pressed in wrongly, slither into a flabby inessential part or scrape the bone and miss the heart? Besides, she never knew when he dozed or woke except when inebriated and snoring. And then the breath was punctuated with rumblings and flutings so loud he was always on the point of waking himself.

He was strong. Her bones and flesh knew that. Would there be time to push in a knife of any sort before he turned and murdered her instead?

Could she poison him? He took more and more laudanum. It created dreams, deadened pain in the head, indulged bad temper. Could she put in enough for him not to know the difference? But what if he did know it?

What if she put vitriolic acid in his wine instead of in the ink and he tasted it and realised? Then it would be like the knife foundering on the bone, preparing them both for what *he* would do.

It wasn't easy to shut off a brain that was maggoted and troublesome even when asleep. In any case its dissolution would be the most mighty rupture for everyone.

She'd let the fantasy run its course until it settled into more failure, inveterate helplessness. It no longer soothed.

The money from the Savelli did not go far. She had put a little of it in her hemp bag under the bed, not fearing that Robert would look, for he was not a nosy man. She would not dip into these small savings even to pay pressing debts. If she intended to live in Venice for any time and eat, then she should find more pupils to tutor or get back to her writing, let her body and mind heal with concentrating on something outside herself. Dean & Munday had been silent, so she must assume they were unwilling to make a loan. She'd never really supposed they would, but it had been worth a try. Robert mustn't know she'd written. She would write again, a more persuasive letter.

But what arrangements had *he* made? Did the ordinary demands in life mean nothing to him?

One day she'd said, 'Signora Scorzeri has become very brusque. Have you been paying her any money?'

'What money?' he said. 'She is not rude to me.'

'How much do we owe?'

'I have no idea. It doesn't matter.'

'I could do more teaching. There are other pupils out there.'

'You enjoy serving the nobility? I thought you'd have more pride.'

'Pride and poverty don't go so well together.'

'We differ there. I think they go very well. If you are rich you have nothing to be proud about – it's all too easy.'

'Francesco Savelli is rich and does not find life easy.'

'No, because he is mad.'

Suddenly he looked at her with such quiet mournful eyes she turned away and bit her lip. He could still do this.

Good to start another book or better to complete the one she'd brought from England. Then she could send it to London and hope that Dean & Munday would want it and pay.

So, while he sat at the bar of an open-sided tavern where their stripling canal debouched into the Giudecca Canal, his blank notebook in his pocket, with the kind of expression on his face that pulled in company to share his rough wine – or more often him to share theirs – she sat down with a new sheet of paper. She would redo the novel begun in England and call it *Isabella; or, the Secrets of the*

Convent. She would change the villain to Scaligeri since she expected no Italian readers. The name sounded brutal.

'The count towered over his victim,' she wrote, 'the girl shuddered, her hair falling across her ashen brow. "My lord, I am in your power but I will not be crushed. I am my father's daughter."

'His cruel glinting eyes flashed in his hard swarthy face and . . .' and so on.

When Robert returned she had no time to put away her papers before he entered the room. His footsteps were heavy, she should have heard. But she'd been so absorbed that nothing had disturbed her.

'You live in that world,' he said.

He glanced over her shoulder and she was not quick enough to prevent his reading,

'At that moment she looked not like her noble father but like her beautiful dead mother. The count stayed his hand and seemed to hesitate. Then, instead of smiting her, he grasped the locket round her white throat. As he wrenched it towards himself it swung open to reveal a lock of golden hair. "It is hers," he muttered, more to himself than to the lovely girl cowering at his feet. "There is none other like it."'

Robert grunted, then walked off. She'd have laughed if the movement hadn't hurt.

The year had really turned. She felt rather than knew it for she'd lost count of days and months. Spring must come, even in this dank cold place. Today its promise was in the air.

Suddenly out shone the sun through the mist, which became clean and lively in the light. The southern lagoon was flat and a black gondola was being rowed quietly across it, the gondolier taking those long elegant movements that made him seem the lord of much more than his black wooden craft. The blue ripples that fanned out behind him ambled slowly towards the shoreline, pausing only at the clam nets.

There was little difference between shore and water, both seeming of the same silky substance. On the wooden posts the water and light flickered. The lagoon islands were dark shapes in the glittering sun. A place much painted, never caught because never still for long enough. No, John Taylor would not have done justice to this dappled glinting scene.

The clearing white air intensified her longing to be free. Yet still – and she hated herself for knowing it – that longing was less intense than her fear of being left, of leaving what was wounding her.

Why was she so caught by Robert's huge and hideous egoism? A being like that would never disappear into mist and water. However he thinned, he would always be there, his flesh more solid than other people's, his words more vibrant, lasting longer on the air. His genius was himself, for what was genius but madness crossed with selfishness?

She shuddered. She could never be free with him, never be free of him. If he left she would yearn for him, if he stayed it was a kind of hell.

She looked at the elegant pulses of light cascading down the wooden poles in the lagoon, then at the local people attracted out by the milder weather, the men and women sometimes in their separate groups chatting and strolling or sitting on wooden benches together. The loneliness embraced her. Only a young woman sat apart disconsolately with a small demanding child on her lap and a tall man stood alone interrogating the slowly moving clouds.

After her walk almost the length of the islands across the little bridges, she returned to the apartment. Robert was not there. She looked into his study. On the floor was crumpled and torn some of the paper they'd carried with them across Europe. It wasn't expensive Venetian paper, nor was it cheap. She picked up a piece and spread it on the table.

'The dried corpse of greatness floating on the sea of misery,' she read. 'I seek the bloodless, tortured lips of the sun to hear his pure words.'

She looked at another piece. 'The frozen sun on the murdered town, howling in purity.'

And again, 'The sun slumbering in the deep ocean in the awful cave of writing.'

'The ocean slumbering in the sun's awful cave.'

'The sun howling in his sepulchre leaving a sunless wordless vapour.'

Robert had been writing variations of the same thing over and over. Writing maniacally with different-sized letters and various scrawlings. There was no developing, no moving on. Fear clutched her as never before.

In the morning she walked to the end island by Le Zitelle where a Turkish woman in an attic room made up cheap material into shifts and shirts and mended torn stockings. On her way she looked out once more on the waste of water, the sun rising and making red patches on the silver surface. She had not known an expanse of water and sky could be so embracing, so stifling. Like a large white hand with rosy clutching fingers, bent on taking the life from the living. Was she thinking of Robert's beautiful dead woman who deserved to be dead or did she make this Fury herself?

When she met Giancarlo Scrittori again her bruises were healed, but she was conscious of looking thinner and more faded in her summer dress. He said nothing but guided her to a café where he could make her comfortable; he intended to detain her a little for he needed, he said, some English expressions for a letter offering ivory snuffboxes and silver-gilt toothpick cases to an English customer. She'd not known he dealt in such expensive commodities and there was something odd about the repetitions in the letter he showed her. Probably it sounded more elegant in the original Italian.

Perhaps he was succeeding at his trade despite his initial misgivings. She saw now that he was more expensively dressed, with a new summer cloak in the latest shot material. She smiled appreciatively, but the smile must have been weak for he returned a look of compassion.

'You are like a small bird wintering here, trying to hide yourself.'

She frowned at such clear reference to her drab clothes, remembering their first meeting when he'd propelled her to his cousin's shop in San Paterian.

He noticed the reaction and rushed to counter her thought. 'Because I have not met you in the piazza. I see you like a migrating bird that comes but does not quite settle, so always acts to show it is only passing through.'

'You are interested in the habits of birds?'

'I have interest in birds, yes – I believe so does Signor Alessandro Balbi whom your husband met. He knows far more.'

She was surprised. 'How do you know they are acquainted?'

'People talk a lot here,' he said with a broad smile. 'But you on that low island must look at birds all round you. There is not much else there, I think, but a few artichokes and vines and broken boats to occupy the eyes.'

'Great churches.'

'Churches don't move and fly.'

'No, you are right and there are days when only birds can be seen, when the Euganean Hills disappear and a mist obscures where land, sea and sky meet. Everything becomes grey-blue. Then I enjoy seeing seagulls swooping through what you call the *nebbia*.'

He ordered two more coffees with a nod of his head. The owner was apparently another 'cousin'. 'Seagulls, yes of course, everywhere, though different ones. You can see difference? No? Then you must watch, when the tide comes up and land emerges in the lagoon, so much birds coming and going. Sometimes common gulls with black head, grey sides, sometimes what the great Linnaeus called *Ichthyaetus melanocephalus* with black head and red beak, and another with yellow. You can see this if you look close. It brings pleasure, Signora, to notice such things.'

'I am sure it does, but . . .'

He interrupted. She was startled. Perhaps he was used to combating melancholy and surmised it in her. Had he too grown up with a Francesco at home or been more around the Savelli than she realised? 'Ducks, you have seen ducks, *fischione* and *mestolone* – how do you say? Big duck, long neck, dark green head and yellow eyes, black, white, red feathers, you have seen, I think? And egrets surely?'

She laughed. 'I lived in London.'

'But there is sky even there and a river.'

'Yes, both, and both a little murky, as you will know. You have the eye of a painter when you talk of birds.'

'No, no, I just watch and see, and maybe describe. I do not paint or imagine. I am not an imaginative man. But let me go on. It is, as you say in England, to ride my hobby horse.'

Despite being entertained she wanted to leave, scorning the desire even as she felt it, for she knew she wanted to go to be miserable somewhere else, and alone.

'You look, Signora, even from La Giudecca, and you will see big *gheppi*, much flapping of wings or sometimes no flapping as it lies on the wind watching. *Svasso maggiore* comes in summer and he is not yet here. But there are others, perhaps a *falcon* or *chiurlo*.'

She smiled at his enthusiasm, how he tumbled out these strange names. 'No, Signor Scrittori, I have not seen any of these. Just smelly pigeons and sparrows and magpies and perhaps an egret, but then I wouldn't recognise them. I don't know so many other birds anywhere.'

They had got up and were now outside the café and, as they prepared to part, they spied overhead as if conjured up by his watchful eye a flock of long-beaked birds flying out towards the sea. '*Smerghi minori*,' he said.

She looked up and went on watching even as they fled from sight. She almost forgot her companion.

'You are looking with some wistfulness – is that the correct word? – at those big birds. You want to be them but they are so unconcerned with us down here, so arrogant. But you are now like the little *capinera*, Signora.'

'I don't know the bird but think it must be grey and small and dowdy.'

'I did not mean such thing,' he said earnestly. He looked so contrite she had to smile. 'Only that like the bird who stays here sometimes you may need to fly away a little, get out of this so small place.'

'I think I understand you. But we, Signor James and I, do not really know where to go.'

'Go somewhere in nature, for pleasure. Perhaps you will see a flamingo. They are nearby. They are very beautiful.'

'I am not sure that birds will cheer my husband. He is a little distracted at the moment.'

'No, well, plants then? I will show you both the plants of Dr Roccaborella, his drawings in the Marciana library if you wish. I know the man who looks after the collection.'

'Ah yes, the representation, not the thing.'

'No,' he said gently, 'it is no *sostituto* perhaps – but it lets you really see the thing when you do see it.' He paused. 'To see clearly what is there is best, I think. Francesco Savelli sees in his head and makes in stone what is not there and perhaps need not be seen by others. And I think your husband, Signora, is very admiring of this work. He has called more than once on the Conte and leaves him more agitated than before his visit. Signorina Beatrice has told you, I think.'

No, Beatrice had not mentioned it and had been right not to do so. Yet Ann resented her silence. It was not good to be in a web she couldn't see, unaware of the fine lines of connection. It made little difference in fact. She should have known Robert would not leave well alone after viewing the savage Madonna, and that Francesco Savelli would respond to his intensity. That each would aggravate the other.

As for the advice of going somewhere to look at nature, natural things or natural copies of any sort, it was difficult to follow. Robert was in no mood to be taken out of himself by pictures or scenes or flaming birds.

But with some surprise she did in fact persuade him to accept a cheap outing. It might lead to cheaper lodgings at the same time. If it did, they would need to steal away from La Giudecca on a moonless night, for their creditors would not be keen to wave them off before a settling of bills.

On Giancarlo Scrittori's suggestion they'd walk in the woods of Carpenedo, get away from the oppressive Venetian buildings which kept in the mounting heat, possibly see flamingoes. She doubted Robert's interest in such creatures. But they could at least eat pheasant – it was reputed to be tasty over there by Mestre, and much cheaper than in Venice. He might be better with a good meal inside him.

The day had been muggy and lowering, the *felucca* that took them there filthy, and they'd seen no flamingoes. They might have been present, pink in the misty distance, but human eyes couldn't spy them.

Instead, coming out of the small bedraggled wood, they faced a half-dead tree thick with cormorants. 'They are waiting for us,' said Robert. 'Look at their great forms against the sky. They eat the dead.'

Back in the apartment, with no preamble, he said, 'This place is the pit of Tophet.'

She went on folding clothes on the dining table, bracing herself. He so rarely engaged her nowadays that such a strange opening must herald more.

'The pit of Tophet,' he repeated to himself. He stopped and banged his fist on the other side of the table so hard he jiggled the heavy wooden bowl in the centre. 'You don't need brimstone and flames for it. You can forge tortures for all the damned, for yourself, without moving outside.'

His eyes fell icily on her, then he looked away, gnawed the knuckles of one hand, stopped and rushed on, his voice rising with each word. 'There's enough pain, disappointment, anguish, tears, sighs and groans to do away with Tophet. You don't need penal fire.' He looked at her belligerently as if she'd argued the point. 'Eternity adds little to malice.'

What on earth was he talking about? What or who was Tophet? Who had Robert been consorting with that this weird, presumably Papist material was addling his brain? Surely he'd not gone into any of the baroque churches he so hated and been accosted by some mad unfrocked monk.

He went on, his eyes now unfocused but his hands clenched. 'Only the Almighty executes a relentless doom. We don't need him, we can do it ourselves to anyone, *to* ourselves. Hellfire and cannibalism. We all want it, we would will everyone to damnation if we could. You know that's true, Miss Ann St Clair. I know you feel like that. But you have no will.'

She was about to protest, to cry out against it all, but he silenced her. 'You want to control but can't.'

He'd been standing hunched over the table, now he sat down heavily, talking again more to himself than to her. 'The pleasure of hating, carrying fire, pestilence and famine into the soul. I know, I know.' He turned to Ann but his focus was beyond her. 'You all look with such narrow, jealous, inquisitorial watchfulness over the actions and motives of the best of people; you wrangle, quarrel, tear one

another in pieces, making a target, a mark to shoot at. I don't understand all he says but this is what he means, what I mean.'

'Who, Robert?'

'Francesco Savelli, of course.'

She was glad she'd been warned by Giancarlo Scrittori. Else she'd
have been bewildered. Suddenly aghast, she blurted out, 'You have
brought him here, to this apartment?'

'I have and why should I not? Isn't this our "home", our haven?'

He was suddenly furious with himself, with the world, with her.
He picked up the wooden bowl on the table. He was about to throw
it. He locked into her eyes. He would hurl it at her. It would do
damage. She winced but stayed standing by the pile of folded clothes.

Abruptly, as if his arm had suddenly been paralysed, it went limp
and the bowl clattered on to the table.

The aborted act of throwing had sapped his vitality. He bowed
his head on to the wood and put his hands round his neck. 'That
young man understands what I am doing. He understood *Attila*
without being able to read it and why I am beyond it now. He admires
me. ME. Is that so strange? Let others mock.' His voice was high and
choked.

She couldn't comfort him. And he wouldn't have accepted
comfort.

Late one evening in the following week he remarked that there was
something – he hardly remembered – he had to tell her.

'What?'

'Oh,' he said as if an afterthought – but how could it be? how
could it? 'There's a letter at the *poste restante* somewhere.' He spat
out the word 'letter'. 'A letter for Miss Ann St Clair, no longer Signora
James apparently. It was a brilliant invention, of course.'

He had a right to his fury. She'd kept the secret of her visits to
Palazzo Grimani, her occasional dispatching of Signora Scorzeri's
boy. So now they could be traced. He had a horror of this – because
of her they would be known by 'authorities'.

For once his rage didn't matter. There was a letter for her.

Who could be sending it? Could cousin Sarah have followed the trail through Moore & Stratton? After all, the pair had first come together with their help. For it had been through someone at this office who knew someone who knew a cousin of Charles Hardisty's who knew an Aunt Louisa whom apparently she shared with Sarah that she'd first been brought to her cousin's door. But she doubted that Sarah would expect there still to be contact after so many years.

It must then be Dean & Munday – perhaps, after all, they were willing to advance money despite her having sent them nothing, or perhaps Mr Munday was asking for some speedy work because another hack had failed to deliver. That was as unlikely as a loan.

From wherever and whomever it derived, the letter made her heart beat quickly. It came from outside the iron circle of her present life.

'I must get it at once,' she exclaimed. Then she added for no decent reason, more as a kind of echo of what she believed a normal person would say, 'It might be from my mother.'

'Perhaps she's dead and leaving you some money.'

'She would not then be writing.'

'You assume it's she who is writing then? What a lot you seem to know,' he said wearily. 'Anyway the *poste* is closed the rest of this week. The boy said the office would be open on Monday morning. What did you pay him to do this dirty work?'

'Did he say anything else?'

'No, why should he?'

'You didn't tell me this at once.' She tried to keep her voice level.

'I'm telling you now. I thought you hated your mother.'

She let the idea hang in the air. 'Hate' was too uncomplicated a word for Caroline. 'I doubt it's from her. How did you hear of the letter?'

He was going back into his study, annoyed at the questioning. 'The boy came to me,' he said without turning. 'He thought a husband might be told the business of a wife of whatever name she chose. You kept that a secret, didn't you, Madam?'

20

She walked passed San Moisè towards San Luca near where she'd been sometimes to buy cheaper week-old vegetables for Sunday. She felt conspicuous. People were staring at her, as Giancarlo Scrittori had been too polite to do on their last meeting.

No Venetian signora would take so little care of appearance, let hair straggle from under a cap however sultry the day. Happily, Mrs Bigg-Staithe was no longer there to titter and turn away, for she'd long since travelled on to the more popular destinations of Florence and Rome, her spouse brimful of Robert's opinions.

She would pass as a local peasant if she weren't so clearly foreign. The bones of her skull, her hair, her browning but still pasty face, her manner of walking, everything screamed it. The hot summer had finally struck. So care did not seem so necessary to an Englishwoman. It was different for natives.

Her pupil had gone off laughing and smiling to the country house leaving the troubled Conte in the care of the useful Signora Zen, the toothless housekeeper, and the other servants. With the pretty girl had gone the contagion of beauty, the sense that it rubbed off – even if the mirror always told another tale. She would visit the house again when everyone came back after the sultry dog days – if she herself were still in Venice.

Even Giancarlo Scrittori had gone somewhere north in the mountains for a week or two. She missed him but was glad not to provoke his pity and relieved to see no more newspapers. She had no interest in England's shoddy affairs.

She'd crossed to the Piazza San Marco early on the Monday morning, long before the *poste restante* office at Palazzo Grimani could have opened.

She was not the only person to arrive early. People received bank drafts and promissory notes through the office as well as personal letters, and there was an air of anxiety among those who anticipated the opening.

While she waited, she strolled on through the small *campo* of San Luca into Campo San Paterian past Tommaso's shop, already welcoming business with its open door. The jacket she'd enjoyed buying there was now much worn but some cheap cotton muslin she'd had made up near Le Zitelle had been supplied by him after Giancarlo Scrittori had quietly explained her circumstances. It helped keep her cool in the stifling rooms.

At precisely the correct hour, to the surprise of the people waiting, the outer door of Palazzo Grimani was opened by a swarthy man – a Turk or Arab? She'd not seen him when she'd come later in the day. He asked each person's business in guttural Italian, then silently waved them on. A serious bustle agitated the air, and the faces of those who mounted and descended were preoccupied.

Despite her eagerness to know who'd sent her letter and what it imported, she was not the first on the stairs. Behind her as she went up sounded other footsteps. She calculated perhaps two men: there was no rustle of skirts and the tread was heavy. She was hot and held her breath as she ascended and listened.

By the time she reached the office she was gasping for breath. Happily the room was airy with good natural light. It fell on ledgers and inkstands, quills and papers, tied together in tape of different faded colours.

While her agitated breath became more regular she moved into line behind a squat elderly man and broad middle-aged woman sweating in tight purple bombazine. The latter was expostulating with the clerk. As far as Ann could make out, she was insisting there was a letter for her from her husband Signor Moro in Genoa enclosing a banker's draft; they must be hiding it. As her voice rose, another man entered slowly from an interior room. He was flaxen-haired with chilly eyes, an optical glass hanging on a chain round his thin neck. The woman turned to him and began her tale again but more ingratiatingly, in lower pitch. Under the scrutiny of the blue eyes the words began to slow. Gradually they failed. The German, or Austrian, Ann supposed, then came round the counter and politely, firmly, moved with the woman towards the door. She appeared surprised but accepted, her anxiety as well as desire seemingly quenched by this authoritative show.

Just the elderly man, then it would be Ann's turn. She held back; it seemed an age till he stopped mumbling his business and a package was produced and signed for.

It was her moment. As she stepped forward to give her name and ask for her letter, she turned slightly, realising that the next client was not as thoughtful as she had been.

A man was standing too close. He was in line but courtesy demanded some distance even within the office, for transactions were often private and signatures guarded. She glanced at him, surprised. Though he was looking away, something about the shape of the head, the stance, the side of a moustache, she was not sure what, made her think of the man she'd wrongly supposed Giancarlo Scrittori's friend so many months before near the Gesuati. Perhaps it was his foreignness that was not quite the usual Austrian version and yet was not quite English or French, perhaps Dutch? It could, of course, quite easily be the same man, for in this small town foreigners did their business in only so many locations; the post office would surely be one of the main meeting places.

Perhaps he knew no better than to crowd a person, for he'd stood close to Giancarlo Scrittori on their first encounter. That was why she'd noticed him.

It was not sufficiently threatening to protest, just irritating enough for her a second time to raise her eyes towards his face then lower them to indicate displeasure. But he was still looking away and didn't catch her glance. She turned her attention back to the clerk.

She prepared to present her credentials as Ann St Clair but found she had no need to say her name; the clerk, who'd recovered from his episode with the vociferous lady and been bored by the old man, was now offhand. Almost in silence he looked at the name on her papers, then ordered her to sign and pay her postage fee. She wanted to see the letter first, but had not the skill to argue. She leaned over the counter and signed where she was told.

Her heart beat in her ears as she took the letter.

Whoever had sent it, he or she was addressing her as what once she'd been, not what she pretended to be.

Her name Ann St Clair was followed by the address, the *poste restante* in Venice. The hand was unfamiliar, not Caroline's for sure. From notes she'd had to take to Mrs Graves, she'd come to know it. Like a person's voice, writing was not easy to forget, even after many years.

The letter was fat. Fat enough for a bank draft? A postmark, almost obliterated by some other stamp, told her that the letter had come from London, presumably a clerk at Dean & Munday's had addressed it – for they remained the most obvious senders.

Without looking at him further, she brushed past the man who was standing a little further away now. Perhaps he'd not realised his discourtesy. She went swiftly down the stairs.

Outside she leaned against a wall and felt the sun directly on her face. She opened the letter carefully so as not to tear any of its contents.

It was not from Dean & Munday.

To her surprise it had come from Moore & Stratton in the Strand. The sender was a Mr Laurence Holt. He wrote solely to enclose a second letter.

This one was smaller, the paper thinner and the hand spidery. It was addressed to Mademoiselle Ann St Clair at Moore & Stratton. For a moment she was too perplexed to act, then she began taking it apart. She had to be even more careful than with the original letter for she could expect much writing on the flaps. But, as she unfolded them, she saw they were empty. There was no further enclosure.

What she read in the middle of the opened paper was short and in stilted English, underneath a carefully printed Parisian address.

It said, 'Mademoiselle Ann St Clair, your mother is very ill, soon to die. I wish you come before too late.' It was signed 'A Friend'.

Her back was heavy against the wall. She felt a hard stone pushing into her skin through her muslin dress. She stood straight, then swayed a little and leaned back again.

How long did dying take? How long had the letter been waiting for her? She had not been to Palazzo Grimani for some time, and she'd not sent Signora Scorzeri's boy for over a fortnight. The letter could have been sitting in that office for many days.

'I'd be dead for all you care,' she heard her mother say distinctly. She'd complained so often her complaint had ceased to impress her daughter. Was it true?

Had not Caroline said she died with Gilbert? Well, he and she had been there long after his death. Caroline's stories were the memories of Ann's childhood, much stronger than anything that had actually happened to her. If Caroline died in body, her words would still be left over. What death was now being proposed?

Caroline and Gilbert: her parents' narrated life washed over Ann like an immense red and yellow wave as she stood there on the hot stones of Venice. It obliterated closer time and space.

The music, the paintings in Vauxhall Gardens where he'd taken Caroline. He as the accepted lover and husband, yet all meetings as trysts. 'You know,' and Caroline bending over the table to look right through her young daughter who was sullenly sitting opposite while her mother consumed her apple pudding, 'you know, he knew my innermost thoughts and I of course knew his. He knew, oh I admit it, my melancholy tendency, my loneliness – for what thinking being is not alone . . . ? and he admired all of it, all of me. He could awaken me to such joy.'

Here was grown-up Ann leaning against a Venetian wall near Palazzo Grimani going back to Vauxhall which she was quite sure she'd never visited, knowing it was far more distinct in her mind than the Accademia or Frari or anywhere else beside her now.

She propelled herself automatically through the dingy narrow *calli* round Palazzo Grimani and down towards the finer area of San Marco towards the *traghetto* that would take her over to La Giudecca. All the while Caroline in her head went on talking while her daughter clutched the letter that summoned up all this over-coloured memory.

'Such sights as we saw together, the jewellery at Cox's museum, so costly, so glittering, the silver and gold tiger, yes life-sized, the curiosities of Montagu House, the silver swan that could incline its silver neck and pull out a silver fish from the glassy shifting water. Imagine that! And Gilbert, dear Gilbert with only eyes for me and caring nothing for such a mélange – he used the word – bought me a bright silver, gold and crystal pendant.'

'So where is it?' child Ann had asked.

'One loses even one's most valued possessions.'

She believed in the absent pendant, just as she believed in the thin sliced ham at Vauxhall.

Only once when younger, much younger than thirteen, perhaps ten, though already a reader of stories and already suspicious, she'd asked if Caroline loved Gilbert.

'Ah,' said Caroline, 'I loved and what is most wondrous, he accepted my love. He was so grateful for it. When I brought myself to admit it, he took me in his arms and said that he knew I had risked so much by loving, for most people resisted the great happiness of love. I did it willingly.'

'Was that because you were so old?' asked Ann for she'd not failed to notice her mother was more ancient than the mamas of other girls at school.

Caroline had boxed her ears so that they tingled even when she lay on her back in bed.

The memories, the ridiculous wordy memories – that sliced ham, that swan, the tiger, the gold, silver and crystal pendant – began to subside only as she crossed over the canals in La Giudecca towards the apartment. What of all this *could* die?

Without much desire to see her mother, she would travel to Paris – realising now that she and Robert had passed through the city the year before without knowing that Caroline was living there. She was going in response to that conventionality of which Robert had so often accused her.

Of course here was, too, the escape she'd longed for. But she'd go resenting him and resenting the time away from him.

He would say he was glad she was going, he would be free of her clinging – love, he supposed she called it. He would not mind if she did not come back.

She would smile a bitter smile. But she would return. She had to. She would not abandon a part of herself.

When she'd entered the apartment and knocked on the open door of his study she'd told him her news. It was then out of sheer weakness and fatigue that she fell on to a chair in the sitting room and sobbed. He slammed the door from the study not to hear the noise. She carried on long after the emotion that brought it on had ceased.

21

She enquired about tickets and bookings from the few offices still open in the heat-racked town and requested a pass for travel to France. Everything took time.

She must use the interval to find them lodgings out of Venice, somewhere where the water didn't stink in the high heat and the rooms were cheaper. Without her in this city Robert would fall even further into debt: he had no notion how to rein in expense.

When she was gone he might leave and live somewhere else: he might not be there when she returned. He might not. And she would not know where he had gone.

Then she would not be free of him – that was a hopeless dream – for she would spend her days imagining him sitting, smoking, talking, drinking, becoming again for someone else all those people he had lost. A Bianca? The idea, so tenacious, could still kindle that passionate anguish that surely by now should have been cold dead, not just resting.

She trusted Tommaso for, when she'd come to buy his cheap muslin, he'd not urged her into anything more costly. He was from outside Venice and might be able to suggest other nearby towns where she and Robert could live more cheaply.

Padua, he'd said at once. The place was full of students. They didn't want expensive rooms. He'd heard she taught English to the Savelli Signorina; she might find pupils there among the young men.

If they moved she'd have to give up her lessons with Beatrice. No Padovan student could mean as much to her as this young girl. Her heart felt heavy at the idea of losing her company – at starting over, and being still with him. Yet Beatrice had hidden something from her she should have known.

She determined on the visit. If they liked the town they could move and start over again.

Perhaps Robert would grow calmer. Perhaps some of the savagery had come from the Savelli influence. Perhaps in a new place he might be renewed. Perhaps he could work his charm once more and gain them some more credit. Perhaps.

She doubted all of it. Since the departure of the Bigg-Staithes, he'd made less effort in his manner and dress. Signor Balbi was not a poor man but he was a traveller and was not arrayed so finely as his fellow citizens: sometimes he appeared shabbily clad, so perhaps he noticed less. But surely even he had seen the change in Robert.

His paunch was smaller, no longer firm – she supposed it was because he drank more than he ate. The bald part of his head looked unpolished, and his tawny hair once so cared for round the rim was now too long. It made him seem an old man – or a mangy dog.

She pretended they were going to Padua to see art as well as find other lodgings. But as usual he showed no interest. The glories of Venice had not awakened him; he anticipated no more pleasure from old art in more decrepit towns. But Signor Balbi had said he should visit Padua, he had relatives at the university there whom his friend might like to meet, and Robert remained polite in his response to him.

Giancarlo Scrittori had once said they must see the Giotto frescoes in the Scrovegni Chapel. Like Robert she felt beyond looking at painting, but there might be something comforting about a quiet Virgin well executed. And Christ? There was only one passion in his life – and it was all over quite quickly. Then what rewards! She had less time for Christ.

From Mestre they travelled in a closed public carriage, early because the heat was already mounting. It hardly went down even at night but still the early morning was the best. Other passengers smelled worse than their hens trussed up and shitting into a basket under the seat.

And what did they themselves smell like by now? They were so far apart and yet they must smell the same, two English strangers fed on foreign food.

When they arrived in Padua they found the door to the chapel with the frescoes firmly closed. A sign declared the doorkeeper away on a private *festa*. A few other people stood outside as well, disappointed by the closure, a couple with a child, the woman in a close bonnet despite the warm day, some young Germans — brothers perhaps — with a squat clerical tutor. All of them waited irresolute as if they expected the doorman to return despite his notice.

While they stood there, another foreign visitor walked up, a tall middle-aged man with a trimmed beard, moustache and tightly curled brown hair thinning at the temples. He looked at Robert and Ann because, she first thought, he too was English. But he did not speak to them. This was a blessing, since Robert was in such a painful, smouldering mood he would have found casual talk impossible. He'd taken the journey badly.

The stranger was familiar — but she was unsure of her judgement. She'd thought the man with Giancarlo Scrittori was the same as the person in the post office. Now she thought again that this was the same man. That the first two figures were the same was possible. That all three were the same was improbable. Surely the man before her was neater than the cloaked figure near Giancarlo. But he was very like the man at Palazzo Grimani who'd stood too close to her and whom she'd seen a little more distinctly.

Most probably her eyes were playing tricks. Was everyone already falling into types in the way old people saw them, indistinguishable from each other across time or place?

The German youths were expostulating with their tutor and each other, uncertain what to do next but eager to be off somewhere. Robert started to move away, Ann followed.

They walked through the town, decaying picturesquely in the sun. It lit up the once magnificent porticoes, sagging in front of dilapidated buildings. They passed by the flower market, selling tall closed blooms she didn't recognise and little bouquets bound in pink ribbon.

A smell of newly made bread floated on the air. On the stalls were pastries in different shapes and small cakes covered in sugar. Rows of crudely painted earthenware pots stood on trestles, with gaudy glass ornaments from Murano. How Robert used to cherish cups and bowls, handling them as a connoisseur! All in another life, another world of tea parties with Mary Davies and Richard Perry, of coffee and pots of ale with Frederick Curran and other rollicking friends in Cheapside.

She tried to hurry them past the stalls since they had so little money to squander. He might spy some flowers and be tempted to buy.

She need not have feared for he seemed in a daze. The beggars, who usually claimed his attention, pleaded and tugged at his jacket in vain.

Yet he did not walk at his natural quick pace but sauntered. She wanted time to check the places Tommaso had suggested. She'd not stressed cheapness when she'd enquired about lodgings but she doubted either he or Giancarlo Scrittori, whom she'd earlier questioned, were much deceived about the state of things. The change from the *turquois* jacket to cheap imitation Indian muslin told its tale. Such places as Tommaso recommended would be on the periphery, beyond the grassy spaces. They must leave time to visit.

Robert was not to be hurried. He gestured annoyance when she tried to urge him on by taking his arm. He tugged it out of her grasp. Then abruptly and for no reason she could see he sped up. She had to scurry behind him.

They were now passing the cathedral, an ugly plain facade before an open square. Meaning to visit briefly, they found themselves instead through a thick velvet curtain in the baptistery. Robert carelessly handed over coins to a sacristan. She wondered how many but dared not ask. A few candles were already alight in the gloom. The sacristan added another.

They had entered a different world, marvellous, crude and ridiculous. She looked around, then at Robert, expecting him to register contempt.

'Giusto de'Menabuoi,' said the sacristan. Ann had never heard of him, Robert didn't listen. She swivelled her head round the sides, then wished to flee from what she saw.

To her surprise Robert didn't turn away and scoff. He appeared enthralled by the deranged and whirling vision covering all four sides: an apocalypse, a revelation of Revelation. She felt danger at once. This rapt attention couldn't be good. His nerves were strung so tight they must surely slacken or break. She remembered Tophet.

She followed the channel of his eye. There was a leopard with seven snaking heads emerging from it. Why this confusing of forms, this mixture of reptile and mammal? Why had the painter not made the whole monster scaly like a snake or crocodile? It wasn't disturbing, just absurd. Perhaps it was biblical; she knew her ignorance.

She moved away to glance at a demanding Christ, one whose glaring expression proved him aware of the trouble he was already causing and would go on causing. She continued her tour, staring briefly at the hundreds of ranged male and female saints paying court to something or someone, the Madonna perhaps, it was unclear.

All the while Robert remained transfixed before the revelation. She returned to him, eager to persuade him to leave. The frescoes were perhaps more interesting than she'd first thought – but she'd had enough.

'It is blasphemy,' he said in a hoarse voice. He was looking at bishops' mitres on the heads of beasts.

'Symbols of power, that's all,' she said.

'Not that.' He glared at her incomprehension. 'No, the blasphemy is the whole thing. It's against reason.'

She was aware of a figure in the shadows. A light from the few candles the sacristan had lit now let her catch the glint in the eyes of a man who was looking at her and Robert rather than at the pictures. It was the stranger whose stare she'd caught outside the Giotto chapel, the foreigner she kept seeing, or imagined seeing.

Such recognising, real or mistaken, was a gothic trick she often used in her novels, putting her mysterious characters over and over again in dim churches and on misty mountains and in caverns, showing up, pop, like a jack-in-the-box whenever the plot required them, then spiriting them away when they'd served their turn. Her mind must be infected.

Yet the stranger really was staring, surreptitiously perhaps but definitely, and she was sure she discerned in the flickering light that distinctive almost imperceptible moustache and small beard. He stayed in the dimmest part of the chapel. Could she trust her senses?

What could he be about? It was no surprise that foreign visitors to Padua or any other Italian city should go to see similar sights. One would expect to find the touring traveller, guidebook in hand, in front of each Titian or Giotto, trooping from one masterpiece to the other before heading home with relief to tell his tale and hang his copies on the mansion wall. Nothing strange therefore in meeting the same man at different shrines.

And yet she and Robert had come reasonably fast from one chapel to another, and they'd not paused to look at the flower stalls. It was curious that anyone else would take the same route or be so insensitive to the unison of light and smell – would have come straight through the market to arrive here at exactly the same time.

Still, here the stranger indubitably was – she was now sure of it though he was still lurking in the dimmest corner where a candle hardly shone on the painted wall. It was silly to be jumpy. She'd thought at once about what they owed Signora Scorzeri. But that was crazy thinking. No one would have travelled all the way from Venice to Padua for the sake of hounding them for debts that couldn't have been worth such trouble. Certainly not a stranger. Had Robert really offended 'authorities'? Was there something in his past that justified his occasional furtive looks into dark corners?

It was dim in the baptistery, yet the stranger's fair colouring showed in the wavering candlelight. The man could be Austrian or German, there were many about in northern Italy – and yet, she thought again, there was something different in him that argued against this.

If he were indeed interested in her and Robert, it would perhaps be in part because he'd heard her voice in front of the Giotto chapel or in Palazzo Grimani. This would argue him English after all and perhaps in need of English company. But he had been here a long time already. That is if she were right in her sightings and not being madly suspicious. In which case, he could have made himself known before. From even the little she'd seen of him he didn't seem a diffident man.

No good explanation sprang to mind, but she remained convinced he'd been listening to them earlier: he had had the look of someone who understood what they were saying.

She'd no more time for pondering the mystery, for Robert once more dominated her mind.

She went up to him and touched his arm. 'Shall we go? We have quite a bit to do.'

He shook her off roughly, then turned to stare at her with eyes full of blazing hate.

She took a step back. His looks had almost the same violence as his physical assaults, eye and fist equally powerful.

Again the self-questioning. Why was she here in this dreadful place instead of on the road to Paris with or without a pass? What was the hold of this incubus over her?

Or was there no need for one: was she spoilt for ordinary life now? Did she not need Robert as an addict needs opium, a drunkard his killing brandy?

She walked away to gaze at the large figure in heaven. In her disordered state she could read meanings everywhere. The seated man with the burning eyes huge and majestic in the midst of a circle of little people. If he had been fairer and balder, he could have been Robert. How mad a thought was this! Supporting this immense figure, this rampant potent man, was a serene blue-clad Virgin.

That is what Robert had needed, the virginal mother, large enough to lean on, calm enough to rely on always, but quite secondary, totally enclosed in the majestic circle of his divinity, his genius.

She moved on, trying hard to stop her mind allowing such imaginings. There were simply biblical stories told in pictures. She'd been taught some of them in school but most by Martha in a rudimentary way; they weren't part of her as they were of Robert – and of Caroline, she supposed. She was glad for this escape at least.

Now she noted on the wall a whole procession of diminished women, a woman coming out of the man, a man with many wives, a man willing to sacrifice his son, asking no permission of the mother who'd borne him, a drunken man being copulated with and covered by his women. All these men, Joseph, Christ, Noah, the empty angels, all had piercing glittering eyes that followed the watcher. The Virgin's eyes followed no one outside her world. She had no need to look at others – for her man, her god, was above her.

The candle was guttering and the sacristan must be eager for them to go. But Robert was insensible. There he was now by the apse, transfixed by another ridiculous beast with seven serpent necks. She returned to stand by him. She didn't dare touch him.

'He made a third of the stars fall down on earth,' said the sacristan, presuming their ignorance. He said much more but her Italian was not good enough to penetrate his accent and keep up. Robert heard nothing. He looked fixedly at the beast like a dragon with a monstrous bat's wing.

She could make no sense of it, much less of Robert's fascination. Apparently one of the dragon's seven heads wanted to grab a child from a woman but was prevented by a god who took it instead, leaving the woman to go off into the desert. It was an unsatisfactory story as plot or morality. Perhaps she was not giving it enough attention.

She turned back to look at Robert. He must not see her – he hated to be stared at.

She saw enough to understand he was not, after all, much interested in the beast, the woman, the child, not even the stars. His eyes were, she now noticed, fixed on another panel, on the books.

'Words,' he said loudly. 'It is about books, potential books, words too sacred, too pure to be written down. And Christ, all about the word, of course, of course but not words at all, just purity in letters.'

He looked wildly, not at her but through her and around. She gazed from him to the pictures. Something was very wrong.

'See, there are seven angels in seven attitudes. The first played his trumpet and hail, fire and blood rained down on the earth and a third of all the green things died, the grass, trees and stems and leaves, in his mind, do you see? The second angel played his trumpet so that the seas stirred and boats fell under the waves for a flaming mountain was thrown into the sea and the sea turned to blood. Look! a third of ships and sea creatures were destroyed in the blast.'

He said 'look' and 'see' but the command was not addressed to her or anyone else. He was speaking now with horrid rapidity. Had he understood all this from the sacristan? Surely not for, with her better Italian, she'd caught almost nothing of what he said.

'The third angel played his trumpet and a burning star fell from heaven and a third of the earth's rivers and springs became poison, so that anything that drank dropped down and died. Always a third, you see. Not *all* as you'd expect. More than decimating, less than destroying, so clever. The past not as bloody as the present. The fourth angel blasted away and a third of the sun and moon and a third of the stars were darkened. So that the night and the day lost a third of their light. Again not all, but just enough to make everything dark, dreary.'

Ann's anxiety was mounting under this torrent of speech. But he would not, could not stop, and she feared to intervene. He went on rapidly in a low gravelly voice, 'The fifth angel blew his trumpet and made a star fall on to the earth. When it hit the earth it blew apart and thick smoke darkened what was left of the sun and the air. And out of the dense smoke came manlike grasshoppers with scorpions' tails and stings. From these stings the people left on earth would suffer horribly for five months without dying. All numbers now, all unkind numbers. The little brown people cowered against it but did not die. What was the point? They had not suffered enough, that was the point. The sixth angel turned away from the human beings and attended to his own kind, angels who'd been kept in chains on earth by a river. Who had had the power to keep them there? A cavalry with swords and sulphur which emanated from the horses' mouths.

With this a third of humanity died. So that's it.'

He seemed to look at her, address her, but his eyes were still not focusing on her face.

'Nothing matters but the seventh angel. Do you see? Do you see? That seventh angel speaks to me, me. They would snatch the book from him if they could. But look here, the last angel coming down on a cloud from heaven, then placing his right foot, only that one, on the inkstand. In his hand, see, he holds an open book, with writing not to be read. It's a book of purity that could be held only by a being who had one foot on the earth, never both. Worldly words could only have made a common world, no heaven of earth. All illusory. No one could receive them. Only my own maniacal will could have kept me from seeing this. The image is dead.'

He was clawing the air with both hands, gesturing to himself alone.

Ann tried to look in case there was anything, anything that could be done to divert this dreadful flow of words. She saw that in the painting, between the angel and a man who leaned forward from the land, was a little angel with a pen. He seemed to be writing with small scratches in a smaller book which the man held to his mouth, appearing to nibble at its top right-hand corner. She could make nothing of its nonsense. Nothing she could say to interrupt. Robert was still talking on and on.

'There are seven thunders, light and fire erupting. But there, quietly, this man through the little angel has written down what he has heard in the thunder – on the book that he is now eating. He must, of course – he must ingest – keep the words inside himself, not let them out; otherwise the small book cannot echo the huge angelic one. There will be no Huns to fall on his Rome. No need, no chance.'

There was an eighth angel but Robert ignored him. Ann saw that the rest of the paintings depicted blood and scourges with the remainder of miserable humanity obliterated. But it was not these that mattered. For all the meaning they held they might have depicted Attila and Napoleon. It was the book and its meaning that clutched at Robert. The work could not and should not be written.

Was this what he was seeing, insanely interpreting rather: that what he had wanted to do could not be done? Could he really be taking this absurd scriptural jumble seriously?

His voice that had been rising despite its gravelly timbre had now reached its zenith. He stopped suddenly. After such revelation the only way forward was to pitch even higher, making with the stretched strings the great note that would harmonise with everything in the world, that would make the sun and moon one with the earth, the light, the flowers, everything.

He now knew that nothing could be conveyed to others. He must simply swallow his words. Only then would the book of the pale man and the huge book of the dark angel be one and the same. There would be no uprising of the truth through him, only in him.

Robert did not feel he'd seen a vision, only that his mind was moving in distinct levels. Layers shifted, collided, merged, coalesced, separating but making no pattern that would be static, that could be expressed. His mistake – he knew it now – had been the desire to tell what he knew, especially to women. The seeking was right, but the telling was not. And if there was to be no telling, then why?

Ann was terrified. Wanting to intrude. Against all sense, all experience she tried again to take his arm. Doing so, she angered him beyond reason. Her insensitivity was breathtaking. He jerked her away and lurched towards the velvet curtain shrouding the opening. Pushing it aside, he propelled himself into the outside world taking great gulps of air. Ann watched him go. She could almost see his frayed nerves jangling about his silhouette, while feeling her own.

Where would it end? It was sheer fantasy to think she could destroy such a being, however much she wished it. Every bit of him was alive – that's why he couldn't be still. If you cut off his head, his fingers, his feet would still live on.

But neither could she save him.

In the short interval in the chapel beyond his going and her following she tried to respond to ordinary social needs. She thanked the sacristan who'd been silently watching the show. She proffered the usual Italian exaggeration, the intensive thousands, but knew he expected more money for his time of patient listening. She felt sick. She must go to Robert.

Yet something held her momentarily back. The stranger still loitered in the chapel, watching perhaps. He must believe them both sick or crazy. He *must* think something, have some response, for he'd stayed to witness the whole pathetic performance. Had he been entertained? She looked over at him – there was more light in the room for the velvet curtain hadn't swung back completely into place. He'd fastened his eyes on a depiction of the life of John the Baptist. But of course he'd have heard everything. Why hadn't he walked away?

As she pushed back the curtain further to leave, she saw him move towards the sacristan, obviously preparing to pay him. Perhaps he was, after all, English and wanted to compensate for the rudeness, the insanity, of his countrymen.

Robert was standing a little way off with his back to her. He was smoking his pipe. The smoke rose into the hot air above his head. His body was still trembling, the motion interrupted by sudden jerks when he pulled with his left hand at the long hairs at the back of his neck.

She must get help but where could it be found? Would the Contessa be able to assist? She must know about diseases of the mind. But Robert would never regard himself as needing help and perhaps the Contessa never saw her son like this. There was a gulf of rank between them. She doubted she could find help in the Palazzo Savelli.

By now the stranger too had exited. To her surprise he walked over to Ann and Robert and accosted them.

'Excuse me for addressing you but I couldn't help noticing you were English,' he said in a voice that was clear and precise but a little strange, as if he'd learned to talk in different regions, letting no one accent predominate. 'I am taking this opportunity to insist on speaking my language by asking if you will join me in a glass of wine. You see that *taverna* there, down the side street. We might pass a half-hour there if you would honour me . . .'

The invitation was addressed to them both but Robert, still standing separately, continued to smoke and stare elsewhere. His face in profile was listless though there was a twitch in the exposed eye. He was in earshot but would not hear. Before she could answer the stranger, Robert had walked a further few paces off.

'You are English, then?' Ann said, her eyes trailing after Robert.

The man looked at Robert and, observing he couldn't hear, addressed Ann alone. 'Yes and no,' he answered, 'I'm originally from the north, but I have been in England, mostly London, very often, and regard English as one of my native languages, if one may have more than one. My mother was half-English. My name is Aksel Jakobsen.'

It was kind of him to venture so much and there was no easy response. They both fell silent. The man glanced again at Robert, then she felt his eyes on her. He pitied her of course, her drabness, her humiliating worry. She felt ashamed. She hoped a look would convey all: apology, misery, even now fear.

It would be good to have company, to drink sociably, but how could Robert help exposing how mad he'd become, how enthralled to this madness they both were? For, after all, she could only reveal herself as contingent and unwomanly. But did it really matter what a stranger or anyone thought? Could she possibly still care?

'Thank you,' she said, 'that would be a pleasure. Though we are both tired and not good company. We are Mr and Mrs James, Robert and Ann James.' She felt an urge to burst into hysterical laughter at the normality of what she said.

The stranger made no effort to force himself on Robert, who continued smoking at a distance. Nor did he indicate any surprise at his lack of response.

'Are you returning to Venice tonight?'

'Oh yes, we must.'

He understood: it would be cheaper to travel late than to find lodging from home.

'When we have rested a while, may I accompany you? I too want to return this night. I am travelling by boat down the river. It is already hired and there is room for more passengers. I am staying on La Giudecca.'

'But that is a coincidence. We too. I think perhaps I have seen you somewhere . . . but I cannot be sure of course.'

He bowed and was silent a moment. 'I lodge near the Zitelle.'

Robert was still ignoring them both, his back now turned to them. He shuddered at intervals.

Ann and Aksel Jakobsen walked past him towards the *taverna*. She willed Robert to follow but feared to glance round to check. When they had already made some distance, he started from his reverie and moved in their direction. Like a reluctant bulldog on a leash.

It was an uneasy gathering. The stranger talked of commonplace matters, nothing more of himself or his business in Italy. Politely he enquired about Ann, her life, her plans. He seemed interested.

'I am leaving shortly to see Caroline – my mother.' She corrected herself hurriedly, she was off her guard today, far too much had happened. 'She is ill in Paris and I must go to attend her.'

'Your father is dead then?' he said.

'Indeed. Sadly I did not know him. He died before I was born.'

In all the way back, Robert ignored the new acquaintance who had paid for their easier journey home.

When they landed on the *fondamenta* by Sant'Eufemia, he immediately walked off and was enclosed by the dark. Ann was left to make thanks and farewells.

In other times she would have asked this strange, forbearing man about the possible earlier encounters. He'd not responded when she mentioned the Palazzo Grimani. Perhaps she had after all been wrong. More likely, she'd been less memorable to him than he to her. She had little energy left to interrogate coincidence.

She doubted she would see him again: he would surely never seek them out after such a display of craziness and discourtesy as Robert had made. Also, she planned to leave for Paris so soon. They were birds of passage, people passing through and on.

When she reached their apartment, she found Robert stretched out snoring on the floor. Disgust and envy flowed over her in equal measure. She had not slept properly in weeks and here was this body that sat so heavily on her mind lying prone, unconscious. Her eyes took in the scene: evidently he had stumbled against the door which had opened with his force; then he'd crashed on to a chair, now pushed against the table, slipped, fallen – and slept where he fell.

The open mouth was a cavern stretching down towards the stomach, the lower lip pendulous, quivering slightly with the breath. She could step on that face. But it would not give in to her step. She had no weight for it. It would rise up and knock her down. Then it would mock her as the victim she continued to be.

22

It was the time of leisure, of idleness, of heat. No Venetian who could afford to leave for the mountains was still in residence.

But, strangely, Aksel Jakobsen remained on the island. Perhaps he didn't possess quite the means that his hiring of the boat from Padua had indicated. Or perhaps his leanness made the heat less troublesome to him than it was to more ample persons.

Now that she knew who he was and had learned a little of him he seemed to have come out of the shadows. While she waited for her passes and passports and went about her business, she saw him often and acknowledged his presence with a greeting, rarely more, at several places: in San Marco by the basilica, by the shipyards near the Arsenale, and by the few open fish stalls of the Rialto; she spied him looking at prints and copies of paintings in a window in Sant'Anzolo.

On two occasions she even found him staring at clam fishers out in the lagoon near their apartment. She was afraid to invite him in for a glass of wine or water for fear of Robert's brooding presence; it could be felt even through the study door. Out of politeness, however, she pointed at their rooms. Aksel Jakobsen remarked that there, up so many flights of steps, they must have a good view and some breeze. She lamented they had neither.

On the second occasion near the apartment he'd been useful. She'd been arguing with Signora Scorzeri by the canal, promising yet again to begin paying arrears of rent from some imagined store. Signor James expected a bank draft very shortly, she had lied – or so she supposed since she saw no evidence that Robert had arranged for money to be dispatched – how on earth had he expected to live? She was not good at such blatant deceiving and Signora Scorzeri was letting her anger mount. Then up walked Aksel Jakobsen. His presence curbed the *padrona*'s speech: she was forced to restrain her frustration as she acknowledged the gentleman and let herself be introduced.

He appeared more prosperous than her scruffy tenants; perhaps he might be appealed to in future if he really were their friend. Or he might want rooms himself. He must be looking for something, for why else be staring across the water at this shabby end of the islands?

Summer turned into *Ferragosto*, the Assumption of the sinless soul and uncorrupted body of the Blessed Virgin, rising direct to heaven. Napoleon had decreed the Virgin be demoted, that her day be changed to celebrate Saint Napoleon instead. Reasonable enough: the Lord had raised him up in troubled times; as such he demanded reverence. But Napoleon had lost his day and the Virgin was reinstated.

Unexpectedly, Beatrice had sent word to Ann that she and her mother had returned to their palazzo just for a short time; she didn't explain why. She would welcome a lesson with the Signora, welcome it very much. It was hard for Ann to think of parsing the language of 'The Giaour' at this time but the cool interior of the Palazzo Savelli would ease her head: it now ached almost continuously. To get away from the apartment where the silence between her and Robert was oppressive or interrupted by a snarl when they were forced to meet would be something.

Her passport, she now knew, needed signing by an official who'd left the heat of Venice for the cooler foothills of the Alps. There was nothing to do but wait. She'd written back to the address in Paris to say that she would come as soon as she could. Caroline had so often been dying she doubted it was the emergency the 'Friend' implied, but she would hurry.

Most often now Robert was in his study sleeping on his chair or moving around nervously. Once she'd said it would be better if he came to bed. But he did not. Best not contemplate the life they'd lead when she returned to Italy. No point in saying 'if'. To think of the future was to enter a desert at night.

So the visit to Beatrice was an oasis. She freshened herself as best she could in the morning's oppressive heat. She'd hired a girl to bring up water and was paying her from her small hoard, but she was not always on hand. Signora Scorzeri was unwilling to do anything extra for them now. When the girl was absent and the boy reluctant – she'd always paid him promptly but perhaps Robert had berated him for delivering the letter from the post office – Ann had to carry up water herself; the exertion made the sweat run down her body. In such circumstances it was difficult to make oneself truly clean.

Their rooms had high beamed ceilings but heat lingered throughout and insects swarmed in through the open windows when she tried to lure in a little breeze by flinging wide the shutters. There was usually a wind blowing on the island but it hardly penetrated their apartment even on these occasions. When the wind strengthened it was a hot dusty one that brought no coolness.

Sometimes the heat was interrupted by great electric storms that washed over everything. But when the rain and wind and lightning had swept through, the oppressive heat settled back again and a smell of broiling earth and sludgy water rose into the air. It was rumoured that the Patriarch of Venice was able to allay storms by pouring holy water on to the waves. But he was out of town; like most of the officials, civil and clerical, he too disliked the hot months and spent them in the mountains.

She could only do her best. Having washed as well as possible, she changed into clean clothes, wiped the sweat off her face once more, and pinched her cheeks to try to hide the strain and pallor. She hoped she didn't look as dreadful as she felt. There was little point in saying goodbye to Robert. He would stay in or go out in his own particular way. If he'd felt it unnecessary to mention his visits to the palazzo, she could emulate him.

She went down the stairs and let herself out of the building. She passed Signora Scorzeri, who was just leaving to see relatives with her pretty grandchild Rosa and a bunch of flowers in her arms. She huffed when she saw Ann but, with the child in her hand and her festive intent, it was not the moment to raise again the matter of unpaid rent.

Ann was glad she had a reason to cross the canal. The struggle presented by travel in Venice along the liquid roads was all that could momentarily dampen her uneasy mind. The difficulties of life and the heat, with the expectation of more of both, were, she felt, all that stood between her and accepted despair.

At the Palazzo Savelli she was let in by the black-clad servant, more silent than ever, her face tight against any greeting beyond the obligatory *prego*. Even that was just a mutter. The footman and the other servants were nowhere to be seen; perhaps some had remained in Friuli. The house was unusually still, chilled despite the mounting heat outside. Ann luxuriated in the sudden coolness. She felt the sweat between her breasts begin to evaporate. It was a welcome change.

Feeling a little more comfortable but aware that she might none the less appear more hot and bothered than she wished, she walked slowly through the cavernous hall and towards the stairs that rose to the room where she and Beatrice usually delighted to take their lessons. She was surprised and a little hurt that the girl didn't come out to greet her. She'd made a special effort to travel from La Giudecca in a time of holiday and on a day that promised at its meridian to be as sultry as any they'd suffered.

Then Beatrice burst through the opposite door from the room where the Contessa usually presided over the card or tea-table. She ran down the marble steps and along the hall towards Ann, holding up her skirt, yet nearly tripping in her haste. As she came close, Ann saw that her face was swollen and blotched by crying, her dress disordered.

'My dear Beatrice, what – ?' Ann began. The girl stopped her by coming up and whispering in her ear, 'Oh, Signora, I cannot after all have lesson today. Excuse, excuse.'

'Of course,' said Ann, 'of course, do not worry. But what has happened?'

Beatrice moved away slightly but went on whispering, now in a high tone that made her words quite audible beyond themselves if anyone had been by to listen. 'There has been a terrible thing. Francesco has hit our mother.' She added quickly, 'It was his sickness, not Francesco, who did it. But Mama is distraught.'

She took Ann's arm and held it tightly, 'I can tell nobody else but you – for I know that you will understand. Your husband, Signora, and my brother. It is no good.'

The girl looked at her with such appeal it lessened the pain of what she said. She, Ann, would understand: Beatrice and she both knew why it was no good . . .

Beatrice squeezed, then lightly embraced her. She slipped back up the stairs and into the room, leaving Ann alone.

She would like to have helped this girl for whom she'd come to feel so much affection, but there was nothing she could do. She had no solution to provide and no energy to use for anyone beyond herself. She was as helpless in the palazzo as in the depressing apartment on La Giudecca.

She turned round and walked slowly back along the hall towards the door. She was let out silently by the servant who'd so recently let her in. At first the woman kept her eyes fixed downwards, then, as Ann moved outside and on to the stone steps, caught her eye and gave her a sad, toothless smile.

She returned to the apartment, her mind brimful of dread. It was a dread so obvious, so palpable that anyone on the boat or *calli* on her route back could have seen and smelled it. Fortunately so few people were out in this heat; the rest kept themselves for the night. Her dread enveloped her as she dragged her weary feet upstairs.

By now it was the hottest time of the day. Few with pale skins and a memory of cold and mist could bear it easily. She knew how provocative it must be for Robert, the heat and his choler agitating each other. She knew all this so well.

Had she left him alone he might have gone on melting through these sultry days, getting thinner, more listless but disintegrating slowly – like a large vegetable growing over-ripe, mottled and loose, finally decaying.

But she didn't leave him to go on his own way, to his own particular destruction. She simply could not bear it.

So, instead of letting well – and bad – alone, she went into his study, not waiting for an answer when, after several small, then increasingly louder knocks, no answer came. Not accepting that the lack of response was a blank and utter rejection of her.

She knew that what he'd recently written was nonsense – she'd read those crumpled pages with their repetitive inanities. Yet on *this* day she went right up to him, leaned over his shoulder and reached for one of the leaves he'd pushed aside. At that moment he was making no pretence to write.

She meant to look and soothe. So she said to herself. She meant to touch his shoulder and stroke the back of his head where the hair was too long and a little matted with sweat. She might have done all this, but did none of it.

Instead she put her hand on his arm as she leaned forward to his desk.

How could he want this, any of it, what she was doing or had planned to do? Want it from any woman? How could he respond? Violence was all he had, all that was left of his power. He was no vegetable rotting beyond movement, he never would be. What he did on this and on any occasion was reactive, intuitive and inevitable.

It was afternoon when she limped down the many steps, dragging the palm of her hand against the uneven wall. The young Frenchmen had unexpectedly returned to claim their rooms but they were out now for she'd heard them earlier tramping down the stairs, laughing together as usual. So the building was empty. She could have no fear of being accosted by Signora Scorzeri.

She had to be outside, to gulp the heavy air. A *temporale*, a giant storm, was about to break through the oppression, to counter a tension that made the whole sky and earth and water into one large, complicated knot of anger.

Let it burst and rain down water and stones and pitch to wet them all and wipe out this filth and horror.

Drama or melodrama? Did her predicament translate too easily into hackneyed words? She'd once thought Sarah naive to associate her stories with her life. But the reverse?

She stood looking towards the pictured Venice. Not her Venice.

Against the odds she'd become fond of it, the tawdry glamour, its gaiety, its insouciance about its failure of nerve. An Englishman would have cringed for years. Venetians never did.

She liked the decaying buildings, their roots deep in the slime that was kinder than water to the wooden stakes. She liked the great high decorated palazzi – called palaces by the awestruck English though in reality nothing more than big terraced houses quaintly painted. She approved the laconic acceptance of the secular in the religious, the churches adorned with figures of those who'd paid for them as often as the saints they honoured. All wonderful.

She wished she'd been born of this city, been one of the gay painted people who did as they pleased and were pleased with what they did. They kept the outside embroidered with ceremony and tact and exclusion. For her it would never be homey, homely, never home. With all her heart she wished it could have been.

'It's a charnel house,' Robert had said. He dismissed it with a theatrical wave.

'There are no more dead here than anywhere else.'

'There's a whole damned island of them. They don't all fit in there, Signor Balbi said so. Corpses float about in their own boats or are tipped out in the lagoon. Look down, you'll see skulls through the water. It's a place with no future.'

'A great past,' she'd said, mistress of banality as she was.

'A past with no future is nothing.'

She waited for his words to leave her mind as she struggled

through the rising wind, stumbling while she held tight to the scarf she'd tied round her head to cover her face and its darkening bruises.

The voice subsided but she couldn't rid herself of one special word: you will not *muzzle* me. You will not. She would not. No, indeed. She would not try. Dangerous dogs that have tasted human blood are greedy for more.

She had no idea how long she stayed out. The great wind huffed and puffed and promised a deluge, delivered lightning, but in the end paused, hurling only a few large drops on to the dust. She felt the storm still rumbling and lurking nearby but, for the moment, it hid. The stinking smell that had come with the clammy weather, the careless supervising of intricate canals and crumbling outlets, rose up between the buildings and along the waterways. It infiltrated every sack and pocket of unused air in the city. The sewer of the mind sent its filth through the body but was no match for this enveloping and clambering stench.

She couldn't return, not yet. She could cross the Canal again – perhaps to check if her passport had been signed. She knew the answer. But she would go none the less, for where else was there? She needed a purpose.

As she limped down behind San Zaccaria through the delta of narrow *calli*, in the distance she spied a man she was sure was Giancarlo Scrittori, in black mantle. She'd thought he too was out of the city. She must avoid him; he shouldn't see her like this. She could hardly speak to him through a muslin scarf and he'd know she was holding her ribs. She kept her eyes on him, hoping he would soon move away from her path.

But instead he was joined by another, shorter, fair-haired man. He embraced Giancarlo. The Italians were more tactile than the English, less bashful about endearments between men. But this embrace was something different, longer, more intense. She was glad she'd not been recognised. She could savour her envy alone. Then they pulled apart as they were briefly joined by another man. She saw only his back. He was tall, familiar perhaps – or was she eliding differences in her damaged state? Was everyone except herself and Robert becoming images of each other?

She waited and at last all three moved off, the two shorter men arm-in-arm.

She went on her way, found the consular office closed as she'd expected. Then she loitered where she could before turning back towards the water and the crossing. She must return to the apartment – she had to, this was her life and her cross. The walking had made her mind a little less numb and she was thinking that, if she were not to kill herself or him, they must somehow live without this dreadful conflict.

That she hated him she knew perfectly well. It made no difference.

Best to stay with practicalities. Surely it would be only a few more days before she had her papers. If she didn't find more lodgings in another town before she left, perhaps Robert could simply go somewhere cheaper in Venice. He could ask Signor Balbi, who'd seemed to enjoy his friendship – though it was some time since Robert had mentioned him. But he was hardly speaking to her. Perhaps something out by the Arsenale or Sant'Elena might be found. It was said to be less costly around there. She didn't know how he would pay Signora Scorzeri but . . .

On her mind whizzed, countering hopelessness with hopeless plans, her eyes swelling black and purple underneath the muslin scarf. She even thought she might return with money, for in Paris she could reach Dean & Munday more easily, perhaps send them *Isabella; or, the Secrets of the Convent* which she could finish on the journey at stops on the way.

Yet all the while she could see no future, just a black tunnel which she would enter.

23

It was evening. She'd been out from after midday until dusk. She'd had no sleep the night before and little rest today. She'd sat for a while on the step of a humped bridge with no railings like a peasant woman come to town to sell her country wares, suddenly fatigued, impeding the way of more elegant walkers who nudged and almost kicked her as they passed.

Her body ached all over. Not only the damage but the pain of shrinking, of shame. She was wearing away, her ribs sticking out uncomfortably. There was a flatness, almost concave quality, to a belly where she'd once been perhaps plump, if not full. She knew the thinness for what it was – as a woman knew her state when in the first stages of pregnancy her body filled out just a little, but not enough for others to see or pry. A mind could do this. A mind impaired by lack of sleep.

She had to go back, she said to herself again. If she stayed out she would need to eat and she had little money with her. If she'd had more, she could perhaps stay a night in an inn and try to think. Maybe order a gondola to take her out on the lagoon and let her sit there. Or go to the Lido and . . . But for any move, anything at all, she needed to go back for money, for some things. She feared what she would see when she returned. But what worse could happen? What else *could* happen?

Well, she knew exactly. He could conclude the farce.

She crept in. She would get her money from the bag under the bed, then she would do what she would do – whatever it was.

As she mounted painfully to the top, she heard the Frenchmen going out of their apartment. They must have returned while she was out. They were speaking quietly and stifling laughs as they went down the steps and opened the outside door. She didn't hear it bang after them. Perhaps they were careless, as young men could be.

She reached the apartment and opened the door, leaving it ajar to let in some air. In the sitting room silence engulfed her.

There was no snoring from the bedroom or the little study, so Robert was not asleep; no moving, no breaking of things, no throwing of crockery or wooden bowls or books, nothing to suggest that other objects within the world beyond her body could staunch his anger. Nothing.

He could not be here. Her heart jumped. She could have a few minutes alone, perhaps hours. She could work out what to do in peace. And when he returned she would be gone or she would fake sleep and he would leave her be.

As her mind settled, she noted signs of him in the sitting room despite his absence. A chair was tottering against another as if he'd pushed it roughly out of his way while he moved from his study. He must have gone out and still not be back. But his Swiss gold watch lay on the table beside some breadcrumbs and a hungry procession of ants. His winter greatcoat, so little needed these broiling months, was on the floor. There'd never been anywhere to hang it properly, so there was nothing strange in that. She picked it up automatically, righted the chair and draped the coat over its back. She looked at the watch again. Why was it there?

The door of the study was closed and no light came through the crack. She could peep through as she often did but she would not invade his space. As she determined this, her fury rose. Was she of so very little account, so very contemptible that she didn't even dare to touch the man, to press open his door?

Through the crack she could see nothing. A new unpleasant smell, beyond unemptied chamber pots, assaulted her nose.

She pushed tentatively at the door and looked in.

He was hanging there with the girdle from his morning gown tied round the high ceiling beam. The face was towards her. It was mottled red, the tongue turned some terrible colour and sticking out. There was blood, dark blood, on the hands and on his shirt. The expression exaggerated what she'd seen before, the grimace, the devil, her devil. The breeches dirty.

On the floor by some broken quills, scattered as if thrown down rather than falling, she saw the knife they used for chopping fruit when they ate in their sitting room. It was covered in blood. She moved towards it, picked it up, looked at it briefly, unseeing, then brushed it against her light dress so that it was stained by the darkening blood. The knife was still dirty.

She laid it back down on the floor. Her hands were sticky. She was aware but did nothing to clean them. There was nothing clean on which to clean them.

Her eyes roamed away from the hanging thing but could not fix. Her throat was filled with phlegm. She squeezed it to stop herself from vomiting. She blinked several times. She was so very tired. Was this a nightmare? Would she wake?

Then her eyes found the papers on the floor, an oddly limp pile, some scattered, one caught on the high-backed chair, itself tumbled over. She picked up one sheet from the floor and looked at it. There was writing on it. It had been written by the living hand, the one that still kept its blood inside.

She stared at the words. Robert had written his name over and over again in capitals.

Her name, her name, must be there. It must be. Was she not part of him? But she looked down the page and on the other scattered sheets on the floor, now desperately. She was not there.

He has done this thing to get away from me, she said aloud. From me.

Her eyes swivelled to the stack of limp papers which she assumed had formed his book, his work, what he had written before the sun seemed to sear his brain and stop the flow. They were wet. That's why they looked limp. A smell rose from them and assaulted her nose. She became aware of it. He had pissed on the pages.

He had stood there drunk on wine perhaps or fuddled with laudanum or whatever he had picked up in Venice to take him out of his right mind. Yes, she could see it. He had fumbled with the buttons on his breeches. Then he had pissed on his life's labour. She could as well hear the splash.

She went back into the sitting room. The door to the apartment was still open. She left it so and sat down.

A Voyage Home

24

Robert was there. But not there. Present as he always was, bony but bulbous, now filthy, obscene, overpowering, powerless. Dripping and trickling.

She felt no conscious shock though her cheeks were wet as well as red and bruised.

She did not cut him down. She could not. Outside, the summer storm was rising again. That was why it was so very hot, so oppressive. It was about to thunder. This time it would rain as well.

Then Aksel Jakobsen was there.

'I was passing,' he said.

How could he be?

'I saw Signor James on the *fondamenta* not long ago. He was walking strangely. He seemed giddy, I thought he would fall into the canal, so I followed a little. Then I went off and returned, perhaps to be of help. I saw you enter. You screamed.'

'I have not screamed. It's the wind outside, a storm is coming back.'

She was speaking lucidly. She could hear herself at a distance. So how had she not heard a scream, if there'd been one?

'His wrists are slashed as well and his breast, there's blood. He must have tried other ways. Look, the kitchen knife on the floor. He bungled it, he failed. He did too much. He always does too much . . .' She was shaking as she babbled. The door to the study was ajar. Anyone could see inside.

'Be quiet please,' said Aksel Jakobsen.

She could understand neither this man's words nor his tone.

'Signora Scorzeri, she's out now but she will return. She comes back late from visiting her sister, with Rosa. She will think I did it or helped him do it. She will. I will be the murderess. She has heard things. She will know.' Her teeth rattled, as if they were someone else's, loud and metallic.

'Know what, Ann?' Aksel Jakobsen asked. She heard him, heard him use her Christian name, so familiar, as if they were old friends or kin. But they were neither.

What was happening? What was he doing in the room?

'Know it was I. She will know. She will think we quarrelled, then I stabbed him and strung him up to make it look different. She will think so.'

'But you did not. Remember it. Whatever Robert James believed, thinking and doing are distinct. You did not do this. You are too weak.'

Again this naming. What was happening? What was she hearing? Why was this man so familiar with her?

Neither of them moved to cut the body down, to clear up the mess, to staunch the smell, to move the knife.

How did Aksel Jakobsen know what had happened? How did she? She looked back into the sitting room and saw Robert's gold watch still on the table. He'd taken it off to make the cuts on his wrist after he'd tried to stab himself. She could see his actions. She put her hand to her mouth to stop a cry.

'You are right. It looks bad for you. Venetians love a scandal. You are a foreign woman, both of you connected with the Savelli. They are not popular with the Austrians. There'd be no appeal to passion or provocation. The *bocche del Leone* are abolished but there are other ways.'

There were no real flowing tears despite wetness on her cheeks. Why, when they were right and proper, were there no tears? How could it be?

'What shall I do?'

Dazed, she looked at Aksel Jakobsen. He was much taller than she was. She registered mainly that fact. Also older.

'Leave,' he said, 'leave now.'

'I was going to . . . I had prepared.'

'I know. Your mother.' He paused only momentarily. 'Come, I will accompany you. It is time I left this town. I must return home. It does not suit here.'

'You? Why?'

'A whim,' he said. 'Come now.'

'But people will ask after him. He had a friend, Signor Balbi, a traveller, even the Count Savelli . . .'

'Nobody will miss him at once or care for long, except perhaps the Jews in the ghetto who lent him money.'

Too much to take in.

Aksel Jakobsen went on, allowing no time for response, 'The Savelli will not grieve. The Contessa will be relieved. Only the authorities matter. Signor Scrittori will try to take care of them. He helps the Savelli. He is, I think, your supporter. He has influence with the foreigners. Come.'

She was too dazed for surprise. How did he know Giancarlo Scrittori, any of her life? Debts to Jews? Still, she registered that he mentioned no other woman. How pitiable . . . But no time for further thought.

The body was still – not swinging, just dripping its horrid waste, its appalling filth.

She shook her head. It hurt. But the action disturbed her mounting fear. 'We must take him down, we must . . .'

She wouldn't look at the face, it would be red, yellow, white, dreadful. She'd imagined it many times, but never quite this – many times dead, but not ghastly. 'Dead' had just been a word.

'There's no time.'

'I can't go.'

'You can.' He spoke urgently or roughly, she couldn't judge. 'Leave him. It will be some proof to those who cut him down.'

He said 'him'. But there was no 'him', just 'it', 'it'.

She looked below the face in the dim light. Something, a ray from the half-shuttered window, shone on the knots. 'There are so many knots in the cord he tied. Why so many?'

Aksel Jakobsen allowed no irritation in his voice. 'It pushes the head forward to make it snap. But the drop was not enough for any snap. The neck could not break. By then he was dying.'

While he spoke he was collecting together the clothes he thought useful from the sitting room and the bedchamber, a worn jacket of indeterminate colour, a faded blue scarf, a thin patterned shift, but not the heavy shawl he saw lying on the floor sodden with waste that had seeped from the body.

'Get your bag, your things, papers. Anything. Quick. And wipe your hands.'

He had become so thin. Why the blood, why so much blood? Did he want the knife to work? Had it almost worked? That old blunt knife. Did he want her to be blamed? Was she so important to him after all? A kindness to implicate her or a final cruelty?

Mechanically, she walked to the bedchamber, knelt down and dragged a bundle from under the bed. The few things she'd planned to take to Paris. Then she fished out her hemp bag from further back. It held the little money she'd hoarded.

As she tugged at the bag, some of her writings tumbled out. 'Isabella approached the horror with pale trembling fingers,' she couldn't avoid seeing. She tried to look away, but it was painful to swivel her eyes.

She crumpled the papers with the clothes and stuffed them into the hemp bag along with the money. She handed it to Aksel Jakobsen, who put in what he'd collected. He'd not said a word about her bruised face, though the muslin scarf had slipped.

She must go back into the study. She must force herself. She had to get one of the old passports which might still be with Robert in his writing desk. As she entered, again she registered the fallen high-backed chair. He had sat in it to write, using her old shawl as cushion. Or rather he had sat, got up, sat, then stood on it.

'The chair fell over. Maybe he did not intend to succeed. It was just a message. Maybe for me.'

'He would have kicked it,' said Aksel Jakobsen, who'd stepped into the room behind her. 'He need not have kicked. Hurry and be quiet please. Or it will be too late.'

'The smell. Why so . . .?'

'Of course there is smell, look at his breeches.'

Tears welled up. 'He would have hated this. He would not have wanted . . .'

Or did he know?

'The wrists and breast failed, the hanging worked in the end. So he died in filth, but it would not have been quick,' said Aksel Jakobsen. He had said this before. She heard no expression in his level voice, only the words so clear, so measured, so cruel. 'Who does not die so? I said, hurry!'

'My papers, a passport.' But she could not approach the desk.

Aksel Jakobsen saw her flinch and hold back. Gently he guided her arm towards the desk. She need not touch the body. 'You must. Any papers, even old ones, might be useful.'

Her hands trembled as she fumbled with the drawer. It was not locked but was hard to open. He saw what she was about and pulled it out for her. It stuck halfway but it was enough. She grabbed the old documents. Some unstamped were in her maiden name, some stamped in her 'married', all false to the woman she now was.

She saw one underneath: in the name of Peter O'Neil. It stirred a vague memory. It had been carried here and must have been used somewhere or intended for use. This was no time to look further at what country it was for or where it might have served.

Aksel Jakobsen glanced at it. But Robert's past life could have no meaning for him.

He held open her bag as she stuffed into it all the documents that related to her. Robert's canvas satchel lay nearby. It would have been more sensible to take it since it was roomier. But that was impossible. She left the drawer as it was, half open. Then she skirted the body again and went back into the sitting room. She wiped her hands on a cloth sagging from the table. She grabbed the gold watch and pushed it down the side of her bag.

With no further look at the body, the rooms or their trunks, she followed Aksel Jakobsen through the door, out of the apartment and down the uneven, always damp stairs. Signora Scorzeri and little Rosa were still away visiting, the happy Frenchmen were out. Somewhere in this or the next building she heard a girl lulling a whimpering baby.

Aksel Jakobsen propelled her over the wooden bridges towards Le Zitelle. Her ribs ached when she had to go fast. She'd almost forgotten the look of her ravaged face. Of course it hurt. But her body had been, for these past minutes, quite quiet. Clouds were scudding across the sky.

'Wait,' he said as he went inside a scabbed, once yellow building behind the church. 'Stay there.' He handed her the hemp bag. 'Hold it over your stained clothes.'

She stood and watched the gulls behind a boat spilling rubbish.

Aksel Jakobsen returned with his own stout leather bag and a cloak, though there was no need of such a garment in these sweltering days. He also had a heavy tarpaulin, more useful since surely soon the wind would bring the rain so long promised. It would be a torrent. How was he ready so speedily? Did he know what would happen?

A question flashed through her mind – attached to no purpose or consequence: had he been there when it happened? Had he played a part? Had he . . .? Her mind raced wildly. What had this man to do with it all? If nothing, how did he know she was not guilty? How had she become 'Ann'? The naming had been inadvertent, she was sure. It was unusual to use a Christian name so easily, especially between a man and a woman. What was he to her?

There was no time to untangle the threads. A numbness was invading her thoughts even as they dashed along. Her body, once quiet, was now desperate to shout while she kept her mouth tight shut.

She concentrated on her legs, making them move, further and further away from the apartment with its ghastly tenant.

That was all Aksel Jakobsen demanded of her. She must do what he wanted. He was in control and should be. She had no need to tell him of her still painful ribs or any other ailment. She put one finger to her face and felt the bulges under her eyes. Perhaps they would never settle. She would always address the world with bruises. And with the bloodstain on her hands.

'We will go to the *squero* in San Trovaso. There are men there who hire fast boats and ask no questions. We cannot use gondoliers. We must hurry. Hold your bag higher.'

They were rowed away by boatmen who'd been lolling on the *fondamenta* in the twilight eager to avoid passengers until they saw what Aksel Jakobsen was offering. On the way, without especially looking at her, he whispered, 'I pass as Signor Stamer, Aksel Stamer. That is my name. Remember it.'

They found the place in San Trovaso and the men who asked no questions and were paid handsomely for their silence. For a special price they would even try to ride the storm at night. It had not yet come in its full force.

They would take their passengers to Mestre or if possible to one of the swampy hamlets further south that served Venice. Aksel Stamer knew he could hire a carriage there. It was best to avoid places where people were well fed and curious.

'Put the scarf round your head, cover your face.'

Why? she wondered. To help the bruises and the swelling – or because the sight irritated him. Or was it to prevent her being recognised – by herself or with him? But there could be no hue and cry yet. It was impossible. And it was dark or almost so. A single fisherman slouched over a rod on a small wooden jetty. He did not look up as the boat set off.

She wrapped the scarf round her face and head leaving enough of her eyes free to see, then held it tightly at her neck. She dug her nails into the palms of her hands and bit her lip to divert attention from the scenes passing through her head. But they remained as clear as ever, far clearer than anything her eyes could see outside. Her now bulky hemp bag was slung round her like a peasant's bundle, masking the stain on her clothes.

'They will expect us to go north at once. So we are going across and down. We will take passage as soon as we can and leave Italy.'

'They? You mean they will come after me, look for me especially?'

'Of course. They love entertainment in Venice.'

They caught the high water and went towards the mainland on a tide, two men rowing. Salt water splashed her eyes though she sat in the cabin. The cheap ring on her hand had always been loose. She pulled it off now, leaned painfully from the cabin and threw it into the water.

They arrived in Mestre just as the storm struck, confusing water, land and sky. They could go no further south. It was no matter, for it was now dark. Beating rain sent people scurrying into doorways. Even the water rats abandoned a dead dog for their damp holes.

It was immense, overpowering. Ann and Aksel Stamer huddled together under his tarpaulin beneath the overhanging roof of an inn, closed like most places against the summer weather of stagnant heat and violent tempests.

When it was over they shook themselves, scattering droplets of water. Steam rose from them as heat mounted again, even at night, and dried their clothes. The bloodstain was far less obtrusive now. Their bags had escaped the worst.

'We will hire a carriage at once. After that we will travel more cheaply with others. But it is well to get out of the Veneto without delay.'

Through the rest of the night he made arrangements and before dawn broke they were on their way. The earth was drying: Ann smelled the unaccustomed dust after so long surrounded by water.

In late evening their carriage put them down in a small inland town with a tower and turreted walls covered with ivy. She never heard the name. There was an open theatre where some strolling players were preparing to perform. In the dark she heard singing across the square from the inn where they'd taken a room.

In the early hours of the morning, another great storm arrived in lightning and thunder but no rain. She saw the towers against the white flash. She mentioned the players to Aksel Stamer, who she saw had been out in the town. He nodded but said nothing.

As they travelled onwards in carriages and carts, all arranged by Aksel Stamer, he was almost silent, as if he'd said all he needed to say just once at the start of their strange journey. So silent that she began to fear. She asked questions to try to make him respond, but she got almost nothing back.

'We go south towards Naples and across the water. No one will think of that route.'

She expected him to suggest a resting place, for she was tired, but he did not. 'If we can travel at night we should do so. You can sleep in snatches? You can do that?'

He didn't ask how she fared, how she managed to rush and scurry while being so pained in body and mind.

After one long stretch he looked at her. 'Make some changes. It is best,' he said.

He handed her a bundle of things he must have acquired somewhere, as she slept perhaps, but she didn't remember a time when this could have happened. Perhaps in the little town where they'd had the first comfortable night? He was all surprises.

'These should help.'

The bundle contained loose trousers, a long linen smock, a hat with wide floppy brim.

Two days on and he was holding a sheet of news. He glanced over it at her. 'Yes, they may be looking,' he said. 'But we will soon be out of Austrian jurisdiction. I doubt there will be such efficiency then.'

'What does it say, let me see.' He didn't reply but simply folded the sheet and put it in his pocket, then closed his eyes. 'There are always fires in Venice,' he said.

Why should she not see it? She wanted to know only what they'd done with the body, what they'd done with Him. But she hesitated to address those shut eyes or interrupt a mood meant to close her out. She must be obedient. Could they really be looking for her? Or . . .? She stopped herself.

'We take a boat to the island of Sardinia when we reach the western coast. From there to France.'

He had spoken to her. She was grateful. Too grateful. Silences pressed on her.

'My money will be nearly gone,' she protested. 'I have nothing for the passage.'

'Of course. It is gone. No matter.'

'I had enough to get to see my mother. I had saved it from teaching Signorina Savelli. I will get more when I reach Paris. I can pay you back. I have nearly finished some work and can send it to a bookseller.'

She kept talking, giving needless information in the hope that she'd interest him, get him to respond, see her as what she had been, a writer of tuppenny trash yes, but a writer and a woman, a person, a personality. After all, he'd engaged her in conversation once in Padua when she'd not asked for it. He'd seemed to want to know of her and her life. Why not now?

'I had been going to my mother who is dying,' she said. He knew that already. She knew he knew. That is where they'd begun.

'Oh yes,' he replied, 'your mother, yes, you called her Caroline.'

Why did he remember her name? She'd used it in error when they spoke in Padua. Then she'd corrected herself. Why retain such a detail?

It had been a shock that he'd addressed her as Ann – although now he hardly ever used a name at all – perhaps a precaution? – but to mention her mother like this was strange. Or did he simply know no other name for a woman he could have no real interest in?

Was he concerned with names? Although he'd urged her to bring her papers, he'd not wanted them on the journey when she offered them; none the less, she saw him looking at them when she took them from her bag to pull out her scarf. He seemed neither interested nor quite indifferent. What was he doing with her? Why was he taking this tortuous way back to London to help her when he himself was not in danger?

He'd said Denmark once. Was that really where he was from? Why did he not speak and tell her everything?

'Nonsense,' he said when she repeated her offer. 'There will be no need to pay me back.'

As she thought or rather whizzed fragmented thoughts round her head in those moments before snatched sleep, she became more and more convinced that, however bizarre the idea, Aksel Stamer must know her mother. He'd not talked at all about Robert James, about the gruesome death that sat constantly in her mind. He'd asked nothing about him, nothing at all. This vibrant wonderful man had just become for him a body.

She was suddenly furious. How dare he be so careless, so unaware of what had gone out of the world?

What had? She hardly knew herself.

But her mother? Who could be interested in Caroline? Except for the marvellous Gilbert. That was years ago when Aksel Stamer must have been just a youth. Could he have known Gilbert – though no one had spoken of him, unless she'd said something? She couldn't now recollect. Might his weird silence be bitterness, disappointment, for something, someone lost? But no. He, they, should be thinking of Robert. Robert.

Yet she knew in some shifting corner of her head that this marvellous, this tortured soul was fading just a little into a swinging lump. But it had not swung; it had been inert when she saw it. She was imagining it, imagining him swinging and twisting through the air, still alive and struggling. Not alive, though, dead.

She held on tight to all the Roberts. For the first time in so many years they had the potential to make her laugh long and loudly with a most careless joy.

25

Aksel Stamer decided the route they would travel and the means. He chose out-of-the-way paths. Sometimes these required a guide to negotiate, so faint were the tracks. At times he hired carriages for them both, at others he put them in uncomfortable open wagons – a more elegant traveller would have dismissed them as farm carts.

So demanding was the way that there was no time, no opportunity to talk of what had happened. Their business was to be unobserved. They must travel the most direct but safe route and be as inconspicuous as they could.

So he said, on one of the rare moments of communication. With these aims, comfort had rather fallen by the wayside.

Sometimes he seemed on the verge of saying something more but mostly he respected her privacy and pain. For, though her bruised eyes had healed, it would take more than a few weeks of bumping on dusty pitted roads, some miles of mountain and dried-up river, to make the rest of her body sound. The mind was another matter.

She never understood the route they took or why they seemed to travel so far across such forbidding terrain, but she questioned nothing. Once she did look her surprise as they turned on to yet another winding road off the main highway. They had to cross this stretch of country, he said, because on the other side of these mountains was a port with boats to Sardinia. Perhaps he'd seen something in a newspaper, perhaps someone had mentioned an incident in Venice and he'd added precautions. Or was it simply because she lacked correct papers? As he did surely, for he'd left on impulse. Hadn't he?

'It is an empty island,' he said. 'From it we can travel with more impunity to France. Then we will have nothing more to fear except importunate officials.'

She was still too dazed to notice much but she registered that he said 'we'.

After a pause he elaborated. He knew this because he had been to Sardinia and down through France already. He gave no further information.

For now they had to go through the lands of Tuscany and part of the Papal States, skirting those places and towns known to care especially about documents. The avoidance made for very rocky travelling.

When they learned that brigands lurked in the steeper, more menacing parts of the Apennines, Aksel Stamer hired men with guns to attend them on their way. They had no boxes for robbers to pilfer and no air of prosperity but it was best not to take chances and render themselves vulnerable, he said.

She found to her surprise that he himself carried a gun. Had he brought it from his rooms near Le Zitelle or had he stopped somewhere to purchase it along the way, fearing particularly lawless stretches of the road? She knew she was no longer an observant traveller.

Most likely he'd bought it somewhere when they'd stopped and she had tried to sleep. Could it be for her defence if the occasion came and they were apprehended by agents of the law? But why would he do that for her? Why risk his skin for hers? Always when her still fuddled mind formed questions about the immediate past, their present and future, they settled on this single one.

But she didn't worry much. Anxiety was deadened now that the worst or – she always paused at this point – had happened. She might be captured, locked in prison, hanged or executed or whatever Italians did with wicked strangers. But, while she was with Aksel Stamer, fear seemed groundless.

What he did to facilitate their journey, their escape or rather *her* escape, he did quietly and efficiently, without consulting her. She was glad to be free of the burden of choice and grateful for his care.

She knew him no more now than she had when she'd first spoken to him in Padua, but she felt, especially in the earliest days of their travel, a kindness that gave her confidence.

Even in the height of summer the Apennines were chill at night. Mrs Radcliffe had placed the castle of Udolpho in these picturesque hills, somewhere vague but vertical and very wild. She had sent her Emily thither with the villainous Montoni for company. But, after her experiences with the Grand Canal in Venice, Ann was less eager to use Mrs Radcliffe as her guide.

Indeed, the thrills of gothic now seemed poor things beside the real life imprinted on her mind. She remembered how Sarah had wanted to connect them. The writing she'd planned to do on what now seemed – hilariously – the more sedate journey over the forbidding Alps to Paris was forgotten. She'd no invention in her, no spirit to push Isabella through her imagined trials. As far as her author was concerned, the heroine would be locked away in an Italian convent forever.

In all their time through Italy she'd not needed to produce documents. Or rather, whenever anything was required at the gates of a city they could not miss or when entering a new judicial territory, Aksel Stamer had shown the officials something that was necessary and they'd been waved on their way, not with enthusiasm or especial courtesy but with indifference. He seemed to have a sheaf of passes and papers and, so far, one always appeared to the point. Remembering the difficulties that she and Robert had encountered through the Alps and into Italy she could only admire the dexterity with which he moved them through gates and barriers.

Did he pay large bribes? She couldn't tell. He didn't have the air of a man with great resources; yet gates opened for them and they passed on. She'd no wish to pry but once she saw a little of one paper he proffered. It appeared in a strange language. At each barrier he told her to be silent.

When she did try to consider rationally what they were doing and open her mind to the journey itself, it was France that bothered her.

Surely there at least the proper papers would be necessary. Her application for a passport still sat on a desk in Venice while the official with the potent signature cooled himself in Belluno or sipped his grappa in Bassano.

It was so different from when she'd journeyed with Robert many months before. She and Aksel Stamer never stayed in the best or, after the first night, even in decent inns. Instead he chose places in the shade, hostelries and refuges not much frequented by the prosperous traveller.

She continued to dress in the smock and baggy trousers he'd told her to wear soon after they'd left Venice. In one mountain village he'd helped her to add a few other items, so that she was at least clean and free of the vermin that attacked travellers in public coaches and dirty inns. He'd cut her hair short with some ingenious scissors attached to a hunting knife. She looked at the knife. His special knife.

With her shorn head she was noticed by no one. When by chance they encountered other English travellers, she had simply to be quiet. Aksel Stamer sometimes said a few words to them but his taciturnity prevented talk beyond pleasantries, and they were always sure to be on their way before any more was needed.

In taverns they ate silently together and even slept in the same room when essential. She was always exhausted now and he was discreet. She feared nothing. Why should she? On the road sometimes she was sick and they had to stop. He held her forehead as she vomited up her bread and cheese and olives.

On La Giudecca he'd simply dashed away from her up to his lodgings to fetch his big leather case for the journey. He must have packed with magic speed or else he kept his luggage always ready. He could be on the move at once, always anticipating emergency.

It surprised her just how much he had in this capacious bag, not just for himself but for general comfort. Not only his razors – he'd shaved off his small beard but kept his moustache – his toothbrushes, Waite's powder, rose balm and personal items, but other things for use on the road. He had pieces of cloth to put over infested cushions when they stayed at particularly filthy inns, a towel that could be washed and dried and used repeatedly, a leather bottle and metal cup, even spoons and an ordinary peeling knife for when they had to buy their food at stalls and journey on.

She had made the arrangements for travel with Robert from London to Venice and had thought herself reasonably prepared. But this array of good sense and prudence rebuked her care. Robert would have been more comfortable on the journey, and she more tranquil, had she thought to augment the clothes and papers, the writing desk and books, with a little salt, some tea, a small lamp, pieces of flannel, some castor oil and bark.

If instead of fugitives fearing the law they'd been common travellers with proper documents, they could now have crossed to France directly, taking a large and stable boat. They'd have expected to arrive with a flock of other passengers ready to do business or pursue pleasure. But it was impossible.

Aksel Stamer had been clever through the Italian states – quite how she couldn't tell – and the way had always been eased by some means of money or subterfuge. But he was not a miracle worker. To enter France openly from Italy they needed more than he could give. The passports she'd loaded herself with when she and Robert had first set out had taken weeks to acquire in London – and then they'd not had the proper signatures in Paris. Even if there'd been no further fear from consequences in Venice, it would have taken many more weeks to obtain what they needed and to explain how they were where they were, if indeed it was possible at all. It was to Ann a marvel that they'd got as far with so little documentation. It would stop now surely.

Why would it be easier in Sardinia?

'Sardinia is in turmoil. So it is less efficient there. I know. But we will have to take some chances. I hope you are ready,' said Aksel Stamer. He didn't wait for an answer.

By the time they reached the coast her bruising was gone and her ribs had ceased to ache. Perhaps the movement had done them good. But her whole body held some deep-down pain. Was some essential organ damaged? She wore the baggy trousers he'd provided and her hands were ringless. No one thought her a man but no one much worried what she was. Just a nondescript sexless servant.

They boarded a sailing vessel from down the coast below Civitavecchia with undocumented men returning to Sardinia from work. It creaked on choppy water and slid sickly on the calm. Aksel Stamer looked green at times but walked up and down, to settle his stomach. She couldn't do the same. She sat huddled with their baggage as her own stomach churned, her eyes open and staring. Richard Perry shivering between two corpses on the North Sea swam against her mind. She shut him out; he led to Robert.

They landed on a desolate stretch of land, a place where no passes were demanded and no one touted for business from gullible strangers.

The other passengers shouldered their bundles and, paying them no attention, vanished into the scrubby interior. Aksel Stamer looked perturbed. It was the first time she'd noticed anxiety in him. Clearly he'd thought that something or somebody would have waited there.

'We will have to walk, I am afraid, just a little way. You will need to be strong and brave.' He looked at her but she could not interpret his expression – dubious, kindly? He showed no irritation.

She'd be a burden to him if the going became even tougher. She'd tried to do her best. She'd hidden her woman's weakness inside the loose dress of a peasant boy and she took larger strides. Yet she knew she went too slowly when they should have hurried; she needed to rest when he could have soldiered on. Now in this unknown land, this country with no map, what could she be but a drag on his swifter feet?

For a while she kept up with him. He was carrying his large leather bag and another lighter one he'd added on the way. Then he shouldered her hemp bag as well so that she could walk more freely. He was much encumbered. Both suffered from the heat that grew more intense as they left the sea.

Soon they came to a small village with a cobbled street running

through it towards a church topped by a large bell. Aksel Stamer left
Ann to wait for him on a tree stump in the shade. He would find help.

He returned soon with some provisions but had not managed to
to hire a cart or get a man to help. The villagers were all absent or
asleep or just lethargic. Not even curiosity had made them volunteer
to accompany the strangers. But they had at least sold them a little
food and drink. There would be more friendly towns further down
the valley, he said.

They set off again. But before they left the edge of the village she
stepped awkwardly on a stone at the side of the cobbled part of their
way; she slightly twisted her ankle.

She feared to become lame, increasing his burden, slowing him
down still further. The pain made her feel feeble but he didn't register
her state or the delay. Instead, he simply waited till she was ready and
could move on, then went, as slowly as she wished.

They came to other villages. Here they could eat and spend the
nights and sometimes obtain a cart for part of a way. Wherever they
stopped, his ready money and air of quiet command produced beds,
but so far no comfortable means of transport.

'Since we have had to go slower, it means we will – for just one
night – have to sleep in the open,' he said. 'It will be cool in the hills
but not cold, cooler than down here. Then we can walk the last
section when your ankle will be rested. I know the way. I know the
people.'

There was no answer wanted or needed.

It was a strange journey. Strange being in the open, travelling with a
man so little known.

He was sensitive. He walked off as she squatted behind a bush that
hardly screened her to open her bowels. She was glad that it was not
now the time for letting blood, not here in the open. Indeed, in these
uncomfortable strenuous weeks this hadn't troubled her as it often
had in the past. She was relieved to find that, after the churning open
sea and rumbling mountain carts, her stomach had become comfortable, seemingly content with its new diet of goat and boar meat, beans
and dry bread.

When it came time to rest for the night, he found her a spot where the sandy soil was firm underneath and soft on top. He made a cocoon of clothes from his leather bag, leaving hers to serve as a pillow for her head. He gathered a mattress of dry leaves, cones and grass.

'Perhaps if we had prepared for this we should have brought along a mule to carry bedding,' he said. 'If they had no cart to lend us, they might have had a mule.' Was she supposed to smile at this? She never quite knew with Aksel Stamer.

Soon it was dark, no reason not to take off her baggy man's trousers and lie beneath her cloak. It was clammy underneath, but throwing it off would expose her to the biting insects of the night and, if by amazing chance she slept into the dawn, to the stranger's gaze.

Long before morning the slight chill made her draw the cloak close round her. Still exhausted, she slept again.

Already when the light came Aksel Stamer was standing, silhouetted against the dawn. She couldn't tell whether his eyes were on her or were just looking out to where the sea would be, watching an egret on a protruding rock. He was like a stone statue, set up to guard the living. She realised he'd lain only partly protected and comfortable to leave her the snug place.

Her ankle throbbed just a little but she wouldn't complain. Bats were circling back to their caves.

By early afternoon it was hard to remember that it had ever been chill. These September days still boiled at the zenith. The air grew heavy and humid and the sandy earth fluffed and swelled hotly about her feet. A cricket chirped incessantly.

It would be nearly autumn in England. What was it here? In these slopes of dry flowers that looked like spent dandelions. Apart from the crossing, this night had been the only time of real discomfort on the trip and he'd eased it as far as he could. Still, she felt dishevelled. Would she ever be really at ease again – back in the world of eating and sleeping on down, washing, sewing and chatting, with protocols of politeness and all the proper defences of clothes and manners against the other sex?

26

The man – she thought of Aksel Stamer as this now, not Robert – strode ahead. He'd told her to take even longer strides while she was in male attire, there was no need to mince as a woman must. But she couldn't easily adjust further. Her body held its residual pains.

Despite the discomfort, the oddness of it all, there was magic too. Sometimes distant voices and cattle bells dented the stillness.

They came in time to a little chapel in some woods with a cave nearby, a special cave. Of course a hermit's cave.

'Look,' he said.

'How did you know it was here?'

'I told you. I came this way once. Come, look.'

The cave was of soft stone. It seemed to mingle shells and dust. Someone had carved grotesque faces or skulls on the wall, one face simply an oval with a great gaping mouth in perpetual howl. She could hear water dripping in distant caverns into pools she'd no wish to see. Were there blind white creatures there?

'There must have been rituals, ceremonies here, something secret with the dead,' she said.

Aksel Stamer shrugged. 'There was perhaps some mystery,' he said, 'or perhaps just a private place where men hid while their enemies sought them.' He turned away.

She wished she'd not spoken. Such gothic imagining had annoyed Robert. Perhaps had helped drive him mad. She chastised herself. She would never again use that word so lightly. It was not 'madness' in him. He had never been mad. If anyone had been it was she.

A wooden bench was set against the old stones of the chapel. It had gaps in the slats where the wood had rotted and weeds grown through. Aksel Stamer sat down and encouraged her to sit beside him. For a while in the dappled shade they sat together companionably like a long-married couple. She thought once he looked towards her as if he would speak, but he said nothing. She had no urge to chatter as she'd so fatally had with Robert. No need to push this man on to say something. His silence was unthreatening, part of a laconic self. At times like this, his quiet strength was comforting.

He stood up too soon. She was still tired as they began walking once more. The air smelled of rosemary.

There was a poplar in the path. Surely she could lean on its smoothness just for a moment. The tree almost invited her back to rest. But on he went ahead of her. As she looked towards him she saw a black-and-orange butterfly just to his left as if leading him forward. He brushed it aside. Others came to join it.

He said something, she didn't hear. She tried to catch up but failed. Then he turned and said '*Aglais urticae*.'

Did men always know the names of things? Aksel Stamer and the butterfly, Giancarlo Scrittori and the lagoon birds, Robert and his pots, Gilbert and the shells. Was that their power? She tried to press Robert into generic men. But he resisted.

On they trudged. Aksel Stamer making distance between them, then slowing as she struggled to keep up, despite the longer strides she was forcing herself to take.

Now the trees were looming in the dusk. Everything ached about her: blisters welled up on her feet, first one then both. The lady's boots were not stout enough, intended for stone pavements and city halls not for this tramping over uneven ground. She steadied herself with a sapling, a feathered branch. She would not ask the man to slow down. For, underneath all, there was only one thing that mattered, that Aksel Stamer be there, that he not disappear, that he not abandon her.

But then, as she looked up from keeping her eyes on the uneven ground, he really wasn't there. Her stomach rose to her mouth. She sat down on a stone to swallow and catch her breath. To be abandoned here in this wilderness.

Then he appeared to the side of her through a grove of olive trees, carrying his leather bottle with its metal cup dangling from the rim. 'Here is apple juice,' he said. He unhooked the cup and poured out the liquid. It was yellow-green, with a frothed top. It was cool and delicious.

Then suddenly it was Robert's constricted throat that was trying to drink. She felt the juice fall from a coloured glass into that mouth. Tears sprang to her eyes. She could swallow no more. Yet what she'd drunk still kept its delicious, delicate taste.

Aksel Stamer saw her emotion. He looked away. She hoped he'd simply judged her tired.

A little breeze came down through the olive trees and holm oaks and tugged at her straight, now straw-like hair. It was short but perhaps not short enough. For it flapped against her flaking face. Appearance was nothing, sensation everything.

A spasm of self-contempt overwhelmed her as she thought of what she, like other women, had once feared of men – a rape, an attack, for God's sake, even an intimate robbery. What was there about her things or her person to take now? Was there anything that anyone would want?

She got up and handed the leather bottle back to Aksel Stamer. He drank the rest. She heard the liquid pass down his throat

Soon they came out of the dark green, almost indigo canopy of the shore pines and into an area of sand and scrub intersected with shallow rivers and rivulets. The few freshwater ponds were almost dry, as was the salt marsh with its white powder shining with crystals. There was again the faint smell of rosemary.

Venice with its wet floors and dripping walls, its endless tides over slippery feet, its humid sultry air and floppy gulls, was far from this thirsty scrub. It didn't call her back.

The stern back almost faded into the undulating dunes as she tried harder to hasten her aching legs. Follow, always follow.

'We are nearly there,' he said over his shoulder.

What if, when they got to the other coast, no boat came? What if it happened as it had when they first landed, that nothing was as he expected? What if there had never been a boat? What if Aksel Stamer too was mad and they were walking into a desert? Where was this place?

Would she never learn just to obey – or not to follow?

The dunes stretched on, in and out of headlands. A stray juniper interrupted the waste, a few sandy thickets. On the ground were pieces of bare distorted wood. The few growing things were stunted.

'How will we know where we should be?' she asked as she caught up with him.

He didn't answer. Of course not. She spoke to hear a voice in this emptiness.

What was the matter with him? He didn't seem like a human being with ordinary emotions.

At last they saw the sea. It was still, almost thick, substantial.

'We must wait by three huts on the promontory. There is only one place like that.'

She could have wept with relief at his words. Yet she made no sense of them. This was like Giancarlo Scrittori with the lamb and goose in San Marco so very long ago. But that had been playful. She looked at Aksel Stamer with incomprehension. He caught the look but didn't interrogate it. Then he spoke again slowly, gravely as if talking, any talking, used too much energy and he feared to expend it. 'We have to find the place, Ann.'

He used her Christian name as he had on La Giudecca. Was it still her name? She was unsure. Her old passports were in her bag under her clothes. They had her name – her two names – on them.

When the stream they had crossed so much earlier – then re-crossed repeatedly as it meandered, following some hardly defined path – entered the sea, they waded through the shallow water holding their boots. The sand below was light brown and blue catching the whiteness of the sandy beach beyond as well as the light azure of the sea. Ann felt herself black and parched as she looked down at her bare feet. Like pieces of chipped wood.

They couldn't drink the water: it had become salty.

'When we meet people from now on, it's best if I say you are my sister,' he said, with the slightest pause before the last word. 'Please put back your skirt when we stop.'

'But our ages are different.'

At last he smiled, or rather his face creased just a little. 'Not so different. I had . . .' He hesitated and looked pensive, then added, 'And do we not look somewhat alike?'

She caught his eye. Her mind tumbled over its half-realised thoughts. Why did he not say 'daughter'? Would that not be more reasonable, more suited to their years? And why the pause? She was sure she'd discerned it.

She wouldn't ask. He would never respond.

By now she felt weary beyond the bodily weariness of aching legs, sore feet, sprained ankle and burnt skin, even beyond the weariness of worrying about how she'd be answered. A new anger was starting to seep through her at this man who was taking such immense, peculiar trouble to save her. From what now? They were well away. She was filling with fatigue and fury.

She sat, then lay down.

Then he was rubbing her ankle, pressing in crevices with his thumb. She felt comfort steal up her legs

For the last part of the journey he took her hemp bag on his back again and found her a stick which he peeled with his hunting knife, so she could limp just a little and take the weight off the foot with the weak ankle.

They stopped for her to change back into woman's clothes. The stays of the bodice rubbed unfamiliarly against her healed ribs.

Let it not rain, please let it not rain! The sandy rubble would become mud and squelch over and into her ageing boots. The skirts she had now to wear would be a weight of wet. She half-closed her eyes from weariness and the sun, and saw instead a sea of shining mud. But it didn't rain.

Then there, just before the huts and at the edge of the promontory, they spied a man sitting on a pile of broken wall, the remains of a ruined house.

'Stay here,' said Aksel Stamer pointing to the ground. She could have been a spaniel. 'Just come when I beckon to you.'

She obeyed. She'd almost forgotten how much she disliked obeying, but not quite, the feeling was still there, intact. She stood as she'd been told, and waited.

The two men came together. She saw them nod, but didn't see whether they shook hands or not. They were of equal height. Not so. Aksel Stamer was taller. She had remarked his height earlier. He was not broad, just tall. They were talking now. Then they looked back at her. The man wiped his brow and stared again. Aksel Stamer showed him a paper and the man took it, glanced and gave it back. He shook his head. Why was Aksel Stamer doing this? Could such a man read?

Again they both looked at her.

After a while Aksel Stamer came towards her and nodded for her to move forward. Before she reached the stranger, he whispered in her ear, 'You will have to be what name I say you are. We have no passports for this part of the journey.'

'But I have my old papers,' she protested. Then her cheeks grew hot. She remembered why they were journeying in this tortuous way.

'I have sold them,' he said curtly. 'You are better without them.' Then he shrugged. 'They were no use in any case.'

He must have taken them from her bag when she wasn't looking – or sleeping. She had not given them to him, she knew that. Did he think he simply owned her? Was it to do with her 'crime'? So she would never again bear that incriminating 'married' name? Yet how on earth could people on this forsaken shore know anything of what happened so long ago in Venice? And what *had* happened there?

'You have yours, though?'

He shrugged again and walked ahead to the man, not turning round.

The boat they aimed for would be a sizeable one, suitable for crossing the open water. It lay further down, south of the promontory. The stranger had given directions, but would not accompany them. They had to reach it by themselves.

It was hard to do this when, after a short pause, her body expected rest. As if she'd promised it to her recalcitrant legs and was now forsworn.

They continued trudging over the dunes, a few shells cracking as they walked. The sharp edges almost punctured the thinning soles of her boots. The frayed silk scarf she used now against the sun was caught by the low thorny bushes as they passed.

She slowed down again, so that Aksel Stamer went on way ahead of her. She saw he was sitting upright on a rock protruding through the sand. The sun shone on his old leather jacket, making its dark folds look silky. She reached him and sat down beside him on the dry sand, exaggerating their difference in height.

In silence he pulled out a small piece of dry bread, some olives and a thimble size of goat's cheese, then poured from his leather bottle half a tin mug of warm water.

She put small bits of each in her mouth. They tasted of heaven.

'Those plants we passed earlier are asphodel,' he said. 'They flowered long ago. Here they eat the root.' He paused. 'Children heat it sometimes and explode it like fireworks.'

What was he talking about?

To lie in asphodel.

'That man you spoke to,' she said, 'what could he be doing here? There's little farming. A few goats are all I've spied these past days. Is he a fisherman?'

Aksel Stamer stared out towards the sea. 'He was a miner,' he said at last. 'Now he owns boats.'

'Mining for what? There's nothing here.'

'They mine for lead.'

How does he know these things?

He surmised her question. 'I told you. I have been here before.'

'Why, when?'

'I was travelling.'

As earlier, the rest made the aching more palpable, her sore feet more demanding. But still she stood up and went on, hobbling, lurching over rivulets.

Finally they saw it round the low dunes. A large old fishing boat with wet black nets coiled on its deck. In it two men sat waiting, quite still.

Was it a small thing for these men to carry to sea a suspected murderess and her protector, neither with papers for the foreign land? Or was this their traffic: ferrying fugitives back and forth?

Was her life more ordinary than she'd supposed?

When they arrived near the French coast, one of the men rowed them ashore in a sort of India dinghy. He set them down on a deserted inlet by a village called Cassis, he said. Aksel Stamer handed over more money in silence. No one noted their arrival.

By now the long journey, the privations, the fear, the aching muscles, the dirty hair, the baggy trousers, the returned skirt round a thinner waist, all of it had begun to dissipate the horror left in Venice. Pain and strain changed things, diminished disturbances of the mind. Something was appeased – at least by day.

'My mother will probably be dead by the time I reach Paris,' she said.

'Probably,' Aksel Stamer replied. She thought he smiled but her lips were still so cracked from the dry air she couldn't smile back to make him smile again – perhaps he'd never done so.

He glanced at her, then rooted in his bag and pulled out his small jar of rose balm. He put a small amount on his finger and stretched it out to her. She took it off and smoothed the waxy substance on to her lips.

He'd never said why he was going to Paris. Most probably he needed to get papers there to cross back to London, unless England were really his home.

Or did he want to see Caroline? It was possible. The suspicion had been lying in her mind. But silly, gossipy, cruel Caroline?

Or had he been a friend of Gilbert's, a young relative through the half-English mother? She'd mentioned him and his repeated words a few times on the journey. She couldn't remember what she might have said or not have said in these long extraordinary days. She registered no response.

She'd not said much about Robert. In fact when, by her face perhaps or some gesture, she'd started to betray that she thought of him and was about to speak, Aksel Stamer seemed to notice, then drew attention to something outside themselves: some stooping woman with a bundle on her back, some quaint feature of the passing landscape, some animal scampering into the bushes. It was not the copious detail of Giancarlo Scrittori and his seagulls, little beyond pointing and an adjective. See the sunset over the hill; look at the girls loading the donkey with more than the poor beast's weight; notice the tracery round the door of this poor inn – it was once a lord's palace, and so on. The asphodels had been such a moment. The tactic did not quite serve, but it staunched confession.

By the end she herself had become so mute she'd ignored the few chances for conversation. She had no worry: time enough to talk when they reached Paris and they would both see Caroline alive – or hear of her dead.

Then would be the moment for thinking back on those terrible events in Venice. Then would be the time for explanation.

27

As they came to the end of the journey, near places where she and Robert had been together, she heard her own voice speaking through his. Within her own head she'd become like one of his comic characters, those people he conjured up to amuse his followers, then dismissed as the shallow, simple souls they were. He'd never done intricate personations; or rather, he revealed a secret: that the intricate were really simple. If they thought otherwise, it was vanity. She knew she was simple now.

She stilled the voice that was hers only through him. But there was something she couldn't control. Why, now that beds were softer and food more edible, did the nightmares become more vivid?

For so many months in Venice she'd dreamt the same dream. She was lost in obscure streets, rushing, running breathless to be home, a home that was always an elusive Robert. There was danger too, violent danger but it was there in his absence, not his presence. His person was never reached. She feared she would be dashed to pieces from a fall before she found him, drowned in whirlpools, or asphyxiated in brown duck feathers. Now as she travelled these dreams had almost stopped and in their place arose the image of that hanging body, washed with a horrid yearning. Underneath was the dread that this yearning would be fulfilled and she would embrace and be embraced by the corpse.

When she reached consciousness with the morning, she was flooded with gratitude that desire could not be, and had not been, acted on. Then she found tears on her face for Robert in all his forms – and for her profound, remorseful relief that he was gone.

As with the old dreams, the day diminished the new ones and she found that his image stayed behind in the bed, shared on one occasion with a lady's maid from Marseilles. She could not have credited it. She thought Robert had moved inside her forever.

Signs streaked behind her eyes at intervals, of course. The high-backed chair in his study that had held his body, then fallen. Like the sofa of Princess Caroline which everyone remembered long after ceasing to think of its owner. Like Gilbert's solid-silver swan. Like Caroline's coloured shawls. Why did her mind fix so helplessly on these unseen objects?

Something was amiss with it. There was a lump within her head. It had settled just beneath her temple and at times travelled to the nape of her neck. Heat flashed and subsided.

During the last part of their long journey through France, they'd stopped when demands for papers and passes required payment, bribes, or counter-signings by more expensive dignitaries. Aksel Stamer dealt with it all, producing whatever would serve or knowing how to circumvent what would not. He made people accept that they'd landed properly at Marseilles from a regular packet boat – not been dumped by Sardinian fishermen on a deserted beach.

She let him handle all of it, documents and identities, with the trust of a child or beast.

So they reached Paris.

By now she was trembling. Why? So many dreadful things had happened that an encounter with an old woman who'd always been indifferent to her, just a distant figure in false red curls, could not provoke this emotion.

Perhaps to help her struggling mood, Aksel Stamer became more forthcoming. 'Paris is filthier than London,' he said, 'it's laid out impressively on a grand scale as Napoleon wanted, a Roman imperial capital – but all show. Walk away from the wide boulevards and there's filth and narrow streets. Yet there are still swans on the Seine. Look, one is moving its head up and down. It looks like a clockwork fowl from this distance.'

She couldn't reply, not even to that detail of the mechanical bird; she felt too listless. He looked worried then. He had gone too fast for her, he said, it had been too much, he should have thought.

It was he who suggested she acquire new clothes now they were in a city. He didn't choose them as another man had done, or lovingly finger the feminine material, but he took her where the young maid at their inn knew there were clothes bespoke for someone else and not collected. She could have them quickly altered to fit her. He paid for what she wanted.

Back at the inn the same maid helped her make her short hair passably like a modern woman's.

Then, dressed in new light jacket and skirt, her *turquois*-coloured one beyond cleaning or repair after serving as pillow and sunshade during the long weary miles, her hair surmounted by a clean trim cap, she was ready to visit Caroline and – watch the 'dying scene'.

The phrase came unbidden to her befuddled mind. What could be happening? She could no longer distinguish fictive from real, life from a play, or indeed waking from dreaming.

One thing had taken hold in her mind. Aksel Stamer had come for Caroline. Why else had he grown gentler to her now they were in Paris?

She'd worked some of it out. He'd heard the name Ann St Clair in Palazzo Grimani when he – for it was he – stood too close as she picked up the letter from 'A Friend'. Ever after in Venice he'd been haunting her, ready for the moment to make himself known. On the journey he'd looked at her papers, some with her unmarried name. He must have used this name to acquire – somehow – the right documents for France. Her head ached and she could think no further.

She must go to Caroline and see what Aksel Stamer made of her – and she of him.

He was with her as she walked the last paces to the address in Le Marais given by the 'Friend'. He too had bought new clothes and looked smart in contrasting coloured waistcoat and jacket and new linen. He was as at home in this urban place as thoroughly as he'd been in his worn leather jacket on the sand dunes and in the woods of Sardinia.

It was a street on its way down, hotels turned into modest if not quite impoverished apartments.

They arrived at the right number. The shutters were closed on the first floor, green shutters with flaking paint. It was the kind of detail Ann saw while failing to take in the whole.

She swayed: was the idea of seeing Caroline after all these years so very moving? She was surprised. Aksel Stamer gave her his arm to steady her. 'Be careful,' he said, 'it need not be frightening. You are a brave woman.'

She had a pocket dangling from her belt. He raised it and put in it a fat pouch. 'For you,' he said. 'I will leave you now. You are home, or nearly home. God bless you.'

She didn't at once understand his words. Then they struck her. Struck her a blow on her face. As shocking as the fist she so well remembered.

'You . . . you are going? What will become of me?'

'Don't become, Ann, just be.' He kissed her lightly on the cheek, turned and left, walking briskly back down the street.

She was so surprised she had to steady herself against the door, the dizziness, the sick feeling expanding. Sweat was falling from her brow although the day was cool. She put her hand to her face and touched it, almost expecting to find a bruise beginning. She felt only heat and damp.

The kind delicate kiss, the pouch of money, the departure before he'd seen Caroline, before she'd shown her gratitude, before they could talk about everything, above all his going, his going. What could it all mean?

She pulled herself together as far as she could and tried to stop swaying. Then she jerked an iron ring by the door. A bell clanged deep inside.

Silence.

At last she heard footsteps.

She waited.

An old woman with careworn brown complexion and deep-set eyes came to the door. Her neat cap was laced and clean white, so good for a maid. Ann was about to introduce herself when the woman spoke without greeting or smile.

'So you are come, Mademoiselle. At last. She has been waiting long.'

Caroline was alive then and attended, it seemed, by a very creditable if discourteous servant.

The pounding in her head increased and again she had to steady herself against the wall as she mounted the stairs. Her hesitation made the maid look back at her. Did the woman assume she was upset? She'd crossed all of Europe for this moment. Perhaps she was.

'*Bien*,' said the maid. 'Follow.'

They mounted one flight, passed the room with the closed green shutters, and went on up the second flight to a bedchamber.

It was dimly lit: pink curtains covered the windows towards the street and kept out the sun. Framed sketches of flowers and ferns were on the wall. The kind of thing Caroline used to draw in Putney while sitting on cushions and being waited on by Martha.

The room smelled of decay, of bodily effluent, not too intense but not quite masked by a scent of some kind of flower, lilies she thought, with perhaps lavender in the mix. It conjured up the lily and lavender and rose from another era. That body. Odour was a strong mnemonic.

The bed was large and whatever was in it lay to one side, its outlines softened by the white coverlet. A woman, a corpse? Not the latter for there was loud, hitched breathing coming from it. There was hardly any flesh to see between a frilled white cap and high tied collar. No sign of that false red hair Caroline used to wear.

One arm lay outside the coverlet on the bed with the sleeve pulled up. Had it clutched at the bedclothes or the face, crumpling the sleeve as it did so? It must have gone limp and been left unattended.

On the table were phials and gallipots. Accoutrements and signs of the dying person? Everything said so; yet Ann would not believe for, if this were her mother, she would not die. The mantelpiece in the Putney house had been cluttered with medicine bottles, very pretty with their coloured mixtures young Ann used to think, but smelly too. Concoctions for a weak heart and delicate nerves. Sometimes they were frightening for they grew things inside as if living creatures were trying to escape. Away in her bedchamber she'd imagine the dangling limbs easing out the cork, floating free, massing and slithering up the stairs – but by then she'd let out a scream and Caroline would shout, 'Quiet, girl, I must have my sleep.'

'Your daughter,' said the servant to the thing in the bed, 'your daughter has come.' She retreated, leaving Ann in the room.

She felt so strange, so dizzy, she simply couldn't comprehend what she was seeing. She gazed at the body. Slowly it became an old, old woman.

It was not, could not be, Caroline. Yet the medicines, so common from her childhood days, and the servant's words, declared it surely was. Her heart staggered. She was hot. A white flame zigzagged round her head. Was she about to faint? She bit her lip and crushed her nails into her palms.

The woman was so much older than she'd ever imagined. How old was she? Caroline had been an elderly mother but this person was extreme, old enough for the flesh to be decaying before death. It sagged from the shrivelled arm like the tattered remnant of a flag on a wooden pole. The hand was ridged and splotched.

Time is short, said Caroline. But of course she said nothing of the sort. Too pithy.

I doubt it, replied Ann. Did she speak? Was either of them talking?

The lips were dry, her own lips. Had she said anything? It is too much of a coincidence, my being here and you dying.

What was the matter with her? With them both? No one had spoken at all.

'Caroline?' she said, her voice sounding hoarse and distant.

The face twitched and eyes opened just a little under the frilled cap, no longer dirty green but yellow. They slowly closed again.

She had no wish for memories and yet they came. The last time with Caroline, the real one, not this thing. 'You are hard,' she'd said.

Ann saw the scrawny old hand lift up from the coverlet and tug at the rolled cream ribbon at the neck of the nightgown. Her mother's hands had always been veined – but she'd never imagined them turning into these tortured claws.

The mouth from the bed opened and a phlegmy, gurgling sound emerged from layers of thickened liquid. No word came.

Then there was Robert hanging and twisting in this sombre room against the polished wooden bed and little table with its spindly curved legs. Ann shook her head to expel the sight. She was here, in this place without him. It smelled of effluent and the sickly lily; that was all that laid one scene over the other.

She looked again at the face, then the hand. Dying, yes. Perhaps after all. And if so, if this were indeed the dying scene, it would be long. There was no hurry.

A glass jar was descending over her, cutting her off from everything without: this woman, if woman she still was, and this suffocating room. The sides reflected herself. She swung in the jar with that familiar body which was this body too. Swung in it like the foetus in the Conte's studio in Palazzo Savelli, twisting slowly in its pickling element – or the trapped and growing thing in Caroline's medicine bottles. All of them both living and yet too dead to struggle out.

Was all this confused emotion just to fend off a dying woman? She litanised to herself, A mother is dying, my mother is dying.

The stern maid came in and removed thick strands of sputum from Caroline's chin. They had glistened even in the dim pink light but till now Ann hadn't noticed.

It was the epitome of old age, its horror and disintegration – or rather its failure to disintegrate fast enough so that the living need not see it and could go on their way in ignorance. Why was the thing still alive? Ann felt only the horror of decay, no pity.

The yellow eyes opened again, stayed open this time, seeing or unseeing? Ann couldn't know.

She should lean over and kiss the wizened cheek like a daughter, like girls did in her stories when faced with the dying stepmother they must forgive on the final page. But she couldn't do it.

'Caroline, I have come. I have come from Venice.'

The mouth moved a little. But not to say words. Instead it gasped. Did it want water? But she couldn't see how such a body could swallow. Indeed she didn't really believe in any live thing under the white coverlet, for, though the mouth and eyes moved, and once the hand, everything else was still. If those eyes hadn't opened and the rasping sound weren't emerging from the mouth, she would have thought all of it now quite dead.

Then the claw hand clutched at the sheet.

The servant was in the room, pushing Ann aside. She moistened a piece of cotton with vinegar and held it to the lips, then withdrew it so that they glimmered like thin pieces of lard. There was more thick liquid too, so the body could still create. The eyes swivelled towards Ann, then returned and closed.

The servant left the room as quietly as she'd come. Or perhaps she waited in the shadows, ready to help her mistress since the daughter could or would not. Ann didn't turn her aching head to see.

There was silence again as she stood, victim to such oscillating feelings from hate of this thing, to a new painful compassion for all crumbling bodies; from relief that her own unsatisfactory self, though ageing, was not like this, to horror that she too would be there, that she too would and could become such a foul thing. It was not her flesh; it would be her flesh.

Was she as self-obsessed as Caroline that such thoughts swam into her head? She had no urge to weep but a great one to howl at such desolation. There was no Robert for her to humour, no Aksel Stamer to protect her. Only herself and her future alone in a stuffy room turning slowly from Ann into Caroline.

The eyes were now more human, and, yes, she saw they were becoming Caroline's, just a tinge of murky green in the yellow. But the room was pinkly hazily dim, she may have imagined it.

With the partial recognition came all the old emotions.

She stared at her mother. What would she say? Would she speak of Gilbert, now in this slow, extreme moment? Surely, for so much of their life had been around this man, his memory, his legacy – it was his money and his spirit that had kept them going all those years in Putney, so unhappily conjoined.

Ann would stop her if she started to speak his words again: she couldn't bear that.

'Gilbert, my father,' she said.

A flaccid snort, then a low, tremulous whisper: 'You're no child of his.'

She was too surprised to respond. What could the woman mean? It was an absurd confession made for effect. Had she imagined it? Was it a line from one of her novels?

'Then whose, then what?' she said.

There was no reply. It was obviously a lie. There was no more reason for truth on a deathbed than anywhere else.

Why would there be? Caroline didn't believe in a last judgement; there was no crucifix in the room, she'd not changed. Why give a lie to a life by confounding it with a final truth?

She wished she could speak to Aksel Stamer. But he'd gone, defeated perhaps by what he feared to see of Caroline. His long travels thwarted at the end.

Her head was thumping and banging and her knees and ankles growing weak. A result of all that walking on Sardinian sand dunes, the one ankle never quite right despite his kindness. She steadied herself on a bedpost.

The breath from the bed grew noisy again. If there were to be confessions, she wanted to mention Robert, for surely she'd killed him in one way or another. She'd run right across Europe to avoid his avengers. Caroline would like to hear that.

The thin slippery lips moved. Was there to be a surprise, a forgiveness, an absolution, even a benediction? Ann swallowed her revulsion and put her ear closer to the face, keeping her eyes averted.

She could make out nothing of the words at first. But Caroline was trying to express something.

'What are you saying?'

The lips moved and a thin sound emerged through the phlegm.

With difficulty she made out some syllables.

'Did you see her?' whispered the voice.

Ann was puzzled. She was sure this was what had been said.

But why? She moved away, then held her breath. Sweat was pouring from her forehead, running into her eyebrows; yet it could not be so very hot in the room. There was only a low fire gently hissing in the grate.

She brought her ear closer again. 'Who? Who do you mean, Caroline? Mother?' She used the word after some hesitation. She was assuredly *her* child. Then she waited.

'The Princess in Venice? Did you see her?'

A momentary eagerness entered the yellow eyes as Ann raised her head to look, then the thin lids came down.

She pulled back, wiped the sweat off her forehead with her sleeve and stumbled out of the bedchamber.

By the time she reached the rooms that Aksel Stamer had taken for her and himself she was swaying, sweat was streaming from her face, down her neck and from under her arms along her sides and between her breasts.

He was not there. He had said goodbye. And yet, she'd hoped.

Robert James or Aksel Stamer: for so long she'd thought of one or the other, always pulled along or pulling, that now being alone was impossible to grasp. She sat on the bed, and let herself collapse into sobs.

She cried on and was still crying as her head fell on to the pillow and the room turned itself on to its side. Her tongue was growing large and furry in her mouth, filling her head and blacking out her eyes and nose. She could hardly breathe or see or hear. The sides of the glass jar had contracted and were pressing on her temples.

The fever – for she knew it for what it was now – had been approaching for a while. It was not new; she accepted its thirst, hot headache, pulsation and near delirium. Perhaps it came from the many biting insects in Sardinia or southern France, a malaria from the swamps, a kind of typhus, a disease of the foul water, perhaps from the detritus of all her life.

She had no power to think further. Darkness was coming over her and she was burning into it.

28

Tentatively Ann opened her eyes. They felt sticky and raw. For some minutes she tried to think where she could be and what had happened. She'd been in and out of consciousness for some time, that much she knew, but how was she in this particular room in unfamiliar clothes? They felt damp, almost wet, beneath her.

A young servant girl came into the bedchamber. She seemed familiar. She saw Ann had woken at last. She'd hardly moved but her eyes flickered.

'You are so weak, Madame,' said the maid in slow French.

Ann found it hard to grasp what she was saying. Yet the language and her presence brought with it some sense of place.

With sense came anxiety. How long had she been here, in this bed? Who had been caring for her? Even more insistently as consciousness flooded in: what was this care costing? She recollected the pouch of money Aksel Stamer had given her but had no idea how much it contained, how far it would stretch – or where it was.

The young girl saw her unease. 'You have been ill these three days,' she said. Ann could still not quite comprehend her words and didn't reply.

'You are hungry, yes?'

'No, no,' she said, rousing herself and finding her lips could speak, though the sound she made resonated in her head more than in the room. Where were her purse, her things?

'Did the man . . .' she began.

'Your brother, Madame?'

'What?'

'Your brother, Madame. He left money for lodging however long you are here, it is enough, all paid.'

Of course. Aksel Stamer was her brother.

'He is gone?'

'But yes, before you came back. He had to go for business. He explained.'

'Explained?'

'He had to go.'

'Go where?'

'You are weak, Madame,' said the young woman primly. 'Rest and we will give you some gruel. The doctor says once you were sleeping all would be good. He sees such fevers often. They go in five or six days, maybe a week, then weakness. You have been lucky.'

'Days?'

But the maid was leaving the room.

Ann closed her eyes and dozed. She heard a voice speaking distinctly. Whose? Why were there so many men in the bedchamber when she wanted only Sarah?

Cousin Sarah.

Over the last months, she'd rarely thought of her cousin; now she longed for her motherly plumpness, her kindly voice. If only she could be one of Sarah's little brood and snuggle up to that comforting bosom. Yet she could not fix her cousin's face and voice in her head, it was crowded with men no good for her: with Robert and Aksel Stamer and Gilbert.

It must have been Gilbert who spoke of death, for Ann remembered how often Caroline had told her he knew all about life and death. But she hadn't heard his accents apart from Caroline's voice. It couldn't be he.

It was Robert then, thinking of mortality. Or was it just her own voice grown gruff?

She was lying in a bed and whether she was becoming weaker or stronger she couldn't tell. The maid had said she was getting well. But surely death had not yet packed his bags and walked off.

'I think of death often: it gives me strength. With it I have a free mind, don't you see? A free mind and a strong heart to think and feel, a firm hand to write and tell others of infinity. We are all moving to death.' So said the voice.

'Well, yes,' ventured another, and this was surely hers but not quite hers here in this bed. More like her voice when she'd been one of the circle in William Bates's house in Fen Ditton. Could the other be young Gregory speaking to her? No, not after all this time. 'But surely we would kill ourselves if we thought it so admirable a goal.'

The first voice looked contemptuous, for it was a voice with a voice's body. 'You cannot truncate the journey. Whatever we do we are on the road, we have to be. Death is plenitude. Death will come soon enough and we will yearn for it but never be ready.'

The woman who was herself and not herself was now sipping coffee in a Holborn coffee shop; she'd put down her cup and thought it best to say only 'Hmmm' to Robert and Gilbert.

'Death is the only perfection. It is the only primordial. It makes water and earth and space and time more vivid. We are mere clock-work swans on a glass sea. We stop when the mechanism tires.'

'Yes, yes,' said a young man who had materialised beside the voice, 'the freedom of disintegrating, of being in nature, being in all things.'

Ann would normally have said, How do you know, not having died? But instead she picked up her cup and looked towards Robert's shadow. He absorbed her look and the young man's views, then deflected them graciously.

Now the words were coming thick and fast in bundles as if someone were throwing her life at her from a great height, so that the bundles exploded their contents round her when they reached their goal like the bulbs of Sardinian asphodel. But the contents were just fragments, words, images, nothing secure.

'Absurd is a bird,' sang out the young man whose features she couldn't see.

'Jesus Christ is metamorphosed,' said Robert's voice.

'Fucking and frigging should be free, free as any other bodily function,' said the young man.

'Like childbirth that comes after,' said the Ann in the coffee shop.

Everyone turned to look at her. Robert was cross at the attention she received. 'You want a mama, not a living man,' he snapped. There was no menace in his words unless you looked at his eyes which came now yellowy, rheumily into focus.

Ann slept and woke, then slept again. She sensed hours, perhaps days, going by.

When she woke definitively she was a little refreshed, her voices gone.

But her fever or simply exhaustion from all the past was still there wracking her. She couldn't say how much was disease of the mind, how much the body, how much each feeding on the other. The eyes, tired and sore, felt like hers but they looked out on a body she now hardly recognised.

She shuddered at her hands. They'd become thin and veined from travel and unaccustomed dryness, from a lack of lady's gloves. They were like Caroline's.

She was glad there was no glass close by the bed or she would have been tempted to look at her face, and who knows whose reflection she might have seen? Or the mirror might have become a pool in shadow giving back nothing. She shuddered again. She'd been so out of her skin and mind these last weeks, so caught in a state or place between dream and real that she was reluctant to test memory or fear. She felt unsure of everything.

Best keep inside and quiet until she knew who and exactly where and, above all, what she was.

What she did know for sure was that she was alone. Aksel Stamer had really gone – he would not suddenly appear, stern and comforting.

How long had she been sick, how long had he been away? The maid had said a few days, maybe three or four. Then others had followed.

She struggled to raise herself and get out of the bed. There was fresh water in a bowl and she sprayed it over her face and neck and arms, too tired to do much more, then used the chamber pot. There were her clothes, the ones she'd bought with Aksel Stamer, only they were freshly laundered and ironed. With pauses she managed to dress herself in clumsy fashion, not all ties tied or buttons looped. The clothes now hung loosely on her.

On the side table there was cold chicken and an egg, an odd combination, perhaps leftover of meals that had been kindly brought to her by someone expecting her to wake, then not touched, left to congeal and dry, one day, two days, more? Or perhaps the maid had brought this in while she was sleeping for the last time, having left gruel earlier and found it uneaten.

Surely she could not eat anything, certainly not this incongruous collation. And yet, although no tempting smell rose from the chicken or the egg, she had a sense somewhere about her, not necessarily in her mouth, that she was ravenous and she rather thought she could dispose of anything at all.

There was noise outside in the street, and it brought to mind the inn that Aksel Stamer had found for her, for them both, though this was not the room she'd first been in, she was sure. She contemplated it while swallowing every last morsel of quite tasteless chicken and egg. Chicken and egg. A laugh rumbled up from her belly but didn't quite reach her mouth. Chicken and egg. She stood up, meaning to go to the window. Chicken and egg.

Then with a rush, as though they'd been waiting in the next room and suddenly flung open the door into her head, back came Robert, the dreadful face and dripping body, and Caroline, the near corpse curtained in pink.

She sat down abruptly and raised her hand to push them aside.

She tried again to take stock.

Beside her old hemp bag new clothes were laid out; they'd been near those she'd just put on but she'd not seen them at once. They included undergarments, fresh tan gloves and a bonnet with blue ribbons. There was also a set of toilet items, brush, comb and smelling salts in a light-brown leather case. No one except Aksel Stamer could have bought them for her. He must have put them there while she was with Caroline since by the time she returned to the inn he'd left. Why? How did he know what to buy a woman? He'd spoken of no wife, and he didn't appear like a man who'd been married. Yet no bachelor would know so accurately what a woman needed.

She was moved. Especially the undergarments. Martha had tried hard to keep her neat but the mistress had so many wants in the Putney house and she often went out with puckered stockings because they were the wrong length, her bodice ribbons knotted rather than properly tied.

Beside these items lay the pouch, still full of money. She was in an honest house.

There was no mention of the gifts in an open note which she now saw by the washstand. Aksel Stamer's hand? She was uncertain for she was not familiar with it.

The note told her that, when it was appropriate and when she wished to return to England, she should go to the Paris Sous-Préfecture Police Office near the Pont-Neuf. There she could pick up the passport in the name of Ann St Clair. It would have come from Marseilles where they'd landed from Sardinia. She knew they'd done nothing of the sort, nor been in quarantine there as would be implied; once again Aksel Stamer had worked some magic.

So Ann St Clair she was again. Signora James was as dead as Signor James.

The passport should be signed by the British Ambassador and she could go to his office between eleven and one in a morning. The directions were precise, and she would follow them – she recalled the painful delay in the Alps when they lacked correct signatures; but that was in another life. Then she should return to the Police Office with the passport and go on to the Ministère des affaires étrangères in Rue du Bac. Ten francs from the pouch he'd left should be handed over at this stage. For the journey to the coast she should take the diligence: it was quite comfortable.

He'd thought of everything; she'd only to follow the detailed instructions. He had not known she was so ill – he must have believed she was just weak and emotional when she leaned on him outside her mother's house, dwelling on the past and imagining the future with Caroline. She wished he'd stayed. She missed him beyond anything.

Still feeble and nervous, none the less she felt the strengthening effect of the food. She believed she could walk unaided and, by taking a cabriolet for part of the journey, get to the Marais. She'd come to see Caroline and must see her again now she was more prepared for the sight. She put the pouch of money into her pocket. She was ready to go out.

An older more portly servant entered her bedchamber. What was Madame about? It was too soon to get up, to go beyond the inn. It was folly. Madame should be in bed another day or days. She would bring soup. On she clucked, standing squarely in the doorway.

'No,' said Ann, 'no, my mother is dying, I must go.'

A dying parent was compelling. There was no answer to it.

The servant still looked disapproving but made no effort to argue further. Ann wondered fleetingly whether she was anxious that her patient return to pay. She had only her bundle and her new clothes but she purposefully glanced at them so that the woman would follow her direction and take them as some surety – if indeed that was the problem. Then she remembered that the young maidservant had said all had been paid for by her 'brother'. How could it be when he'd not known she would be ill? Did he have some special credit here? Ann felt so unsure of everything that she was unable to judge whether this stout middle-aged person were the mistress of the house or just another maid. Dress, gestures, speech, nothing was giving up its usual meaning.

She hesitated but the woman stood aside even as Ann tottered a little in her steps. She must be acting more normally than she felt. And, if this were the ordinary world, would Aksel Stamer perhaps come back into it?

29

Without having much idea of the time of day she managed to get down the stairs and make her way out into the street. She felt autumn in the air or it might simply have been the chilly temperature of this northern town after the sweltering travels they'd taken.

She was weaker than she'd hoped and after a few paces she almost slipped on some buttery milk thrown out by a careless milkmaid. She returned to the inn and asked for help and instructions. She'd almost forgotten how to take charge of herself.

Part of the way she used the conveyance, then walked with increasing steadiness towards Le Marais. She concentrated on bricks and pavement and on passers-by, hawkers, horses, manure, beggars, carriages, anything external to keep herself intact and upright. The vibrancy of everything almost overwhelmed her.

Then she turned into quieter roads; the bustle subsided. By the time she reached Caroline's street, she was alone except for an old man with a bundle of firewood on his back trudging slowly away from her, away from that house.

When she arrived before the door, the building seemed to her more humble, more pitiful than it had appeared a few days or a week – who could tell her? – before. It was not poor exactly, not dilapidated, but it was greyer. A few geraniums would have brightened it, made it come alive as a house.

There was nothing cheering on Caroline's two floors or above. Indeed, now she looked again she realised that the green shutters were still closed and the curtains in the bedchamber drawn. They didn't look pink from this angle, perhaps it was a lining that obscured the colour; they were thicker than she remembered, more definite in their exclusion of the daylight outside.

She still didn't know the time, the weak sun and shadows were telling her nothing. She didn't even know what day it was. But the crowds in the main streets she'd passed through must indicate late morning or midday and a workaday world. Why not pull the iron ring or knock?

She did neither at once. She stood anxious, just as when she'd first come here but with no Aksel Stamer to lean on. She'd hardly leaned on him on the journey, not even when her ankle and blisters had given her such pain. But yet he'd been there to catch a fall, had she been the kind of woman who collapsed. His subtle care had let her stay upright. Until they reached this door in Le Marais.

She knocked. She waited. Nothing happened. Then she pulled the iron ring. This time she heard no answering clang within the house. Could the bell have been broken in so short a time? She knocked once more with greater force. After another pause she heard the sound of footsteps approaching.

The harsh-faced maid opened the door and looked stonily at her. Again no greeting of the sort commonly given even to an importuning stranger or doorstep hawker.

Ann hesitated, then blurted out, 'My mother?'

'She's not here, Mademoiselle Ann. She's gone to the mortuary, Saint-Denis.'

Ann looked uncomprehending. The words meant nothing.

'Why?'

'Why, why, Mademoiselle? Why? Because she is dead and that is where the dead go.'

Ann leaned against the door frame with such suddenness that a splinter pierced through her dress and into her arm. She winced.

A silence followed. The maid made no move to let her enter the house, even stand in the passageway. Nor did she speak further.

'Dead,' said Ann at last, fact or question she didn't know.

'She told you so, I think,' said the servant unsmiling, 'when you came once.'

'But I have been ill.'

'So I see.'

Silence followed again. They stood at the door both staring into a distance, making no contact of eye or hand.

In Venice the dead went in their own boats, floating out to their special island.

At last, the woman spoke, 'She left you . . .' she paused, then turned and went down the passage into the gloomy interior.

Ann roused herself, presuming she was to follow. Still she expected somehow to see Caroline, even the old repellent Caroline, for such a woman could not be dead, dying yes – that had been going on for years – but not dead. It was impossible. After all, she'd lived on through all Ann's delays in Venice and her circuitous journey. To die now?

They mounted the first stairs and entered the green-shuttered room. An oil lamp was burning in the gloom. It made the room seem full, giving a momentary illusion it was inhabited. The illusion came even more from a huge armchair covered in brown velvet, still squashed where a body had been. Coloured shawls were folded and placed over its arms. Caroline had not lost her liking for violent drapery.

The chair had a looming presence. Ann hoped the servant wouldn't ask her to sit down: she had a horror of sinking into this dreadful furniture.

The maid left her standing while she crossed towards a small bureau in the corner of the room. She pulled a handle which clicked as a drawer opened. Then she lifted out a little silver box patterned with two stags. With a jolt, Ann remembered it from the Putney days. It had stood on the table beside Caroline with a book and a flower in a vase that Martha always put for her. Why as a child had she never risked those contaminating finger marks and disobeyed her mother to look inside, even when Caroline placed the locket within it?

Perhaps it would contain the memory of her birth and childhood, or explain that sudden strange statement that she was not Caroline's and Gilbert's child. It must do.

She rallied herself before her hand could take it. She knew it would contain nothing of the sort.

Only in her novels did such boxes hold secrets of birth and lineage. In real life they held rings, pendants, brooches, perhaps for other mothers a lock of a baby's hair tied with shiny ribbon.

Instead of giving the box into her hand, the maid put it on the little side table beside the great velvet armchair. The table was the one that had been in the bedchamber, moved now down here to be with its chair. With a crooked index finger the maid pointed at the box, then looked at Ann with eyes much shrewder, sadder, than she'd expected. 'She left you that.'

Trinkets, thought Ann. Cheap trinkets.

She was ashamed of her bitterness, but it would well up.

She still had the sense that Caroline was there, upstairs in bed waiting to hear what her unsatisfactory daughter would do. She thought of the Princess. Oh, Caroline. She didn't know for whom she sighed. Chicken and egg, she thought suddenly and felt a terrible laugh welling up. She pressed the back of her hand hard against her mouth.

'I will take Madame's clothes,' the servant was saying. It was not a query, but Ann nodded. Clothes of the dead, if Caroline were dead, were dreadful things. She used them in her novels, when they rose up to speak of wicked deeds or refused to sink into the mire or lagoon or stay hidden in trunks and caves.

The maid had turned again to the bureau. Ann thought she was being dismissed, instructed by this gesture to find her own way down the stairs along the corridor and out before seeing anything more substantial of her mother's life. In fact the maid had gone back to open another drawer in the bureau. From it she took some folded paper.

'This letter is for you. She write it before you come,' she said in heavily accented English. 'Then when you don't come again, she write some more. With difficulty, Mademoiselle Ann. She was not then in her real mind.'

She stopped and stared at the chair and the little side table next to it as if her mistress were still sitting there. It was on this table with its spindly legs then that Caroline had written. She had lain back in the chair, pulling herself up to write every sentence. Then the shrivelled arm and hand had finished off the note from her bed. Or more likely she'd dictated it. That claw-like hand could never write.

Ann dragged herself into the present. Her mother was not there. She was dead – or at least this woman before her thought so – and her body had left the house. There was no point in going upstairs into the suffocating room with its closed pink curtains, even if she were invited.

'Why did she die?' asked Ann.

'As to that, Mademoiselle Ann, when a time has come. She was ill for long. I write to tell you so. And you took much weeks to come.'

'No,' interrupted Ann, for she dreaded another silence, 'what did she die of?'

'Her 'eart, of course. She tell you.'

Her brain was still sluggish. The maid's English when she used the language was hard to understand. She heard the word 'art'. She thought of her mother's sketches on the wall of the bedchamber. Surely they had been just a habit to pass the time, of no merit. Even Caroline could not have put store on these.

'Her art?'

'Mademoiselle,' said the servant impatiently. 'She has told you. She has weak 'eart. She tell you many times. She tell me.'

Ann understood at last. She spoke on impulse. 'Yes, often, but I never . . .'

'No,' barked the maid with sudden assertion, returning to French to interrupt, 'Madame Caroline said you never – *jamais*.'

'*Jamais*.' The word hung in the gloomy air flecked with dust.

Ann stared at the maid, startled at what she was seeing. She had never believed in the loyal affection of servants – it was a trope of story-telling, nothing more, though Martha had cuddled her when she was small. But, then, as Sarah had said, everyone loved a little child, it meant nothing particular. For people of their class like her mother, no aristocrats with generations of faithful retainers, there was only resentment from those forced to serve them. What was happening here, then?

The maid's fierceness could not easily be explained except by affection – unless of course she always faced the world with such scowling hostility.

Whatever its cause, the sudden emotion cracked something inside Ann. She felt overwhelmed by the drama she was in: the dead mother, the estranged daughter, the dingy lodgings, the loneliness of both of them. Tears welled up. She had rarely cried except in self-pity in these years when Robert had taken over her life, and then not in front of strangers. She had little idea how to control her face for social tears.

The maid looked at her, then muttered, '*Trop tard*, Mademoiselle Ann.'

'But when?' The question hung in the air. 'When did she write it, the letter?'

'She wrote most of it not so long ago, when she began to be very ill. I was to send it to you when she was dead through the office in London which knows where you are.'

'Why didn't you send it before then?'

'She wasn't dead.'

'But you wrote to me all the same.'

The maid said nothing.

Ann stared at the letter. What could her mother be saying to her? What could be said only when Caroline was dead? When had the letter really been written? She looked in horror at it as if it were a living thing, part of the wicked old woman who'd been on the bed, only just alive.

Old age was so ghastly, so ugly, it should not speak. The dead should go away when they died.

She must take the letter and leave, but something restrained her. This maid, this scowling old servant, was the last link, the last to know Caroline. Perhaps there was more than could be put into the letter.

'Is it about me, about Gilbert, my father?' she said, knowing how selfish she must sound. But her mother had already given her a character; the portrait could not be further blackened.

For the first time the maid gave a smile, so wintry that Ann found she preferred the scowl.

'No Gilbert, Mademoiselle Ann.'

Again the maid looked her in the face with those weirdly shrewd eyes.

'What do you mean? What?'

'As I say, Ann.'

The name had been used without any title, just as Aksel Stamer had used it. Here it was done with such familiarity she was even more startled. But before she could ask more the maid had put the letter down on the table, leaving Ann to pick it up. Then she turned on her heels, mounted the stairs, and left the room.

Ann was alone to find her own way out.

She waited a moment in the stillness, knowing full well the woman would not come back. She dreaded above all things following her up to that awful room. Was the maid sitting there alone by the empty bed?

She collected her wits as best she could and, avoiding any image of herself that might appear in that silver-edged mirror that hung on the wall here as it had hung in Putney, stumbled her way down the stairs and along the dark corridor, her eyes still hazy from tears. She felt with her hand the rough wall of the hallway while with the other she clutched the box and letter.

As she opened the door holding her precious things in one hand, some tears fell on the paper.

When she was in the street, the door not quite closed behind her, she drooped the letter from one hand and flapped it to dry the paper and prevent tears seeping in to the words. Tears might destroy part of the message.

For surely this was a message. Surely this was her life. It must be the life of Gilbert and Caroline and Ann, whatever the maid said, whatever Caroline mumbled. Although she feared to read the contents, she must not smudge the words.

Would they explain what had happened to Gilbert? His death was so confused in time and place and manner. She even wondered briefly whether perhaps Caroline had murdered her idol and was here confessing.

But this was too close to her own sordid experience, to those cheap tales in which she'd dealt.

No, no. She knew with the speed of lightning, so shocking that she nearly dropped both box and letter and fell to her knees. Only with difficulty did she refuse to allow the thought to conquer her whole mind and body and knock her right down there on the Paris pavement.

She knew that what the servant had said was truth, surely and absolutely. Gilbert was not dead because he had never existed.

30

She returned to the inn; there was nowhere else to be. After telling the young maid she would order dinner later, she went up to her chamber. It had been aired and put to rights: beyond some bottles of green and black medicine there was no evidence it had held a fevered patient. She would have it only for that night as a convalescent; after that she would – and the stout older woman was all apologies, for she'd obviously been paid well – have to move to a much smaller room or share with a respectable widow from Grenoble.

She was not fit for company; she would take the small room.

She didn't know how long she'd need to make arrangements for travelling to England. She had no wish to be anywhere in particular. Nowhere was home. But she would go back soon. She would follow the instructions Aksel Stamer had left.

She sat for some minutes on the bed with the silver box and letter on her lap, collecting up the rags of herself.

The box was easy to open, its pitiful contents as simple to decipher. They were just what one might have expected. First there was the locket Ann had always thought depicted Gilbert. Even now she believed she'd seen his picture there, but memory was duplicitous. She knew that. She pressed the locket's catch. It clicked smoothly and sprang open, indicating that its mechanism had been often used and oiled.

The face of a woman in early middle age stared out at her. Surely it could not be Caroline herself when young, for no one wore a locket of her own features, did she? For a wild moment Ann wondered if it could be herself, the daughter so neglected. Common sense returned. Caroline hadn't seen her in her present age and there was no resemblance in colouring or shape of head. How ridiculous to entertain such a notion, even fleetingly.

Curiously, it looked most like the maid from the apartment. Or rather the artist had caught something in the eyes of this younger woman that reminded Ann of the old one she'd just seen, that shrewd look, part cunning, part wise. Strange.

She was quite sure this female image had not been there when her mother had had the locket in Putney so many years ago, the locket she'd assumed held the image of Gilbert. She remembered now a detail: she'd not seen the image clearly for it was dimmed, unclear. Caroline had said it had become blurred with tears. Of whom could this clear female portrait be? Some relative of Caroline's she knew nothing of?

Apart from that there were some earrings made of enamel and silver, the necklace of red and indigo glass beads which Ann remembered Caroline wearing, a few insignificant rings, and the crazy peacock-feathered brooch that she used to put in her hair or on a turban when other mothers had taken to a laced cap long before they reached her age.

She opened the locket again and gazed at the portrait. Foreign, she was now sure, but Italian or French? Surely if they had had exotic relatives Caroline would have made something of them. Perhaps it was a connection of Gilbert's. But there was no Gilbert.

The more she gazed, the more she became sure it was a younger version of the unfriendly servant who'd just directed her to a mortuary which she would not visit. The servant who had tended her mother in what for once had proved to be a real illness, and closed her eyes when she achieved the death so frequently announced.

She did not even know the woman's name.

Evidently she was not just a servant. She'd been a friend doing the duty of a servant, a companion to that thing in the bed, part Caroline, part monster of old age, part another incubus of Ann's own making.

Again she'd got it wrong. Even in death Caroline had the power to fool her. Or was she so wilfully blind that no one had to take any trouble to impress what they wanted on her mind? Did she always meet any deceiver halfway, even three quarters?

Perhaps it was bodily weakness, not feebleness of intellect on this occasion, that made her almost see and yet never quite see. After all, by the time she visited her mother, she'd been running a fever. That must count for something.

But wearily she knew this was not the first time, and she doubted it would be the last.

Gilbert and Robert, all hints and mirrors and smoke, adding up to nothing – or next to nothing.

She got up, went to the window, looked out on a small dingy courtyard where someone had placed a plant with spiked green leaves. A piece of paper printed with large bold writing was being blown lazily by the breeze along the ground against a wall. It might have been used to wrap flowers, more likely a pastry sold on the streets, before being discarded. Possibly it was a playbill or notice for a travelling circus that every footman and maidservant had read, then maybe attended, before the paper was torn and dirtied and used elsewhere.

Why be observant of the inanimate, so blind to the animate?

She sat down again on the bed. She could delay no further. She must read the letter.

There were several scrawled pages within the folded outer sheet. They were numbered, otherwise there was nothing to indicate when they were written or in what order they should be read. Yes, she could delay after all. Though this writing might contain the riddle of her life, it was not inviting. She didn't want to read it.

She went down the stairs until she met the young maid who'd first spoken to her when she'd been recovering in bed. She remembered her now as the girl who'd helped her with her hair and dress when she and Aksel Stamer had first arrived from their long journey. It seemed so very far in the past.

She ordered coffee and a baguette to be brought to her room. Napoleon had standardised shapes of bread – it was necessary to declare what size she wanted. This took time. Then she had to wait for the order to arrive before she could begin on the letter.

Would it contain the destruction of Gilbert and did she fear it? She doubted that. His words had always delivered Caroline's infuriating complacency or a reproach to herself. Something else was troubling her. She tried not to let it be heard – but it was insistent.

Why would a strange man seek her out in Venice and save her from the dreadful fate of being apprehended by the authorities and perhaps condemned to death or a life in prison? Why would he struggle with intermittent kindness to carry her across Europe and deposit her here by the woman whom she'd once thought might be his goal but who was perhaps simply a cover for what he'd wanted all along?

Would this letter mention a very young Danish man who had visited a Herefordshire rectory more than thirty years before?

The coffee and baguette arrived after a long half-hour during which she'd simply watched the torn paper take its erratic path around the courtyard to be trapped by the dusty spiked plant. A weak sun formed a weak shadow on the top of the far wall.

Sarah had once said she should learn to do nothing. Was this the nothing urged on her? It did not feel good.

She opened the package and read the first words. The beginning was abrupt. 'Ann: when you read this I shall be dead. You will be rid of me and I shall be at peace.'

Blood rushed to her face. Was this to be an embittered document, pouring hot coals on the head of a daughter who had not been dutiful because, in her view, a mother had failed first? It was quite possible. Caroline always had an acute sense of what a child owed a parent, nothing of the reverse. She knew her Bible: children must honour parents, it was a commandment. There was nothing, nothing, she'd once said – while jabbing a finger on a black embossed book she showed no other sign of respecting – about parents honouring children.

The letter continued, 'For the last years I have suffered, it is hard to describe how much I have suffered. First there was . . .'

Ann read on, skipped a little, then more, read with mounting disbelief and dismay. For it proceeded as it had begun, sentence after sentence, paragraph after paragraph, page after page, almost a kind of diary of symptoms and pain and physical decay.

It was not the document to explain all, indeed anything of what a daughter wanted.

Ann had to drink her coffee and order more to push herself through what she'd begun by skipping, only to find that the whole simply varied a single note. Caroline said almost nothing of their shared past. Instead she gave details of a body and mind rotting. Perhaps to describe such disintegration had been comforting, even enjoyable. Why else write this stuff? It could give pleasure to no one else, not even malicious enjoyment to an enemy.

The letter assumed in the reader – and Ann could have been the only one intended – an extraordinary interest in the minutiae of a last illness. Caroline must have begun writing as she realised that this time she was indeed dying of something nasty in her nether regions, some growth or decay causing symptoms Ann would rather not have known about. Much of blood, phlegm, regurgitated food, bleeding bowels, diarrhoea, vomiting after purging, leeches and cuppings, moments of delirium, of the rise and fall of pain from obstructed organs, even of failing continence, of all the nostrums and medicines tried from different apothecaries. And through it all the efforts that the maid – no, the companion – Madame Renée had made to find a cure; then, when nothing served, to ease the symptoms and calm the patient. All this translated into a dignified failing of the 'heart'.

What a document! Who would want to expose themselves like this? Caroline apparently.

Ann remembered being ordered to look up Buchan for diagnoses and remedies when her mother had declared her headaches or belly pain worthy of more consideration. The volume had often been open in the house; though, when it came to treatment, it was usually Martha who provided simple relief.

The corpse-like body on the bed and the Caroline she once knew were coalescing, so that she could now see the skull beneath a living face, the dying beneath the living mother. She felt disgusted and dirtied. As if she'd taken down that dripping hanging body in Venice and embraced it after all.

The last few words were written in disordered hand. They mentioned Madame Renée but were hardly legible. These must have been the sentences Caroline had struggled to write from bed. With her own decaying hand. There'd been no amanuensis.

It would be a long while before she could erase the details from her mind, such vile expulsion of humours from phlegm to bile. How utterly unsuitable for a daughter. Had Madame Renée seen this letter? Caroline had set such store by her and she'd been fond: for how else explain her scorn of Ann? If she'd read all this, what would it have done to her feelings for her friend?

Perhaps nothing at all – for she must have heard the details and seen the proof. Caroline was not someone to keep complaint within or for her paper.

The two of them would have talked often of this and other things, shut up alone in the gloomy house. Indeed now, with sudden illumination, Ann understood the preposterous query of her mother's about the Princess Caroline.

The two old women were gossips. For all the sternness of countenance she'd shown to Ann, Madame Renée was simply someone who enjoyed living with Caroline and talking with her as Mrs Graves and Mrs Pugh had done so many years before in Putney. And the ridiculous royal family of England was still the best story going in Europe. With the consonance of names it was irresistible.

Through Ann her mother had wanted to give something special to her devoted friend and carer, a kind of gift. With a child there could not be adult gossip, just make-believe. But, with another adult, it was the very stuff of intimacy.

To this woman she'd told what she could never quite bring herself to tell her daughter, even when close to death: of the deflation of Gilbert the marvellous.

It remained startling. For surely after all that time and so much loving detail Caroline had made Gilbert live – not just for his supposed child but for herself. She must have known this image so well he could enter her dreams in every shape. She had no reason to murder him like this.

What a torture it must have been! Ann would never know how it came about. Had she arrived suddenly in her right mind after a lifetime of deception and fantasy, then asked Madame Renée to tell her daughter the ludicrous truth?

How on earth had Madame Renée borne it? After all her imaginative living, her absurd lying, had Caroline found some love in this unprepossessing Frenchwoman who had cared for her in her last disintegrating days, so wanted with her at least to tell the truth? As a result, did Ann feel a glimmer of affection for Caroline? She interrogated herself, then felt relieved that she did not.

But she was thankful to Madame Renée that she hadn't tried earlier to find the absent daughter, for the caring must have been arduous, however much help they had. Presumably the income Caroline had always received – Ann had believed it a legacy from Gilbert – had continued.

But possibly, until close to the end, Madame Renée was not apprised of any daughter.

Perhaps after subsiding into partial truth Caroline had reverted to being a maiden childless lady, destroying at once both unreal father and real daughter.

But then she'd recollected, and Madame Renée had done the rest.

Interesting to her that, with no further proof, she'd so quickly accepted the Frenchwoman's remark. Had she suspected something earlier? Underneath layers of acceptance, of exasperation at all this reverencing and adoring, yearning and God knew what other emotions, surely she had wondered about this man who spoke only through Caroline? No tangible thing of him remained. She was never shown a letter written by him and of course the miniature, the prized miniature – she blushed for her gullibility – had never been clearly seen. How strange her mother had not simply found an image for her mantelpiece, even an unflattering one, and called it Gilbert. Unattached miniature portraits were easily bought – why did she not rest desire in any man of halfway decent, and clear, features?

Perhaps invention needed to swing free. Gilbert lived in words, and not just any words – in those serialised romantic novels and stories young Ann so soon rejected from the *Lady's Magazine* and which Caroline declared she never read. He was an old-fashioned construction, a hybrid, a woman's imagining of a respectful gentleman who never was or possibly could be. Then her creation had soared through her ordinary life and tinged it with a romance, an impossible love without ending.

It had no need, had no place, for anyone else, certainly not for a daughter. The protagonist was always young and would never need a great girl hanging on her girdle. By my soul, this Gilbert had said, I can neither eat, drink nor sleep for I can love no other woman but you.

31

She would not lacerate herself by seeking out Madame Renée and asking more questions. She would not stay to bury her mother. She had abandoned one dead body: she could leave another. If Caroline had left any money she would not want it, though Madame Renée might have feared she would. It was right that it go to the person who'd cared for her.

Aksel Stamer had put a substantial amount in the pouch and had apparently paid the lodgings ahead of time. He'd assumed she might have to stay a while in Paris for her dying mother, then a week or so to ensure her papers were in order and her travel plans fixed. With this money she could make some amends to Madame Renée.

She called the young maid again and asked for writing paper and a packet. She then took one of the high notes and placed it in the packet, accompanied with a note. She avoided a temptation to suggest a headstone marked 'Caroline and Gilbert, imaginary lovers' but simply informed Madame Renée that she would like her mother's remains interred in Mont-Louis outside the Paris wall.

The next day she had the young maid – her name was Marie, she'd made a point of learning it – move her belongings into the smaller room. She began preparing for departure in the way Aksel Stamer had instructed her.

In the evening, still feeling weak, she walked with hesitant steps through Paris. The autumn air had now a definite chill. Had they observed her closely, people might have judged her a little tipsy. The clothes bought when she and Aksel Stamer first came to Paris fitted ill, she'd become all angles and bones.

She should have used her waiting time to visit the Louvre, to see the ransacked treasures of Europe not all returned since Napoleon's fall, but she lacked the energy. Instead she sat in the Luxembourg Gardens watching clouds. Had Aksel Stamer really left the city? Would he perhaps come by and find her sitting there?

He had gone just when she most needed his stern presence. Her fever had left her but she was still in the glass jar. Who else could break it open and let her out?

As hard as she tried not to think of them, she couldn't erase Caroline and Gilbert. She shook her head, focused on a yellowing tree and shuffled her feet on the ground to shift the images.

But they wouldn't go. Her mind fixed randomly on items – the thin sliced ham in Vauxhall Gardens. Where had that come from? Had Caroline read of it or had she visited with someone else? Was she there to pick up passing trade? The thought evaporated, as too far-fetched. Caroline, so fastidious about herself, was never a whore. And yet no identity was certain now. Not only the sliced ham but the fine wine, the special shells. What of them? With whom did she eat whitebait? Surely not alone. The Royal Hospital at Greenwich had been too grand for Gilbert's taste, said Caroline, too royal.

It was and always had been only Caroline's voice. Did she invent the words as well as read them or hear them from another man given Gilbert's name because of some unspeakable betrayal?

It was all flooding back to her, creeping over the edge of her glass jar. The gold, silver and crystal pendant from Cox's, the silver swan. Had any item ever been touched? Did any exist? The pendant had not been in the box of trinkets and she had never seen it. But in her mind the images of a silver swan, a shell and sliced ham went round and round dragging their names behind them.

She began to wonder about everything. What of her own memories? Was everything *she* remembered real? That amazing irruption into her dull childhood: the visit to Mrs Wright's waxworks? That must have happened for the humiliation remained intense – humiliation was always real. They'd laughed at her for thinking the waxwork seated on a settee a live person. She remembered, too, the slaps and boxes on the ear from Caroline, the reproach of stupidity when she failed to shine at music after a few lessons, her idiocy, her ugliness when no one dressed her limp hair, her hanging lip when she'd had a cold, her simple bodily presence as she grew – awkwardly – into a woman. Yes, all of that was real enough.

Already as a child she'd noticed some discrepancies in the story her mother told. To meet his death, in one account her father had been translated into a soldier. When she'd doubted it, she'd been slapped for insolence again – she remembered the feel of that though Caroline's blows were never hard unless she was in a passion.

'Maybe he simply choked to death on a small cake with his coffee,' she'd said. Another slap followed. A feeble one but yet, as others followed, in the end she cried. Then they stopped.

Ann had meant the question sincerely, for she had herself nearly choked on scalding milk and dry bread one morning.

But other memories began to totter. Thoughts and words and images were sliding and slipping, growing nasty and self-mocking, as she sat on the bench apparently doing nothing, a youngish woman approaching middle age alone. With tears running down her cheeks.

She took out her handkerchief and wiped her face. She must pull herself together and at least control her demeanour. No wonder people, on seeing her, had quickly looked away: a mad foreign person in the park in the thin evening sunlight. It was not done.

So why stay here? Surely it would be best to go home. The papers would be in order. They had only to be picked up. That was it. It was time to go home.

But where was home? London, she supposed. But not Holborn or St Paul's Churchyard or Paternoster-Row. Maybe Sarah's little house in Somers Town where she could not stay, but which would take her in for a dinner as families do, a dish of tea, some chat between childish interruptions and maternal fussing. It was not and would not be her home, but it was *like* a home.

For once she would travel alone. It could not be difficult. She had her instructions and she'd made so many of the arrangements when she'd journeyed with Robert, at least the sensible ones, for he'd always taken expensive passage and argued ideas not fares with people only interested in fleecing them. She could get to London without any more drama.

She would not be quite alone, however. The shade of Aksel Stamer, that kind, stony-faced man, stayed with her. She knew she was letting him inhabit places where he'd no secure business to be. But she was still weak from illness, that had to be some excuse.

Perhaps the suspicion, hope rather, would in the end be baseless. But for now she was aware she was replacing Gilbert with Aksel Stamer. But he was acts and gestures, hardly words at all.

She let him circle inside her head. What was he and what was he about? Why had he thought a Paris swan like a clockwork bird? Had he seen Caroline's silver swan at Cox's?

He seemed to have enough money to commandeer service, send servants to get passes and ease their journey when needed: could his money have been the source of Caroline's income all those years?

Why, then, had he lost touch? Why not come to see them long before now?

And why had he left so abruptly after travelling so far?

When faced with seeing Caroline towards her end, could he have lost courage, fearing to assume the care of yet another burdensome woman? After all, he'd been forced to drag one across Europe. He could simply have had enough of women hanging on him and want the freedom of the man alone.

His going could be as significant as his coming all the way to Paris, all the way to the very house.

Had she herself been dismissed? Was she supposed not to see him again? She feared that might have been his meaning. Perhaps he was glad to be rid of her.

But why had he bothered with her in the first place? How had he found her in Venice?

Of course, of course. He'd been at Palazzo Grimani at the *poste restante*. She knew that by now. He'd stood close to her and could have heard what she and the clerk said. She always called herself Signora James, but on this occasion to receive her letter she'd clearly given her name as Miss Ann St Clair. That was why he knew her.

After that he'd put himself where she was. In Padua where he didn't seem the usual tourist.

That he was Stamer not St Clair was a problem, but at least an initial was shared, and she knew he passed under more than one name, like Robert James. He'd begun as Jakobsen.

She didn't look like him, but not quite unalike, especially now they were both burnt by the sun. He had remarked it, she remembered. She had flat English features, that compression of eyes, nose and mouth; Aksel Stamer had something of the look – though in truth not much. But then children did not always resemble parents. Except that she had Caroline's hands . . .

And the age? He would have to have been so young when . . . she could not quite say it. He was older than she was but not by enough. He would have been twenty years younger than Caroline. It was too much for a man. But it was not impossible. Make his age greater, Caroline's less.

She was growing weary of her thoughts. Her mad circling thoughts. She berated herself.

She got up, still a little unsteady, then walked slowly back to the inn, wondering as she went along whether she had become infected with her own plots after all. Her girls found noble fathers in every decent older man they met, while harbouring fears or strange desires for villains along the way. Fathers revealed themselves in words, in letters found in old carved chests deep below ground.

But these were novel tales and the girls were seventeen. She was twice their age. And the letter, the significant letter, had said nothing. Was she finding a father in anyone a little kind? Was it really all an effort to eliminate that very real man in her life, that Robert James?

Aksel Stamer had not encouraged any such imagining. He had given no hints as to why he was with her. Once or twice, especially towards the end of their journey, she thought she'd seen a furtive smile directed to her when she was not looking at him, but it might have been a trick of the light. These moments had been rare. Nothing like the resplendent gaze of Gilbert on his Caroline. And so little speech. Yet so kind.

She must go back to England. Earn a living. Aksel Stamer's gift, though generous, would be soon spent. She would return to the life that in retrospect did not seem so very dull.

Aksel Stamer had arranged so much for her it was hard to start again making her own decisions. But she must decide whether to take the route to the coast through Beauvais or Amiens. When she'd passed that way before with Robert, she'd wanted to see the fruit trees, the cornfields, the vineyards, the buildings, the people. But now she'd surfeited on travelling and looking. She had no appetite for touring abbeys and palaces.

London

32

London was what it had always been, big, dirty, bustling and fretful.

She went to a cheapish inn she knew in Judd Street and took a room for a few days while she decided where to seek more permanent lodgings. Her furniture was still in store in Holborn and she would need to bring it out when she settled. For she must live and work, she supposed, though nothing was clear.

One Caroline was dead but the other one was very much alive. While his daughter-in-law was wandering scandalously round the Continent, old mad George III had died and his disreputable son become George IV. So had not Caroline been Queen Consort these many months? To the new King's horror she began a noisy progress towards his country.

The ministers of the Crown rushed to France to drive her away. They offered money, bribes, anything to keep her out. But she was undeterred. She was Queen of England if her husband was King.

The people were overjoyed. As ever, they loved the royal shenanigans. Caroline was far more entertaining than her fat spouse who was most of the time too drunk or embarrassed to show himself to his subjects. They wanted her in London: they wanted to be enrolled in the Order of St Caroline with Count Pergami and the rest of her flamboyant entourage.

So back she'd come with the summer, as large as life and far more popular than she deserved. She stood for everything that everyone desired, against all they hated – and people had much to hate in these oppressive postwar years.

She'd demanded to stay in the old Queen's palace but ended in South Audley Street instead; shop windows exhibited effigies of her person in royal robes with crown and sceptre. She mortified the government as they tried and failed to prove her any worse than her outrageous spouse.

How young Beatrice must be enjoying all this, Ann thought as she heard the news. Venice seemed so very far away; yet she could picture her pretty pupil receiving foreign gazettes through Giancarlo Scrittori, poring over them with much glee and little improvement to her 'pure' English. The Contessa would gently chide her, while her eye as ever would be fixed on her dreadful darling son. It could not have been easy for a girl to grow up with such a brother. Some entertainment was deserved.

Ann was desperate to see Sarah, yet she didn't go to her at once. A cleft would have opened up through all these agitated months and she was afraid she couldn't account for herself, afraid perhaps of her cousin's pity if she heard the half of it.

Finally she did call at the little house in Somers Town. Sarah was away from home with the two older children. The nursery maid who'd been there when Ann had left was now looking after the younger ones. She was helped by a rather sulky girl, who stood close behind her as she opened the door. Unless Sarah had a baby with her, at least there appeared to be no new infants. Something to be relieved about.

They were gone to the menagerie at Exeter Exchange, said the maid. It was William's birthday and it was a treat for him. They'd left the little ones at home. She would tell her mistress that the lady had called.

Ann was not recognised. Was she so changed?

'No, please say nothing. I will call again very soon.'

'But, Ma'am, I must say someone has visited.'

Ann could see the maid had an inkling she knew her voice. It might be the strange abrupt cousin from so long ago, but she was not sure: the clothes, the hair, the figure were all wrong, only the way she talked had something familiar about it.

'I will be here again very soon,' Ann repeated. With that she left. The maid stared after her.

When she returned a couple of days later she was shown in by the same maid whose name she really should have known. Jennie, it seemed. With a pang she remembered Madame Renée.

Clearly the young woman had obeyed her instructions, for Sarah was amazed to see her cousin. So expressive was her wide white countenance that she couldn't hide the dismay with which she contemplated the gaunt face and thin figure before her. But she uttered nothing except excited words of welcome.

'Come in, come in, sit, eat, drink, be warm and comfortable with us. Tell us everything. Why did you not write more of yourself?'

Ann should have been full of travellers' tales, *her* tales, but she was still in the glass jar. She said almost nothing.

She'd brought no exotic presents – it must seem odd to go so far and come back with so little for those who stayed behind. She'd only a silver box on which two stags touched mouths in a kind of kiss. She handed it to Sarah with no explanation. Her cousin exclaimed as one must do with gifts, but asked no questions.

When silence followed the initial greetings, Sarah chatted on. She told her cousin little things about the children, how one twin was much quicker than the other but both were adorable, about Charles being promoted for his careful recording work at the India Office, about some little changes they were making about the house, even about the day out at Exeter Exchange they'd just taken for William's birthday, the excitement and wonder of Charlotte at the bear and lion and tiger as well as a midget on stilts. With the tact for which Ann was so grateful, she never in all the time said, And where is Robert?

'I am looking for lodgings,' said Ann.

'Of course, and you are back for good? Let me help you. Why not find something near us? And please stay here while you look.'

The little crowded house almost spoke its welcome, but Ann could not trust her grave presence to its warmth, even if there'd been room, and surely there was no nook or cranny without its little body stuffed into it.

Sarah saw her hesitate. 'We can move a bed into Charlotte's room. She will like an aunty to chat to at night.'

Ann doubted it and could not imagine herself much company for a child, but she found the offer soothing.

'No, Sarah, I will not impose like that. I am already looking at apartments that might suit.'

'Then I will accompany you in your search. I can see where you would be most comfortable. I am good at finding out the possibilities of a room. Oh, I would enjoy it.'

'No,' said Ann again, 'do not come with me. I will look for my own lodgings but, when I have found somewhere, please come and see it with me. I don't know that I'm capable of judging what is comfortable.'

'Dear Ann,' said Sarah, and pressed her hand.

Her lowness of spirits was so palpable it repelled some acquaintances. A few weeks after she arrived she met Mary Davies going to the booksellers. She stared at Ann complacently from her healthy plumpness. She was better dressed than Ann remembered; she understood why when Mary announced she'd moved her talents to John Harris, who appreciated them rather more than Mr Hughes had done. They talked a little of nothing in particular and made no plan to meet. Ann learned again the lesson of all returning travellers: that those who stay at home are little interested in what they did not see or choose to see. Even she perhaps, stationary in London, would not have wanted to hear of the huge sea wall, the cormorants, the Titian *Assumption*, the forsaken chapel, the dripping hanging body and the old, old woman. No, as she reviewed the past year, she was sure that she would not.

She found rooms in Bloomsbury near the Judd Street inn where she was staying and not so far from Somers Town with Sarah and Charles and their brood, near enough to walk over for a dish of tea or share an afternoon dinner when she would not be in the way.

It was wet and cold for the season and the building she'd chosen looked grimy. The smoke over the city was thicker than she remembered and it mingled threateningly with the low cloud to form a pall on the houses. Venice had been freezing or at the least very cold and damp much of the time, misty so that she could hardly see a gondola bobbing on the lagoon. She told herself to hold on to the bitter cold of a town that denied it was ever cold, the houses so beautiful, so palatial in the heat but chilly caverns in the long winter. She must try not to exaggerate the greenness of the past. Yet now it was Venice's twinkling water and swooping seagulls in the azure sky she remembered most.

In this prelude to the northern winter, it was hard to capture the dried-out rivers of Sardinia, the sweltering stones of Italy, the fragrant smell of pine, earth and salt. Images yes, but the full experience on her mind and body had gone with the sunshine.

Anyway, there was something deathly about that intense pure sky, at least for a northerner such as she. It was too close to an infinity a mortal couldn't share. Surely the grey covering and scudding clouds were more honest, more human in scale, nearer to the quotidian experience of everyone.

Still, underneath the remembered blue sky and the experienced grey one, the body twisted in her mind and dangled through her thoughts. The dying mother had largely disappeared. Buried, she supposed, in a respectable grave with a Frenchwoman to mourn her. And the father who had shifted his shape, who still lived: it was impossible at once to destroy him. Through Gilbert's ludicrous words and Aksel Stamer's crazy possibility, wasn't he still there?

In the daytime memories and visions could on the whole be contained, even banished with determined effort, but they were not to be shifted in fitful sleep.

It was early December by the time she moved fully into her new lodgings. They were satisfactory but not as fine as the old ones had been. The money from Aksel Stamer was almost gone and she must soon start making her own living. She couldn't be sure of earning enough for anywhere too lavish.

Cousin Charles helped with the move by organising the retrieval and delivery of her furniture from store near Holborn. Sarah came round, bringing some hothouse flowers that must have cost her trouble to find and afford – and some new teacups and saucers to welcome her in. Perhaps she knew how saturated with memory her thin Spode ones would be.

Ann bit her lip to prevent being too moved. Her feebleness irritated her. She wanted to be light and laughing with this kind cousin, but all she could do was turn a grave face towards her and mouth appreciation.

'You must see your friends, cousin Ann. You are too much alone.'

'I see you.'

'Oh, we are family, Charles and I and the children. We don't count. Move back to London properly. You were so snug here when we first met.'

But she didn't feel snug any longer and she doubted she ever would again.

Why had Aksel Stamer gone so suddenly? She feared she knew.

Sarah had brought over from her house as another present to brighten her dull rooms a pretty glass with flowered and bevelled edge; she'd placed it in an angle that proved unflattering and cruel when Ann caught herself within it. Now she saw this image she wondered if Aksel Stamer had simply been appalled at her hollow gaunt appearance, daughter or no daughter, and fled before it.

How did others see her? A thin faded spinster, a bastard presumably, certainly a whore – by conventional standards for she'd been with two men and married neither. Luckily they'd not made her with-child – there was a relief; she would not have grown easily into a mother, no aptitude, no experience. None the less, to those who knew, she was as damaged in reputation and character as in appearance.

Yet Sarah, the conventional wife, never seemed to mind – there was the miracle.

How had she never before appreciated just how wonderful this gentle cousin was? Perhaps by contrast Aksel Stamer was, deep down, an ordinary man who was simply disappointed at women who did not look bright and modest and walk with masculine strides. He had helped but wanted no more of her.

But, as it all twisted round her mind, she found it hard to contradict that moment when he soothed her ankle. Was she misremembering the time and its emotion? After all, she'd been half-dazed with tiredness and pain. If it was not a father's love, it was at least a rare tenderness.

It rained incessantly. Or so it seemed. The London streets were mud and dung through which the butchers' and bakers' hacks shambled. At night the pattering of drops on the roof slates kept her awake. And then in the dark early hours of the morning the sweetness of what she had lost overwhelmed her, while the horror of the losing burnt on.

She couldn't hide herself away. If she didn't at once take Sarah's advice and seek out old acquaintances, she must at least deliver her work. She still had with her the pages of *Isabella: or, the Secrets of the Convent*. They were crinkled and creased, being wet then dry, then wet again, and some of the ink had smudged. She'd carried these bedraggled words all across Europe. She would need to rewrite or copy the material before she could present it anywhere.

As she spread out the pages she felt traces of fine sand and smelled the faint odour of rosemary and pine needles.

Although she'd been gone so long she still retained her reputation for fast writing, for meeting deadlines, for doing what was required, no more, no less. But she needed to keep up with changes, with public taste.

When she'd visited Mr Dean and told him what she was writing and planned to write, he looked at her quizzically. She supposed it was her altered appearance or perhaps this time away had made her seem a revenant to those who stayed.

She offered her castles and chains and weeping girls. Of course, of course, they were always welcome, she knew that, but she must know too that something else was now wanted. The times required more moral teaching.

She was surprised. Was this directed at the author or the work? She hoped the latter.

'You mean,' she said, 'you think I am a little behind the public taste? People want less sensation and more goodness, more virtue?'

'No, Miss St Clair, certainly not. More sensation *and* more morality. It may seem contradictory to you but you can do it, I am sure. Young Mr Munday and I will always want what you write.'

Mr Dean patted her arm in an avuncular way, felt her thinness and gave her an encouraging smile.

But no one would encourage long without proof that she could make him money. No more than other booksellers like Mr Hughes or Mr Newman did Mr Dean or Mr Munday give favours. And they were never a certainty. She must move with the times and move quickly. She had a horror of poverty. It was her only spur.

Mr Hughes probably still held his weekly dinners for authors but he proffered no invitation to her – in any case she'd never been a regular. When they met in the street after her return, he was polite and uninterested.

It was just as well. Mr Hughes knew Richard Perry and Luigi Orlando, and they would ask after Robert if she were there. She had no stomach yet for sociability. No prepared story to tell.

The flowers Sarah had delivered had long wilted and Ann had bought no others to cheer her lodgings. They were an extravagance just at this time. The room was not unpleasant but not light, in fact a little dismal even when it was bright weather outside. She'd done so little to decorate it. Some coloured cushions and prints might make a difference.

Sarah called round but didn't stay. It was nothing to do with the discomfort of the lodgings but Amy had gone to visit a very sick sister and Jennie couldn't look after the children alone; the girl employed to help was worse than useless. Sarah laughed. Again, there was no time for any real talk, just that sizing up of each other without comment.

She was not eating well. Since Aksel Stamer left she'd hardly taken or bought food sensibly, preferring instead to live on what was hawked in the streets, the pies and buns of dubious nourishment. Sarah had brought round some homemade stew, being sure her cousin was not living properly. 'You must eat, Ann,' she said as she went down the stairs, 'put some flesh back on your bones.'

33

So this was her life.

After Caroline, after the glorious Gilbert – Gilbert who had never added up – how could she have been so credulous, she who prided herself on seeing through deceit, she a maker of stories? After Gregory Lloyd even, after Robert James, and after Aksel Stamer, here she was.

Caroline had loved somebody, an elderly Frenchwoman it seemed, and not her. The selfishness she'd resented was impressive – her mother had needed no Gilbert by the end – though it had once been her bulwark against a nasty world. So she'd simply destroyed him for her daughter and herself.

Ann sometimes feared she'd inherited this selfishness, at other times knew it for a skill she lacked but should learn. Often she'd no idea which was true. She had no illusion she knew what and who she was. Now there was no one left through whom to find out more.

She should have been relieved to be back. Apart from work there was much to do in London. She could go to the theatre, she could shop in the bazaars and markets and look at the windows in Bond Street; she could walk in St James's Park and Lincoln's Inn Fields; she could visit Montagu House on Monday, Wednesday or Friday and see the Parthenon sculptures so cried up by poets, meet Mary Davies and other genteel hacks at an East India tea-room or in Lloyd's Coffee House where people still collected for the Patriotic Fund though Napoleon's war was long over. It was a life as others lived it.

And yet the melancholy was enveloping her more and more. As

inexorable as the fever that had descended on her in Paris. It inhabited her rooms, as if she'd rented part of them out to this lodger who was each day taking up a bit more of the space, making it danker and darker and less fit for anyone else to live in. It had crept inside her glass jar.

Nothing was how she'd anticipated. The horror of both her dead had not gone. In her head she was at a perpetual funeral. But people at funerals were always a little glad, a little gay within their black velvet and crisp bombazine. It was worse than that.

One night she was on her bed fully dressed, not bothering to light a candle, not preparing for sleep, though she was usually so fastidious about keeping the bedchamber as the place for rest. Instead she lay there as a stranger might, letting Robert flow over her, Robert as he'd been before his ideas were litanies, before they both became itinerants not inhabitants, before he thought that God had forsaken Attila and himself and was shitting on his worlds.

Was it right to forgive him in this way – for surely that was implied? Would it not be better to hold on to the outrage, to continue to hate the thing? But she could not avoid the truth: that she forgave him everything. He was violent because he couldn't stand losing the vividness – vividness that he'd momentarily given her and she had lost with him.

No, there should be no forgiveness, no excuse for him or for her. Since it was – also – her fault. She had thrown away the only person who'd enthralled her, who'd overshadowed Gilbert in all his imaginary splendour. If she hadn't murdered him literally, she had done so in other ways, by hating him and wanting him dead, and more, by being dull, by being ordinary and needy.

She deserved all the violence she'd suffered.

If she deserved it, what was the point of lamenting? She was better not being. Robert had had the courage to see that – for himself, she knew it now. But she averted her eyes from the memory of what that courage had achieved. It was a man's way to go so explosively.

The images hovered before and behind her eyes. There was no

point in closing or opening them. What she saw in front and inside the lids, dissolving and recomposing, was sometimes so bright it scorched her brain.

Then suddenly Aksel Stamer was present, stern and tall. Yet he was merging with the butterfly he named. It gave his silhouette a dazzling, translucent, shimmering quality. It was no image for a man so grounded on the earth, so stolid in mind, so present even where so little expected.

She bought pens and sheets of paper and set to work copying *Isabella; or, the Secrets of the Convent*, trying to move the elements of her work around to look like invention. It was hard going. Indeed, there were times when nothing seemed worthwhile, not even making a living. A hopelessness tinged everything.

Why struggle on? Robert had shown the way.

It was no disgrace to yearn for blackness, that perpetual night he feared but never quite believed true – he was always a Catholic boy. She would never leave life in his disgusting manner, but there could be grace in the going. It was possible to drift away more easily, with less repugnant display. Had he died quietly and alone on the Lido he might have been covered in sand and beauty, like the white bones she'd fixed there in her mind for so long.

She began to imagine her own scene, a scene as it *should* be. After days of silence, Sarah would come to visit her lodgings. She would find her peacefully on her bed on a check blue-and-white coverlet. Nothing would be disgusting, none of that dreadful incontinence of the hanging corpse. She could buy enough laudanum to do the job. She'd know the amount. She was susceptible to its power: she was a poor sleeper but with only a small portion of this drug she fell into the limbo she craved. It would be easy enough to take more and go beyond.

She would finish the book she'd agreed to write. She had a sense of duty – God knows where it came from. Wryly she noticed that, unlike Robert, she would not leave a few incoherent scraps and a fouled pile of paper, but a simple, tidily written manuscript of absolutely no value, competent, decent and ordinary. *Isabella; or, the*

Secrets of the Convent would be on the table beside a note for Sarah and Charles asking them to deliver it to Dean & Munday and receive the payment.

She collected laudanum from two apothecaries in Camden and Bloomsbury. She hid it in case Sarah came and suspected what she might be about.

Then she decided not to leave a note. What did it matter what happened when she was not there? Or perhaps she would leave something cryptic, so that no coroner could report that she was a suicide in sound mind.

The main point was that she would go without fuss. She'd like to have been anonymous but that could only work if she took a room in a distant inn. She wouldn't fancy travelling on that special day; she'd wish to be at home, she was sure of it.

She thought again of the note, whether or not to leave one. She must not appear to have died through any extravagance of emotion but through reason. It was quite simply that she had had enough. 'Thank you very much,' the note could say. That would be short and to the point.

But to whom could this note be addressed? Those she would 'thank' in that tone were all dead.

No, she would depart without undue seriousness or levity, without glamour or staginess, just go because it would be pleasant not to be here. She would declare no desperation or fashionable *ennui* from too much high or intense living. She would simply admit to being bored with being herself, having had such a bad hand that she'd always been in debt to every passer-by who wished to play with her.

She knew of course that no imaginary watcher would think her death pragmatic or sensible. It was not in the nature of the comfortably cheerful. Was it not enough that she thought so?

But she remained unsure of practicalities. Did they still bury bodies at crossroads at midnight? She rather thought not, at least not often, though she'd created such bizarre burials in her tales. A mare would shy at the spot, at that place where no Christian rites had been said; quaint will-o'-the-wisp lights would emerge to lure travellers to their doom. Nothing like that. England was an improving if less heroic nation. Here her act would be accounted less blasphemous than wayward. There would be no essential ghost in these modern times, no thin veil over a spirit as it crossed that boundary, no stake to keep it hidden, no traffic back and forth tramping and impacting the grave.

She was glad this was an enlightened age. She'd have no aptitude for being spectral.

Whatever she left or didn't leave, it should all happen on a day when Sarah, after the interval of silence, would call and find her, not the maid who occasionally whisked a duster round the rented rooms and termed it cleaning.

She could already hear Sarah, kind, uncomfortable and sorrowing. She shook her head to remove the words for she didn't deserve their pity. Or she deserved it more than Sarah and Charles ought ever to know.

'My poor cousin was disordered, infatuated,' Sarah would say, 'else she would never have left us. For it is against all sense, all nature, all religion to do this. She cannot have meant it, poor darling. She must have mistaken the dose.' She would pause and look pensive. 'Did we do enough, Charles?'

And what if Aksel Stamer, the inscrutable, the icy, the kind, was indeed her father and came back to find her? He had struggled to Paris with her, why wouldn't he come to London from whatever chilly northern shore he now strode along?

She stared at herself in the unflattering glass, catching and fixing her reflected eyes. They stared back at her with a haunted look. It made her dizzy to keep her real ones on the reflected ones, which faded in and out, yellowing into Caroline's but never quite disappearing.

She'd forgotten to breathe as she gazed. Now she started again. The image was still there. *She* was still there. She could send herself mad by staring at herself.

Was she perhaps a little mad? Poor old Ann. As mad as her mother who'd lived with a ghost all those years.

But that was not mad, it was breathtaking. What a sublime invention! You had to admire it.

Then she simply postponed killing herself. She'd assembled more than sufficient laudanum for the deed, but instead of using it for its original purpose, she prudently took small doses and achieved a deeper and longer sleep at night. It made a difference.

Time too was making an alteration. Her morbid state of mind was still there, she knew, the rank poison had entered her veins and stuck. But it was thinning. The glass jar might have cracked.

She was not quite sure why the change occurred but she knew that on some days she actually felt sorry for Caroline, the old story-teller and gossip, maybe even a little guilty.

To be more precise, she found her anger turning to scornful pity. It was not a nurturing emotion but improved on rage.

She'd linked suicide with reparation. But, when she consulted common sense, she knew her death would make not one whit of difference to Robert's. Besides, there was no need for guilt at what had been accidental for her: no sin or crime had been committed. He'd made a choice and in that choice had ignored her. So her act would not be linked to his.

No, if she'd destroyed her life – and she still might – this too would have been her choice and not necessity. It would be a way of silently absenting herself from further disappointment, having calculated that the past had on average held more pain than pleasure and was likely to continue in much the same way in the future. The guilt – for there was some, it couldn't be denied – came from knowing that, although she'd not killed him, she'd none the less wanted to do so, and that, if he'd not tumbled out of life, she'd still have been resentfully enthralled.

Then one day, turning the matter over in her mind, she realised she'd procrastinated too long.

Once this verb rather than 'postpone' was used, suicide was no longer a near option. It had become close to comedy.

34

She must start writing faster, recoup her reputation among the booksellers as a diligent inhabitant of Grub Street. Messrs Hughes & Newman and Dean & Munday must be fed with gore and goodness as they wished, and she should start stimulating herself to deliver. At least *Isabella; or, the Secrets of the Convent* was ready and could be printed. It was time to begin on *The Ladies of Zitelle; or, the Prisons of Venice*. One of her nuns could discourse on obedience and humility during a short interruption from torture. Another might be pecked to death by a mechanical swan whose clockwork never wound down.

She would get out. She'd stayed too long cooped up in her new lodgings. Perhaps she'd invite a friend to drink tea from Sarah's nice dishes while storing away those delicate grey-green cups of Robert's.

It was now late winter, no sign of spring. Leaves were turning into slush and mud on the ground as frost hardened and melted. She was cold in her rooms. She must buy something thick. It was never easy to keep warm while needing to sit still scratching at paper.

Happily, ideas and plots came fast to her as they usually did: she smiled to note she retained that despised facility for the clichés of language and story, that *chiaroscuro* of a world inhabited by nothing real.

She was not quite returning to her old life. The last time she'd lived it, she'd moved on to a plane of drama and tension she still missed but knew she should now avoid. It had cost too much.

This would be easy, for Robert James was gone. When she was at her sanest, he dwindled into a memory of vanity and vexation and (she had to admit it now) mutual torment. Even the spectral Gilbert had faded, his link with Robert left obscured, uninterrogated.

Only Aksel Stamer, the unlikely father, was still present.

Yet, although she entertained the fact and although he'd done so much for her, only explicable through close kinship, she couldn't quite think him back into her childhood, let alone her birth or conception. The idea of Caroline in middle age having a love affair with this young foreigner was truly too preposterous.

If she *had*, wouldn't she have embroidered this astounding event and not invented Gilbert at all?

For assuredly Aksel Stamer was not Gilbert. There'd been no cross-fertilisation there, the one so loquacious and loving, the other so reticent and stern.

It was all so double-dyed she resolved several times a day on the same course of action: not to think of the matter, to accept the unknowable, to be undemanding of herself, others and life, to skirt round pain and just carry on.

After Ann had eaten a number of the rich stews and meat pies so kindly sent over to her lodgings, Sarah expected some return. She was curious about the time abroad, an existence so very far from anything she'd experienced. She was careful of her cousin's feelings, her fragile state of mind; she didn't probe minutely.

Her interest lay not with the lagoon city and its paintings, the stuff of the two letters she'd received, but with Ann and her life. She wasn't sad to find that Robert had not returned with her cousin and unsurprised that he'd burnt himself out – with fever, she supposed. That type usually did. It was indelicate to ask the circumstances, they might have been painful for Ann to rehearse. That he was dead – and this Ann had finally confessed – was enough. With all her heart she pitied her cousin having to cope with such a dreadful thing in a foreign land. She could not imagine it. Weren't they Catholics there – what did they do?

She knew she'd have been utterly bereft without Charles in any emergency – but, then, she'd never have allowed herself to be in such a predicament.

She'd said it before and would say it again: her clever cousin was a child when it came to dealing with life.

Ann appreciated the reticence but – and she knew it ridiculous – was hurt at the seeming lack of interest in Robert's death, despite her firm intention to hide the details. That he was out of their lives was evidently enough for Sarah and Charles. It should be enough for her, too. And, beyond Robert, she gave Sarah little material on which to hang her questions. She made no mention of Aksel Stamer.

So Sarah beat round the important topics. How had Ann managed out of England? How had she liked being somewhere else? Whom had she met? Ann answered vaguely and described again some curious aspects of Venice, the need to travel everywhere by boat, the gaiety of the conquered city.

Sarah turned her eyes on the youngest child – the baby had grown into a little boy. He was, yes, the bonniest of the tribe. His little chubby legs and flaxen curls added up to a bundle of joy, it was hard to concentrate elsewhere.

Ann halted her account and regarded the child. She didn't usually notice children, had hardly done so when she first visited on her return. They never took to her; she lacked the expression or gesture – or indeed the kindly intention: but no small child could know what she thought, or could he?

This chubby little boy was no exception. There was the usual indifference or outright hostility. When asked to greet her, he turned away and buried his face in his mother's increasing flesh. There seemed more of Sarah than when she'd left England and her cousin had been quite ample then. Perhaps it was in part the contrast: for there was less of Ann.

On this visit she'd brought a few presents for the children, aware that on her arrival back she should have come bearing something beyond her careworn self and an old silver box. This time she carried a book, coloured papers, wooden dolls and alphabet blocks. She'd been duly thanked by Charlotte and one of the twins, with prompting from Sarah. William was away at school; Sarah was sure he would be grateful for *Aesop's Fables* when he returned.

But this little chap – was he called Henry? – did not achieve such courtesy with even a reluctant grin. And yet when by chance she came round the door unexpectedly from helping Sarah with the tea things down below – for, as ever, cook was simply too busy to do what was demanded by her mistress, having only one pair of very knobbly hands – he gave her a wide smile of such beauty it stopped her heart. Then he ducked behind a chair, or rather he put his head round it, like a cat leaving its tail in sight, thinking that by removing just his face he became invisible. Then he pulled it out and smiled again. 'Boo,' he said. They were playing.

Ann went out and in, out and in, and each time he smiled and laughed, his whole body wriggling with delight.

Suddenly she caught him up and hugged him. Astonished, he accepted for a moment, then squirmed and pulled away, giving her a serious, even cold look. But it was no matter. She'd seen his smile and it had been for her, no, provoked by her. The act, the embrace had been hers, no need of his.

She'd no time to be as astonished at herself as the child had been, for just then Sarah came back into the room. 'I see you're getting on with Harry,' she said, as the little boy raised chubby arms to be nuzzled by his mother.

'He's a pretty child,' said Ann, blushing as if caught in unseemly flirtation.

'Yes,' said Sarah. 'He is that.'

'Quick, too,' said Ann.

Sarah shrugged, 'As quick as he needs to be.'

They both smiled.

'It's not every woman's nature,' said Ann

'No, not every woman's,' said Sarah and stroked the chubby arm.

A silence followed. Then Sarah commented, 'You know in him I do sometimes remark a likeness around the eyes to you, cousin Ann. He has your way of narrowing just the one. I believe Charlotte has it too.'

Ann smiled. 'I must be going,' she said.

'Will you not wait for Charles? He will want to see you.'

Ann doubted that but replied politely, 'No, no, but I will come again when he's here, never fear. I was grateful for his help with my furniture. It's so long ago but I don't think I've really thanked him enough.'

'It was many weeks since, Ann – it's long forgotten. You must come more and come to dinner soon again. You are still too thin, dear cousin. You eat my pies but I can do more if you visit more. Cook will bake you the kind of pudding you can't resist and we'll put more flesh on those naked bones.'

'I'd like that. But you know I'm already fatter than I was when I returned to England. I did grow thin abroad.' The memory crossed her face. She looked serious.

'Come, Ann,' said Sarah, 'that foreign food. It's not for us north-born people. We are used to something better here.'

She put down the now drowsy child. He stood swaying close to her and the door. Ann reached over and ruffled the pale curls. The child shook his head to push her off.

'We will see you soon,' said Sarah as the door closed.

She'd been to Sarah's quite often since returning but hadn't asked what she'd wanted to. Perhaps she would always delay the moment.

There seemed now in the cold light of London so little possible connection between Caroline and a Danish stranger who'd become exotic through appearing and disappearing along the canals of Venice. She still hadn't mentioned him to Sarah; Aksel Stamer was her secret. Yet perhaps some piece of the puzzle might come from this source if she asked the right question.

After all, Sarah was the child of her mother's sister. That much was true, she supposed. Sarah accepted it, and wasn't there the likeness she'd mentioned with two of her children? Ann grimaced, a little embarrassed to think she might have been pleased at such a blatant compliment.

There did come a time when the useful moment and her courage coincided. Charles was at home, but not in the parlour where they sat or within earshot. The nursemaid and Jennie had all the children under their wing. It was relatively quiet. She would seize the instant. Sarah must know something. There was always gossip if not truth in families.

Ann began. She feared she would embed her thoughts so thoroughly in something else that her listener would not catch the salient point, but she could only do it in her own way. Anything else would be so out of it that she'd stumble.

'Did you ever meet – no, I suppose you didn't for the breach was made by then – did you ever meet my father – you know – ' she hesitated, 'the man called Gilbert?'

Sarah looked blank.

Hadn't she made herself clear? Surely she had. Then – and this was certain – Sarah looked shifty. As ever, her broad pale face registered the slightest emotion. She must be an execrable card player.

'Gilbert?'

'Well, my father.' Ann reddened. It was too much to explain about Gilbert, it was still too raw.

'His name doesn't matter,' she said. 'I think there might have been several.'

Sarah was bewildered.

'No, not fathers, but my father might have had several names. Did you happen to hear . . . ?' She trailed off. There was almost nothing to say without saying it all. 'Caroline – Mother,' she corrected herself, 'told me so little about him. He was or might have been a scholar of some sort, for Caroline – Mother – picked up a lot from him. She used to quote what he'd said.'

'I don't know anything, I'm afraid,' said Sarah, her face hidden as she adjusted the tie on the pinafore of one of the twins, the slow one – Mary? – for they couldn't be long alone without a child coming back into the room. 'They had no contact, my mother and yours, after you were born and long before I think. Some dreadful breach – but nothing was said to me. It was as if your mother was dead. Not that I mean . . .' She too trailed off. 'What more can I tell you?'

Ann gave up. 'It's no matter,' she said, 'just an idle query, but I should know.'

Charles had entered the room more silently than was usual, masked by the children's noise from upstairs in the nursery where they were playing with tambourines, and Ann's eyes had been on Sarah and little Mary. Both women stopped as at a signal when they spied him. It was female talk.

Shortly afterwards Ann got up to take her leave. Once Charles was in a room, although he wasn't a large man, it seemed full, and Sarah always felt she must minister to her husband.

So Ann was surprised to find that, after Charles had politely escorted her to the door, he walked out with her and almost shut it behind him. They both stood on the doorstep. Ann looked at him enquiringly.

Perhaps he didn't want her there so much and would warn her off. She stopped the thought. That was the old abject thinking. Worse, perhaps he had something dreadful to divulge about Sarah – her heart fluttered – or one of the children, which he couldn't speak of to its doting mother.

He lightly nudged her shoulder but didn't talk at once. He wasn't fluent with words and waited that bit too long to reply even to ordinary remarks. She stood expectant.

He spoke at last. 'I could not help overhearing what you told my wife.'

It was her turn to be discomposed. Charles was not blood family, he shouldn't be privy to such awkwardness. Perhaps he blamed her for embarrassing Sarah by enquiring about a shut and possibly painful past. Though Sarah had been bending over her little girl, Ann remained sure she'd been unsettled.

'Yes, but it was idle talk. It's really no matter,' she said, about to hurry off.

'No, no, Miss St Clair, cousin Ann. It is not my business. Not at all. But I think I heard, and it may be wrong, but I think it to be true, that your mother was in Shropshire, in – ' he paused, 'in service. I thought that you perhaps wished to know.' He stopped again. 'And *should* know.'

He looked at her earnestly for an instant, then turned away, patted her arm, gazed again at the door, pushed it open with his foot, and quickly entered. He closed it behind him without a further backward glance.

25

Could Charles be telling the truth? Why on earth would he lie? Caroline 'in service'? Surely she couldn't have been a governess or a companion – and, if not those, then what? How could this news be assimilated?

Her mother had seemed the epitome of a lady, living to be served. And she *had* been served. They were never rich but money came from somewhere to keep them in reasonable comfort, with Martha as housekeeper doubling as nursemaid, a succession of cooks and scullery maids. Caroline had spent her time enjoying an elegant hypochondria, reading and occasionally sketching, sometimes gossiping. And of course she must have worked on her fantasy, her creation of Gilbert.

None of this moderately expensive and idle life fitted easily with the history of a servant, even a generously superannuated one.

From where had she obtained the details with which she'd peppered her talk, the learning, the cataloguing, the sights?

That Gilbert the lover was formed from books and a fertile woman's mind Ann was becoming sure, but his qualifications as a connoisseur and scholar seemed harder to create.

But were they really?

She herself had had so little schooling, some lessons in languages and music, then much reading from the trash of circulating libraries, some few superior lectures in Fen Ditton. Yet she could converse with those who'd read and knew much more. The appearance of learning was not difficult to gain. A few volumes of *Elegant Extracts*, some serious journals, even the better articles in the *Lady's Magazine*, and a good memory would have given Caroline all she needed to impress a child. Her memory was certainly good. There were lapses and gaps – now, looking back, Ann saw more discrepancies – yet the outlines hadn't wavered. Quotations recurred, and the circumstances of their saying.

She couldn't yet laugh, but perhaps, just perhaps, she could smile at such fabrication, just for her – well, for her and the author.

She tried not to indulge the question, but she just had to ask: where on earth would a cosmopolitan Dane of Aksel Stamer's sort have met such a woman – if he had? Would this man have visited and been entertained in a country house in a distant county of England? Or was he too a 'servant'?

That was unlikely. He of all people lacked the demeanour.

The scholarship could have been Aksel Stamer's, she realised with a start. He knew languages, he knew the natural and the cultured world. But yet, yet . . . it was so very difficult to see the two together.

For sure he'd not been the great lover.

The name, the poetic name St Clair, was not his. But Caroline had never made it clear that this was Gilbert's either, or that she, Ann, had a right to a father's name – though Caroline had passed as widow. When she'd become a reader, then a writer of gothic tales, Ann began to suspect the name was not hers by right of birth and family, but simply chosen by her mother for its euphony. Chosen for them both. And since she'd not, at least in Ann's lifetime, married anyone else, there'd been no need to own up to this little fabrication.

Was it possible that Caroline had helped herself to a romantic-sounding gentry name beyond her claim?

Whatever Caroline had been – or wherever she'd worked – she could have taken a few days to go up to London, perhaps many days for it was a long, expensive journey from Shropshire. And there she might have met . . . But again, the ages stuck in Ann's throat. What a strange act for a respectable middle-aged woman, a daughter of the Church.

But perhaps Caroline had not been respectable, then or before – or later. Odd, considering the church upbringing. Ann gave credence to the rector – no, more likely curate – in Herefordshire, for Sarah had confirmed the clerical detail. Such background was suitably modest and explained some of the education she must have had – and her abandonment when she disgraced herself. Caroline had hinted at grand relatives in the north, but that could be discounted – they probably came with the name she chose.

There'd been a large family of sisters. Sarah mentioned them. That might explain why Caroline was fitted for some kind of upper service should she fail to marry. With so many daughters and little income, there could have been no dowry as incentive to any man. So as a girl she might have gone into the household of someone known to her family nearby, even in another county. It was possible. Then, after years of respectability, this virgin had in London – or somewhere far from Shropshire – jumped at the chance of being neither respectable nor a virgin, jettisoning her character in a single, maybe more than that, act of love.

The yearning struck Ann forcibly. Gilbert's speeches, though born of someone else's imagination, had been chosen, rearranged and memorised. Caroline had wanted them spoken by a man and to be true. Aksel Stamer, though lanky now and weatherbeaten, would not have been unhandsome.

And, yet, still she could not combine the two. Again she asked: was Caroline younger than she'd thought, was Aksel Stamer older?

Whoever it was, with whomever she'd done the deed – in a Shropshire mansion, a parsonage in Hereford or a London inn – she would, once impregnated, have lost her place and what could she do then? For a moment Ann toyed once more with the idea of Caroline going down the ranks and roaming the streets in the common way of fallen girls. But it didn't fit. Barring this act, Caroline had lived in imagination, not in the world. And always there was the question: from where had that allowance come? She could have offered nothing that could command such income. Evidently it was not from her own family.

And now she came to view herself in this new context.

If Caroline in service and not young had disgraced herself, she would surely have been urged to get rid of her shame by putting the child in a baby farm where it would most likely die and spare the expense of any further upkeep.

So why did she, Ann, exist?

The question raised the curious possibility that Caroline had chosen to keep the baby. Keep it instead of sending it to probable death in a London backstreet, howling its way to heaven. But not heaven — for she was sure Caroline had arranged no christening.

She had kept the child, she had kept Ann. Caroline had been no mother except in this instance. But this one instance was large. She had given her child life and then preserved it.

36

Below her window Ann heard London's muted bustle: hawkers, carriers and carriages on the cobbles. The world continued on as ever, ignoring her concerns.

She'd been remiss. But not for want of thinking. She wouldn't try to make contact with Robert's parents. She had no idea whether they were alive or dead or whether they or someone else had been the source of his modest funds in London. If indeed she'd been suspected in Venice – and Aksel Stamer's expression as he read a newssheet in those early days through Italy had made her imagine it might be the case – then the suspicion would have travelled across Europe into County Cork with report of an Irishman's death.

Best leave well alone.

She must however seek out his friends, those who'd admired him and fostered his self-regard. Since she returned she'd been dodging places where they might be, reversing her haunting of streets and taverns in which, so many years before, she'd hoped Robert James would be found. She'd no wish to talk and explain, but she owed a duty to these men who'd loved him less destructively than she had done.

His friends continued mostly in London but they had, as a group, scattered without their leader. This much she quickly discovered. Frightened away by baying crowds of Princess Caroline's supporters, who suspected all Italians of being informants paid by the Crown to discredit their heroine, Signor Orlando had fled the city; he'd been heading towards a despised but still alluring Venice while she'd been travelling her erratic route away. John Taylor, who'd let the Italian live with him for many months in his lodgings near St Sepulchre, had moved out and on. Now he stayed in a new-built house near Islington Green. Frederick Curran, always the most elusive of the friends despite his bulk, was no longer to be found at Gray's Inn or in the Queen's Arms or any of his usual haunts. He had, it was whispered, become involved in something dangerous connected with Ireland. Perhaps he'd written an unwelcome truth or used his mighty arm to smash the wrong head. She would find him along with the other Irishmen who'd known Robert. Then she would forget them all. Just like that.

But first she should speak to Richard Perry.

She thought of him wryly as the Beloved Disciple but he was more. She knew that now. He was too modest about his own abilities. She'd read an article he'd written in a review for Mr Hughes, making a mass of complex scientific material available to those with little time and less perseverance. But in Robert's shadow he'd counted himself of slight worth.

He would have the biggest shock.

When she met him by arrangement she could see that already he imagined what might have happened. He was visibly shaken at the outset of the meeting. And yet he clung to the hope that perhaps she alone had become homesick and tired of foreign parts, leaving Robert to write his glorious words where the sun always shone.

This was possible for he'd never thought Ann quite admired him as much as was his due.

Faced with this simple admiration, the improbable hope, she found it difficult to look as grave as she should. She'd dreaded seeing these men; yet now she almost relished the idea of telling them of Robert's death. After all, he'd not written to them as far as she knew – he couldn't have valued them so very much.

They sat together taking tea by St Paul's Churchyard near where she'd first met Robert James at Mr Hughes's dinner. She was acutely aware of the connection.

'Poor, poor Robert,' he said.

He questioned her for a while. She could see he wasn't satisfied with the answers or was unsure quite what she meant by some. He looked askance at her as she fielded both his grief and his curiosity. She admitted Robert's decline but not the manner of his death.

'He could not accept the indefinite because in his mind everything became definite. He had such boldness he saw right into mysteries.'

'He couldn't always convey them to others,' she ventured.

'He could to those with whom he had affinities.' He waited a moment, then added, 'Once he did to all the world. A stranger, a foreign bookseller, came to me soon after you and he had left. He asked after him while holding a copy of *Attila* as if it were a precious jewel. You see, he was widely admired even beyond these shores.'

'Did you think I was in the way?'

'Yes, we all were at times.'

She neither coloured nor responded. After a pause, she said, 'It was an unhealthy place. Italy, Venice, all the north Italian towns. It was cheap living there but there was a reason for that.' She smiled. She was being adroit.

Richard Perry was silent, looking fixedly at her.

'It was a place of agues, plague from the east, and fevers, damp and always harbouring disease, you know, the season of malaria,' she pursued.

Suddenly Richard Perry pushed away the tea things and leaned across the table. He caught her arm. He whispered hoarsely in her ear as if telling a secret, 'His work, his new work, you must have saved it?'

'I'm afraid not,' she said. 'All had to be destroyed. You know in the case of a death from . . .' She trailed off, failing to say the word 'fever' or hint at fumigation, hoping that silence filled in the rest.

No need to lie. Just make others believe something through not saying too much. It was simple.

When he registered her words Richard Perry looked so aghast she wondered about sugaring them, but the terrible image of those sodden papers was haunting. Her pause made him think her too moved to go on.

One of the younger Irishmen who'd sometimes joined their group now came up to them. She'd forgotten his name. He was told the news and they all three sat together, the men in shocked silence.

There were tears in Richard Perry's eyes. 'I shall stay up all this night in vigil. If he cannot have a proper funeral here, I will pay him my own individual tribute.'

'It is such an appalling loss to the world,' said the young Irishman. 'I too will join you in this.'

She roused herself. 'Indeed, yes,' she said. 'But yet his work, even *Attila* – his vision, it was so much more in conception than it could ever have been on paper that perhaps it is as well . . .' She hesitated, wondering why she was hazarding herself again on such slippery ground.

Through his tears Richard Perry directed a sharp look at her. 'But the very fragments would have declared his genius anew. Those fragments were infinitely precious. Don't you understand that the iridescent words would themselves have pointed to the vision beyond?'

He was using Robert's phrases. She recognised them. This was his immortality. So much better in an admiring mouth than on cold paper. As she thought this, tears almost came to her eyes as well. She held them back and kept silent.

After a pause, she said, 'Ah yes, but we remember them, do we not?'

The three of them sat a moment longer contemplating in their very different ways what had gone out of the world.

Irrationally she felt she must help these men, whose minds she could scar by hinting at that hanging. That she restrained herself from divulging the details made her feel responsible for what they would go on believing. 'Truly I don't think he could ever have found adequate words with which to express his enormous understanding of things.'

'We were dazzled,' said the young man helpfully.

'Of course,' said Ann. 'He saw through different, stronger eyes.'

Richard Perry was not appeased. 'But we needed him,' he almost wailed. 'He should not have left us.'

'He wouldn't have wanted to be old,' said Ann. 'He escaped the degeneration he feared.'

'He feared nothing,' said Richard Perry. 'Nothing!'

Another silence followed.

'He must have loved the art,' remarked the young man, who she rather thought was called Fitz something – Fitzwilliam? He hadn't let himself arrive at such a pitch of grief and disappointment as Richard Perry. 'Titian, Tintoretto, Veronese and Giotto, such ability as he would have to describe and appreciate the paradise they made.'

'Oh, yes,' she said, 'he loved the paintings.'

Her fingers closed round Robert's Swiss gold watch in her reticule. She had intended it for Frederick Curran, his old Trinity College friend, but it was better given to Richard Perry, the man who'd loved him most.

She produced it now and watched his face change colour. It was as if till this moment he'd not absolutely understood that Robert James was dead. 'I know he would have wanted you to have this.'

'Did he say so?'

'He did not have time. But I know.'

It was enough. She need not do more. Robert's friends weren't much interested in her. They never had been. Why should they be?

Not even Richard Perry, who'd told her of his great horror and salvation through Robert. It was for his friend and saviour he'd spoken, not for her.

Once she'd delivered her messages, provided her comfort and displayed a welcome inadequacy, even common courtesy was hard to muster. 'You should have dinner with us one day soon,' said Fitzwilliam, who, she saw with some amusement, had inherited Robert's white-lashed boy as servant. Richard Perry remained silent. It was one of those invitations which, when she'd been lonely and yearning for Robert, she'd have taken as so real she'd have been looking out to meet one of them every day, hoping for the promise to be fulfilled. She knew better now.

It was late in the next week when she encountered John Humphries near the Temple in Drew's print shop. She knew he often worked nearby. He no longer saw anything of Richard Perry, he told her, but someone had received her news from this source and relayed it to him. 'I heard you were back, and alone,' he said.

She was struck again by how quickly Robert's admiring group had broken apart without him.

Like Richard Perry, John Humphries looked almost accusingly at her but she didn't let her countenance alter. She was doing well.

'Yes, so sad,' she said. 'But you must have so many memories, so much to hold on to, that he'll live vividly in your mind – as he does in mine.'

He looked surprised. 'I've known him a long time if that's what you mean.'

'Well, yes, I suppose I do. He valued his male friends very highly, I think.'

They turned out of the shop and walked down towards the Temple. A thin sleet was starting. She brushed the wet off her face. 'They were always there for him and some went back to his very childhood, I think.'

'I was not one of those,' he said. 'I am not Irish.'

There was almost scorn in his voice. For him, to be Irish was shameful. But he'd made a temporary exception in admiring Robert.

'No, of course. Mr Curran and his young friends. But I mean only that you have formed over the years, or he has formed, a sort of group supporting and valuing each other – and I admire it,' she added quickly. 'It's not something that women so easily make.'

'Oh, women,' he said and waved his hand dismissively, 'they have no need. They're usually in a huddle with mothers and children, always doing something together, sewing, cooking, raising infants, gossiping. They're always in each other's pockets.'

'But surely that's quite different. Your group is – ' should she have said 'was'? – 'by choice. You are there for what you have in common, not by mere kinship or purpose. Yet your groups are as strong and last as long.'

'I suppose so,' he said, losing interest. He never liked me, she thought, but I didn't feel his hostility so fiercely in those early days. Then he added, 'But women intrude as well.'

'Did I do that?' She forced herself to smile. 'I never had any intention of getting between him and any of his friends.'

'Oh, he would never have let that happen, none of us would,' said John Humphries.

She waited. They were both staring unseeingly into a shop window displaying etchings of British naval battles and warships in full sail.

'He had once a woman, before you, a woman from somewhere in the north, Norway, Sweden, somewhere like that. No, Denmark. She was in London staying with an aunt. They went back to her family together. She was too passionate, so needing of his attention, so demanding of it. She was no good for him. She couldn't understand his genius – as I hope you could.' He looked again at her more searchingly, then turned away.

She'd never heard him say so much when she was present.

'She couldn't keep him, though he stayed long enough,' he added as an afterthought.

'So he left her?'

'Of course. He had to for his own sake. We all advised it.'

'What happened to her?' she asked as gently as she could, her eyes switched back to the window.

'Oh, she died. I don't know exactly when. He came back here alone but only after he'd travelled a while for some months, with Richard Perry, I think. He was a man of deep feeling.'

'How sad. She was very young, I suppose?'

'Oh yes, very young.'

He touched his hat to her and was about to move away, a little bored she supposed, and annoyed he'd been led to say so much. Then he turned back, and she never knew why. 'He found her quite repugnant in the end. You managed him better. You are older. I expect you understood more.'

She thought of the muzzling and said nothing. In any case, more striking images were accosting her brain. Denmark. Denmark. Who went there? It was not in an Englishman's tour of Europe.

She almost pulled at John Humphries's arm, meaning only to touch it lightly. 'She was Danish, then?'

He looked blank. 'Who?'

'The young woman with Robert.'

'Yes, I believe so, something like that. But possibly half-English. She spoke like a foreign woman. She probably understood little of his *Attila* or anything of his genius. How could she?'

He was moving away, eager to be rid of her and the irksome talk. But she wouldn't let him go.

'Did she have a father?'

'What?' He looked surprised. 'I have no idea,' he said, 'why?'

'No reason. I was just interested – in anything that concerned Robert you know, his past life. You cannot imagine how I miss him.'

'We all miss him,' he said and touched his hat again in another effort to leave.

He turned his back on her. She could think of no way of detaining him, when suddenly he looked round and said almost accusingly, 'She was a most beautiful woman.'

Was that by contrast with herself? No matter. It rang in her head that beauty could indeed become loathsome. More loathsome than adders and toads.

Then he added, 'No father, but I think an older brother. He was here once. By chance, I suppose. Curran may have met him. I did not.'

With that he really was gone.

As the weeks went by, she turned these meagre facts over and round in her mind. She knew nothing of Denmark, had only a hazy idea of where it was, where it began and ended, and what extent of land it covered. But to have heard of the country twice in different contexts – was she making significance where there was only coincidence?

There was the hiding out in Esbjerg with Richard Perry, the tale of which she remembered so clearly. The detail of the false name, Peter O'Neil, assumed because of something political. Although no one, not even Frederick Curran, knew exactly what Robert might have written to cause such fear of discovery in a foreign land, or what incendiary thing he'd done beyond any young man's posing. In her time with him, there'd been no evidence of the English law coming after him for activities in Ireland or in London – and what could he have done in Denmark or the German states to warrant any surveillance from the government? He'd said he didn't dabble in mundane politics – although even in Venice there'd been those hints of secret societies. Surely that was just men playing.

So what could it have been?

She tried to slow her train of thought. She was making a plot of life – again. Yet she couldn't but notice it was when her thoughts accelerated in this way that the modest gloom that had become habitual to her was lifted. She would try not to need such stimulation. The gloom was her due; it wasn't so painful it was worth dispersing at any cost. She must take life a little more gently, as Sarah took it.

And yet.

It was interesting that none of Robert's old friends regarded her as in need of consolation. How nice to be a widow and receive comfort! To be a real widow with all the richness of the title. Caroline had never made much of that fiction.

She'd tried but failed to find Frederick Curran, who would in any case by now be aware of her news through young Fitzwilliam. But she must see John Taylor, who seemed to have separated from his old friends. Neither Richard Perry nor John Humphries had mentioned him.

So one especially frosty day she put aside her writing and took a hackney to Islington Green. She easily discovered the house, in a new terraced development beside an open space. It was narrow and quite small but prettily appointed. It would have been handsome if on a bigger scale. Fancy railings up the steps led to a painted door overtopped by a fan of coloured glass. She took all this in, then went back to Canonbury-house to warm and fortify herself with tea before knocking on the door.

She was shown into a neat drawing room by a maid in a white ribboned cap. A plump, or more likely pregnant, woman came almost immediately into the room. Something was familiar about her but Ann couldn't at once place it.

Then she remembered. This was the friend of Frederick Curran's cousin: Lydia something, the woman who'd been making her sheep's eyes at John Taylor in the Queen's Arms. Then, he'd been a lapsed lawyer and an eager artist – rightly, for he was, they all said, truly gifted.

Evidently the eyes had worked their seduction.

It was a changed Lydia she saw, her face less pinched, fuller, but still with something of its discontented look. From the rest of the house came the sound of a baby wailing and an older woman's voice grumbling. So there was not only a wife but an infant – which may have accounted for the marriage of a man she'd thought the least likely of Robert's friends to be a husband. And there might be another one on the way. The nagging within suggested there might also be a mother-in-law. John Taylor had made a family of women. Into Ann's mind swam the contemptuous words of the unkempt artist with the skeleton in the *campo* by San Marco. She blinked them away.

Mr Taylor was not in, she was told, but he would be home for his dinner if she cared to wait. He was always punctual.

The two women sat making stilted conversation until John Taylor arrived at precisely the time Lydia had indicated. The days were still short and it was already dark when he stepped in.

He was not the man she used to know. This one was beardless and very clean. No more than his wife did he make much effort to be welcoming. Ann would have judged him boorish if she'd not noted his lack of ease. It was not simply due to her presence, she was sure.

She told her news. He'd heard a rumour of it. For a moment he put his head in his white hands, on which there was now no sign of paint. Lydia shuffled her feet while the sound of scolding and wailing from beyond the room became louder, punctuated by the pleading of a young nurse or maidservant.

Unlike Richard Perry, John Taylor did not interrogate the manner of Robert's death. He simply accepted that people tended to die in foreign parts. Nor did he ask after the work. More perceptive perhaps than the others, he might have understood before they left that there would be little to show for the travelling.

In the silence she enquired about his painting, his Suffolk watercolours which they'd all so admired.

Before John Taylor had time to reply, Lydia interrupted, with a sharpish glance at Ann, as if she were bringing into that ordered elegant room the old raffish world of unattached men and artistic dreams that delivered no bacon or baby clothes. 'My husband is in a very promising law firm now. I don't suppose he will tell you so himself. We are very proud of him.'

'I'm sure you are,' said Ann.

'You no longer paint?' she asked, turning to John Taylor.

'I have no time for avocations,' he replied curtly.

For all the upheavals of thought and revolution, how little the world had changed. It was depressing and restful in equal measure.

She would seek out no more of Robert's circle. She was tired of tramping around in the bitter weather to be met with such emotional coldness. His friends and companions had cared for him mightily and still did, but not enough, not nearly enough in most cases. Did they not see that some surpassing spirit had gone from the world? Only Richard Perry really understood and he too, she wearily realised, would soon move on. She was hurt for Robert, though not self-deluding enough not to know that, with such thoughts, she protected herself. What had she been about, falling victim to a person so easily erased?

Happily for her brooding mind there was something else demanding her attention, something she'd not yet allowed to have its complete way with her.

Two mentions of Denmark within a year when she couldn't remember ever hearing anything at all about the country in all her past life, except for the story of George III's unhappy sister forced to marry its mad king. Ann sighed. It was an unfortunate exception.

She turned over all the early events concerning Aksel Stamer. Keeping Robert James as far away from her thoughts as possible; he must not contaminate anything.

They had met Aksel Stamer together in Padua. Nothing had been said about any connection. Then there was that earlier probable meeting in the *poste restante* at Palazzo Grimani where she'd gone to pick up the letter she now knew to have been sent by Madame Renée. He'd stood too close behind her in the line, presumably collecting mail of his own, perhaps a bank draft since he seemed to command considerable funds. It was there of course that he'd heard her maiden name, though he made no allusion to this when in Padua they formally introduced themselves both under assumed names and talked over a glass of wine – or at least he and she had made that awkward conversation in Robert's louring presence.

She concentrated on that moment in Palazzo Grimani. How close had he been standing? Too close. That much she remembered. She'd been crowded by his presence. She'd felt him overhearing what should have been private business.

She went over every aspect of the transaction, her moving up to the counter after the garrulous old man had left, her providing the document with her name on it, the offhand manner of the clerk, his rummaging among his ledgers, his passing over to her the letter from London and her signing for it.

Now it became clearer and clearer to her that Aksel Stamer – if it were indeed he (and she was almost certain that it was) – could not have looked at her signature as she signed 'Ann St Clair', for she'd placed her left arm along the record book as she wrote with her right and, though he was taller than she, he would have had to peer directly over her shoulder to see the name. She would have protested at that sort of intrusion. Even the bored clerk would have said something. Aksel Stamer must only have *heard* her give her name.

But she had not given it.

It had surprised her at the time that the clerk, tired from too much talking and arguing with his difficult clients, had simply taken her written document as proof of her identity and not waited for her to confirm it verbally. So how could Aksel Stamer have known she was Ann St Clair and her mother's daughter?

She faced again these strange conjunctions, these seemingly fortuitous mentions of a country hardly on English people's lips in ordinary life. Aksel Stamer was from somewhere called Fyn in Denmark, this much he'd told her. She'd never heard of the place. The beautiful woman who'd not been right for Robert and who'd died pathetically young was also from Denmark. Esbjerg, near where Richard Perry had had his dreadful misadventure with the corpses on the ice, was on the north sea coast not so very far away.

Was she being absurd to make such links? Denmark was after all a whole country, quite large. For by now she'd seen it on a globe in Sarah's house – Charles consulted it for his work and young William pressed his finger along the oceans. A country of that size would have room for many inconsequential coincidences.

And yet.

She went back to that incident in the office in Palazzo Grimani. She'd noticed Aksel Stamer because she thought she'd already seen him somewhere else, a foreigner with features difficult to place in any particular nation, not quite Austrian, not English or French. If he'd not been close enough to see her name there and not been given an opportunity to hear it spoken on that occasion, then what and where?

There was another possible meeting, one much earlier during her stay in Venice, not long after she'd arrived. On this occasion a man whom she'd suspected just might be Aksel Stamer had assuredly been close enough to hear a full and formal introduction.

It was near the Gesuati church where she'd been addressed by the friendly Giancarlo Scrittori as she studied her English guidebook. She'd noticed the man close enough to be considered a companion of the young Italian, so close that she'd awaited an introduction. But he'd not been with Giancarlo and, after remaining near for a little time, perhaps perusing a news-sheet, she couldn't now be sure, he'd wandered off to leave them talking. It was long after this that she'd thought she recognised him at Palazzo Grimani when she'd used her maiden name of St Clair. She'd jumped to the conclusion that this second encounter was where it all began.

Then he'd reinforced her conclusion that it was as Ann St Clair he knew her by asking after her mother and remembering she'd been called Caroline. But he could have learned that during the awkward talk in Padua when she'd mentioned her proposed trip and the dying mother by way of easing conversation. It could then have been a stray and courteous enquiry during a difficult journey. She'd become so unused to common politeness that she may have imbued it with far too much meaning.

The name she'd given by the Gesuati church was the one that provided a respectable identity.

She had said clearly, 'I am Signora James, Signora Robert James.'

She was certain of this for, at the time, she'd wondered if it was the Italian form of address. She had said the name 'Robert James'.

She had spoken it loudly for she was addressing an Italian who might not know her language well, and the last name always gave trouble to Italians. And this man, this foreign man, this perhaps Danish, Dutch, German, Austrian man, was standing close enough to overhear.

Then, despite the erratic behaviour of Robert in Padua, he had forged an acquaintance with them. She had assumed it the kindness of exiles.

But, no, it had continued. He had stayed and developed the friendship when it was clear that Robert was crazy – she'd once but no longer feared to employ the word. No man without a need or purpose could possibly have done this.

Robert said he'd been in Germany – he mentioned Hamburg – though he never spoke of experiences there, not even about his time with Richard Perry in Esbjerg, and certainly never described a woman. In all his disparaging of her, he might have made comparison with this acknowledged beauty but he had not. So what had happened to her? Another supposed fever, an unfinished sentence, a dubious exit?

Who told the truth if they had a chance to hide it? Only the stationary were stuck with the reality of the past. Robert had moved around a good deal. Though he spoke so much of higher truths, he cared little for the lower quotidian sort.

It was *Robert James*'s name that mattered.

Had Aksel Stamer in the past cared for him? He did have a profound effect on men. But, if he'd cared so much, how could he have accepted his death so easily and why had he gone to such trouble to help someone who he could never be absolutely sure was not his murderess?

Perhaps he *had* suspected her – he had after all taken such speedy action to save her from the consequences of something only she knew she hadn't done.

Or, if she hadn't employed the bloodied knife herself, could he have thought that she'd driven this genius to his death?

Hardly that, for he'd seen enough of their life together. In no sense was she his murderess – she berated herself for the word, determined yet once more to keep melodrama for her books.

Not for a second would she let her mind loiter on more furtive purposes or on stronger arms and any knife sharper than her own.

However she looked at it or tried to refuse looking at it, the coincidence was there and, though in truth, so slight and possibly so insignificant, it had, she knew, taken its hold in a particular way. She sighed. It was another train of thought she'd no wish to follow. But knew she must and would.

For, if it had been Robert James, and Robert through her, that Aksel Stamer had shadowed in Italy, not herself, then there was no reason to continue with the ludicrous suspicion that this man was her father. He'd always been too young for the role but, following the mechanical swan and other small inanities, she'd jumped over incongruities once she'd settled on the idea.

She closed her eyes. She'd lost another parent. She was glad there was no one near to laugh at her.

Knowing this, she tried hard, not at once and completely, to accept what was staring her in the face: that Aksel Stamer might be the older brother of the dead Danish lady.

No more searching, she told herself – again. Let life just happen. For goodness sake, let it just happen.

38

The key must be held by his old friends. She still hadn't found Frederick Curran, the man who'd known him the longest. Richard Perry she thought was probably naive when it came to his idol and he'd already given his version of his secret time with Robert tucked away in hiding in Esbjerg, no woman interrupting the cosy intimacy. John Humphries had told her all he'd gleaned, and it had been truly shocking. But still John Taylor knew more than she did. She'd have to brave him again, despite his unfriendly reception.

When she'd known him with Robert he'd been drunk half the time – wine helped him create the blurred effect that heightened the beauty of his English landscapes. It had made him jovial and generous, eager to spend his money on liquor, tobacco and good food and open his lodgings to an Italian stranger. Now he was sober, a lawyer, and a changed man, a family man. She wouldn't go to his house again, for Lydia's presence would prevent her asking difficult questions: she'd make sure her husband remained reticent.

Instead, Ann would go to the law firm of which Lydia had boasted. She wouldn't simply march up the steps and knock with the great brass handle but rather wait outside to waylay him as he came out. Years before she'd done much the same when she'd trailed Robert after a quarrel, as she noted wryly. She'd probably be no more welcome to John Taylor if she accosted him in this way rather than in his drawing room, but at least she could ask her questions directly and at once. If he refused to answer, she could still seek out young Henry Davies. He'd been quiet but always observant. She doubted he'd know more than the others but she had to try every avenue.

She was right about John Taylor. The sober man disliked chance meetings. Unluckily the day she'd chosen was both dismal and obscure, with a gentle snow thickening the fog. She'd have seemed an unwelcome spectre looming from the mist, reminding him of an old, best forgotten time. He proved as unforthcoming in the street as he'd been at home.

'Look, Miss St Clair' – he reverted to formality in this new art-free, wine-free life – 'I knew Robert James less than Richard Perry and Fred Curran. He was a great and a good man and I am sorry, sincerely sorry, he is dead.'

He was pulling on his grey gloves while looking down at his white hands; then with his gloved fingers he stroked his clean-shaven chin. Snow was settling on the brim of his black felt hat. He stared at her, then continued, 'I cannot help you dig up a past he did not see fit to share with you.' He hesitated a moment. A softer expression passed across his face. 'It is perhaps not fair that the most brilliant mind should go first.' His look hardened again. 'Good day to you.'

And with that scant courtesy the conversation was over. It was snowing more heavily now and he was quickly subsumed into the white fog.

She wouldn't see him again. The disintegrating of Robert's circle which his defection stressed was a sad blow. She'd intended to go on to Henry Davies, but she wasn't so sure she could take more rebuffs with equanimity, even to satisfy such burning curiosity.

Yet a few days later she did pursue him. She discovered him in the Castle and Falcon, one of the taverns where Robert and his circle used to meet. When she spied him and even more when she accosted him – she'd been directed to a dark corner of the room or she wouldn't have found him – she understood something of John Taylor's transformation. It was perhaps not all due to Lydia and her need for marriage and money. For Henry Davies was so far gone into drink and drugs that there was no getting sense from him. But, when she told him her news, he understood at last. Then he wept like a baby.

Only sleep could console him. She left him with his head on the bare wooden table beside an untouched plate of parsnips and salt cod, his tears soaking into some spilt froth and ale.

She was disheartened. She would try to discover Frederick Curran and then move down other paths.

For Curran, an Irish printer's boy who worked for Mr Hughes proved useful. When they were all together she'd never much wondered what the men round Robert, including big Frederick Curran, lived on in London – who except John Taylor picked up the bills in the taverns when there was a rushed if lurching exit for the door as the candles were snuffed out? Curran was said to be writing something on political economy that no one knew about, but he couldn't have been earning a living in this way. He'd always been the most eager to argue politics, the least impressed when his friend Robert soared upwards out of the grubby world. Now she learned he'd been receiving income from an Irish bank, Roche's in County Cork. It had recently failed.

She smiled, remembering how he castigated Venice for caring only about money. Perhaps Robert's allowance had come from the same source.

The collapse had hit Frederick Curran hard. He'd gone back to Dublin, then Cork, where it was reported he'd fallen foul of the government through inflammatory talk of masters and greedy bankers feeding off victims and workers. Some said he'd used his bulk against a smaller functionary, but accounts were vague and may have been based on the look of him. Now his whereabouts were unknown, said the printer's boy with a wink.

Once she'd taunted Fred Curran when he spoke of Ireland: that he was homesick for it. He had said seriously, 'I and Robert both.'

So she'd tried all the main friends in London and no one, not even Richard Perry, had pursued her further to find out about Robert's final days. Didn't they care? Robert hadn't wasted thoughts on them; perhaps in the end, despite their admiration, almost adulation, they'd waste no more of their puny ones on him.

Aksel, Aksel. She once called his Christian name out loud in her room, then chuckled to herself. It was as well he'd not come back: she might have addressed him as 'Father' and flown to his arms.

Yet there was a haunting. No kin perhaps, but something. So much remained obscure.

Why had he taken such pains to flee Venice with her? He warned her she was in extreme peril. He was right of course, Robert's very blood on her clothes.

But she had read no news-sheet declaring her a wanted person, an outlaw from justice. Aksel had kept to himself the one she'd seen. To spare her feelings, of course. But still.

Aksel Stamer: the man who inhabited the mystery at the centre of both her plots and who, in spite of all she could do to disentangle the two from each other and him from them, stayed resolutely in place, the only living being among so many ghosts.

He had something to do with Robert James and a beloved woman – that was becoming clear. And if not the lost father, the substitute Gilbert, something to do with her and her murky origins? Perhaps.

She was sure that Sarah and Charles knew more than they'd told her, even after Charles's startling revelation.

But how to ask them the questions that might just elicit the desired answers, the true, the uncomfortable answers? They were so guarded, so fearful of hurting a person they both saw as a lone, defenceless woman.

Besides, there were by now so many characters in the plots it was difficult to put the right questions without revealing her own thoughts – and she'd been wrong so often that these were the last ones she could trust, or wished to communicate.

She'd tried Moore & Stratton in the Strand but they were no help at all. They'd been the agents for some families in the west of England, in Shropshire and Herefordshire, but the old partner who'd handled these accounts originally was long dead; the money to be paid out now came through Coutts Bank and was sent to them for forwarding. Coutts were as tight as closed oysters with information.

She did, however, manage to track down the young man, Mr William Holt, who'd sent the letter enclosing the note from Madame Renée. He admitted to relaying it from a client in Paris. He ventured the information that an allowance was still paid to this elderly English lady from a small and he feared diminishing Trust through Coutts. He would say no more; he'd felt important divulging news to this pleasantly eager lady, but there would be the devil to pay if one of the senior partners found out. So he bid her good day – without waiting for her to decide whether or not to inform him that the recipient of this declining Trust was now a French lady of stern face but tender heart.

There was really no alternative to her cousins. She would try Charles first. But he was rarely at the Phoenix Street house when she called, and they were never alone. Perhaps he ensured that this was the case. He must have thought he'd done her a favour and had by that act fulfilled what he considered his duty.

It was while turning off Gray's Inn Road to head towards Somers Town with a bag of hothouse apricots for Sarah's children that a ghastly thought struck her. She almost dropped her package, seeing in the instant the ripe fruit smash and smear the ground, trip passers-by . . . But she held on.

The thought was that nobody was telling her the truth and that Sarah was not her cousin.

They didn't look alike, and the resemblance Sarah had found between her and little Harry and Charlotte was part of the compliment mothers pay to single women to attach them to their children.

Why had Charles spoken to her? Had it been a kind of warning?

She arrived at the door clutching the apricots in a fluster of enquiry, only to find that Sarah's friend Jane Lymington was there with her little boy. She should have deposited her gift and left but decided not to. She knew she failed to justify her presence by admiring the lad enough or even interacting with him when he lisped his pretty phrases. She'd be forgiven – it would be ascribed to her spinster state by pitying mothers.

She sat in silence as they discussed everything – surely they were not actually talking of the price of eggs?

Finally Mrs Lymington and her little boy left, with a polite but cursory goodbye to Ann. Sarah looked quizzically at her cousin, knowing her usual impatience with social visits.

'You are beginning to know me too well.'

Sarah waited for her to go on.

'I suppose,' said Ann, then stopped and began again. 'I need to ask you a bit more about Gilbert.' She tried to swallow the word – how had it slipped from her mouth? She'd meant to say 'My father'.

Sarah looked anxious.

Then Ann blurted out, 'Are you really my cousin?' She held back tears. Somewhere surely there must be flesh and blood that belonged to her.

Sarah laughed with relief. 'Of course, of course. Whatever put such a notion in your head? What have you been thinking?'

'I don't know. Perhaps I have a craving to destroy everything in the past before I find it being destroyed for me.'

'But it never will be, dearest Ann. Come, no morbid thoughts.'

And that was that again. She got no further.

She would give Sarah and Charles time to get used to her prying before trying them once more. She would fatten herself up in the way they approved and declare herself a cheery body who was walking with her two feet on the earth, someone who could take whatever was told to her without flinching. Then they would not need to be so cautious.

She took up with a few acquaintances and went walking with them in the parks. She even contacted her old schoolfriend, Susan Bonnet from Putney, the girl who'd shared her secret novel-reading from the circulating library. But the friendship could not be rekindled. Susan was now a professional married woman with all the usual empty charm. If Ann scratched her skin and pushed into the flesh, would she reveal underneath the affectation that eager, awkward child? Of course not. As Mrs Jonas Loyn, née Susan Bonnet, she covered her old friend in layers of politeness, of compliment, of social flutter, and a new steely distaste. Ann saw there was no going back to grab at possibilities.

With Mary Davies it was easier. Colleagues, partners in work, carried fewer expectations, and writing was as reliable a topic as the weather over the tea-table or in the print shop. But it remained hard to come close to those who'd stayed quietly in their snug routine while she'd careered over rocky ground in the rickety cart of life. Superiority of 'experience' impressed no one without it.

As time passed and she delivered to Dean & Munday *The Ladies of Zitelle; or, the Prisons of Venice*, then *Eleanora; or, the Black Tower* (with an interpolated homily on the absolute need for chastity in females whether old or young) and began on *The Mystery of the Dunes; or, the Dying Cavalier*, she amused herself with taking tea out with some of her fellow gothic authors when they came to town – for she'd discovered through Mr Munday that a good number of them were maiden ladies from little rural schools or discontented governesses hoping one day to write so fast they could snub their employers and flick the dust of dependence off their shoes.

'All right,' said Sarah at last. 'Charles has said to me that he told you about your mother some time ago. He should not have done so, it was not his place to tell. But he's a good man and he saw your worry. He thought he did it for the best.'

'Of course he did. It was kind of him. But he knew what he knew from you. So, dear cousin, perhaps you will now tell me more, tell me at last everything you know. My mother is long dead.'

They were in Sarah's drawing room, a tea-table between them. The children were out or in the nursery having lessons, all except the slow twin – Mary? – who was sitting in a corner on a little stool fastened to a tray, trying to fold coloured paper into squares and diamonds. She was very quiet. It was unusual to have a child in the drawing room rather than the parlour. Ann hoped she was all right but Sarah had said nothing, so her quietness was probably a response to a house of so many other children and their constant noise.

Sarah looked uncomfortable, as Ann expected. She also looked sad.

'Don't you think, my cousin, there are things better not to know.'

'I do. But we can't rest till we winkle them out all the same. You must be a very sensible person indeed to be intentionally ignorant. And you know I am not so sane.'

'You are very sane, Ann, no one saner.'

A strange thing to say.

They drank their tea in silence, hearing each other's swallows as if they were their own. The little girl was now kneading the paper shapes like dough. She was still quiet.

'Yes,' said Sarah at last, keeping her eyes down as she twisted the tight rings on her plump right hand. 'I will tell you all I know. But Ann, it is not so comfortable a truth.'

'Tell it, Sarah, my dearest, tell it. I have a right to know.'

This made Sarah smile sadly. 'Not a right, Ann. I think people speak so easily of rights they have no claim to. I am not sure there are such rights at all. But maybe, if it will not set your mind at rest, it will at least stop you imagining too much.'

Ann was about to speak when Sarah raised her eyes to her cousin's face and stopped her. 'Oh, I know you do, Ann. It's not possible with so much unknown to avoid speculating, and speculation can be wild. You deal in strange stories. Charles and I have looked at some.'

'All right. Go on.'

Another silence followed. Ann found it hard not to break it.

Then Sarah spoke. 'Before I say more, you must promise me that, after this talk, after you hear what I have to say, you will search no further in this, not seek anyone who doesn't want to be sought, or go where there's been a breach for so many years. I ask this for your own good, dear Ann – and I ask it seriously.'

She hesitated. It was difficult to promise not to do something, not to be curious when she'd lived with curiosity so long. Could it be given up?

'Yes, Sarah, I promise.'

'Good, I ask it for your benefit. I see you will tire yourself out by trying to discover what need not be discovered and you will only do yourself harm, my poor cousin.'

Sarah poured out another dish of tea. It was cold but Ann drank it eagerly for her mouth was dry. Her throat tensed as she swallowed. 'You make me alarmed with this talk. But go on. Just go on, Sarah, I beg of you.'

Sarah glanced at the little girl and found that she'd fallen asleep, her head on the coloured paper. She walked over and moved her so that her curly head lay on a cushion from the sofa, then returned to her seat. She spoke without looking Ann in the eye.

'Caroline, your mother, was not a usual daughter. She was much older than my mother, a bit – I don't know, really – perhaps a bit rebellious. Our grandfather had only a small income and if the girls didn't marry they had to do something to keep themselves. But your mother didn't learn enough to be a governess in a gentleman's family like Aunt Louisa, and she didn't marry when she should. She was unhappy at home – I don't know why. She quarrelled with our grand-father and left his house.

'I know nothing of the next years. But later she was a sort of companion – in a Scottish family settled in Shropshire.' Sarah looked up at her cousin. 'But truly, Ann, I do not know where it was.'

'Don't be so anxious. I've promised and will keep my word.' She hoped she would. Thank God she'd not shared her suspicions of Aksel Stamer with her cousins. They'd have judged her demented.

Sarah saw Ann's emotion but she'd begun and must go on. She put her hand across the table and touched her cousin's arm. They exchanged looks. Ann remained silent.

'I really know very little. But there was in this family a son, a not-well son, I believe a simpleton, somebody not quite usual. He was kept at home, the mother was devoted to the boy. He should have been sent away to where he could have been cared for properly but he was her only son and she wouldn't have it. And it was at home that, despite his baby ways and lack of speech, he grew to be a man – in size and needs. The person there – she was called the house-keeper – was really his carer. She was supposed to keep him from harm and harming others. The husband could not bear to see him.'

As she spoke, Sarah's usually placid face grew strained and flushed; her lips trembled.

'This boy, this man, this mad creature . . .?'

'No, no,' said Sarah, 'he had fits, something had happened at birth. I heard his mother blamed herself, cruelly blamed herself.'

'All right. So this idiot did what?'

'Ann, I don't know.'

By now Sarah was in agonies, twisting the lace on her cuff round and round as if wringing water from it.

Ann's anxiety gave way to anger. She would explode if Sarah didn't vomit out the truth. All of it. 'Are you saying I am the daughter of this idiot? Is that it?'

Tears started in Sarah's pale eyes. They rolled down her burning cheek. She brushed them aside with the back of her hand as she let go the twisted lace.

'Oh, Ann, I shouldn't have said anything. Charles warned me. Why did you push me so?'

'Oh, don't blame me. You've known this all along and never told me.' She felt so savage she could gladly have hit the weeping woman and smashed her china against her prettily papered walls.

'The mother was at fault. He'd grown to be a man with a man's desire, and the housekeeper was not always close at hand.'

Ann got up abruptly and walked round the room, stared at the sleeping child, then sat down. She looked coldly at Sarah, who could no longer control her sobs. Though she was so miserable now, Ann thought bitterly, she was usually so complacent in her tranquil love, her tranquil life.

At last anger subsided. She felt empty. 'Go on, Sarah, please, just go on. I am calm. I cannot be left in any more ignorance. It is not fair.'

Sarah pulled out her handkerchief, wiped her hot face and swallowed hard. She'd never done anything so difficult in her life. Why hadn't she waited for Charles or asked him to do this? But he wouldn't have let it happen. In any case he didn't know it all.

'Something bad happened. Your mother was sent away. Mrs Sinclair, that was I think the family's name, had to dismiss her. I don't know all of it. Then the family moved away. Indeed, I know they did but have no idea where.'

So, Ann thought, I was born of a desperate ageing mother, who may have been seduced or was more likely raped, and a beloved idiot. A fine origin for a hack writer of sensational tales: a crazy coupling followed by years of thraldom to a ghost created after one imbecilic act.

It was indeed marvellous. That all these years Caroline had hidden this truth with such imaginative brilliance. How had she sustained it?

And again she asked: had it been created for the benefit of the daughter born of this disaster?

No, she'd kept it up for herself. Did she go to bed nightly with the shadowy Gilbert to erase over and over the memory of this nameless fool?

Ann remembered her shudder at the idea of sexual congress; maybe Gilbert's ultimate benefit, his genius for a woman, was that he never demanded the duty of a wife, that he could give admiration, adoration and total fidelity that a lady wanted without the baser payment, forever untainted by consummation.

He alone could wipe out that memory.

She didn't dislike Caroline less for what she'd suffered, for perhaps hating servitude and not expecting her rebellion to end like this, desperate for some affection as the creation of Gilbert showed, but unwilling or unable to give it to the daughter born of the worst act of her life – a child who reminded her daily of it. Grimly she wondered if Caroline had been able to chuckle when she heard she'd determined to earn her living writing tales of gothic silliness.

But Caroline had had no sense of comedy.

Sarah was still talking as her own thoughts rattled round her head. She would've liked to ask questions about the man who couldn't bear to see his mad son or the curate who'd not prevented his wilful daughter leaving home – to see if either had any lineaments of Gilbert. But she knew there could be no answer.

'So why Ann, not Annabel or Arabella?' she asked suddenly. 'Caroline said I was named after Gilbert's mother.' She snorted and changed her scorn to a cough. 'Was it the name of the Sinclair lady?' A sudden thought. 'Was it our grandmother's name?'

'No, Ann, our grandmother was called Jane.'

She looked sadly at her cousin. 'Ann was the name of the housekeeper who took you to be christened.'

They sat in silence. The child awoke in the corner and Sarah got up to lift her up despite her heavy weight. She went to the door and called for the nursemaid. When she didn't come at once, she left the room carrying the drowsy child up the stairs. Ann stayed alone with the remains of the cold tea.

When Sarah returned with a basket of mending from the parlour, she found her cousin exactly where she'd left her. She had no more to say, she was empty.

Mechanically she rummaged in the basket for the breeches that had just made a man of William. Already they needed strengthening in the seams and darning where the material had become thin from his tumbling. He was still a child in his man's clothes.

'Ann, I have only one more thing to say. You are my cousin and we love you dearly.'

'Thank you, but I must ask again. My birth?'

'The mistress paid for it, I assume, I don't know details, and the housekeeper, who was so repentant for her lack of care, helped to arrange all. Money was sent but everything else kept quiet. We never knew anything more of your mother. And even I knew nothing of it until Aunt Louisa told me something before she died. It's a cruel thing, Ann.'

'The world is cruel.'

'Not all of it.'

Sarah swallowed hard, smiled and put down her mending. She came round to where Ann sat and tried to embrace her.

Ann pushed her gently but firmly away. She felt near to tears herself. But she'd determined not to cry before anyone again.

'I'm sorry, Sarah,' she said as her cousin looked pityingly at her. 'It's too soon. I know you mean well to me, but you should have told me this long ago. I will need time to take it all in, to learn to live with it.'

Sarah bent her head, perhaps acknowledging this truth. Ann didn't know or care.

'I will go now but come back in a few days and we'll not speak of it further, I promise. I've learned that no good comes of talking once a thing is known.'

It took time, much time. She gave herself some of the advice that Mr Dean now wanted peppering the sensational novels. She had much to be grateful for. Though the truth was grim, she was not a wretch wandering in the streets covered in sores and rags.

Yet she also knew wretchedness could not be measured from outside; she knew that well enough. She'd seen a once healthy body hanging dead through sheer self-torment.

None the less, best to hold on to those sores and rags. She didn't have them.

Shame had been imposed on her from so many sides it was hardly worth interrogating it further. As for the anger, it couldn't last forever.

Comforting to know with certainty that, unlike her, Robert would have preferred to be that beggar with the sores and rags than accept there'd been no mission and he'd simply been thrown on the scrap-heap of life – like everyone else.

She met Sarah again when she was holding a party with other ladies, mothers by their conversation. She joined them. Perhaps her presence drove them away for they didn't stay long after she arrived. But this time she thought she'd chatted quite amiably without being able to add much about weaning and breeching.

As she was leaving, she had a chance to say something she hoped was soothing to Sarah about the revelations it had cost her such pain to divulge.

'Do not be bitter, cousin Ann.'

'I'm not, really. You can't undo the past with rage or pity for yourself or anyone else. I've been a little mad sometimes.'

'You weren't mad, Ann, but maybe your heart was mad for a while. It can happen.'

It was so strange a thing for plump, placid Sarah to say, so much what she might have said herself, that Ann laughed out loud on the doorstep.

39

Obese, extravagant and addicted to laudanum, George, ex-Prince Regent, was to be crowned King in an expensive ceremony in July. His wife Caroline intended to be at his side as Queen Consort. Some people were with her in this. She continued to be most entertaining.

On the day, the 21st, she arrayed herself regally and was driven to the Abbey. At both North and South entrances she was refused entry. So she tried Westminster Hall. Guards held bayonets under her chin until the door could be slammed in her face.

She made a further assault on the Abbey, failed, and was persuaded to desist.

She'd been popular with the disgruntled, but the English are royalist under their prating of liberties: the fickle crowd jeered her as she was driven off.

That night she fell ill and three painful weeks later she died. She believed she'd been poisoned. She'd arranged for her burial back in her native Germany; the tomb should read 'Here lies Caroline, the Injured Queen of England.'

With the rest of the nation and many people on the Continent, Ann read the accounts of such undignified scenes. She felt sad for the lady and for the end of an extravagant, flamboyant era.

Despite such different spheres, the two Carolines had not been dissimilar. Both so self-deluding, so self-creating, facing and overcoming the travails of life by audacious feats of imagining. Both rearranged their past to control the present and neither could deal with those who darkened the brilliance of the creation. Both were unlikely heroines, one squat, plain and, it was reported, foul-smelling, the other plain, injured and neglected. Both rejected the reality of a life that had been damaged by terrible men. Rejection provoked creation of an existence that was, Ann reflected at last, no sadder than anyone else's. It simply came to an end – like everyone else's – and had had some pleasure and much pain on the way. Now both women had to suffer the condescension of the living.

Was it so very bad to be the daughter of an idiot beloved to distraction by his mother and a fictionist of life on so robust and dedicated a scale?

It was perhaps not good.

Ann got up and smiled into her flowered, unflattering glass. She felt pleased that an image was smiling at her. Then she glanced down at Caroline's hands. Whatever they looked like, until arthritis clutched them they would go on scribbling. She thought of the pretty plump fingers of Beatrice as they sewed her sampler. She was glad she'd known the girl.

Now she looked at, not into, the glass and saw less of herself and more of a gift from Sarah. It was a tangible object to hold to, it was seeing the thing, as Giancarlo Scrittori had advised. She'd refused to look into her dead mother's silver-edged glass in Paris. At will she could bring up the dim and beautiful Savelli mirrors and believe she'd just glimpsed herself in passing.

She would develop solitary pleasures, look at the world as it was, alone, while never becoming a recluse. She would not regain the optimism of the young. That was good. Disappointment was hard work.

By late summer it had rained so much that Ann could hardly remember dry ground, the swollen, hot dunes in Sardinia, the bristles of cones, the heavy smell of brittle thyme. Here everything was sodden and, when she walked, the water came up from the pavement and over her boots and pattens, splashing her skirts. Rain flung itself against her small window pane. Some of it got through. She rolled up a napkin to place against the crack where water seeped in. She changed the napkin when it was saturated. Life as she knew it, a daydream of security, pathetic perhaps, but she could laugh – and did smile – at such warm pathos.

It was autumn. Leaves had begun to change but no really chill winds were blowing. Aksel Stamer knocked on the outer door and came up the stairs into her lodgings.

He was older than she remembered but not old enough for what she'd once made of him, a bit careworn, stern as ever, and wet, shedding droplets of water.

From another angle he looked boyish. He carried a copy of *Isabella; or, the Secrets of the Convent*. He was familiar. He was dear to her.

'I nearly told you,' he said. 'It was when we sat on a wooden plank outside the hidden chapel.'

She let him go on.

'Do you remember? Then you thought it a hermit's place when it was merely a shepherd's. I knew it was not fair to constrain a woman with your feelings. I knew that too well.'

'Your sister?' she said.

She had surprised him. They sat a moment in silence. 'Ah, you are a maker and reader of plots. You worked it out. Yes, my sister, my half-sister. Our parents were dead. My mother had a late child, Kirsten Marie.' He hesitated. 'I raised her on Fyn, but I did not do so good a job. She feared me, I think. I am a man. I was perhaps not as tender as I might have been. She was soft, gentle, lovely. Many young men looked at her, but she was also a dreamy, sentimental, romantic child, she wanted to be admired, yes, all young girls do, but also to admire. Not a manly man who might have protected her as I sought to do. No.' He paused. 'Then he – ' he paused again, he found it difficult to say the name, 'then Robert James came into her life. He – well, he – wrote her some verses, very beautiful verses.'

'Where are they?'

He glanced at her, then away, 'I don't know.'

'Did you ever see them, read them?'

'No, no. She, my sister Kirsten, hid them from me as she hid so much.'

'Beautiful'? Indeed. How was something unseen beautiful? She remembered: Robert James could answer that.

'I had journeyed to London. I never met him then. You know this.'

She saw with amazement he was near tears, that man she'd judged so stern, so controlled. And yet she felt something angry still, beneath the grief. She touched his arm. His softer clothes made it less hard than it used to feel.

He went on, in abrupt sentences. 'I loved her like a father – and a mother – she was all I had of family. I protected her too much. I hid the horrors of the world from her. She was educated as a lady, for she was a lady. She did not see the bad side of life. She did not know what men could do.'

'Both sexes are pretty equal in what they can do, I imagine.' She blushed, realising Caroline gave a lie to this platitude. 'My mother . . .' she began, then stopped, swallowed, and, when he did not interrupt the silence, blurted out, 'You know there was no – father.'

'No, well? Perhaps not the one you heard most about.'

'Did you always know? But how could you?'

'Of course not. You once told me something he had said, that's all. Maybe I know men better than you.'

She doubted that, but let it go. He didn't expect contradiction.

When he left it was arranged he would return next afternoon and eat with her, but only when she'd done her work. Women's work – sewing, painting flowers, writing stories – was important to them. He respected it. Soon his visits were regular.

'He killed her,' he said one day.

'Do you mean Robert really killed Kirsten Marie, murdered her?'

'Yes,' he said. 'Robert James hit her – and she so loving and sweet and soft. Then he hurled a large china vase at her. Perhaps he did not mean to kill, but so it happened. And he, even he, knew something was then wrong. He disappeared.'

'He was not all bad,' she interrupted.

Aksel Stamer hadn't listened. He was deep in thought and memory. 'I had gone to Altona – I was in business then, dealing in scientific books. They had come to Denmark. She was headstrong, secretive, as she usually was with me. I should have been there. I should have warned her, stopped her, shut her up if necessary. I had had to do that once before. He meddled in what he didn't understand and left debts, but not enough that people would pursue him. I sought but the trail was cold.' He held his head a moment in his hand. 'I inherited some money from an uncle – it would have been part hers, her death killed him, he called her his angel-child . . . Two deaths, do you see? I gave up my business not long after. I travelled south. I was not at first actively seeking him but my hatred never for a moment diminished. Indeed, I may say it increased though it did not over-power me. I returned north.' He stopped.

She caught the phrase 'at first'.

'If life could be relived,' he continued.

'I have thought as much, at least a few chapters of it.'

'Do you see life in chapters?'

'It has advantages. There can be gaps and new starts.'

'If you had a few chapters to do again differently, which would they be?'

'No, I am wrong. I would do the whole book again.'

'Not all of it, perhaps.' He pressed his hand on hers.

She couldn't restrain herself. 'You should know I'm the child of an imbecile.' She gave a wry smile to cushion her words. She felt the heaviness of his hand.

'Aren't we all?' he said.

'I knew a man of artistry in Venice, of genius. He was considered mad and the family cared for him.'

Aksel Stamer removed his hand, got up and looked down at her.

She willed herself to keep still. She couldn't see his face.

'Francesco Savelli was indeed most gifted. But leave them, him, this father who may or may not be as you say, but whose main act was over in minutes, seconds. Francesco Savelli — let him go with Robert James.'

'Oh, but it is worse,' she said, forcing herself to smile. 'I am the child of two idiots.'

'Remember how the air was full of gold and black butterflies in Sardinia? You didn't know their name. I told you. When we slept outside, I watched over you sleeping. You threw off the covering for a while and pulled it back when you were chill. I watched all night. I appeared hard, perhaps. I would not for the world take advantage of a woman's weakness, of any human weakness when the body or mind is unaware. I called you Ann as I would have called my dear sister by her name. I startled you.'

'With Robert . . .'

He put a finger across her lips. 'Close the door on memory and when it starts to open, press your foot hard against it. Then there is no need to lie.'

He removed his finger slowly.

'You, too.'

'I, too. Certainly I too.'

'But I must know. Did you . . .?'

He placed his hand where her shoulder swelled up to her neck. She wouldn't remove it. She couldn't have removed it.

It was a clear winter day when they walked side by side along the gravel paths in Kensington Gardens as horsemen and carriages trundled past. She looked up. A flock of birds with long silvery necks were flying in formation, sketching and blurring. Her heart leapt at their beauty. She would not ask or seek to know their name.

→>-<←

ACKNOWLEDGEMENTS

I am grateful to all the team at Bitter Lemon for their help and dedication, especially François von Hurter and Laurence Colchester. Thanks are also due to Jane Havell for thoughtful work on the script and to Diana Birchall for her enthusiastic response, and to Claire Connolly, John Gardner, Deborah Howard, and Susanna Zinatu for generously answering queries. My main debts are to Derek Hughes, who read the work almost as often as I did and who gave me the benefit of his care and learning, and to Katherine Bright-Holmes, without whose kind and sensitive encouragement I would not easily have turned from editing to writing fiction.